A Hollow Bone

a novel by

Dawn Hogue

Dawn Hogue

Water's Edge Press

Printed in the United States of America

ISBN-13: 978-0-692-88300-6
ISBN-10: 0-692-88300-2

Library of Congress Control Number: 2017906479

Water's Edge Press
Plymouth, WI

waters-edge-press.com

This is a work of fiction. Names, characters, businesses, places, events and
incidents are either the products of the author's imagination or used in a
fictitious manner. Any resemblance to actual persons, living or dead, or
actual events, is purely coincidental.

The typefaces used in this book are
Adobe Garamond Pro & Yanone Kaffeesatz

Original cover photography by Eric J. Plahna

for my family

"There is a sense in which
we are all each other's consequences."
Wallace Stegner, *All the Little Live Things*

Some say the name Sheboygan comes from
Ojibwe Indian culture. One theory is that the Ojibwe word
jibaigan translates as a perforated object or a hollow bone.
A different theory suggests the word Sheboygan originally referred
to a great noise underground, particularly the sound of a river
making its way from Lake Superior.

1926

Ten-year-old Junie Schneider crouched on her haunches and dug into the sand with a broad stick. She liked to think of this spot on the north shore, which was not far from her home at 6th and Lincoln, as her own. Gulls screeched overhead as if annoyed by the girl's presence. Several feet away, a fish head buzzed with flies. The more she dug, the more water filled her hole.

A few weeks before, she had unearthed a small, olive-brown clam, still alive and oozing mucousy bubbles from its valve. Later, in its new habitat, a cleaned-out oil pan Junie kept on the back porch, the clam had died.

Junie's eyes glistened and her stomach burned as her mother growled. "You can't take things out of their place in life. Good grief, girl. Don't you have any sense? Next time you find something, just look at it or draw pictures of it, but for goodness sake don't bring it home. Now get that stinky thing out of here."

So Junie had buried the clam back at the beach instead of in her yard. She had felt bad that it died, but the little clam was not the first creature whose death had been her doing.

Now she pushed her stick under the jagged end of a white tube that protruded into the edge of the little pool of water, and with the stick, dislodged the tube. Junie set the stick aside and picked up the tube for close inspection. She saw that it was a section of bone about half the length of a pencil. Maybe it had come from the leg of a gull. Junie rinsed the bone in the water, then put the bone to her lips. She blew through its hollow core, and the faintest whistle sounded. She held the bone like a tiny telescope to her eye and squinted at a sandpiper who trotted in and out to the water's edge on a sand spit to the north. She put the bone in her pocket. It would go in her tin. Things already dead could not die.

Junie waded now at the water's edge, her feet accustomed to the cold water of Lake Michigan. Far out, almost beyond where she could see, a faint image of a freighter looked to be heading north. That far off the Sheboygan coastline, ships often disappeared in a haze. A hundred yards south, two boys cast cane poles in the water. Beyond them, the shoreline curved in a promontory that blocked her view of Sheboygan's southerly beaches. Junie shaded her eyes and watched to see if the boys would catch anything. After a while, she decided they were only playing at fishing. Junie sometimes fished too, with her father. She knew fishing was serious business, that it required patience and the ability to remain quiet for a long while. Those boys would have more luck if they moved out onto the pier, Junie thought.

The mid-morning sun was sharp and strong, and Junie could feel her arms redden. A southerly breeze rippled the surface of a small tide pool and disturbed a cottonwood tree that arched over the sand. She stopped a moment to listen to the soft rustling of its leaves. Junie hated to think of summer ending and school beginning. Reviewing her lessons every night with Mother as well. All the combustion of children and their riddles. What boy likes what girl? What girl has a secret? Or darker. Whose father had taken to drink? It was all so silly or so shameful. She often wished that she could learn from her father's books at home. Still, her teachers were kind, and she found them to be far more interesting people than her classmates.

Miss Rodgers, her teacher last year, had brought in seashells from her travels to Florida, which she described in great detail. Junie marveled at them all, from the smallest shell the size of a fingertip to the giant conch coated inside with pink glass. Miss Rodgers let each of them lift the conch to their ear. Listen carefully, she said, and you might hear the echo of the sea. Junie felt afterwards great regret at not having been able to listen hard enough.

Junie waded farther into the lake, staying in a shallow channel, and let the water eddy around her legs, pulling and sucking as she slowly trudged eastward into vastness. Some days she imagined lowering herself into the water, floating on her back, letting her bright blonde hair fan out like seaweed about her head and shoulders. Eyes open wide, staring hard and long at the sun. Years later when she would sob herself to sleep, wishing God would strike her dead in her sleep, June would remember this moment, when she wondered what it would be like to float out past the pier, past the shadows of trees, past daylight and into the night, where the light in her eyes would turn to stars.

1977

Sophie sat with her mother in the oncologist's office, florescent lights gleaming off the glass of his framed diplomas, her mother refusing to look him in the eye. After the necessary comments about what a lovely morning it was, all the saying before what had to be said, they sat there uncomfortably in unreasonably comfortable chairs and listened to the diagnosis: stage four breast cancer, metastasized to the bones.

On the wall behind the women, a hexagon-framed Regulator clock ticked. Sophie swallowed and searched her mother's face for some knowledge. How long had she been sick and never said a thing?

A month earlier, when Angelina had gone on her own to the clinic for a cough that would not go away, her family doctor had taken note of her significant weight loss. The signs pointed to cancer. At first he'd thought lungs, but wisely turned over all stones. It was then that he found the lump. He had questioned her. Hadn't she felt it? No, she had not felt the lump or noticed the shape of her right breast changing. She had not paid attention to her breasts as anything more than a nuisance for a long time. As for pain, she'd been living with one pain or another her entire life. She'd been tired, sure, but she was always tired, "waitress tired." She had laughed and rubbed her slender, ringless fingers. The doctor did not laugh. Then there had been the biopsy, the other tests, and now, finally needing Sophie to be with her, she faced the "cancer doctor." His news was not a shock. She had hoped, of course, for better news, but she was not surprised.

"Mrs. Miranda," Dr. Winter said.

"Oh, call me Angelina," she interrupted. "Or Angel, which is what most people call me." She had not been Mrs. Miranda for years, if she had ever truly been.

The doctor cleared his throat. He preferred to maintain professional distance and rarely called patients by their first names. "Well, then, Angel. Let's talk about your treatment options." Behind his desk, he sat straighter and adjusted his gold, wire-framed glasses. "The standard course of action is surgical removal of tumors, which means, most likely, a double mastectomy."

Angel's eyes widened. She never thought this would happen to her, but then realized that no one ever does. She did not interrupt the doctor, who continued to explain what he would do. Stage four. It couldn't be worse.

"Then, chemotherapy. A fairly aggressive course is indicated." He paused and looked at the women. Behind his kind eyes, he reformed his thought. Beyond the walls of his office, a baby cried.

Angel focused on the doctor's well-manicured hands, a plain gold band on his left hand. He held an ebony pen in his right. As he spoke, she looked up, and finally her eyes met his. Crinkly at the corners, fringed in thick, black lashes, his light indigo eyes were wasted on a man.

"How long?"

The doctor explained the surgery would be done as soon as could be scheduled. Then chemotherapy would take....

"Sorry. No. I mean. How long do I have to live?"

"Mom." Sophie said, half astonished at her mother's directness, half embarrassed to be talking so about life and death.

"I see." The doctor looked down, waited a moment, then looked back into his patient's eyes. After twenty-two years, he ought to have been accustomed to telling people such hard truths, but the task had never become easier. "First, please do understand, your cancer is quite advanced, quite aggressive as well. The therapies, surgery, and chemotherapy, should give you, and this is just an estimate because we cannot really know, but should add six months, a year?"

"And if I do nothing?"

"Mom. Nothing? You have to…."

"Sophie. Please."

Sophie sighed her annoyance but said nothing more.

Angel shifted in her seat, settled her hands in her lap, thought momentarily about her mother, and smiled. In the memory, June Catalano sat stiffly upright in the light maple church pew, her gloved hands crossed over the hymnal in her lap, her eyes fixed straight ahead on the pastor who spoke from the pulpit. Angel willed, in that moment, her mother's hands to take over her own. A calm knowledge settled upon her.

Doctor Winter, as if he felt a change in his patient, decided to speak honestly. "Mrs. Miranda, to undergo chemotherapy would extend your time, but unfortunately, it will only slow down what is inevitable."

"What if I was your mother—or your wife? What would you tell me, Dr. Winter? Be honest."

The doctor did not feel comfortable advising his patient in this way, but he also could not condone futile procedures. "First do no harm" echoed in his head. "If you were my mother, I would say let be what will be and try as much as possible to enjoy your last days."

Sophie squeezed her mother's hand. Angel nodded her understanding, exhaled a long breath, and thanked the doctor for his honesty. All agreed that Angel shouldn't work much longer, that is, she would be physically capable for a while, but doing so might unduly tire her. Angel laughed and said, "Yay, I can retire early."

Outside, Angel pointed to a stone bench set in a little garden twenty yards from the front entrance to the red brick clinic. A gargoyle fountain had not yet been turned on for the warm months, but the little sprite's emerald eyes glinted in the sun. Clumps of daffodils were in full bold yellow. On each side of a sign that looked too much like a headstone were tulips, budded but not yet in bloom. Later, the low growing sedum, golden green now, would sparkle with little starflowers, pink or yellow. The sign read *Garden of Peace*, also more fitting for a cemetery. Did the planner of this garden intend to remind visitors of their final resting place? Well, Angel thought, he did a good job.

Angel felt for the pebble-inlaid bench as if she were ready to collapse. The stone bench was warm in the full sun. Sophie dug her sunglasses out of her purse, put them on, then sat by her mom. Angel's head fell into her hands and her body began silently to shake.

"Mom?" Sophie leaned her head down to her mother's ear. "Mom," she said softly. "Are you okay?"

"Well, shit no, I'm not okay," Angel said.

"Well, I know. I didn't mean...."

An old man bent over his walker and a just-as-old woman at his side, her arm on his for balance, moved slowly toward the clinic entrance. They turned their attention briefly to Angel and Sophie, then continued to make slow progress.

Angel inhaled deeply and looked beyond the edge of the parking lot, the tears welling in her eyes blurring the horizon. The next deep breath quavered. What am I going to do, she thought. What am I...? The tears she had held in escaped now. Sophie, who noticed the quiet tears, waited silently but did not try to comfort her mother.

In a while, Angel straightened and stared wide-eyed into the sun. She took a deep breath and exhaled heavily. She dug in her purse for a cigarette, lit it, took a long, hard drag, and tossed the lighter back in her purse, which she let fall to the ground.

A mother and her rambunctious six-year-old son came out of the clinic and headed toward the parking lot. The mother lunged to grab the boy's hand when he began running without her. "I want ice cream," he shouted. "You promised."

Angel glanced at the mother and child. "That kid's got it right," she laughed. "Ice cream sounds good."

"Mom, come on," Sophie said, thinking her mother was joking.

"No, seriously. It sounds good. Enjoy my last months, right? To me, that means doing whatever I want. Whatever we want. So if that kid gets ice cream at 2:30 in the afternoon, why can't I?"

They chose the soda fountain at Prange's department store and parked on 8th Street. As they walked down the sidewalk, half a block to the front entrance of the store, Angel remembered having a root beer float there one Saturday afternoon with her mother. She'd been eight, maybe, or nine, and she remembered that all the women in their on-the-town dresses smelled like flowers. She had worn a dress, too, and white cotton gloves.

Today Angel's hands were bare, freckled from the sun, dry from work. She wore black slacks and a pale blue sweater. She felt old. In nine days, Angel would turn forty, and Sophie would be back at school. Angel would spend her birthday alone. Maybe her last birthday ever.

The waitress took their order. Angel ordered a hot fudge sundae, topped with pecans and whipped cream, deciding it was ridiculous, under the circumstances, to worry about the size of her waist. Sophie decided on a strawberry sundae.

Angel folded her hands in her lap. She sat tall and lifted her chin. She thought back to how her mother would always chide her about her posture, warning her she'd end up with hunched shoulders if she were not careful. Angel sighed and decided that for Sophie's sake, she would plaster a smile on her face. If she were lucky, it might even look sincere. The ice cream would taste good, and it might even make her forget, at least for a little while.

Angel would tip the waitress well, even if she brought their ice cream with a side of snootiness. She had let bad days interfere with her good service, too.

"Yum," Angel said after her first spoonful. "Yours good, too?"

Sophie nodded. After a few bites, Sophie said, "You know, I always wanted to come here."

"I didn't know that," Angel said, plunging her spoon into the tall parfait glass.

Sophie decided she would let her mother get away with the lie. After all, it was possible her mother did not remember. And Sophie, who sensed the time ahead would require more than one concession, felt she ought now to let go of the long-held memory, her small, pudgy hands clutching her mother's, tugging her in vain toward the smell of caramel corn and freshly baked waffle cones.

In the car on the way home, Angel insisted Sophie go back to school. "I'm fine, Sophie. There's nothing you can do, not right now anyway. I'll give my notice at work, and—"

"He said you shouldn't be alone," Sophie argued.

"That's for later, not for now. I'm fine, just tired, and I don't need you to watch me take a nap. Besides, you'll be home soon, right? When are you done? A month? Then you can nurse me properly. There's no real rush, Sophie. He said months, not weeks." Angel had no way of knowing how tenaciously her cancer would consume her. If she had, she would never have let her daughter go.

Sophie braked for the stop sign. A crossing guard led a group of elementary school children across the street. Three girls walked in a cluster, their heads bobbing in chatty energy, while two boys raced past them. There had been no such kindly old men, or women, in her childhood crossings. The guard, now back on his corner, waved Sophie ahead. Spring was beginning to burst. Golden green tufts crowning treetops glowed in the afternoon sun. Lawns seemed to have turned green overnight. Angelina Miranda leaned her head back and stretched her long legs. Sophie glanced left, then right, then left again before turning onto North Avenue.

Sophie shifted her thoughts back to making sense of this situation with her mother. That sounded callous, she realized. Of course she wanted to be with her mom, to care for her. There was no one else anyway. But near the end of her junior year in college, Sophie had planned on staying in

Madison for the summer. She and two friends were talking about renting a house near campus. They wanted one last free summer before their senior year and graduation and real life. And the next few weeks? Finals were going to be tough, a lot of studying, especially the one for chemistry. Why did English majors need chemistry anyway? It would be hard to come home on weekends. But she supposed she should try, even once.

She could ask Lev. He probably wouldn't mind checking in, but he would be busy, too. And as good a friend and neighbor as Lev Perlman was, Sophie felt sure it would not be quite right to ask for this much. And yet, they would tell him. Of course they would. If Lev found out later that they'd kept something so important from him, he would be hurt. She was sure of it.

"Right," she said, answering her mother's question. "About a month. Depends on…. Might be more like five, even six weeks." Even as Sophie spoke, she knew she was being selfish. But to look at her this moment, her mother appeared no differently than she always did, a bit worn out, wrinkles deepening at the corners of her eyes, the crease in the middle of her light brown eyebrows prominent as always, but life had done that to her, not cancer. At the same time, there was not one strand of gray in her red-blonde hair, and pulled back neatly in a pony tail, full bangs falling into her deep hazel eyes, she looked so young. Jesus, thought Sophie.

"I'll see if I can take one or two finals early. I probably can do that. Then, I'll be home and, yes, I can nurse you properly all summer. We'll make it a fun summer, okay?" Sophie did not believe these words any more than her mother did, but she had to stay positive now. There was little else she could do.

1935

Friday after work, Frank Catalano sat on the concrete front steps of his parents' Milwaukee home and ran his fingers through his wavy, black hair, scratching hard at his neck. The brisk spring air felt good. Ma Catalano's famous meatballs simmering in her equally renowned sweet and spicy spaghetti sauce wafted out onto the porch.

Frank's friend Jimmy Hoffman stretched out two steps below. Jimmy, who still looked like he had in childhood, freckled cheeks and thin, fawn-brown hair, lit a cigarette and flicked the burnt match into the gutter. Jimmy was a hide scraper. Frank's job was to heave the gore-soaked hides into corrosive vats of lye.

"You thinkin' about it, Frank?" Jimmy said after pushing smoke out of his lungs, picking at the chipped paint of the iron railing. "Sammy wrote me there's plenty jobs, but we can't waste time tryin' ta decide. We just gotta say we're doin' it and go. We can stay with Sammy at first. We just gotta—"

"I know, I know," Frank said, sniffing. The stench of the tannery never quite left the nostrils, even on a clear, spring evening like this one. Soap and water cleaned the skin but never the memory.

They had been talking about making a change, getting out of the tannery and heading north to Sheboygan where their high school pal Sammy had ventured a few months before. It was Frank who expressed the most reluctance, but after the day he'd had today, a change could not come soon enough. Frank was glad his old man had not been there to see the foreman get on him about speeding things up. He'd been daydreaming again—had gotten lost in the thought of resting his sunburned arms on the rail of a ship at sea, staring off to the curved and sunlit horizon—like he did when he was a kid, like he did when he felt suffocated by the tannery and the life that lay before him as a shining trap.

Twenty-two-year-old Frank knew the plan to head fifty miles north to Sheboygan to try for work in a furniture factory made a lot of sense. The work would be clean, sawdust and wood shavings, not animal hides and putrefaction. Still, the tannery was where his family worked. Frank's father, Frank's Uncle Al and cousin Paul, and Jimmy's father, too, they all worked there. How would these men take it if Frank and Jimmy insinuated by leaving that they were too good for the job? And Ma? Would she forgive him if he left? He could hear her cries now, knew she would put up an exaggerated fuss, and Frank would feel bad. He always did whenever he disappointed her. But Sheboygan wasn't so far away that Frank couldn't go home to visit his parents and his younger brother. It wouldn't be forever. It wouldn't be like going off to war.

"Still, we don't know nothin' about makin' tables and chairs, Jimmy." Frank's objection was weak, and he knew he was stalling to make a decision that seemed inevitable. Frank knew if he could watch a guy make a chair once, he could copy the process exactly. His head worked that way. He could follow the method, the pattern, the principles of the construction or the design. He was born knowing how things work. When Frank was eleven, he had tinkered with Mrs. Rossi's radio and got it working. She touted the boy "a genius, this one," and ever since, the Catalanos' neighbors had relied on him as their fix-it man. Frank's family had also come to depend on the benefits of his skill, as his "customers" would pay in commodities or trade. Ma canned part of Arne Rabassa's bumper crop of tomatoes last fall, some of which were now simmering on the stove. Frank knew that if he left, his family would suffer. And yet, wasn't he was too young to sacrifice his whole life? His cousin Paul, who was only five years older than Frank, already looked like he was forty. The tannery would do that to him, too.

Many nights, body tired but brain awake, he would lie in the dark in the tiny back bedroom he shared with Robbie, his seventeen-year-old kid brother. Unable to sleep, he would stare at tree branch shadows on the ceiling and invent various futures for himself. Since childhood he'd seen himself out to sea and thought lately he might join the Navy or the Merchant Marines. But wherever it was, he would go somewhere. Somewhere devoid of black soot and the odors of decay.

Frank's mother creaked open the screen door and summoned them both to dinner, and as if they were still ten-year-olds, she admonished them to wash first. Jimmy stood and stretched his lanky frame and thought about what Frank had said about their lack of experience.

"We're handy, Frankie. You are more'n me, but we'll learn. You do one step. Sand a seat or slap on some varnish, somethin' like? They teach you, a course."

"What's it like up there? You ever been?"

"When would I have went up there? I been living in this house with you since we were kids." Jimmy took a long draw, then stubbed his Lucky Strike on the step and tossed the bent butt into the street. "Old Sammy says it's nice. Lots a trees, houses not so close together like here. But people? Probly about the same."

Two weeks later, Frank and Jimmy were working at the North Shore Furniture Company for ten cents an hour. At first they would learn from more skilled workers until they were deemed able to manage on their own. In about a month, if they worked hard and showed what they could do, their pay would be increased to twenty cents an hour. It was a new start and Sammy's place was clean. Sammy's wife was accommodating, but she made it clear that when they were able, the men would pay a bigger share of the rent. In hard times people had to help each other get ahead, she realized, but that didn't mean she was running a charity. Frank and Jimmy agreed that they would soon be able to help out more with the rent and even suggested other ways to help. They could run the sweeper or do whatever she needed.

"As if a man could run a sweeper," she had said, shaking her head. "No. Let's just settle on a fair contribution. She and Sammy knew this boost to their income was an unexpected blessing, so they were ready to accept any inconveniences that their new boarders would cause them.

She needn't have worried. Frank and Jimmy were ideal tenants. They were quiet and respectful. They were clean and orderly, and they never tumbled home drunk or tried to sneak in women.

The small extra bedroom Frank and Jimmy would share for nearly a year was comfortable enough. There was room for two cot-sized beds and a lamp table between them. They kept their meager belongings in a secondhand highboy they got cheaply because it was missing a leg, but Frank had hand-carved a fair replacement, and now it didn't wobble one bit.

They were lucky they arrived when they did, the foreman told them. Sure, they had needed workers, but when you put out a call like that, you get more than you need pretty quick. Tomorrow, they'd have been sent looking for work elsewhere. Business was getting back on track now. The Depression had hit a few of their competitors hard, but North Shore was able to stick through the worst times. Frank had to admit, life was looking good. Jimmy took all the credit for their optimistic prospects. Good, clean work, good friends, and "the beer ain't so bad either." That was true. No Pabst right down the block, but Kingsbury wasn't so bad, and a guy could afford a couple taps after work.

Frank learned the trade faster than Jimmy, picked up the relationship between the materials and the machinery to the finished product as if the process had been wired into his brain at birth. He was proud of his sandpaper-rough fingertips when he worked at coarse or fine sanding and proud of the stain that didn't wash off when he applied finishes. There was not a job in the entire line that he could not do better than any other worker, and within six months, Frank began supervising quality on the line. If it wasn't done to his standards, he would lean over and talk it out. "I can't do it for you," he'd tell the guy. "You gotta just learn it by feeling it in your hands." Frank would teach by saying, "Yep, that's it" or "No, not quite, try it again." The men liked him. They wanted to do well, and production numbers were up under Frank's watch. Frank had never felt such pride in himself.

At night Frank would lie awake, sweet sawdust and oily lacquer lingering in his nostrils, and reimagine his future. Oceans and far away places still pulled at him, but Frank now realized that dreams of seafaring adventures belonged to the enchantment of boys, not to the obligation of men. And now that the death life of the tannery was forever past, he began to imagine himself someday the owner of his own factory. He had already suggested a minor change in design to a side table that had sped up manufacturing, but it wasn't he who benefited. Instead, due to Frank's idea, the owner, who lived in a big house near Lake Michigan, got richer. Frank wanted that big house on the bluff overlooking the lake, servants' quarters over the garage, rooms for six kids or however many would come along.

Of course, he'd need a smart, strong wife first, and when he was ready to look, when he had money enough saved for his own apartment, he'd start looking a little more seriously, especially at June Schneider, who worked in the office and distributed pay envelopes. Such courage it took for him to ask if she would care to take a walk with him one Sunday. When she accepted, Frank could not have known that she had been thinking of him as well or that she had begun to look forward to Fridays, waiting to see Frank's head bobbing over the top of most of the others, his thick, black hair always falling into his deep brown eyes, his long lashes dusted at times with sawdust.

June was pretty enough, in fact quite pretty, those soft brown eyes, her light golden hair waved to the side, a touch of red on her lips, not too much, not too much at all. What he liked best about June was that she didn't flutter her eyelashes or laugh at everything he said, whether it was funny or not. June had a mind of her own, and she would be a partner he could depend on.

So he planned and saved and kept his eyes on the future. He would live meagerly now to live lavishly later. A man could have his dreams if he worked hard enough.

1977

Angel leaned over the mattress, which sat high on the walnut frame, to tuck the fold of the bedspread under the pillows. Reaching to smooth a wrinkle in the middle of the bed, she pulled a muscle in her side and winced at the sudden, sharp pain.

She opened her bedroom window a few inches, enough to let in a gentle, crisp breeze. The squeak alerted her next-door neighbor, Lev, who was outside raking dead grass out of his yard. He squinted in her direction and, finally seeing her, waved. She bent down to the opening and yelled, "You can do mine when you're done." Then she laughed to let him know she was only kidding. He laughed back and said, "Oh, you'd like that, wouldn't you." But she knew he probably would rake for her anyway.

More than a neighbor, Lev had become a good friend, especially after Ruth, his mother, died. He was such a sweet man, always looking out for her and Sophie. Angel smiled, remembering just then the time Ruth had tried to fix the two of them up, like an old yente. "Oh, it won't matter that he's older. Only ten years. That's not such a difference," Ruth had said. Sweet Ruth. Lev would have been mortified if he had known what his mother was up to.

Angel lowered herself to the floor now, her legs pulled beside her. She sighed wistfully and turned the antique key in the lock of the old steamer trunk, then lifted the lid. It had been a long while since she had sifted through the relics stored inside her father's trunk. Today she was in no hurry to do anything but look back in time.

Since learning her diagnosis, Angel felt helpless to do much except look back, and at times she struggled even to put one foot in front of the other simply to move around the house. Her lethargy came not yet from physical frailty but from mental frailty. She still could not reconcile her thoughts to the fact that she was dying. Lately the futility of forward motion strangled her with inaction.

But today she had resolved to do something, anything. For the first time in four days, she showered and dressed. She chose the purple paisley shirtwaist dress she had splurged on for Easter two years prior. She had worn it only once. Why not, she reasoned. It was pretty. A person can dress up any time she wants. Angel need not have worried about the dress fitting. Instead of being too tight, it hung on her loosely. Had she really lost so much weight? When she was dressed, she slicked deep rose lipstick onto her lips, pressed them slightly together, and blotted lightly with a tissue. She smiled at her reflection in the bathroom mirror. Maybe this is what it took, just moving, just getting dressed and doing something.

Now, facing the open trunk, Angel took up a packet of photographs and untied the red ribbon that secured them. Most were three-by-three black-and-white prints, some with scalloped edges. She loved their old-fashioned look. A few faded color photos were mixed in. She had always meant to sort through these pictures, maybe put them in an album. There weren't many. Her parents had not been avid photographers. It wouldn't have taken her long, and Sophie could have helped. But Angel thought instead she could take on the project as a surprise gift for her daughter. She could go to Prange Way, the discount store on the west side of town, and get a fancy album, put all the pictures in chronological order and present it to Sophie when she came home from college for the summer. Yes. She could do that.

Or she could just slip one or two out now, keep them near her on her nightstand, to look at whenever she needed to or wanted to. After all, she would not be able to look at them after she was.... And wouldn't it be nice, when she woke in the middle of the night, sweating from a horrible dream, to have that comfort?

Angel smoothed her fingertips over her own childhood face. Little Angelina, her hair cropped short for the summer, a scabby knee visible, stood between her grandparents. Mother most likely had held the camera. Grandma Schneider always looked elegant. In the photo she wore a light colored dress, cinched close at her waist, neat as always, her hair pinned up. She also stood rigid, as if the camera were going to bite. But Grandpa? Angel could almost feel him break into a laugh. It was just his way. You didn't even have to say anything funny. He was just always happy. Angel sighed. She wished her mother had taken after him instead of Grandma. Grandma was nice. She was sweet, but she was also so awfully serious most of the time. Grandma didn't find pleasure in ordinary things like Grandpa did.

Angel drew her finger over another photograph, her grandparents side by side, lingering the longest on the image of her grandfather. She knew, yes, she knew, the man had doted on her. He wore a white short-sleeved shirt and black tie. Seemed he was always in a tie. Sometimes even in to the garden, if he went before dinner at Grandma's request to snip chives or to gather a pint of raspberries or to pick a couple of ripe tomatoes.

Angel turned the snapshot over for a date, but there wasn't one. Was she about six when she and her mother went to live in Grandma and Grandpa's big house at 6th and Lincoln? That seemed right. That house had seemed like a mansion compared with the tiny two-bedroom house her parents had rented before her dad went to war. Angel shuffled the pictures to find one with a better view of the house, but there were none. Instead, she closed her eyes tightly and conjured an image in her mind. The current owners had recently repainted the narrow clapboards and the scalloped cedar shingles a soft moss green, which Angel thought looked serene against the buttery white of the window trim and balusters of the wrap-around porch. The last time she'd driven past the house had been in October after work. That day, as she always did when she visited her grandparent's old house, she parked on the street, and sat there in her car, and remembered. She had forgotten how the slanting sun through the autumn leaves would wash the house in gold.

Several more snapshots were of Angel by herself. She laughed out loud at the one of her drenched to the bone, her red-blonde hair all wet, curls stuck to her cheek. She still couldn't believe they had let her play outside in the rain in just her underpants, shirtless as if she were a boy. She was probably seven? Times were different then.

Angel looked a long time at her favorite picture of her mother, the one of June holding her as an infant. She actually looked happy. Angel sighed. There was one of both her parents, so young and slim, dressed in their wedding clothes, Mom in a neat ecru dress and Dad in a dark navy suit, a carnation in his lapel. They had been happy. Sometimes. They were. It had not always been the fights and the loneliness.

"But…," Angel said, sounding like a child who has just had her highest hopes squelched. She held the phone receiver to her ear and listened to Sophie explain why she would not be coming home that weekend after all. It had been three weeks since she and Sophie had gone to Dr. Winter's office together, and she was so looking forward to spending time with her. Time, which she had taken for granted, was now magnified in her mind. Even ordinary moments felt urgent. So this waste of an opportunity more than disappointed Angel. It infuriated her and made her restless with anxiety. Angel had hoped she and Sophie could have their hair done or shop for new dresses, anything that would make them feel like grown-up friends, not mother and daughter.

Sophie, who wrapped her words in what she hoped was a believable excuse, had been invited to a party Saturday night. She was dying to go and knew if she were home, not only would she miss the chance to spend time with Alfie Weiner, a dark-haired history major from New York, she would also be stuck in the house all weekend with her mom. She would be doing that the entire summer. She felt she did not need to start early. Of course Sophie did not tell her mother about the party. She said instead that her literature professor had invited her and several others from her class to a poetry reading featuring a highly esteemed Midwestern poet, Daniel Sullivan. Her mother would have no idea that Sullivan was the name of a residence hall.

After the disappointing phone call from Sophie, Angel tapped a cigarette and lit it. Smoking is bad for you, they were saying now, but she decided it was a bit too late for her to worry about that. She needed to finish going through the pictures, at least to get them cleaned up. After that, maybe she would have her hair done anyway. Why not?

The photograph of her parents had reminded Angel that there were no such pictures of her own "wedding," which had been a simple and quick courthouse affair. Thinking back now, she realized she could not even recall what she had worn, Ruben either. But not a suit. Most likely he'd worn blue jeans. For Sophie's sake, Angel was sorry there was not a single photograph of her and Ruben from that day. Angel tapped her ashes in a gold glass ashtray. God, she'd been so stupid, she thought. She remembered the day they'd left Wisconsin on their way to California, driving as if their vanishing contrails meant a literal end to everything they had left behind them. For her part, she had wanted to obliterate her old life. She had wanted it more than anything. Angel felt foolish as she remembered how she had insisted that they stop on both sides of the Mississippi River so she could take a picture from each border. Ruben thought she was being ridiculous. Maybe he was right about that, she thought as she held those two pictures in her hand. Impulsively, she tore them in half, then in half again, and kept at it until little pieces of the past lay at her knees.

"All right, Angel. All right," she said out loud. "Calm down. There's no use getting all worked up over things you can't go back and change." She blew smoke toward the ceiling.

Angel was anxious to get up now, so she shuffled quickly through a stack of pictures of Sophie. Is some dumb poet more important than me, she thought? She held up a picture of Sophie on her tummy wearing only a diaper. She smiled at one of Sophie on her first birthday, chocolate frosting all over her face, in her hair. There was another of her in the bath. In another she was wearing a swimsuit, standing in the tiniest inflatable wading pool.

"Look at the child's wild, dark hair," Angel laughed. "And me. Shit I look so young." She flipped the print over: July 4, 1958. She remembered that day. It had been hot, high 80s, or even 90. Angel wore pink plaid Bermuda shorts and a white sleeveless blouse tied at the waist. She balanced two-and-a-half-year-old Sophie on her hip, held her cigarette in her right hand. Angel's hair was much shorter than she'd kept it for most of her life. She remembered now, Ruben had hated it. He'd said it made her look older. They had fought over it. Over hair, for Christ sake.

Except for the picture of her and her grandparents, the one of her parents on their wedding day, and the one of Sophie in her little pool, Angel put the rest of the pictures back in the trunk, retying the ribbon and placing the packet atop the lace tablecloth that Grandmother Schneider's mother had crocheted. She fingered the lacy cotton now and marveled that a person could create such a thing, but it was what women did. Some of the girls at work knitted or crocheted, and some even sewed their own clothes. Her mother had sewn things for her when she was a child, before she had refused to wear homemade clothes. Ruth Perlman had been a knitter and had made lovely sweaters and scarves. With a sigh, Angel realized she had never really learned how to make anything.

Sophie should know about the tablecloth as well as everything else in the trunk. When Angel put the rest of the pictures in an album, she would also write a few notes about what had belonged to whom. The tin that had been her mother's, the one filled with shells and bones. The girl should know. Things like this mattered.

Angel stubbed out her cigarette in the ashtray and thought with clarity that these things had not mattered to her for most of her life. She knew she had burned through her life like a comet. But now? There was nothing Angel could do to change the present or the past, and what would she do differently if she could? If she could fly like Superman around the earth and rewind time?

If, if, if. There were many, many times she wished she had never run off with Ruben. She was smart. She could have gone to college. She could have met some romantic poet of her own or taken a trip to Europe. She could have had something else. But any time she imagined some different life, even one perhaps that mirrored her daughter's, she knew any such life would mean Sophie would never have been born and that was a choice she would never have made, possible or not.

1936

June Schneider did not have to think twice when Frank Catalano asked her to marry him. In a borrowed car they drove north, staying close to the Lake Michigan shoreline. Knowing June enjoyed the lakeshore, Frank had spent the weekend before scouting an area a few miles north of the city and had found a shady dune that jutted out into the lake, providing both a vista and a shelter from lake breezes that could be cold, even in summer. On the bank, willows arched over the hillock where a gently sloping path led to the sandy dune. Frank unfurled the red checkered tablecloth he had borrowed from Sammy's wife and unpacked the picnic: a well-cured summer sausage, a half horn of colby cheese, saltines, and two bottles of beer on ice wrapped in burlap.

Now, settled on the old tablecloth, Frank rested on his elbow. The woman he could never get out of his mind sat with her toes tucked behind her, leaning on her wrist. They eyed each other reticently, as if neither knew what to do with the surge of emotion that churned within. To blurt out their feelings would be unseemly.

"It is all so lovely," June told Frank, and he was pleased he had chosen this location over a table in a restaurant. A few yards up the shore, sandpipers trotted out to the water's edge, then back again as a gentle, clear wave washed over the pebbly gold sand. Monarch butterflies dipped into milkweed pods. Except for a few wispy cirrus clouds that wandered by now and then, the sky was a deep July blue.

"Are you comfortable? Chilly?" he asked. She said quietly that she was fine. Everything was fine. In later years, he would not be nearly as solicitous with June. Today her affection for him was not something he took for granted. It was, he admitted at times, hard to believe she loved him at all.

After they had eaten, they passed the time talking about ordinary things, including a new employee at the factory whom they both distrusted for some reason. It was the man's unsettling, wide-set eyes, they concluded. Frank shifted and sat with his knees up slightly, his head turned toward the lake. All his life he had wanted to, but he had never seen an ocean. And yet, how could any ocean be more beautiful than Lake Michigan? Today especially, buoyant but calm, blue mirroring the sky, and at the shore, the water crystal clear.

After a moment, he turned and faced June, looking not quite into her eyes, but just slightly lower. "June," he said. "June, I've been thinking for a while now how hard it would be if I had to live without you—if, that is, if you took up with another fellow, or if you moved away, or... I... I don't think I could stand it if you did."

His direct but simple words—the way he always approached important things—reminded June that Frank was no ordinary man. He was not like other young men she had been out with. Sure, some of them had been fun, but maybe a bit too fun. She liked to have a good time, but she was also serious. She wanted someone in her life who would also be serious, someone who would take care of her, take care of everything if need be. When he had asked her two weeks earlier if she would care to go with him on a Sunday picnic, she suspected what he might be up to. The way they'd been lately with each other, each one knowing without saying that the next step was inevitable, she'd known. And now, as the meadowlarks and finches flitted overhead, he was finally going to ask her.

Frank did not get on his knees. He had thought about it, but decided he would look and feel ridiculous. June would not expect him to be that kind of man. She was far too sensible, a quality he admired and expected. Then, as if he were commenting on a passing cloud, he said, "I can't promise you we won't have rough times, but June, if you will marry me, I will be good to you. I...I see a great future...." To go on meant he would lose his stoicism. He was not a man prone to emotion, though there were perfect and lovely moments in life that could sometimes bring him to tears. But more than that, he simply had no words for what he hoped with all his heart.

June threw her arms about Frank's neck, pulled his face to hers, and stopped his words with a kiss that lasted longer than propriety would allow. As for that, their secluded picnic, including the beer, would be scandalous to some, but she had not thought twice about that either.

"Yes," she said when her hands dropped down to grasp his. "Yes."

Eight months later, pregnant with Angelina and her belly bigger than she could have imagined her body would allow, she stood at the kitchen counter and pushed the rolling pin over dried bread to make crumbs for meatballs. Her mother-in-law had been reluctant to hand over her recipe, and she would cling to her sauce recipe until her death, thinking a good Italian girl would have had have her own. As for the meatballs, she couldn't have let her Frank be deprived just because he married a Lutheran girl, and a German to boot. Frank was grateful for his mother's gesture, knowing how hard it was for her to let go of anything, but June, who realized that whenever she used the recipe she would be held to a standard she would never meet, accepted it with concealed bitterness.

Not only that, June was never quite sure how to gauge a pinch of fennel seed or a palmful of parsley. The handwritten recipe said to grind fresh pepper if you have it, about eight turns, or if you don't, then use McCormick. Trial and error would continue for years, and to his credit, Frank never openly criticized the results. Not that her meatballs turned out poorly. June could cook. She was a very good cook, in fact. She had simply not been able to decipher a purposefully indecipherable code.

Now kneading the beaten egg, the breadcrumbs, and the spices into the ground pork, June's baby gave her a swift kick. "Soon, dear child. Soon," she cooed. "Don't be too anxious to get here."

With her pregnancy, June had begun to have dark days, days when she would rather lie in bed all day, the shades down and curtains drawn. Other days, like this mild March morning, the sun was as welcome as ever. June had discovered that if she kept busy with cooking or housework or sewing baby clothes, she felt better. The long winter had been difficult, the long dark days, weeks without sun. It was hard to force smiles. The doctor told her that some women feel melancholy during pregnancy, but those feelings were generally temporary, and once the baby arrived, she would return to her old self. Frank reinforced the doctor's assessment and told her she should not be too concerned. She smiled at them both, but something deep inside told her that she would never be truly happy again.

1977

Sophie waved one last goodbye to her ride before she stepped inside the house and plopped a bulging bag of laundry and her backpack full of summer reading and old papers on the floor. It was six p.m., and while Sophie did not know exactly what to expect, she thought there might be a welcome home spaghetti dinner that her mother had promised a week ago on the phone. Instead of Great Grandma Catalano's meatballs simmering in sauce, instead of an active kitchen and a bright hello, the house was dark and silent. Alarmed, Sophie searched for her mother and seconds later found her curled tightly on her bed, mewing softly in an almost inhuman expression.

"Oh my god. Mom. Mom!" Sophie croaked. She reached out to touch her mother, but the touch, as if it burned, elicited a louder cry from Angel. Sophie's hand flew to her mouth, covering her horror, and for the moment she simply stood there, paralyzed.

Sophie realized she needed to get her mom to the hospital, immediately. Instinctively, she dialed Lev's number, but there was no answer. She wondered if she should call an ambulance. No, I can drive her there myself faster, she thought. If I can….

"Mom?" Sophie touched her mother's shoulder as gently as she could. Angel twitched at the touch and quietly cried out. Her lips white, her perspiring yellow skin tinged with purple.

In the kitchen, Sophie scavenged through her mother's purse, tossing out crumpled newspaper coupons and a wadded hankie to find the car keys. She threw her mother's wallet and identification into her own purse and tossed a blanket into the car, which she drove up onto the front lawn near the front door. She left the motor running, opened the passenger door, and stood for a moment, raising her shoulders in a show of strength. Oh, why was everyone in this neighborhood so old and feeble? She let down her shoulders with a sigh. She was on her own.

Inside, she turned on the bedroom light to make her mother more alert. "Mom. Mom. Wake up." Sophie tried lifting her mother by the shoulder. Come on. Mom, I need you to help me walk you to the car."

Angel's eyes opened, then closed.

"Mom!" Sophie yelled, like a mother scolding an intractable child.

Angel moaned. Her eyes fluttered again and she focused them on her daughter.

"I…," Angel squeaked. Then her eyes closed.

Sophie realized she couldn't do it. Minutes later, after she'd moved the car out of the yard, the siren's sound appeared and intensified until it stopped. The paramedics worked quickly, checking Angel's vital signs. Sophie felt suddenly in the way and backed to the edge of the room as she watched the team of two roll her mother gently onto the gurney and secure her.

"I'll go in our car," Sophie told the ambulance drivers.

They nodded, then like a cartoon poof, they were gone, siren blaring.

In only five weeks, Angel had become skeletal, hollow-cheeked and waxy-skinned. Outside the intensive care unit, Sophie crossed her arms tightly over her chest and faced the doctor under the uncompromising hallway lights that sent glare onto every shiny white wall tile, every square inch of the well-waxed floor, the lenses of the doctor's glasses, the chrome tubes of his stethoscope. She was cold.

"Is she dying? I mean, is that what this is, already?" Sophie could not believe she could even say those words.

"It's hard to say," the doctor said. "Her high blood pressure is quite concerning, as is the fact that, so far, she's unresponsive. We're running more tests to determine if there is anything else we need to be concerned about, but one factor here is that your mom is severely dehydrated, so maybe that's more what we're dealing with instead of the cancer advancing rapidly. Let's see how she is in the morning."

Sophie nodded her understanding and thanked him. He told her that the nurses would take excellent care of her mom and she should try not to worry.

How could she *not* worry? At her mother's bedside now, Sophie watched Angel sleep, or if not sleep then lay absent of consciousness, her hollow cheeks moving slowly in and out with each weak breath, the feistiness all blown out of her.

The nurse had just finished logging Angel's blood pressure and pulse. "Can I get you something? The cafeteria is closed, but there are vending machines in the waiting room at the end of the hall," the nurse said, gesturing the direction. "Looks like your mom is going to be out all night, if you wanted to go home and come back tomorrow?"

Sophie shook her head. "I'm staying," she said.

"That's fine. I understand," the nurse said as she checked the IV connection. "I'm going to dim these lights, but I need to leave this one on, overhead, so I can see when I come in to check on her, okay? Our nurses' station is just outside, if you need anything?" The nurse drew the divider curtain for privacy, although there was no one else in ICU with them.

Sophie thanked her. Now alone with her mother, Sophie stood at Angelina's side and watched her breathe, not quite believing her mother might die tonight or tomorrow and not some distant time as she had thought. They were supposed to have the summer.

Angel's hand was cold, the arm with the IV exposed. Sophie adjusted the blankets to cover her.

"There." Sophie spoke softly. "Is that better? Can I do anything else, Mom?" Sophie inhaled deeply, wondering if she would ever hear her mother's voice again. It was just like in the Tolstoy story she had recently read for class. There was too much left undone, too much left unsaid. Sophie was not ready. How was anyone ever ready for this?

At about nine o'clock, Sophie ventured out and bought a bag of potato chips and a can of Coke. She realized she had not eaten since breakfast. She picked up a three-month-old *Family Circle* magazine from the waiting room and tried to read it while she ate. As she tried to make sense of the words, even the short descriptions of the photographs worked against her will to stay awake. Finally Sophie gave in to common sense and told herself she ought to at least try to sleep for an hour or so. She used the toilet, splashed water on her face, and rubbed a wet finger over her teeth. Back in the ICU, Sophie used the pillow and blanket the nurses had brought her in an attempt to make the olive green Naugahyde chair near her mother's bed somewhat comfortable, and yet as tired as she was, Sophie could not close her eyes, and the large, round-faced clock above the door clicked loudly, making each second intolerably obvious.

1936

Frank and June were married in August. Their small wedding, held in Wally and Grace Schneider's backyard under a shady elm, was officiated by June's Lutheran pastor. Father Conti from St. Rita's, Frank's former parish in Milwaukee, had counseled June towards conversion, but she had refused, so the priest had made it clear that he could not condone their marriage, a sentiment Frank's mother took to heart and never forgot.

Nevertheless, after the cake and punch, and after the newlyweds' parents made civil conversation with each other, Frank drove his bride blindfolded to their new home, a furnished lower flat on North 11th Street. Before he removed the handkerchief blindfold, Frank apologized.

"It is not the grand estate I dream of for us, Junie, but we can make it nice. You can sew sunny curtains. I'll make sure it stays in good repair. But it's ours, and it sits on a nice lot. Well, you look."

She had not expected her parents' roomy and well-kept home, but when she opened her eyes, June struggled to hide her disappointment. The place was much smaller than she expected. Dingy white clapboards needed paint, and the awning over the front door was missing a slat. But, as she forced herself to begin looking at the good points, she noticed a strong elm towered overhead, so it would be a cool home in summer. The neighborhood was made up of other homes like theirs, some nicer, others not as spruce, but yards were neat and children played ball or hopscotch. It was pleasant enough, she accepted.

Frank escorted June up the walk to the front door and commented on the lawn, which looked to be in good shape. "I'll be in charge of cutting the grass and shoveling snow, but because I'll be doing that work, our rent will be a bit less." He smiled broadly, hopeful that June appreciated his pragmatism. She returned his smile. "The upstairs tenants seem nice," Frank said. "They have one boy, about eleven years old. Forgot their names, but I'm sure we'll all get along just fine."

Inside, Frank pointed out the rose-patterned carpet in the living room, not worn at all. Then the newlyweds sat on the sofa, bouncing to test the comfort. Besides two side tables, an arm chair was the only other furniture in the living room, which was small, but would have space enough for June's grandmother's rocking chair. In the larger of the two bedrooms, a white-enameled iron bed was covered in a mint green chenille spread. Yellowing lace curtains covered the double-hung windows. June would pack away all of those things and replace them with her own bedding and curtains, towels, rugs, and doilies, things she or her mother had made, things given to her as gifts. Mother Catalano had given the couple two new goose down pillows. "Hand-made in bright new ticking," she told June several times to evoke proper gratitude.

The coal furnace was in good shape. "Works good," the landlord had told him. With pride Frank drew June's attention to the new the Kohler fixtures in the bathroom. As if he had installed them himself, he showed her the dusky pink tub, sink, and toilet. June approved of the kitchen, which featured a large, deep sink situated under a window that looked out onto the spacious backyard. She turned on the faucet and cold, clear water rushed out. She was happy to see that the shared yard was neat and not cluttered with rusty bicycles and the other detritus of boys. A little vegetable garden appeared to be full of cucumbers and green tomatoes, and spent raspberry canes bordered the alley garage at the back of the lot.

This, June's first home as a married woman, was clean and did not smell of cooking grease or smoke. Gloved fingers run across tables and bureaus remained clean.

"Will it suit you, Junie?" Frank asked, worried she would find something not quite right.

For her part, June understood that her husband wanted only to provide for her and to give her the best that he was able. She put her arms around him, rested her head on his shoulder, and sighed softly. Without looking into his eyes, she meant it when she told him that it would suit her just fine. "We will make it our own, soon enough, and it will be lovely."

The new groom held on tightly to that moment, even more tightly than he realized.

The first months of their lives soon settled into a comfortable routine. June, whose only job now was to keep the house and take care of her husband, often missed the camaraderie of the office. And not just that, she missed the work, too, missed even the monotony of keeping pay logs. But this was her role now, the wife's role, and she told herself she was ready for it. June knew that marriage meant making sacrifices.

After work, Frank came promptly home, except on Saturdays, when he headed to the tavern with Jimmy and some others for a beer or two. Even then, he wasn't excessively late and never came home drunk.

They got along well, each understanding the other's needs and idiosyncrasies, each understanding without judgment. And they loved each other. Some nights they would remain in each other's arms, naked limbs entangled, pores still wide open, hearts still racing, and openly voice their shared dreams. These moments of hopefulness and love sustained June through long days alone.

Every other Sunday after church, the Sundays the newlyweds attended St. Mark Lutheran, June's parents came for noon dinner. June rose early to put a pot roast in the oven, and her mother brought a pie. At first, the conversation between the men was sometimes strained, Frank being the more taciturn of the two, but eventually talk of weather turned to talk of baseball or the Green Bay Packers. In general, Frank liked his father-in-law and they got on well together. Frank wasn't so sure about Grace. He felt he still had a way to go in proving himself to her.

On opposite Sundays, Frank and June attended Holy Name, the Catholic church. While June insisted on splitting their spiritual duty, Frank made it clear it really didn't matter much to him. The couple set aside the Catholic Sundays for Frank's parents, but after the elder Catalanos' first trip to see the newlyweds in Sheboygan, Frank's mother began to find excuses. She was needed at church or the neighbors had been begging them for months to come for Sunday dinner and they could not disappoint them. Eventually, Maria Catalano felt satisfied to say that the drive was too much for Frank's father, who had not quite recovered from a case of pneumonia the year before. Frank came to understand that all visits with his parents would take place in Milwaukee. Frank and June made a trip in October, then again in November, but with winter coming on, Frank did not want to take the chance of driving on snowy or icy roads, not with a baby on the way.

The house was indeed becoming theirs. Frank approved most of June's ideas for improvements and tried to comply with all her requests for this or that to be built, moved, or changed. Despite Frank's reminder that they were just renting temporarily, he sanded then painted the kitchen cabinets with soft white enamel. More proudly, Frank built a crib mainly from discard materials at the factory. He had no plans from which to build, no paper plans that is. His design had evolved in his mind since June first told him she was expecting. He did not yet have the tools to turn out Jenny Lind spindles, but he managed to make a few hand carved embellishments look even more striking, or so he thought.

In December, June crocheted white and red doilies for the holidays, and she looked forward to having a small tree that she would string with colored electric lights and popcorn and cranberries. She enjoyed making the house ready for the holiday. Frank and June's gifts to each other were modest, keeping in mind their meager savings. Frank declared he had never been warmer when he slipped on the brown wool cardigan June had knitted. June treasured the sterling serving fork and spoon. The entire set would come later, her husband promised. For now the touch of elegance sustained her.

By March it seemed spring would come early, and as June stood at the counter shaping meatballs, watching a bird at the backyard feeder, she thought maybe, just maybe, her sad spells might vanish forever.

Angelina Grace Catalano was born on April 24, 1937. Frank chose the name Angelina after his grandmother who had died in Italy, a woman he had never met, but whose stories had come to him through his mother as legends. *That woman was our Helen of Troy. That woman invented Italian cooking. That woman's laugh drowned out church bells.* June wanted her daughter to have her mother's name as well. Together Frank and June thought the names suggested the grace of angels, which pleased them.

From the moment the seven-pound, four-ounce red, wrinkly girl was born, she squawked her existence proudly. She latched on to her mother's breast as if it was something she had waited nine full months to do, impatient with the necessity of growing and developing and needing to be born.

The first few weeks home, June insisted the baby sleep between her and Frank so she could listen to her breathing. Stories, horrible stories, from neighbor women who warned that sometimes even healthy babies die for no reason, terrified June. But the strain of lost sleep eventually enabled Frank to convince June that Angelina would sleep just as well in her crib, that they would also sleep better, and that they all would remain healthy.

The child indeed remained healthy and grew, and June insisted she could see it happening. Despite June's fear that her depression might get worse after Angelina's birth, she was elated that it did not, at least not at first. Bouncing her daughter on her lap or lying next to her on the blanket on the living room floor, June discovered that she had never felt happier or more alive. She often rose early to rinse out and wash diapers, hanging them on the line in the sun to whiten them. She felt a surge of energy, not the opposite. Neighbors marveled at her stamina. One Tuesday, after a rainy Sunday when Frank had not been able to cut the grass, June settled Angelina in the buggy and pushed the heavy, iron-wheeled mower herself, amazed at her own strength. When he came home from work that night, Frank scolded her, saying she should not take on such strenuous work. Secretly he admired her. His old Italian grandmother had nothing on his Junie.

Once or twice a week that summer, June pushed the buggy the fourteen blocks to her parents' house, where she would putter a bit with her father in the garden while her mother bounced Angelina on her lap, cooing baby nonsense. It seemed as if each time they visited, Grace presented June with another little dress. "I know it's too big now, but it won't be for long," Grace said.

As June thought about her life, she understood that it was everything it was supposed to be. It was everything that was expected.

1939

June's pregnancy with Angelina had presented few problems. She had even escaped the nausea most women were stricken with. This time, it was different. She regularly vomited once or twice each morning, sometimes even more if soda crackers didn't calm her stomach in time.

Yesterday had been a particularly bad morning, and June had remained in bed most of the day. After breakfast, Angelina had been content to play with her toys. But in the afternoon, as if she knew exactly what her mother needed, she climbed into bed with June, lying there quietly until the two of them had fallen asleep. Today June was much better, enough to tackle the laundry that had been piling up. She had just come inside with a basket of clothes to fold. In her crib for her mid-afternoon nap, Angelina slept soundly. A few things, a terry romper for one, were still damp, so she draped them over the back of the couch.

June hoped to finish her task quickly so she could lie down and sleep, even for fifteen or twenty minutes, but as she reached into the basket for a pair of ankle socks, a prickling sense of dread overcame her. She sat up straight, took a deep breath, and shook off the alarming signal. Moments later, a searing pain bolted through her belly. It felt almost like labor, with the same need to push. Sweat gathered in pools under her breasts, between her thighs, glistened on her upper lip.

She staggered to the bathroom, felt a sudden urge to go, and lowered herself on the toilet, sinking her head in her hands, panting heavily. I'm going to be sick, she thought, but a minute of deep breaths helped that feeling pass. Her breathing calmer, for the moment, she looked up, listened. No sound. Angelina was still asleep. She tried to stand, but as June pushed from her knees, the pain returned and a trickle of red ran down to her ankles and soaked into the white rug.

She plopped back on the toilet seat and whined a low painful sound, afraid of what she knew was happening, afraid to wake her daughter. June knew she needed help. She conjured strength from an unknown place within her, grabbed a towel from the bar opposite the toilet, and pulled it toward her. She shoved the towel between her legs, clamping her thighs tightly around it, and hobbled to the phone table in the hallway. She dialed her mother's number.

Later, in the hospital, she told Frank that she was sorry. "I don't know what happened. I didn't mean...."

"June, Junie. Shhhhh. It happens some times. It just happens." He did not have the heart to tell her then what the doctor had told him, a ruptured uterus. It had been twins, identical boys. She would never have other children.

1940

After much convincing, June finally gave in and said, yes, they could go to the theater to see *Pinocchio*, which had finally come to Sheboygan. She had argued that Angelina, who was just three years old, would hardly remember the experience, an objection that did not matter, Frank said.

His final argument had won her over. "But wouldn't you like to see it?" Frank said. "Don't you remember how we both enjoyed *Snow White*?" Frank smiled as he reminded her, and she remembered. Of course she remembered. As a lark, Frank and June had left baby Angelina with June's parents and had headed out on a cold February evening to see *Snow White*. It had been so warm and peaceful inside the theater and she had been so happy to be out with her husband, even if it was only to see to a silly children's movie. While not quite the story her mother had read to her from *Grimm's Fairy Tales*, the movie was delightful, those bright colors, the silly dwarfs, especially Grumpy. She remembered vividly leaning over to Frank and whispering to him when Snow White first came into the little house and began putting it right, "Just like men to keep a house like that!" He had squeezed her hand and kissed her cheek. In the dark with the golden glow of the screen on her face, Frank thought no other woman on earth could be as beautiful as she was at that moment.

June now recalled the moment he had kissed her in the theater and how that small act had been remembered later that night, how it had stirred her passion. Back then she thought it all so simple. Simple life. Love. Marriage. Children. June knew now life was never, never as simple as it all seemed it could be.

"I suppose so," June told her husband when he asked again if they could see the movie. "It would be nice to get dressed up and go out. Yes, it would be nice," she said, though Frank could sense her heart wasn't in it.

The picture would begin at seven and Frank planned also to surprise June and Angelina by taking them out to dinner first. A steak at Everetts, maybe? The five-cent-an-hour raise Frank had gotten a week ago was still burning a hole in his pocket.

He had hurried home, had even asked to leave work a half hour early. The boss, in a good mood, had agreed. As always, Frank came in from work by the back door, scraped his boots even when they weren't muddy or snowy, took them off and set them on the boot rack, and hung his overcoat and cap on the peg in the back hall. They would need to bundle the girl up when they left. It was not yet spring in Sheboygan.

The lunch dishes were still on the kitchen table, Frank noticed with raised eyebrows, and on June's plate, a half-eaten sandwich.

"June?" he called. Angelina was alone in the living room. "Hey sweetie," Frank said to his daughter, who sat cross-legged on the carpeted floor in front of the radio. A daytime serial was playing, something of no interest to a child, but the voices kept her company. Wooden alphabet blocks were scattered before her, and she stacked them into short towers. Raggedy Ann lay behind her. The dress and bloomers had been taken off.

"Where's Mommy?" Frank asked, smiling.

The child began to cry. She got up, ran to her father, and threw her arms around his legs.

"What's the matter?" Frank picked his daughter up, wiped her tears, and bounced her gently as he had when she was a baby. "It's all right. It's all right."

"Mommy's crying. She told me go away."

Frowning, Frank set the child back on the floor. "You put dolly's clothes back on. All right? Daddy will go find Mommy. When I come back, we will have a cookie. Hmmm?"

Angelina's tiny chest heaved once more, but she smiled and nodded yes.

He found June in bed. She was not dressed. She had not pinned up her hair as she normally did. Frank wondered just how long Angelina had been alone, but remembered the lunch remains, so he knew June had not been in bed all day. Frank stood a moment, looking down upon her, feeling helpless. As if sensing his presence, as if feeling the heat of his body, June rolled onto her back. Her eyes fluttered open. She smiled.

"Oh, Frank. You're home. Did you have a good day?"

"June!" Frank barked. "What the hell is going on with you?"

On her part, June looked astonished at his reaction. Whatever could he mean? "Frank, I...."

"You leave a three-year-old alone? God knows what might have happened. Jesus!"

June leapt to her feet and ran to the living room. She took her daughter up in her arms and squeezed her, nestling her face in the crook of Angelina's neck.

Frank, now right behind her, demanded an answer. "What were you thinking? What happened here, June?"

June set her daughter on the couch, laid the doll in her lap, smoothed Angelina's coppery blonde hair. "Mommy loves you so much, sweetie," she said. "You be a good girl here for just a little bit."

Frank grabbed June by the elbow and pulled her toward the kitchen.

"You're hurting me."

He ignored her complaint. Instead, Frank pulled pushed his face close to hers. In a controlled but firm voice, he asked again. "June. What is going on?"

"Nothing. That is, I was tired, I guess. I must have fallen asleep. Of course, I never meant to…." June saw the incredulous look on her husband's face. "You have to believe me."

"June. We were going to…. Do you even remember that we were going to take her to the movie? You never even got dressed today, for Christ sake." Bitterly he understood his plans were ruined.

"I, I…well, I know that. I…."

"I don't know what to do, June. What am I to do? I can't be home all day. I have to work. Should I call your mother?"

"I'm not a child," June fired back, feeling as if her husband were scolding her. "I'm not someone you have to manage."

"Apparently I do. You don't see how irresponsible you are?"

Frank saw his daughter now, by his side, so he controlled his temper.

"Daddy," Angelina said, holding the rag doll out to him. The bloomers were on inside out, but she had wriggled the clothing back onto the doll. She looked up at her father expectantly, but shied away from her mother.

June felt the child's reticence. "Come here, sweetheart. Come to Mommy," June said, holding out her hands to her daughter, who shook her head "no" and backed away. "Oh, Angelina. Don't be that way. Come to Mommy."

"She's fine. Just leave her alone, June."

"Don't tell me to leave her alone. She can't just refuse me. I'm her mother."

"Then act like it. Goddamn it, June. Act like it."

His words were worse than a slap. She felt them clench at her throat tightly, and she couldn't breathe. Her knees folded and she fell to the kitchen floor, limp like the doll, her life turned inside out, the bright overhead light on her.

Frank discovered he had neither the will nor the energy to push her further, so he extended his hand and helped his wife to her feet. He led June back to bed, where she gratefully curled into a tight ball. He covered her, put out the light, and let her sleep. He might have to call her mother. A doctor? Someone. Whom would he not feel ashamed to call?

Minutes later Frank got a plate from the cupboard, pulled two cookies from the jar, and filled two glasses half full of milk. Then he gathered his daughter in his arms, gave her a quick squeeze and a kiss, and set her in her chair, where she settled herself on the thick, leather-bound atlas that served as her booster seat. They sat together quietly, except for the radio, which he now realized he had forgotten to turn off.

That night Frank made Angelina her dinner. He gave her a bath and brushed her thick hair, then he tucked his daughter into bed and read her a story. Later, slumped in a kitchen chair, Frank buried his head in his hands. He could not help his tears. They burned, and he hated them. He hated his own weakness. He hated that had no power to make June happy.

They never did see *Pinocchio.*

1942

"It won't be long before we can start looking for a house of our own to buy," said Frank. He and June were on their way home from the park, where they often took Angelina to play. She liked to climb the jungle gym, but she especially liked it when her father pushed her "high up to the sky" on the swings. Nearly dusk, the amber October moon was already climbing. It would be full tonight, Frank thought.

"Oh, do you think so, Frank? That would be lovely." The world was at war, and since the Japanese attack in December when the United States entered the fight, June worried that Frank would want to enlist. He had suggested he would do his duty if the time came. So far, he had not been that foolish. So while other families they knew had waved goodbye to their young men, Frank, at twenty-nine years old, was still building furniture and saving for the future.

That night, as June sat with Angelina, who soaked away the playground dust in the tub, the two recited nursery rhymes. Sometimes Angelina felt the rhymes were silly, but she liked it when they started talking faster and faster, eventually tripping on words, when they'd stop and laugh. It was not often that her mother laughed.

"Let's get that wild head tamed, now." June used a mild vinegar rinse to remove the shampoo residue. Without it, Angelina's thick hair clumped in knots.

"There," June said, lifting her daughter to the mirror to see her clean damp hair now braided into two braids. "How's it look?"

"Pretty. Thanks Mommy. Can I stay up late with you and Daddy tonight and listen to the radio?"

"Maybe for a little bit. You can have some milk and a cookie, if you like."

Angelina's bright cheeks beamed red. She nodded excitedly.

The little family sat together on the sofa, Angelina's head in her father's lap as they listened to Bob Hope's show. Hope, who did his shows live for GI's, was Frank's favorite entertainer. Now and then, June and Frank would laugh at something on the radio, but the child did not understand why, though sometimes a funny sound would evoke a giggle from her.

Later, Frank lifted the sleeping child in his arms and moved her to her room. He laid her gently on the bed and covered her with her sheet, though she already felt warm. As was his habit, he kissed the ends of his fingertips and touched them to her cheek. Softly breathing and sound asleep, she did not stir at the gesture.

At four thirty in the morning, Angelina cried out from her room, "Mommy. I don't feel good. Mommy!" She began to cry. Besides a minor case of the sniffles, Angelina had never been sick before.

"Frank!" shouted June in alarm. She's burning up." In the dim lamplight June removed Angelina's pajamas. A bright rash covered her daughter's arms, neck and chest. "Stick out your tongue, sweetie."

"It hurts. My throat hurts."

"I know, dear, I know. I need you to stick out your tongue. Can you pretend to make a mean face at me? Come on. There, that's it. Good girl."

Her daughter's strawberry tongue confirmed her fear. It was scarlet fever, the illness that she and her sister Joan had contracted as children. June recovered, but Joan did not. To see her own daughter now covered in the speckled rash, skin hot and tender to the touch, was to imagine the worst.

On the phone, Frank answered Dr. Mueller's questions. "Yes, red tongue. Rash. Yes. I see. Yes. We will. Thank you."

In the kitchen, Frank filled the enameled dishpan with cold water and a chip of ice, then carried it sloshing past the bathroom where he pulled a clean washcloth from a drawer. In his daughter's room, he held the basin while his wife dunked the cloth into the water, wrung it out, and ran it over Angelina's skin, repeating the process until the water warmed, when Frank headed back to the kitchen for more cold water.

An hour later, Dr. Mueller arrived. He examined Angelina briefly. It did not take him long to confirm the June's diagnosis. "Yes, it's scarlet fever, all right."

Though she knew it to be true, having the doctor say so sent June into a fit of tearful sobs.

"Now, there, Mrs. Catalano. It will be all right," he said.

"My sister," June stammered.

The doctor understood. In his forty-two years as a family doctor, he had seen many sisters, brothers, babies die from scarlet fever and other illnesses that were not in his power to heal. He patted the distraught woman on the shoulder. "Now, there was a time when there was not much we could do other than try to cool her down, say our prayers, and let her body do the healing. But we've got medicine now. You're not the first scarlet fever call I've had this week. Can you believe it?"

Frank reinforced the doctor's words. "Did you hear that Junie? It'll be all right. She'll be all right. Nothing bad will happen to our baby girl."

Dr. Mueller gave June a paper envelope containing little white pills. As expected, Angelina cried when they tried to get her to swallow the first pill, so the doctor showed June how to crush the sulfonamide tablet and mix it with water and a bit of sugar. "Make sure she drinks the entire glass," he emphasized. June would follow his instructions exactly.

"Can you believe that there was a time when a feverish child was bundled up even more? Insanity. Keep the cool cloths going until the fever goes down. If she's cold, cover her. And, of course, she needs rest. I'll stop back and check on her tomorrow, though it might not be until evening? I've got a busy day ahead and a couple of babies are threatening to be born, too."

Frank saw Dr. Mueller to the door, where he paid him for the visit and the medicine. Unexpected expenses always worried Frank.

Several weeks later, Angelina's symptoms were gone and the blush in her cheeks had returned to a normal, healthy pink. June kept a watchful eye nevertheless. At the moment, she set her daughter to the task of setting the table for dinner. Beef stew was simmering on the stove. June cut butter into flour for biscuits.

"Which side is forks again, Mommy?"

June met her daughter by the table and showed her. "Forks go on the left. Hold out your hands. See how your left hand makes an L? That will remind you which side is left."

Just then a car door closed and June's ears perked up at the sound. Seconds later, her husband was standing in the kitchen.

"You're early," she said, giving him a peck on the cheek, which he returned. He held his arms out to his daughter, who ran to embrace him.

"How are you feeling, my Angelina? Hmmm?"

"Fine, Daddy. I am good today."

At the sink, Frank washed his hands and dried them on the kitchen towel.

"What's wrong?" June asked in trepidation. "You feeling unwell?"

"No, I'm fine." Frank looked at the floor, then raised his hand to his head and scratched. "June." He took a deep breath, which only alarmed his wife even more.

"What is it?" she said now, her demanding tone pushing him to come out with it.

"Junie. I've enlisted. I just couldn't put it off any—"

June did not wait to hear the rest but ran from the kitchen and threw herself on her bed, sobbing.

Angelina's eyes met her father's. "It's okay baby girl. I promise." And then, because he did not believe in lying to anyone, especially not children, he bent to her level, held her shoulders, and said gently but directly, "Daddy has to go to the war. I will be away for a long time and I won't be able to come visit you. I have to fight some very bad men. Do you understand?"

The child nodded but she did not know what it meant to fight bad men. "Why is Mommy crying?"

"She thinks it will be dangerous." His fingers combed her hair, pushed a stray strand behind her ear. "She is right. It will be dangerous. But I will be careful. I promise. Do you believe me?"

"Yes, Daddy."

"Good girl. That's my good little girl." Frank lifted her to him and held her against his chest, burying his face in the crook of her neck. It would surprise him how quickly it happened, that in a few short months he would not instantly be able to picture her or conjure in his mind the way she smelled.

1943

When Frank left for war, June prepared to live as if he would not return. She felt resigned to the inevitability that he would be killed like so many others. He was headed to Europe. That was all she knew, all he knew.

When Frank had first told June of his decision, she pleaded with him to do all he could to back out of his commitment. She could not understand why a man with a wife and child would enlist. Surely he would not have been drafted at his age. He told her that it was his duty. There were others, Joe DiMaggio, for example. He was also 29, and he had enlisted in the Army Air Force back in February. Couldn't she see that everyone was making sacrifices?

At last, when logic could not persuade him, June had pushed it to a fight, ranting and screaming, telling him that he was being selfish. He let her rage and stood there immobile. He would not fight back. When she dropped to the chair, exhausted, he ended her hysteria once and for all. There was nothing to be done, he said. The papers had been signed.

Nevertheless, she took his departure as a personal punishment and chose to believe at times that Frank had enlisted to purposefully make her miserable. Whatever the case, she was sure he would be killed and she hoped it would happen sooner than later.

Frank insisted that June and six-year-old Angelina move in with her parents while he was away. They had plenty of space. Rooms to spare. Grace and Wally Schneider were happy to have their daughter home with them, even happier to be able to be a full-time part of their granddaughter's life.

The swiftness with which June's life turned upside down made her feel as if she were losing her grasp on even the most ordinary filaments of reality. Watching her husband board the bus to basic training was only the beginning of her upheaval. Even without Frank's help, the task of moving from their lower flat was accomplished more quickly than seemed possible. Except for clothes, personal items, and Angelina's toys and books, most of their belongings were packed into her parents' attic.

As she surveyed the little house one last time, ready to hand the key over to the landlord, June thought about their life in this house. That morning, she had unpacked and reinstalled the curtains and bedcoverings that "belonged" to the house. None of this is mine, she thought. She straightened the fraying antimacassar atop the armchair, which was itself a bit more worn, but well cared for nevertheless. Seven years. They had lived here seven years. How quickly those years had passed. Too quickly. A wry smile filled her face. If she could start over, there would be things she would do differently. But there had been happy times, too. She remembered that August day after their wedding when Frank had blindfolded her and brought her here. She had hoped desperately they would not need to live here for long. Now, she was unaccountably reluctant to leave.

Despite it all, the spring of 1943 was otherwise uncomplicated for June. She inquired about work at her old office, and they told her they would let her know if something opened up. She volunteered at the Armory for the war effort, packing bandages. Because she knew he needed her, she worked the garden with her father. They dressed the soil with compost made from kitchen scraps and yard waste, turned the spring clods under, and worked until the earth was loose and warm. Wally Schneider had been raising his own vegetables long before Victory gardens, but he felt a positive zeal this year, unlike he had felt in years. At 68, two years older than her husband, Grace Schneider found the stooping and bending that gardening required too much for her knees and hips and was pleased her daughter seemed to enjoy the work.

The neighborhood was populated by children near Angelina's age or a bit older. She moved from riding a tricycle to a bicycle by the end of the summer, though she would require first aid on skinned knees three times before she could ride with confidence. The alley behind the Schneiders' house was the perfect place to set up racetracks or play tag without fear of passing cars.

Angelina, or as Grandpa Schneider called her, "my little Angel," and then eventually just "Angel," made the transition with no difficulty from their two-bedroom lower flat to the big house with large, fenced-in yard where a tree swing hung from a tall old elm. She loved being doted on by her grandparents, especially her grandfather, who would slip her lollipops when the women weren't around, telling her with a finger to his lips that it was their secret.

As for June, she was surprised by how much she missed her husband and amused that he came to her in the oddest moments: frying an egg, darning a sock, or washing a window until it squeaked.

At the end of June, Wally came into the house with an overflowing bucket of shiny strawberries and pronounced a bumper crop. With boyish glee, he put the family to work. June was to get the ice cream churn from the basement and wash the inner bowl and paddle. Grace was set at making custard on the stove. Angelina helped her grandfather prepare the berries. She rinsed them, he topped them and cut them into quarters, and she lightly mashed them. Then, after measuring a scoop of sugar, the child stirred the crystals into the berries until they glistened in the big glass bowl. Then Wally readied the churn, packing the outer bowl with chips of ice and salt. Once the custard was inside, Angelina helped to turn the crank, though she found it was not as easy as it looked. Everyone took a turn. It was the Schneider ice cream rule: if you don't turn the crank, you can't eat the ice cream.

"The harder it gets to crank, the closer we are to scooping it into our bowls," Grandma told Angelina. Grace even washed the cut glass parfait glasses and they used iced tea spoons, which made the experience feel like they had gone back in time. "Just like an old ice cream parlor," Wally said.

June said it was the best batch ever. "You sure didn't skimp on the berries, did you?" she said.

After her last bite, Angel licked the glass, sticking her tongue in as far as she could.

"Let's make some more, Grandpa," she said.

The old man could not have loved the little girl more than he did at that moment.

After Angel—for now even June was calling her Angel—had been tucked into bed, June sat up with her parents until she couldn't keep her eyes open. Her father listened to the radio for news of the war. While he never spoke about it, Wally had fought in the Argonne in World War I. More than the women, he worried about Frank. Most nights June's mother read *The Saturday Evening Post* or *Life*. June crocheted doilies or knitted mittens or caps, mindless tasks that kept her hands busy and her mind from worry. As long as she was active, June could manage the days.

The nights were much harder. It wasn't that June minded living with her parents. They were kind to her, even kinder to her daughter, and she loved them. But she missed her own home. She missed being a wife.

A letter from Frank arrived near the end of August. He had enclosed a wide blade of grass from France. *Angelina*, he wrote, *grass is green here, just like it is in Wisconsin. There are dairy farms, too. Down the road from our camp is a nice little farm, and when the breeze blows west, we can sometimes hear the rooster crow in the morning. Would you believe even he speaks French? He says cock-a-doodle-ze-doo.* Frank told his family that all was well. They had seen some fighting, some of the men in his company had been injured, but no one had died, not yet. This part of his letter was a lie. The men often replaced the truth with fiction in their letters home, replaced the unspeakable with stories that some would later come to believe in themselves. He reiterated the well-worn phrases the Schneiders heard each evening on the radio. Now that the Americans are here, the war will end quickly.

June had put the blade of grass in a half pint mason jar, screwed on the zinc lid and put it on her bureau near the string of pearls Frank bought her before he left, the pearls he said she would wear when he returned and took her dancing.

There were no other letters.

In September, Angel started first grade at Grant elementary school. Though it was only one block away, Wally walked her to school each morning and home each afternoon. The two were inseparable.

June's periods of melancholy continued, and her mother attributed them to loneliness and worry over Frank. Her temper short, June would bark at Angel, provoked by the most benign behavior, a child simply being a child. At other times, June's mood swung to the opposite side, the manic energy driving her to pull the draperies off the rods and wash them in a tub outdoors or pull up the rugs to beat. June's mood swings created tension between June and her mother. Grace simply could not understand why her daughter couldn't behave normally.

Without Frank around, June felt the weight of raising her daughter alone and she resented times when Grace stepped in to instruct or direct Angelina's actions. One afternoon after school, Angel, who had been taught to change into play clothes before coming to the kitchen for a cookie, was sitting in the kitchen with her snack.

"Why haven't you changed your clothes?" June screeched. "You think I like doing extra wash? Go get your play clothes on." Angel, stunned, looked back and forth between mother and grandmother. "Now!" commanded June, at which the girl, lip quivering, bounded from the chair and up to her room.

"June, it's my fault," Grace interjected. "The cookies were still warm and I just thought...."

"She knows better, Mother. She has to learn to be responsible."

Grace did not add another word, but turned back to peeling potatoes.

It hurt Wally even more to witness these scenes, and he wished he could say something to his daughter, but he had no idea what to say. "A wife needs her husband" was all Wally would say to Grace at night in bed. She agreed, but believed it was something else. What else, she didn't know. Still, Grace prayed each night that God would watch over her son-in-law and bring him safely home.

1977

Near dawn Angel became ether and dreamt of her grandmother's house. She became a spirit undulating through memory. Angel floated above her mother and watched her strong arms snap the crisp, white sheets, then let them billow down upon mattresses. They smelled like sunshine. They smelled like memory. Angel hovered past Grandmother, who sat on the front porch with her feet up on the white wicker footstool. Grandma hummed an old tune and worked her darning needle over the wooden egg, a pile of frayed heels beside her. A memory of cinnamon transported Angel to the gleaming white kitchen, where Dotted Swiss curtains puffed like sails. Angel saw herself at nine years old with Grandpa, who had just cut a generous piece of his still-warm cinnamon bun for her. It was slathered with thick, white icing. With a quick laugh, his blue eyes crinkly, he swabbed a glob of icing from her chin. She reluctantly moved on then to search for her father, but he was not in the house. She would have to fly beyond for him, to where she felt but could not see him reaching out to her. A faint echo of his voice reached her, but as she rose to an upstairs window, she felt an intractable weight pull against her. And the weight clicked. Shh tuk, shh tuk. Her hand pushed through the open window and reached toward the green leaves that rustled lightly in the breeze and the ethereal blue and the cotton clouds, but the weight clicked and tugged, clicked and tugged.

Shh tuk, shh tuk, shh tuk, shh tuk.

Angel forced her eyes open. They hurt. Her lids felt heavy, sticky, her vision cloudy, but in a moment she saw Sophie curled up like a cat in a chair nearby. And unable to keep her eyes open, she fell back into the dark, weighted now like lead.

Later that morning, Dr. Winter arrived. Sophie watched him read the chart, examine Angel without speaking, lift her limp wrist for her pulse. He motioned to Sophie to meet him in the hallway.

"I'm glad to see she's doing better," he said, "though I am concerned about the severity of her dehydration."

Like a child caught in a lie, Sophie confessed as if the doctor were her parent. "She had been alone," Sophie said. "I was finishing my last few of weeks of college."

Knowing she would spend the summer watching, waiting for her mother to die, Sophie had tried over the previous weeks to distance herself from any thought of her mother dying. Instead, she kept a mental image of her mother gently napping on the couch, watching TV all day, soap operas and talk shows, playing along with *The Price is Right*. In Madison, Sophie and her friends wrote final papers, studied for exams, and strolled State Street at night, especially on the weekends, when they and cadres of eager young men would close the bars. The dictum to live life to the fullest pronounced upon her mother weeks earlier had been something Sophie felt she had a right to as well. Then Sophie recalled the weekend she had stayed away, selfishly choosing to go to a party instead of visiting her mother. What if Angel had been so depressed at that point she had just given up? Sophie felt the weight of blame. She looked into the doctor's stark blue eyes, impossible to lie to. I don't need you to make me feel worse, she thought.

"Yes, well, all that is behind us now. Her vitals are improving, so that is what matters." Additionally, he said, after they got Angelina's fluids back to normal and electrolytes stable, got her eating a bit, she should be alert and feeling much better. They would also be moving her out of ICU this morning.

Confused, Sophie said, "Then she's getting better?"

The doctor apologized for being unclear. No. The cancer would not have gone into remission. If anything, this episode likely accelerated her decline. It was impossible to put the truth into words that did not sting.

Sophie nodded affirmatively.

"I'll be in tomorrow. In a few days, if she takes an upswing, we will have to talk about a nursing care facility. Unfortunately, her insurance won't cover her stay here for more than a week at most. And really, they're better equipped to help you and your mom elsewhere, especially with end of life matters. Riverbend or Sunnyside? The nurses have some materials you can look at."

It was all so awful, the way they talked about these things. "End of life matters." No, thought Sophie. Dr. Winter didn't mean to sound cold. What else could he say? He was trying to help. But where was the heart-rending "I'm so sorry" tone she needed to hear? A verbal arm around her shoulder? An "oh, you poor thing"? Everyone had been nice, but they were all just doing their jobs, and in their jobs, people died all the time. They were used to it, she figured. Well, I'm not used to it, she shouted in her head. More than that, Sophie began to feel the depth of the vast chasm of her ignorance. She assumed her mother would remain here, in the hospital. Who tells you about these things? Sophie agonized. She tucked the pamphlets into her purse for now. She would look at them later, think about what she was going to do. Sophie realized these decisions would be hers now.

Sophie was grateful they had moved her mother to a private room and grateful for the Lake Michigan view, even if all she could see was a sliver of steel blue through the gaps between the neighborhood homes and trees. Sophie opened a window just enough to get fresh air, and while the day was cool, it was also sunny, so the lilac-laden breeze that puffed at the green-and-brown print curtains felt warm.

Whether it was due to the scent of lilac or the buzz of a lawn mower or the sweet chlorophyll from fresh cut grass, Angel's senses stirred and she awoke in a peaceful haze.

"Hey sleepyhead," Sophie said when she noticed her mother's open eyes. "You going to stay with me awhile this time?"

"Smells...good."

"It does, Mom, it does. How're you feeling? I should go get the nurse."

"Tired." Angel closed her eyes.

"That's okay. You sleep all you want. The doctor said it will probably take you a whole day to get back to normal." Even as she said it, Sophie knew she had no idea what normal would be now.

"Let's get you situated better," Sophie said, and she cranked up the head of her mother's bed and fussed with the pillows so that Angel could see outside better. "How's that?"

Angel did not answer but opened her eyes again and looked around the hospital room. Then, realizing where she was, she said, "I'm in the hospital?"

"Yeah. You don't remember?"

"Unh-unh. How long?"

"Last night. The ambulance? Mom, you really don't remember?"

Angel shook her head, then yawned and stretched her neck. Sophie held her mother's hand and rubbed her loose skin. When Sophie pushed too hard against a bruise on her forearm, Angel winced.

A few days earlier, Angel had fallen. She had hit her head. Later, she had awoken in a dark house, streetlights casting shadows over her belongings, her furniture, her knickknacks, her things that would soon be nothing. She who would soon be nothing. Angel had found the strength to get to her knees, then to her feet. She had wanted water desperately, but halfway to the kitchen, she'd felt her knees wobble. Afraid she would fall again, she had headed back down the hall and had dropped into bed. Hours later, she had awoken, shivering, and felt around her ankles for the quilt. When she had become conscious again, she realized she had lost track of time. Was it a day later? Two days? At some point, she had shuffled to the bathroom and, with her cupped hand, gathered cool water and slurped handfuls. She had not been hungry. Even water nauseated her. Back into bed she had lain upon iron spikes. When she closed her eyes, she knew they would never open again.

Nurse Mary swept into the room, her wide hips in crisp, light blue poplin ready for anything. "I thought I heard some twittering in here," she said. With a swift confidence that Sophie admired, Mary checked Angel's pulse. She gently set a thermometer in Angel's mouth and rubbed her patient's wrist as she waited to read it.

"How are you feeling?" Mary asked.

"Alive, I guess," Angel mumbled.

"Well, mainly, you're not so dehydrated anymore, so that's sure to help. You thirsty?"

"Cotton mouth," Angel laughed weakly.

Mary shook the thermometer after reading it. "Normal," she reported. "Now, are you warm enough? I can—"

"Yes. The sun feels good."

"That it does. That it does." Mary checked the fluid level in the IV bottle and laid her hand on her patient's. Angel's fingers, thin, the nails yellowed, the skin transparent. "You just rest. Stay in bed like a princess. Isn't that a deal?" Mary chirped brightly.

Angel smiled.

"That's my girl. You stay positive, en so. Just let us take care of you. You've got a wonderful daughter. You're lucky."

Angel looked over at Sophie, who stood by the window, the bright light a halo around her head.

"Yes. Very lucky." I am just now realizing how lucky, Angel thought, and time is robbing me.... She squeezed her eyes tightly shut and clenched her teeth. It's just not fair. Not fair at all.

That evening, Carole, the night nurse, wheeled in a cot for Sophie. Compared with the green chair, the thin mattress was the most comfortable bed she had ever slept in. Yet despite the fact that Sophie had fallen asleep the moment she had settled her head on the pillow and breathed in the disinfectant clean of the pillow case, she had slept in fits most of the night, restless legs out and back under blanket, the clock, tick, tick, ticking.

At one point, she had stared wide-eyed at the ceiling and recalled her phone conversation that afternoon with Lev. When he'd asked her what the doctor had said, she told him, kept her breath calm all the while. He, silent on the line, listened to her tell it all before he spoke.

"Listen," he had said. "Whatever I can do, whatever it is. You just ask. Okay, kiddo?"

It had taken all Sophie had not to burst into tears at that moment. If an adult, a real adult could take all of this from her shoulders? She thought of turning it all over to him, letting him lead. She'd be there for meetings with the doctors or the nursing home or later with the funeral director, but it would be Lev handling the details. And just like he had done when she was a little girl, he might now and then smile in the way that reminded her that the two of them were partners in crime, like when he would give her an extra scoop of ice cream when no one was looking, or when she was twelve, he had taken her without her mother's knowledge to see Wilson Pickett at the Armory. Sophie remembered her mother saying she didn't know what all the fuss was about, that she personally enjoyed a lot of "Negro music," but she might not have wanted her twelve-year-old daughter going to a concert, even knowing Lev would let nothing happen. Still it was the joy of their secret Sophie had cherished all these years. Lev had always been more than just a neighbor, and she knew that he meant it completely when he said he wanted to help, but Sophie also knew she would ask Lev for nothing. Not now, anyway.

She had squandered a month. It was now her responsibility to make up for her failure as a daughter.

1945

After Frank came home from the war, the family continued to live with Grace and Wally, and each day seemed like a year to Frank, who felt impotent to provide for his family the way he wanted to. Despite Wally's insistence that it would take time to learn how to live again, Frank was in a hurry for time to speed up. After basic training, Frank had been eager, anxious to begin. Then, on the ground in France, there were moments that suspended themselves in time, silent amid the roar of guns, blurred amid the chaos of motion. Other moments had become lost to him, though he would not know until later that those moments had simply buried themselves in his subconscious, where they would lay until some long, dark night, when they would climb into his dreams. The glorious effort he had signed up for had been filled with useless bloodshed. And yet, the Allies had defeated Hitler. Of that, Frank was proud.

Frank had laid for a month in a convalescent hospital in England before being deemed healthy enough to go home. Shrapnel lodged in his lower back and down this right thigh had been removed. Completely, he had been told. How was it that at times he still felt the raw burning, as if the wound was new? As a result of his wounds, Frank walked with a slight limp, especially when the pain throbbed. He heard Wally's gentle voice in his head: it will take time, it will take time. But Frank's capability for patience had been diminished by the war.

Frank went back to his old job, and on his first day back he saw that others he had enjoyed working with were no longer on the line. Unfamiliar faces, some of them women, stood where he used to stand, the future so confidently before them. The new boss at North Shore didn't know Frank or what he was capable of, and he took Frank's limp as an indication of deeper wounds.

"Are you sure you're ready, soldier?" the thin-faced young man in wire spectacles said.

Frank wondered what weak deferment had kept that little shit out of the fray. "Fine. I am fine," Frank said. "I'm ready to get back to work."

Frank was given the task of puttying nail holes and sanding rough edges, getting case goods ready for finishing. "Women's work," Frank scoffed, but he did it, gratefully, at least at first. He missed being able to lead the men on the line, being able to teach them. The drudgery of this new work and his nearly constant pain, combined with Frank's loss of his own place in life, continued to wear on him and made him irritable at unexpected moments.

Over coffee one Sunday morning, June asked Frank if he had heard from Jimmy Hoffman lately. Jimmy, younger and more eager to fight, had joined the Navy the day after the Pearl Harbor attack. He had nearly died in the Pacific and spent six months recuperating at the Naval Hospital in Portsmouth, Virginia. His amputated right arm and disfiguring burns to his face, neck, and chest meant Jimmy would never work again. At the hospital, they had fitted him with a prosthetic, an unnatural peach extremity with a hook for a hand, he wrote in a letter mailed to June. *The cute red-headed nurse is doing the actual writing, though. Ha ha.* He told his old friends how he struggled to learn to pick up a pen, though doctors said that with practice he would once more be able to tie his own shoes. June could easily read the doubt between the lines.

In November of 1944, Jimmy's mother had called to say that he was now back home in Milwaukee and would live with them. "June," she said, her voice a slight quaver, "He talks about Frank all the time, about all their fun times. When Frank comes home, tell him. Please tell him. Tell him to come down for a visit, June." And June, who had not heard from her husband after his first letter, said she surely would. Yes, she surely would. Frank swirled the one slug of coffee left in the cup, grounds stirred up. "No, I haven't," Frank said sharply and in a way that indicated to June that he didn't want to talk about it. What was wrong with him, he wondered, that the thought of visiting his lifelong friend petrified him? He should drive down, he knew. Soon, he would go soon. There was too much to do right now. Frank knew it was wrong, but he could not help thinking it was nevertheless true that very often human beings were repulsed by each other's misery.

At night, the house still, an occasional creak of wood, a roof timber, an owl screeching off in the distance, Frank would wake in a restless sweat, heart pounding, ears ringing, and he would rub his eyes, his wet, stinging eyes. The pictures, like a newsreel, were the same. Jimmy lying in mud, arm blown off at the elbow, the sky around him raining fire, Frank himself in a bunker, shivering in the cold, slush creeping into his boots, his bowels cramping, beside him the soldier he had left the bunker for, the soldier he had pulled back by the ankles, the faceless soldier who had crept out on his belly to retrieve and throw the fumbled grenade.

1946

Almost ten years to the day that she had married Frank Catalano, June stood in the tiny living room of their new place, a two-bedroom house on 10th Street, and resigned herself to the necessity of unpacking. With Frank at work and Angelina at her mother's, June took a deep breath and wondered again how Frank had thought this wreck of a house would be acceptable. Besides the cheap rent, the house had little that appealed to her. A new set of curtains would not be the magic touch this time. After three days of wide-open windows and scrubbing every inch, floor to ceiling, June swore she could still catch a whiff of the greasy cooking odors that had nearly made her sick when she had first walked through the front door. To his credit, Frank had not expected her to do all the work by herself, although his idea of "good enough" did not match hers. But he'd been down on his knees, scrubbing, scraping. June had never sent so much dirty water down the drain. The one time she complained, he had raised his voice. Did she think he liked it that this place was all they could afford?

"We'll get our own house soon, Junie," Frank said as they backed out of her parents' driveway after picking up the last of their things. Even he no longer believed it as he once had. And on her part, June had heard the promise so often that it now sounded hollow. Memories of the many nights they had lain in bed almost as one when they were first married, planning out their life, dreaming of what they wanted, both yearning equally for what they believed they deserved, came to her now with such a sense of grief she felt as if some part of their life, and therefore some part of her, had died.

As June unpacked the boxes she had stored in her parents' attic, she was surprised at how many of her old things she had forgotten about completely. Unpacking them now held little joy for June. Part of her discontent came from her sense that Frank himself had changed. Since the war, he was moodier and more solitary, which she supposed was to be expected in a man who had seen all the ugly things he must've seen, though he did not talk with her about any of that. When she asked directly what it had been like, he shrugged his shoulders and said "War is war."

Several months before she knew Frank was safe, June had listened to the minister tell about his own brother, who had returned home with the right side of his face badly burned. With pity, June had imagined what that man's wife must have felt. Worse, the story, as part of a sermon on patience, had triggered weeks of nightmares in which Frank, a paralyzed and disfigured corpse, stomped clumsily toward her trembling and helpless body. In these dreams, she would scream as he approached, but she was never able to make him hear her. She was never able to make him stop.

The mantle clock with no permanent home sat on the kitchen table and chimed 11:00. June had wound it that morning after rubbing it with furniture oil. Time was getting away from her. Her plan had been to at least have the bedrooms ready to sleep in that evening and to have the kitchen ready to make a simple meal of eggs and bacon. Her father would be dropping Angelina off at four. She had invited her parents to dinner, promising nothing grand, but they had declined and she was grateful.

June lined the kitchen drawers next and organized them with neatly folded dishtowels, cooking utensils, and silverware. She unpacked glasses, washing each one before setting them in a cupboard that she discovered was too small for all of them, so she wrapped the extras back in the newspaper that still lay in crumpled balls on the table next to the clock. Frank could take the box to the basement later. Even though she had already made several trips down to make use of the washing machine, June did not like going into the basement. It reeked of mildew. At some point, she'd need to attack that problem with a bucket of bleach water, but not now.

June was about to make herself a peanut butter sandwich when she heard a crash, the sound of breaking glass, and a woman's scream. She left the open loaf of bread on the counter and hurried to the front door. Through the rusting screen she saw a bright green Oldsmobile up the curb, smashed into the black streetlight pole in front of the neighbors' house across the street. Steam rose from the crumpled hood. Neighborhood kids began swarming to the scene.

A woman in a calico apron waved her hands about her head in alarm. "Someone call the police," she shouted. June would have done so, but the telephone company had still not arrived to connect their service. A young woman in a smart yellow dress now stood by the aproned woman, and the two were shaking their heads. June guessed this was as good a time as any to meet her neighbors. As she crossed her front yard, the driver's side door creaked open and an old man in gray trousers and suspenders emerged from the car, sweating and shaking, but not bleeding. Three boys wearing striped shirts and sitting on red bikes surrounded him.

"Gee, mister," one of them said. "You oughta look where you're going."

The old man glared and thrust out his arm to scatter them. They leaned back, snickered at each other, then wheeled backwards out of his way. By then June was on the sidewalk opposite her house, and a police siren screamed louder and louder as it approached. June saw the man's knees wobble, and she reached to support his arm. The woman in the yellow dress ran to his other side, and together they helped the man to a chair on the aproned woman's porch. Once the police arrived and began to question the man, June introduced herself to the two women.

"Is this a normal occurrence?" she asked as a way to start a conversation.

"Well, good Lord, no," said the aproned woman, who seemed offended by the question.

June, who had not meant anything by her remark, felt stung by the woman's harsh response and began to compensate with apologetic phrases, which made her feel even more awkward. Sometimes, June thought, I just can't seem to say anything right.

Later, when June told Frank and Angelina all about her exciting day, she did not tell them about the aproned woman but said only that she'd met a young woman from two doors down who seemed very nice. Together, after the tow truck had dislodged the Oldsmobile from the light pole, after the police had finished their report, and after the old man's son had arrived for his father, the two of them had laughed about the dangers of getting old. At least someone around here, June had thought gratefully, has a sense of humor.

The move to 10th Street also meant Angelina would have to change schools. With only two weeks before the first day of school, the girl barely had time to adjust. She had loved her grandparents' neighborhood. In contrast, the homes in this area of the city were so much smaller and closer together, and cars lined themselves along curbs because the houses lacked garages. Instead of cool lake breezes, this place sometimes smelled like asphalt or garbage. One always knew what the neighbors were cooking for dinner, whether roast beef or cooked cabbage. This neighborhood also seemed overrun by boys—red-headed, white-fluffed, shaved-bald boys who sneered as they whizzed past her on their bikes. Their imperious surveillance of the "new girl" did not make June's order of finding a friend easy at all. There were days when June just gave in to Angelina's complaints and let her stay indoors. However, on her first day of fourth grade at Washington Elementary School, Angelina's fear of the neighborhood children finally overwhelmed her and she threw a rare tantrum, something her mother had no patience for.

At breakfast, Angel had refused to eat, saying her tummy hurt. June tossed a full bowl of Cheerios in the sink. "It's a sin to waste food, Angelina. You've been told that before. If you weren't going to be late this morning,

I'd have forced you to eat every last little soggy bit."

Angel sobbed the obligatory "I'm sorry."

"Sit still," June scolded as she pulled her daughter's hair back tightly and secured the ponytail with a rubber band. "You're acting foolishly. It's just school. My goodness."

Even now on the sidewalk, Angel stood so strongly resolute that June was forced to grasp her daughter's stubborn hand too tightly and nearly drag her the three-and-a-half-block distance to school. Before they made their way up the walk to the school doors, June took her daughter's shoulders, stooped to her level, and looked her in the eyes. Completely disregarding the children and parents surrounding them, June said in a quiet but stern voice, "Angel, you will stop this nonsense right now. I am not going to be embarrassed. For goodness sake, you think I like this? We are all making sacrifices. So, just knock it off. Do you hear me?" June handed her daughter a hankie and stood up straighter than a rod, smoothed her skirt, and tucked a loose strand of hair behind her ear.

Angel sniffed hard, wiped her swollen red eyes and looked up at her mother with clenched teeth. I hate you, she voiced in her head. At that moment, she swore she would never speak to her mother ever, ever again.

Angelina Catalano was introduced to the class by her teacher, a short, pudgy woman in a plaid dress, belted severely at the waist. Dark horn-rimmed glasses suspended by a gold chain lay across her full breasts. She smelled of sweet powder. By the end of the year, Angel would grow to love Miss Carlson.

Angel was assigned the last desk in the row by the windows, and that fate, at least, pleased her. She felt safely alone at her desk. All the while the teacher spoke, Angel stared into the bright sky and dreamed of running away. She would go back to Grandpa's house and throw herself into his arms. She would tell him about the boys. About the girls who turned up their noses. He would listen. He would take her away from the ugly little house where doors had begun to slam. He would take her away from the nights when she crawled under her covers to drown out the screaming and all the words she could never unhear.

By the end of September, Angel had still not succumbed to the routines of fourth grade. Nor had she made a single friend. But she had learned to walk assertively past the boys who stared. They never confronted her so she understood they were harmless after all. It was the girls she feared. Three in particular, who with military precision found ways to accidentally bump into her. Afterwards, she would hear them laugh. She would not tell her mother, who could not begin to fathom why Angelina's adjustment to her new school continued to be so difficult.

Many mornings Angel complained that her stomach hurt. Twice June had kept the girl home because she had thrown up her breakfast. Then later she would be fine, and there seemed to be nothing wrong with her. Frank, whose own adjustment to civilian life was taking too long, according to June, attempted to fix the problem by telling Angelina to "snap out of it." He had no idea how to manage the girl's phantom illness.

"Do you think we're just going to baby you?" he said, holding her out in front of him one morning, his hands on her weak shoulders, her head drooping.

"Look at me," he scolded. "Look at me when I talk to you." When she did not raise her eyes to his, he shook her hard, then with a quick shove, backed away from her.

"She's all yours, Mother. I don't know what else to do."

At dinner that night, the parents nearly mimicked the catatonic girl. They ate bitterly, chewing and swallowing in silence.

Later, in her bed, Angelina let quiet tears soak into her pillow as she had every night since they had moved away from her grandparents' house. But tonight she felt her loss more deeply, for it was layered with the knowledge that she was no longer a child and her father would no longer love her the way he had once loved her. Her days of dolls and teddy bears and stories on her father's lap had gone away to France with a man who had not come home to her.

Not long after, light filled Angelina's dark room when June opened her daughter's door. "You asleep, baby girl?"

Angelina did not answer, but June came in and sat on the edge of the bed anyway. "Come on, I know you're awake. Sit up a minute. I want to give you something."

June reached to turn on the bedside lamp. The room glowed soft golden pink. Angelina hoisted herself up but scowled at having been disturbed. "You're sad, huh?" June said. "About leaving Grandma and Grandpa?" June had finally put the symptoms together and had surprised herself with how long it had taken her to understand her daughter's melancholy.

At her mother's words, Angelina sobbed loudly. June drew her daughter to her chest and let the girl cry. Her own silent tears fell, not for Angelina, but for the realization that there was nothing she could do to make her daughter happy. A parent's ability to bring joy is limited, if indeed such a thing exists at all. When Angelina had cried it all out, June took a hankie from the pocket of her robe and shook it out for Angelina to use. After the girl had blown her nose, June tipped Angelina's blotchy freckled face to hers and looked into her puffy eyes. "You feel a little better?"

Angelina nodded.

June slipped her hand back into her pocket and pulled out a small cardboard jewelry box. "I have something for you," she said.

"What is it," Angelina asked.

"Promise me first you'll try to be less sad? Try to be happier?"

The girl did not know how one could promise to be happier, but she said she would try. Then she lifted the lid off the box. Inside was a crude necklace, a shell, it seemed, slipped onto a long brown length of twine, its ends tied in a tight knot.

"What is it?" Angelina asked again.

"Well," June said, "it's a piece of hollow bone. I found it on the lakeshore when I was a little girl, just a bit older than you are. After we moved back from Grandma and Grandpa's house, I found it when I was unpacking. I had kept it all those years in an old cookie tin, but I guess I forgot I had it. See? I have made it into a necklace for you. You can wear it all the time, even in the bath, if you want to. You don't ever have to take it off."

June slipped the slender twine over her daughter's head. "There," she said. "It falls low onto your chest, as I hoped it would, so you can wear it secretly."

The twine would soften over time, but at the moment it scratched her tender skin. Angelina brought her fingers to the bone. It felt cool and smooth. She looked into her mother's eyes, which gleamed with water.

"You can wear it," June continued, "to remind you to be strong, strong like bones, which are very hard to break. I know you're sad right now, and I wish I could tell you that you won't ever be this sad again, but it would not be true. I think sometimes that's what life means. Life is just people trying to be happy in between all the sad times."

June shook her head, squeezed her eyes tightly before opening them and, smiled a wide, confident smile. "Now, remember. When you wear this, think about how strong a bone is. A bone lasts almost forever. You are strong, too. Stronger than you know. Can you remember that tomorrow? When you wake up for school? Can you remember that you are my strong, brave girl? Daddy needs you to be happy again, sweetheart. I need it. Can you do that for me?"

Angelina clasped the bone in her trusting fist and nodded that she would.

"All right then. You go to sleep. I've got to go out in the garage to see if your father's done tinkering out there. I think we all need to get a good night's sleep tonight." June clicked off the lamp and padded out of Angelina's room, closing the door not quite tight behind her. Her chest heaved, and she held back a sob. Bones broke all the time, she thought. They snapped like dry twigs and splintered into irreparable pieces.

It was well into the night before Angelina let go of the bone. She would not take it off until she was a teenager, on the night she had sex for the first time, when shame compelled her. She could not bear to have her mother so near.

1946

Frank laid his hand upon his daughter's head, leaned down, and whispered so he would not startle her. "Time to wake up, Angelina." The morning showed no promise of sunshine, and Frank suspected he'd be sorry he had put off replacing the torn wiper blade. "Come on. Rise and shine, now." Frank clicked on her bedside lamp and Angelina's eyelids fluttered but did not open.

The child's coppery blonde hair lay in wavy strands across her pillow. Frank realized he would have to try to manage that mess into a ponytail, or maybe he could just leave it long. He opened her closet door and found a plaid dirndl skirt and a white blouse with a sailor collar and laid them on the end of her bed. A quick shake of the girl's shoulder finally got her to open her eyes.

"Come on, now. Time to get up. I don't want you to be late for school."

"Where's Mommy?"

"She's sick, so I'm going to make your breakfast and get you to school today."

"What's wrong with her? Does she have the measles?" A boy in her class had the measles and had been very sick.

"No, no. Don't worry. She just has a headache and a tummy ache. She will be better later. Promise. Now, no dawdling, you hear? I still have to go to work."

Angel slid out of her bed and plodded to the bathroom. Back in her bedroom, she got dressed, hung her pajamas on her door hook, and made her bed. She was sitting on the floor putting on her socks and shoes when her father returned to check on her.

"You made your bed?"

"I always make my bed."

"I guess I thought Mommy did that for you. Well, I'm proud of you. Good job. Now, what will we do about that hair?"

The girl gave her father a quizzical look. "What do you mean?"

"How does Mommy usually manage that mop?"

"She sometimes wants to brush my hair, but mostly I do it myself."

Frank smiled, relieved. He had no idea his daughter was so self-reliant. She was more grown up than he realized.

"I guess I don't know a lot about the morning routines around here, do I? I suppose I did breakfast wrong, too. I scrambled you an egg and made you jelly toast."

Angelina smiled. "Thank you Daddy. Mommy makes me eat Cream of Wheat, and I hate it."

In the kitchen Frank poured Angelina a small glass of milk. She gobbled her breakfast quickly, and he drank his coffee, black.

"School starts at 8:30, right?" Angelina nodded.

After she brushed her teeth, Angelina saw that her father was busy packing her lunch, so she thought she would check on her mother. She opened the door and tiptoed in. Leaning over, Angelina called softly, "Mommy, are you sick? What's wrong?"

Moments later, Frank's hands on the girl's shoulders startled her. "Come on, Angelina. Just leave her alone."

Frank clicked the door shut and herded Angelina out the door. Their movements, their morning footsteps, their presence moments earlier—none of it had caused June to stir from her stupor. Normally June would be able to pull herself together in time for her to get Angel ready for school. Aspirin and a lot of water early, then an hour back in bed, would normally put her in reasonable shape for the day. But not this morning. This morning, for some reason, she could barely move. Even the thought of moving made her queasy. When Frank arose at 5:30 to get ready for work, she'd run to the bathroom, barely lifting the toilet seat before she wretched.

"Good god, June. Again?" Frank said, standing behind her as she rinsed her mouth, spitting the vile taste into the sink. Frank helped her back to bed. Her skin clammy and green. An hour later, she was no better.

On his lunch break, Frank sped home to check on his wife. At 11:45 the house was silent. He wasn't all that surprised that June was still in bed. In their bedroom, Frank opened the drapes and both windows. The air outside was light and temperate, a pleasant fall day after all.

"Too bright," June complained. "Just let me sleep."

Frank was beyond tolerance now. He pulled the sheets back, exposing June's thin, pale thighs and the sea-green nightgown that had wrestled itself around her waist. She fumbled to recover the sheet, but couldn't reach it, so she made a mewling half cry.

"June!" Frank barked.

Startled now, she rolled to her back and looked up at her husband, who stood over her, fists at his waist.

"You have to get up. Get a shower. If you can't, I'm going to strip you down and put you in there myself. This is ridiculous, June. You can't even get up to get the girl ready for school. What if we had a houseful of kids? I can't go to work and take care of all of this, too."

We don't have a houseful of kids, though, do we? June thought bitterly. We will never have a houseful of kids.

June still felt nauseated, but she finally realized that she would have to manage nonetheless. It wasn't that she didn't feel bad about this morning. Did Frank think she enjoyed feeling this way? She knew she shouldn't drink, but she couldn't stop. She used to be able to manage with a small drink that calmed her brain and allowed her to sleep. No longer. Frank didn't understand. She didn't even understand. Telling her to stop, to just figure out a way to get happy? That solved nothing. And it didn't help.

She remembered that day he had ransacked the cabinets looking for her hiding place. She had pleaded with him, had cried as if he were killing her when he had poured the bottle down the drain. She tried after that to quit. But the cure was horrible, awful. If her stomach was bad this morning, it had been worse then. She eventually did stop. Over two months. Then that poor woman from church and her two-year-old son had been killed in a car accident. June had not known her well, but she had spoken to her a few times. She was so nice.

June sat on the edge of the bed, wiggled her toes into her slippers. "Angel's okay?"

"Of course she is. She thinks you have the measles."

"I wish."

"What are we going to do about this, Junie? A doctor? What can I do? I guess I... I just don't understand. Haven't I given you a good life?"

"That's not it, Frank. That's not it at all."

"Then what?"

She looked into his questioning eyes and shook her head. I don't know, she thought. June slipped her robe over her arm, got a clean bra and panties out of her drawer. "You're right. I need a shower. I'll be quick. Wait for me?"

He said he would.

June came to the kitchen feeling ashamed, but she presented her "it's going to be all right" face all the same. Frank had made her a double cup of English Breakfast tea, which she preferred over coffee, just a splash of milk stirred in, and a single piece of buttered toast. He had made himself lunch.

They sat across from each other at the kitchen table, as they had many times, but today a chasm separated them. June sipped her tea, said it was good, and thanked Frank for making it. He said she was welcome. She nibbled at the toast. Frank kept his head low, looking up now and then, but he was not like her. He could not force the muscles of his face to anything but consternation.

"June. I've got to get back to work. Are you feeling better?" He really wanted to know if he could trust her to be alone today.

"The tea is already helping. I'm fine. Please don't worry. When you get home, everything will be ship-shape and dinner will be ready," June said.

Frank saw now that her hand trembled as it reached for the cup. "You don't have to cook. I can make something."

June heard the lie when she told Frank that she could manage. Still when she saw the doubt in his eyes, she resented it. "Really. I'm fine now. I'm just so embarrassed. Maybe I had a touch of the stomach flu or something. This is just not like me."

Oh, June, Frank thought. He looked now into her soft eyes, her face still pale, though scrubbed clean and without that morning's clammy pallor. Oh, Junie June. He loved her, loved her deeply, but there were days he knew he also hated her. He couldn't help it.

Frank finished the last bite of his peanut butter sandwich and got up to rinse his plate, which he left in the sink. Drying his hands on the kitchen towel, he said, "I'll be home normal time." He hated to walk out the door. He was never sure if he could trust her. While she was in the shower, he'd taken a quick look in all her old hiding places but had found nothing, so he knew there must be a new cache. He did not enjoy spying, but she forced him to it. He had his daughter to look out for. Christ, he had *her* to look out for. It was for June's own good when he poured her whiskey or rye down the drain.

Before he left, Frank kissed his wife on top of her head.

She looked up from her chair and smiled. "I'm all right, Dear. I'm just fine," she said. "Don't worry."

As Frank closed the door behind him, he knew he would do nothing but worry.

1947

Those who went to work on January 31 were those who lived close enough to walk and had the will and fortitude to push themselves forward through two, even three-foot drifts. Those already at work were stranded. The night before, the Catalanos had watched the snow pile up out their living room window. By bedtime, when Frank had predicted the storm would end, glittering snow continued to swirl in tiny vortices lit by yellow streetlights. They were engulfed in white. When the snow finally ceased, WHBL reported that eighteen inches of snow had fallen on Sheboygan in the past twenty-four hours. Frank said he was surprised it was not more.

The next morning Frank headed out to clear the snow. A three-foot drift blocked the back door, which Frank pushed carefully so he wouldn't bend the aluminum doorframe, creating a space just wide enough for him to step out and sink his first footstep into the deep drift. He imagined himself a Jack London type as he trudged his way to the garage where he kept the shovels. When he had cleared a path to the garage, June and Angelina, bundled in winter layers, came out to help him. It took the three of them all morning to clear the drive, the sidewalk, and the front path to the house. Their street would not be plowed until after lunch the next day.

Later that afternoon, Frank and Angelina set to work on a snow fort while June watched from inside. She'd had enough fresh air for the day. Angel called to several neighborhood children to come and play with them, and suddenly Frank was surrounded by crimson-cheeked children lobbing snowballs.

"Take that, Mr. Catalano," a freckled, red-headed boy shouted. The snowball landed squarely in Frank's chest, and Frank, playing the role, acted out his mortal wound and fell onto a bank of soft snow. The boy's "hoo-rah," rang out joyfully. The resurrected Frank then sent a retaliatory missile back in the boy's direction, but missed. Another one aimed at Frank hit Angelina in the face. Suddenly the game was not fun. She began to cry. The snowball, fortified with a bit of gravel, had grazed her cheek. The scratch bled bright red.

Frank sent the kids home and ushered Angelina inside, where June rushed to her side. "Oh, baby. It's okay. Let Mommy take a look." June patted the wound with a wet white cloth. "There, there. It's not so bad."

The child was not consoled. Her face stung and she was shivering cold.

June glared at her husband. "My god, Frank. Her fingers are white. She should never have been out there so long. And this scratch? Why weren't you watching out for her? Do I have to do everything?"

"Now June. She'll warm up. The scratch—"

"Don't. Just don't. You were having so much fun playing with those other kids, you weren't even paying attention to your own daughter. She might have frostbite, the poor thing."

June whisked Angel off to the bathroom where she filled the tub with warm water. After Angelina had warmed, all rosy and glowing, June said, "Your father should have known better than to start a snowball fight. I just don't know what he's thinking sometimes."

Angel squinted up at her mom and felt she should not say anything, not even to defend her dad. Playing outside with her dad was the most fun she'd had with him in a long time. She had not wanted to come in.

After dinner, already in her pajamas and robe, Angel lifted the glob of melted marshmallow from a mug of hot chocolate with her tongue. June had gone to bed early. She'd said the day had been too much for her.

"How's the cocoa, sweetie?" Frank asked.

"Mmmm. It's good. You make it better than Mommy."

"Well, I probably make it the same. I just put in two marshmallows instead of one," Frank winked. He gently touched her cheek. The puffiness was nearly gone now.

"Still hurts?"

"It's not so bad."

"It's your war wound. Means you're tough, tough as any of those boys."

"Mommy was mad."

"Yes, she was."

"But Daddy, it wasn't your fault. It was a accident."

"I know, sweetheart, but your mom needs someone to blame. It makes her feel better. Now finish your cocoa and I'll read you a story before bed. Would you like that?"

Angelina nodded and turned up the cup to drain the last drops, and then licked away her chocolate mustache.

Nine-year-old Angelina was too tall and lanky for her father's lap, so she snuggled near him on the sofa, a blanket over her legs, and listened to her father read her the story of Caddie Woodlawn, which was one of her favorite books. She felt her father's deep, rich voice in her muscles and in her bones, and before long, Angelina was sound asleep.

For a long while Frank made no move to put her to bed. He did not want to break the connection of her beating heart and his. These days moments like this with his daughter were rare. The wind howled, and now and then the walls of their flat creaked. How cold and empty his life would be without his Angelina. But despite the child so near him, Frank had never felt lonelier.

1948

Angel had become friends with two boys who lived three houses to the west, Tommy and Dickey Stowe, and Alice White, a girl her own age, had recently moved in across the street. June thought Alice was a nice girl, but she was not sure she liked Angel playing with boys. Frank thought no harm could come of it. They were only children. Two girls, two boys. That did not seem abnormal to him. Where he grew up, kids were just kids. June had never had a boy for a friend, even in high school. Boys were foreigners and she did not trust them. They were wild and took careless risks, played violent games. Frank dismissed her worries.

During the school year, when the children were not busy with homework, they rode bikes up and down the sidewalks and alleys. They met other kids at the playground and played stick ball or kick the can. When school was out for the summer, Angel played outside all day unless it was raining, and even then, if there was no lightning and if the rain was warm, their little gang would skip and run about, getting soaked to the bone. The kids even made meals part of their play and, at times, begged their mothers to pack them picnic lunches. Angel and Alice reigned like queens over the boys, who didn't seem to mind the whims of the bossy girls.

Sometimes Alice went along when June took Angel to visit her parents. Alice loved going to their house. Grace and Wally treated her like a special guest, and there was always something sweet to eat.

Lake Michigan was only ten blocks away from Angel's house, so on hot days the children would ride their bikes to the lakeshore, where it was at least five degrees cooler. They waded on the shore or played tag. Sometimes the boys fished while the girls built sand castles or wrote in the sand with sticks. Their parents had warned them to never go too far into the water, never without an adult there. It could be dangerous.

Tommy Stowe, the eldest of the crew at thirteen, was famous among the gang for saying out loud that parents don't know everything. Angel was now eleven and she had begun to feel more grown up than ever. And while she would not admit it, even to Alice, Angel realized she loved Tommy. She loved his blond, almost white hair, the freckles on his sunburned face, the way his turquoise eyes looked like the summer sky. She would lay awake some nights, her legs aching and restless, and imagine that they were grown up and married. She invented her entire house, their house, all the shiny rooms.

August 17 was particularly hot. "Come on," Tommy said, egging on the others. "It's not cold." He splashed handfuls of water toward them on the shore. "Angel, Angel," he sang. "Don't be scared. Come in with me." She shyly watched him wade farther and farther out into the lake off the North Point shore. Whenever she tried to move toward him, her feet planted themselves deeper and deeper into the sand, but the cooling water that rushed in and out over her feet did feel good. The lake roiled in waves today. Angel loved their sound. She shaded her eyes from the bright sun, then watched as he shrugged his shoulders, arched his back, and dove under the surface. Her tense shoulders relaxed when he surged up almost immediately and turned to her, a broad smile beckoning, before he dove back under. "Come on in Angel, Angel."

But then, they no longer saw him. The children scanned the water's surface, but they could not see their friend. Angel's heart pounded with anxiety, and she called out "Tommy! Tommy!" Dickey strode forcefully into the surf, the water much stronger than his thin nine-year-old legs could manage. "Tommmm-y!" the children screamed, standing helplessly.

A man on the beach ran in. The children pointed to where they last saw Tommy.

"He was over there," Alice shouted to the man, who began to search, his head up and under the water, up and under.

Soon, another man dove into the churning water.

"I see him," Dickey shouted, and pointed to where Tommy's limp body emerged forty feet away.

The men swam quickly to reach him. One man locked his arm around Tommy and brought his unconscious body to shore. The other man then tried to resuscitate Tommy. He breathed again and again into the boy's mouth. Minutes earlier, a woman had run to a nearby house to call an ambulance.

Later, at home, June was irate. "It could have been Angel," she shouted. "She's never going to the lake again, not without us, and she's not ever getting in the water."

Frank glowered. "You're overreacting, June. Accidents sometimes happen to people." He snapped back the lid of his Zippo and drew the flame to the cigarette between his lips, inhaling deeply.

June reacted with a jerk of her head. "You sound like you don't care about your daughter at all. What a callous father you have become," she said. She wanted to say more, do more. She wanted to pound her fists on her husband's chest, to beat him with her fury. But she checked herself. Angelina was only feet away.

And Frank, instead of fighting back, instead of reasoning with his unreasonable wife, scowled and walked away. He had things to do.

"Doesn't anyone care about Tommy?" Angel screamed, clenching her fists. "Doesn't anyone care about my friend? Is he going to be okay? Can't you call his mom?" Neither of her parents responded. An hour later, her face buried in her pillows, her fingers grasping the hollow bone, Angelina cried herself to sleep.

After Tommy's funeral, the Stowes moved from 10th Street. No one knew where they went, but someone heard they moved back to Nebraska where they were from originally. An older couple bought their house and painted it a garish blue. The man was unfriendly. He didn't like kids, not even riding their bikes on the sidewalk past his house. The lady was never outside, so no one knew if she was pleasant or not.

1977

Mid-morning Sophie had snuck home for a shower and clean clothes. She packed a few things that she needed and tossed some of her mother's favorite magazines in a small bag. On the way back to the hospital, she stopped at the McDonald's on North Avenue for a cheeseburger and fries, which she ate in the car in the parking lot. Sophie thought she would feel too self-conscious sitting inside alone. She peeled back the yellow tissue paper and opened the bun. With her finger she scraped off the little chunks of reconstituted dried onion. She bit into the warm cheeseburger and chewed mindlessly. She ate the hot, salty fries by twos and threes. When she finished, she stuffed her trash into the small white bag. She'd throw it away at the hospital.

Sophie spent the afternoon in solitude, trying to read *Wuthering Heights*, a book she felt she ought to enjoy reading—it was a classic after all—but somehow Heathcliff annoyed her. By the time she'd forced herself awake three times, Sophie realized she should just give in to a nap, so she curled up on her cot, pulled the mint green blanket over her head, and fell soundly asleep.

Around 5:30, Angel woke up and announced she was starving. "Where's Mary?" she said when she saw Carole, the evening nurse.

"It's later than you think, my dear," Carole said, checking Angel's pulse.

"Guess so," Angel said.

"Your temp is normal. Blood pressure is nearer to normal. Any pain?"

"I'm feeling not horrible at the moment," Angel said, and Carole agreed that not horrible was good.

"Now Angelina," Carole said, "you feel free to choose whatever you like from tonight's menu, but if you'll take my two cents, I'd try to keep it light."

Angel considered Carole's advice and ordered chicken noodle soup, but light or not, she was also going to indulge in chocolate cake. Both Carole and Sophie had given Angel an "are you sure" look when she mentioned the cake. On her part, Sophie wasn't about to deny her mother anything she asked for. Not anymore.

After Carole left, Angel asked about Sophie's day. Sophie told her the house was fine. She'd brought in the mail. Nothing important. No bills. "I did a load of towels and I tossed out a carton of milk that had soured."

Now with her dinner in front of her, Angel sipped the hot soup. "I think it's just Campbell's, but it tastes good," she said. "Want some?"

Sophie said no thanks. She really wasn't hungry, but still ended up finishing her mother's chocolate cake after Angel could manage only one bite.

Later, Angel insisted that Sophie climb up onto her bed and cuddle with her.

"We're not both going to fit, Mom."

"Come on. Humor me. Just try. For just a little while."

Sophie took off her shoes, looked behind her toward the door, fearful that someone would walk by and put a stop to their nonsense. Not only was Sophie sure that getting into bed with her mom was "illegal," but she was also worried about hurting her. Nevertheless, Sophie climbed slowly and cautiously up into the hospital bed and lay down behind her mom. Angel reached back and pulled her daughter closer.

"There. Now we can cuddle for a while. We don't even have to talk. I just want to feel you near me."

A bit later Sophie said, "Tell me a story, Mom. Tell me something you've never told me."

"Oh, Sophie," Angel said, sighing deeply. Angel felt as if she wanted to blurt out the entirety of her life, all the stories, all the pain, the happy times, too. The regrets, so many. But too late for that now.

They lay there quietly for a while, each listening to the other's breathing, each feeling the other's warmth radiate. At one point, Sophie thought her mother had begun to fall asleep, but she hesitated to move even though her left leg had started to go numb. Just when she felt she would try getting out of the bed, her mother spoke.

"I was a horrible mom, wasn't I Sophie?"

Where was this coming from? Sophie wondered. "Don't be ridiculous," she said.

"I'm not. I'm being honest. Remember that time I forgot to pick you up after Girl Scouts?"

"You were tired. You fell asleep."

"I was drunk, and you know it."

"I survived. It's okay."

"Then, you nearly were blind, and I didn't know it."

"I was never nearly blind."

"You needed glasses."

"Sure, well, a lot of kids need glasses."

"You remember that? It was funny. Ruth came over, told your grandpa and me that we needed to get you to an eye doctor. That you had put on Josef's glasses, just to be funny, and you said, 'Bubbe, I can see better.'"

"'I tested her,' Ruth said, 'gave her things to read, with and without the glasses. An old man's glasses, the girl needs.' That Ruth. I loved her, but she could sure give it to me good sometimes. I felt really bad, though. How long had you been squinting to read or to see the blackboard?"

Sophie wished her mother would end her self-prosecution.

"Again, I turned out fine. Right?"

Angel reached behind her and squeezed her daughter's hand. "Sophie?

I was a good mom sometimes, wasn't I?"

"Of course you were. That is, you are."

"Tell me something," Angel said. "Tell me something you remember about me from when you were a kid, something that was good."

"There's lots of things, Mom."

"But what meant something to you? Tell me one thing."

Sophie snuggled closer. It was nearly dark outside now, and the overhead light cast mother and daughter in a glaring spotlight. "I loved how you made it a big deal every year to watch *The Wizard of Oz*. I loved that you made a huge bowl of popcorn and that it was okay that it was all we had for dinner. I loved that we took all the blankets and pillows and piled them on the floor and watched together."

"That was fun."

"I liked when you read to me." Sophie recalled the worn copy of *Grimm's Fairy Tales* that had belonged to her Grandmother Schneider, the tales her mother had listened to when she was a child.

"Hey, did you realize that the story 'Briar Rose' is really 'Sleeping Beauty'?" Angel said. "Do you remember? No, you wouldn't. You were only three. I took you to the theater to see *Sleeping Beauty*. We were still in Austin. You were so afraid of that evil witch, can't remember her name. She was so big on the screen, black smoke billowing about her. Did she have horns, or…? Anyway, you were so scared. You hid under the seat until she was off the screen. I shouldn't have laughed. But it was cute. You wouldn't sleep in your own bed that night. You cried. So we slept in my bed. I remember that," Angel said wistfully. "Those days went by too fast. Seems like before I knew it, you were all grown up and didn't really need me any more."

"That's not true."

"Sophie. We both know it's true. Don't humor your dying mother. Let's tell each other the truth while we can."

1949

The war had been over for four years, and a surge in manufacturing meant more work, which helped Frank build their savings. In addition, the government was offering easy terms on loans through something called the GI Bill.

The house they bought in the spring of 1949 on North 13th Street, a block south of North Avenue, was built before the war. While the lot was still much smaller than her parents' house, the one-story golden brick home was so much nicer than their place on 10th Street. And Angel would not need to change schools. She was far beyond the tantrum stage, but June appreciated that the girl had made friends in school and that moving away from them would be a hardship. Not only that, but before they knew it, Angelina would be headed to high school and North High was only a few blocks away. June was happy that she would not have to worry about Angelina having to walk too far, especially in cold weather.

The other houses on the block were well kept. Theirs was by no means the largest, but it would suit them well. This would be a good place, June felt. The two bedrooms were fairly large, and both had closets. The living room was spacious and it featured a large picture window. Western sun would warm them in winter. She could imagine sitting there sewing or knitting. She might even put a bird feeder out if Frank allowed. This house held so much promise that June felt she could easily put her dark days behind her. She hadn't felt so alive in a long while.

June threw her energy into planning the décor. Frank bought her a new electric sewing machine and she joyously zigzagged hems in crisp yellow cotton for the kitchen curtains. I should be teaching Angel how to sew, she thought now and then, but decided she would do that later. Right now, it was too much fun sending the lengths of fabric so quickly under the needle bobbing up and down.

The first few weeks in their new home were truly blissful and the couple felt younger than they had in years. In bed at night, they felt once again they could think about the years ahead.

"Maybe," Frank said one night as he lay nested behind his wife, her still-damp skin warm against his, "maybe that big house could still happen."

June drew her husband more tightly towards her. "Frank. Let's just be happy for now. Let's just take this blessing as it was meant to be."

The first Sunday after their big move, June insisted on inviting her parents for a housewarming party. Frank objected, saying they hadn't had time to fix things up properly. But June said she didn't care about that. The house looked good enough for her parents and she was excited for them to see it.

Wally and Grace arrived with a housewarming gift, a set of Royal Doulton china that June had longed for.

"Oh, Mother. It's the Woburn pattern I've had my eye on. Oh, Daddy. Thank you. I'll cherish them. Thank you." June embraced both her mother and her father. "Oh, Frank. Isn't it marvelous? I've never owned anything so fine." To Frank, the statement felt like a judgment.

"Women do go crazy over such things, don't they Frank?" said Wally to his son-in-law.

"They do indeed, Wally. It's a very generous gift, and we appreciate it." Frank hoped he sounded sincere. He hoped he did not sound bitter. It should have been me buying those dishes for her, he thought.

Angel watched excitedly as June unpacked the entire service for eight: dinner plates, salad plates, bowls, cups, and saucers. She held up a dinner plate, the bright, noonday sun behind it. Translucent light glowed in the undecorated center of the fine bone china. June ran her fingers along the edges of the plate. The red-and-black art deco design was bold, and June felt the boldness in her hands. These dishes represented the kind of life she'd always wanted, the kind of life Frank had always promised.

"We will take great care of these, won't we sweetie?" June said to her daughter. "They will be yours someday."

Frank grabbed two cold bottles of Schlitz from the fridge and offered one to Wally, who took it gratefully. And yet when June snapped the cap off a beer with the church key and brought the brown bottle to her lips, Wally frowned. When women drank, it was unseemly, somehow.

Later, out on the front porch with Frank, Wally presented another gift. "Frank," he said, "if you don't mind, I'd like Angel...." He cleared his throat. "I'd like Angelina to have the red maple bedroom set she used at our house. We bought the twin bed set for June when she was a girl, and it has held up well. Couple nicks and scratches in the vanity, but not bad." As if anticipating rejection, Wally continued. "Now Frank, I know you're a skilled woodworker and would probably want to make her something yourself, but it would please me for her to have it."

Frank shook his father-in-law's hand in sincere gratitude. "Sure, Wally. That would be fine. Thank you." June's parents were kind and generous, and if he were honest, they had never done or said one thing to suggest they felt their daughter could have or should have married someone else or that another man could have provided a better life for her.

That night before bed, June Catalano served her tiny family the remainder of her mother's rhubarb pie on the new plates as a special bedtime treat. She had warmed the pie in the oven first, then drizzled the slices with cream. Next to the shiny new china, their worn silver-plate forks looked suddenly shabby, and June decided at that moment to begin saving for a proper sterling service. Frank had not yet been able to add to the serving set he'd bought her in 1936, but she would make it a priority to do so now.

After their pie, and despite her protests, Angelina had been sent to bed. June sometimes missed the days when she bathed her daughter and dressed her for bed. It had been a long time since she had been that kind of mother. It was late, nearly ten p.m., but June wanted to tidy the kitchen before they went to bed. Frank offered to dry the dishes and June, surprised, accepted. He felt foolishly nervous as he picked the first plate out of the dish drainer. It wasn't the royal crown for Christ sake. Still, he swore he would not be the first person to break one of these dishes.

"Wasn't it a wonderful day, Frank?" June said. She faced her husband and smiled into his eyes. He returned the smile and gave her a quick kiss on the cheek. In moments like these, June seemed so much like the girl from the office, the girl with a quick smile for everyone. He enjoyed these moments with apprehension, with a knowing expectation that they could sour without warning. Frank could not let go of the dark memory of a Sunday morning a few weeks before, when they had not gone to church, when June had stayed in bed "sick" until well after lunch, when he had lied again to his daughter. Again and again.

"I was thinking just before, we really should get a nice set of silverware now. This old set looks just horrible. What do you think of that idea?"

"It's not a good time for us to be spending money on things we don't really need, June," Frank said, breaking his wife's mood. He hadn't meant to, but it was often up to him to be the practical one.

She rarely used a childish pout—in fact it wasn't an effective strategy with Frank—but June was so disappointed in Frank's response that her bottom lip drooped on its own. "Why not? Can't we afford it? You were just telling me how well the bank account has grown, and that we'll be able to manage the mortgage without scrimping."

"When I said that, I meant that we can have meat more than two times a week, or that if we need a new car, which we do, we can manage those kinds of expenses. Silverware is just not a necessity. It isn't, is it Junie? Someday I'll get you every little thing your heart desires, but...."

Why did her chest contract and her eyes sting? She missed living with fine things, and she wanted it all at once. The war, the waiting. She was tired of waiting. "Of course. You're right."

"That's my girl. We need to be sensible. My good old sensible Junie." Frank gave his wife a brief hug and a pat on the back. They finished the dishes in silence.

In bed, after a quick good night kiss, June turned her back to Frank, who lay quietly on his back. June wished she had never said a word to Frank about the sterling set. What he didn't know wouldn't bother him. He didn't know a lot of things. She would simply begin to set money aside from the household budget. That's how she had saved for the silk stockings, the secret gift to herself that still lay wrapped in tissue in her drawer under a sweater. When the time was right, she'd put them on. She would feel powerful. Frank would never even notice.

1949

August had been abnormally cool, but September raged back as if proclaiming its right to be summer. Even with the shade trees and the window fans, the nights had been hot. One night the temperature hovered near 80, and June said she could barely breathe. She had begged Frank take them to her parents' house, which, being closer to the lake, would be somewhat cooler, but Frank, irritated, had said his family would sleep in their own damn house. He'd been irritated more often lately, and June did not know why. Before coming to bed that night, June had checked on her daughter. Angel lay on top of her sheets wearing only her underpants and a camisole undershirt. June had tied Angel's hair up into a topknot to keep it off of the girl's neck, but in the moonlight that flooded through the wide-open windows, June could see the girl's face glistened in sweat.

It had been a long evening. June lay bitterly at the edge of their bed, grinding her teeth now and then when she thought of how stubbornly Frank had refused her request. By midnight it had begun to cool down. Around two, June had finally given in to sleep.

A week later, Frank raged into the house a bit before noon. June was bent over the bathtub scrubbing away soap scum when she heard the back door bang. She left the sponge lay in the tub, rinsed her hands, and dried them on her apron.

"What's wrong? Why are you home?"

Frank stood in the kitchen chugging a beer, looking over her head as if she were not even there. He slammed the bottle on the counter and dug another one out of the fridge, snapped off the cap with the church key, and took a long glug before setting it down. His dark, bristly cheeks and chin shone with sweat. When they were first married, Frank would never have gone to work without shaving. But now he often let his face go for two, even three days. The dark shadow on his face made him appear dejected, even if he was not.

"Frank." June was insistent. "I said what's wrong."

"That shit-faced new foreman...." He went back to the beer. If nothing else, it was cold. He wasn't feeling his nerves go numb yet. He might need another, or even two more.

"Frank!"

"What!"

"Are you going to tell me...."

"I shut down the line and tried to explain to that idiot that the setting on the rough sander was wrong. I showed him the burn marks on the slats. He could plainly see that I was right, but he tells me, he says, 'Sure, soldier.' He always calls me soldier, and I hate it. He's a pathetic twit. He tells me, 'Sure soldier. Now, this is not your place. You need to get back on the line. If there's a problem, I'll take care of it.' And I held the chair slat up again, right in his face. 'It's not a matter of if,' I said. He put his arms up and tried pushing me back, but I stood firm. He couldn't push over a two-year-old. At that point Clarence was behind me, telling me to come on. He said the mistake wouldn't come out of our pay and we shouldn't worry about it. When Clarence said that, the little shit smiled, almost like Clarence had given him an idea or something."

"Oh, Frank," June said. She took the empty bottle from his hand and rinsed it out. Frank said he needed another one, and she did not argue with him. "Then what happened?"

"Then? Then I don't know. I guess I…I honestly can't remember. But all of a sudden the guys were pulling me back, telling me to settle down. And there he was, that shit-faced ass, on the floor, his mouth bleeding."

June gasped.

"I hit him, I guess. I…I don't know what came over me."

"So…?"

"Well, I'm pretty sure they're not going to welcome me back," Frank said, pulling out a chair and slumping into it.

June decided in that moment that recriminations would do no good. She laid her hand on Frank's shoulder and stood behind him for a minute, saying nothing. Then she said quietly, "They have never appreciated your talent and ability." Before the war, it had been almost like Frank was the boss. But after the war, everything at North Shore had changed. After the war, it was almost as if the old Frank and all he had done for them had never existed. She leaned over, kissed him on the head, and whispered, "The little shit deserved it." Frank smiled to hear her use such language. It felt good to have her appreciate the situation he was in.

The result was that Frank calmed down. She made him a cold lunch, sliced pork roast and tomatoes. She brewed iced tea. He drank it gratefully. They sat a long while at the kitchen table, talking about what would happen next. Frank said he had nearly two weeks pay coming. They couldn't deny him that.

After only two days of job hunting, Frank came home with steaks from Miesfeld's and said he planned to grill them outdoors. When June questioned his sanity, spending money on steak, he countered by saying, "It's a celebration, June. I'm the new clerk at Wilson Hardware. I know it doesn't pay as much as I was making at North Shore, but I think I'm going to like the work, helping people find the right tools. Not only that, but I told them I was not bad at fixing things, so that could be an opportunity, too."

June could not object. It was his decision after all. A wife could not tell her husband what kind of work to do. Her full set of sterling, even a new spring suit for church. None of that would be possible, at least not for a while.

That night, despite the welcome breeze out of the north, June could not sleep. Frank's snoring had become intolerably loud. As happened now and again, he stopped breathing. In a few seconds, he gasped again for breath. June reached out and firmly pushed against his lower back. "Roll on your side, Frank," she said, not bothering to whisper. Then again, but louder and with irritation, "roll on your side." He snorted and responded in his sleep to her command. His snoring quieted, but her mind did not.

The Big Ben on the nightstand said 3:15 when June got out of bed and padded in her bare feet to the kitchen, where she pulled the step stool open and climbed up to the cupboard for the bottle of rye.

1950

June wrung out the dishrag, laid it over the faucet to dry, and wiped her wet, red hands on her blue-and-yellow pinafore apron. She smiled weakly. She had woken with a raging headache that still lingered.

"Thanks for drying the breakfast dishes, daughter," she said as she reached out and swatted Angel on the behind in a teasing way. "Now get out of my hair for a while. I'm going to put my feet up and read the new *Redbook* that came yesterday," June said. "Your dad's working at the store today, and I'm looking forward to a quiet Saturday."

Angel thought about getting her bike out when she saw her friend Alice White coming up the street. She had come to show Angel her new puppy. "His name is Peety," Alice said. "Go ahead. You can pet him. He won't bite. His teeth are sharp, though."

Angel had never owned a dog and thought Alice's mixed message was confusing, but she leaned down to pet the puppy, whose wiry coat was softer than it looked. The puppy cocked his head and turned his milk chocolate eyes on Angel, who felt at that moment a quickening warmth spread under her skin.

"See?" Alice said. "He likes you."

The girls walked the nine-week-old salt-and-pepper mutt down the sidewalk, stopping now and then to try to teach him to "sit." After numerous attempts, the girls could see Peety was tired of their game. They sat for a while on the curb and took turns holding the puppy, cooing and talking baby talk to him. In Angel's arms, Peety fell asleep.

After a while, Johnny Steinmetz rode by on his bike, then skidded at the end of a gravel driveway and turned around. He laid his bike on the grass between the sidewalk and the street so he could pet the puppy.

"Hey, cute little guy," Johnny said, scratching the puppy behind its ears. "You're a nice little fella, ain't ya?" Then Johnny straightened up, got astride his bike as if he had to be somewhere in a hurry, and said authoritatively, "You oughta take him home now, Alice."

"Why is that, Johnny? We got a right to be out here. You're not the boss."

"You seen the sky? It's gonna be a storm. A big one."

The girls glanced up. The sky to the east, still bright and blue, was being chased by billowing clouds coming in from the southwest, and the sky in between was slowly turning green.

"Jeepers," Angel said. "When did that happen?"

"My mom sent me out to find my brothers and bring them home. You seen 'em?"

The girls said they hadn't, and Alice, now fearful she wouldn't make it home in time, picked up Peety, cradled him in her arms, and began running toward home. "See you tomorrow, Angel," she yelled on the run.

Angel, who thought Johnny was awfully cute, was in no rush to go home. It was just rain, and she'd played outside in the rain plenty of times. Storms, even the loudest thunder, didn't bother her—well, not anymore. "Want me to help you find your brothers?" she asked Johnny playfully. She imagined Johnny trying to pedal with her balanced on his handlebars, his arm brushing against her leg now and then, she giggling when the bike steered wobbly because of her added weight. And the two of them would call out for his brothers: "Stevie! Joey!"

Just then, Angel heard her mother's voice screaming, "Angelina!" Angel looked towards her house, then back at Johnny. She wanted him to tell her, "C'mon. It ain't so bad. Let's stay out awhile longer." He did not.

"I guess I can find them on my own," Johnny said. "It'll be quicker. You better go home, Angel." She shrugged her reluctant assent.

Johnny pushed off and pedaled while standing tall, peering out as if he could see over rooftops and treetops. Angel watched him until he rounded the corner and disappeared. Even then she was in no big hurry to get back to her house.

"Get in here," June said at the front door, grabbing her daughter by the wrist.

"Ow," Angel yelped. "That hurts."

"Didn't you hear me calling you? Didn't you see the sky?"

"It's going to rain. I heard you. What's the big deal?"

"Watch your tone. Who do you think you're talking to like that?"

Inside, June shut the front door tightly and glared at Angelina, who hung her head, no longer defiant.

"All right. I've got all the windows closed and locked. There is a bag of things on the kitchen table. Grab that and go to the basement, unless you need to go to the bathroom, then do that first. But hurry."

"What's the matter? Why are we...?"

"Don't argue with me. That's a tornado sky, and we don't have time to stand here discussing things."

Angel used the bathroom and then, feeling her mother's urgency at last, scooted quickly back to the kitchen and grabbed the bag. She was near the top of the steep steps to the basement, its musty odor rising to her nostrils, but her mother was not in sight.

"Mom?" Angel called down the stairs, poorly lit by one dim ceiling bulb at the foot of the steps. There was no answer. She called again, louder, more insistently. "Mom. Where are you?" Then Angel heard her mother's footsteps in the hall behind her, and soon June stood right beside her daughter.

"What are you waiting for? Let's go." June took two steps, closed the door, and then, with a small box in her arms, she followed Angel into the basement. The box held her family photos and a few personal items, the only things she owned that could not be replaced. She set the box on top of the washing machine. Then, hands on her hips, June looked about the dank, dark space. In the middle of the room, she pulled the chain on another light.

"Set up those lawn chairs, Angelina. We don't have to sit on the concrete floor to be safe, I don't think. But let's back up into the corner away from the window.

Earlier, June had brought down blankets and a jug of water. She now laid a blanket on one of the chaises for Angel to use as a cushion. The girl stood by passively.

"Here, give me that," June said, as she took the heavy bag from Angel, who gladly relinquished it. "Well go ahead. You might as well try and make yourself comfortable."

From the bag, June dug out several books for Angel and handed them to her, though she realized now it would be difficult for her to read in the ever-dimming light. The sky above them was even darker now. June took out the portable radio, set the bag near her on the floor, and settled herself in a yellow chaise. She turned the radio dial. The twanging tuning waves sang and cracked until she found WHBL. "We can at least hear if there's anything going on." The reception was poor and the announcer's voice cut in and out now and then. "They're not even mentioning the storm," June said. "Well, even so. That's a bad sky. We're right to be cautious."

"How do you know it's going to be a tornado?" Angel questioned.

"Saw one once, when I was about your age. We were in Iowa visiting your grandmother's aunt and uncle. They have—that is, they had—a big farm near Ames. Anyway, we were outside having a nice picnic. Fried chicken with potato salad and lemonade, and the sky got green and yellow just like this, with the same black clouds that looked like they were racing toward us, going to swallow us up, and Grandma's uncle leaped up from the table and rushed us all into their storm cellar. Just before he closed the latch, he saw it across the cornfield. I peeked out and saw it, too."

"Like in *The Wizard of Oz*?"

"Exactly like that. Yes, exactly. Things were fine. It was a nice, sunny day, and then almost as if summoned by a genie, it was there, so loud. Oh, it was loud. We were down in that dark storm cellar so we couldn't see anything, but we could hear. I can't think when I was more excited, or afraid."

June's body cast a faint shadow on her daughter, who stretched her legs out in the chaise next to her. June reached over, patted Angelina on her firm thigh, and sighed. "I'm sorry if I barked before. I guess I just got scared. Little bit like Aunty Em, en so, with you not in the house with me. Right, my little Dorothy?"

Angel scrunched up her nose and nodded her head.

"But you're safe here with me now. And if nothing knocks our house over, we'll be fine once the storm passes."

Angel had not been afraid until that moment. Why had her mother said that about knocking the house over? Could that really happen? She sank lower in the chair and wished she had brought her own blanket. The one she rested on smelled like mothballs. She wished her father were there with them. Mostly because she worried her mother would not know what to do if things really got bad.

June assumed Frank was safe. Or maybe he was in the car on the way to them? She honestly did not know. At this moment, all she could think about was herself and her daughter. It was all she could control.

June saw the worry in her daughter's eyes. "Daddy will be fine. You believe me?"

"I guess so."

"Oh, honey. I wish you were little enough for me to hold on my lap. I'd wrap a blanket around you and cuddle you. If there were loud noises, I'd sing over them, some silly song, like 'Itsy Bitsy Spider.' But you're not. You're a gangly girl now, all legs and arms, taller than me pretty soon, I'll bet. And you don't even need your old mom, do you?"

"I need you," Angel said, but she knew that in most ways, she did not.

She was nearly thirteen, after all. But it wasn't just her age that had made her independent. Out of necessity Angel had learned self-reliance long before now. Even as a young child, she had begun by making simple snacks on long afternoons when her father had not yet come home from work and her mother had cloistered herself in her dark bedroom. Eventually Angel grew more confident and she would either get dinner started or cook it entirely. The first time Frank had come home to his eleven-year-old daughter standing at the stove, she had been browning hamburger for spaghetti sauce. At her side, he had smiled and expressed pride at her ability.

Later, after Angel was in bed, her parents screamed at each other. "The girl is too young," he had shouted. "It's your job. When will it end, June? When?" But Angelina had not felt too young, not then, maybe not ever. From the time she had begun to think of herself as herself, Angel had felt much older than she really was.

"Of course I need you," Angel repeated. She knew that there were things her mother needed to hear.

"I'm glad," June said. "So glad. Do you know? I hope you know just how much I love you and that I would die if something happened to you. I just don't think I could go on if something happened to you." June reached out, grabbed her daughter's hand, squeezed it but did not let go.

"Are you afraid? Want me to sing?" June began, "The itsy bitsy spider crawled up the water spout. Down came the rain and washed the spider out."

Angel laughed and squeezed her mother's hand. "You're weird, Mom," she said, but June just smiled and kept on singing.

Frank came down the steps about forty minutes later. He was happy to see his girls safe and sound. No tornadoes had been spotted in the area as far as he had heard, but it was raining buckets out there. Awfully windy, too. He told them he wouldn't be surprised if there were some big branches to pick up later. He hoped none of the big old trees in or near their yard would topple over.

He took off his wet jacket, shook it, and laid it over the stair railing.

"Boss wasn't going to let us go, but since all the customers had fled, it seemed senseless to stay. Guess he agreed, so we closed up for the time being. I'll go back later, when things blow over. Glad to see you two are being sensible."

June got up and unfolded another lawn chair. She gave her husband a kiss on the cheek and told him she was relieved to see him. "I handled it all, Frank. I have everything under control. I even called Mother and Dad, just to make sure they were headed to their basement, too. You were the only one I worried about, and now, here you are."

"Proud of you June. Angelina, you, too. But I wasn't too worried. You're my capable girls."

In fact, his stomach had churned with anxiety all the way home, not knowing if June would be able to think calmly or act rationally. Lately, even little things, everyday annoyances, seemed sometimes to push her beyond her limits. Frank got annoyed, too, but not like June did. When she had been sewing just last weekend, June broke a needle and started cursing at the machine. But here she'd managed everything so well that it made Frank think he might be overstating her nervous tendencies.

Just then the lights flickered and went out. "Well, we've lost power now. I guess I expected that could happen," Frank said.

It was nearly as black as night. Angel rustled through the bag and pulled out one of the flashlights, stuck it under her chin, and turned it on. "Boo," she said.

"Ha ha. Very funny," her mother said. "We should probably not use those if we don't need to. I don't know how good the batteries are."

Frank agreed, so Angel switched off the flashlight and the family waited out the storm in the dark, only the dimmest light coming through the six tiny windows, and that perceptible only after their eyes had become accustomed to the dark. June recalled the Iowa tornado again, told of the loudest roar she had ever heard, a sound they had felt in their shelter under the earth. When they came up out of the storm cellar, a thirty-foot spruce near the road had been uprooted. The only other thing that looked awry made them all laugh. The old outhouse had toppled over.

Frank told of an awful storm that hit his platoon one night in France. They were on the move and had nothing but the woods to protect them. The men hovered under tarps that on a calm night would have been made into tents. He explained how they had huddled together in groups to keep warm, and how no one slept even though they were beyond weary. They just waited, the howling wind and cold rain beating against them.

Angel said she was glad she didn't have memories of storms like that. Her mother said, "Don't you remember? When you were little and the thunder was loud? You would cry, and we'd put you in bed with us?"

Angel said she didn't remember. But she did.

"This is just like that all over again. Isn't it?" June said.

Frank laughed softly. Couldn't this be the way they were with each other all the time?

Angel wished the storm would last for days.

1950

Frank and June were in the backyard. He had been setting wooden frames around the peony shoots. Before long, the plants would grow up and through the latticed frames that would keep the giant pink blooms from toppling over onto the ground. June was taking the clothes off the line. They stood now in the bright sun, facing each other, almost as adversaries, his hands on his hips, she pulling off clothespins, tossing them in the red gingham bag that hung on the line, and folding each undershirt or blouse before it went into the basket. Folding now meant fewer wrinkles later, her mother always said.

"Now, June," Frank said, "Angelina's really too old for a party and a cake with candles. That's for children. Right? You agree, don't you?" Frank said, his voice louder and more impatient that it needed to be. "We'll get her a nice gift, but can't we just have a quiet party, just the three of us?"

June's blue eyes burned cold. "No Frank, I don't agree. She's still a child. She's…. Really. I don't know why you care so much. I'll do all the planning, all the cooking. All you have to do is show up. I'll be sure there is a bucket of beer."

"That's not fair, June. You make it sound like I don't care about Angelina. I want her to have a happy birthday, but this seems so childish. She's almost a teenager. We can have a nice dinner and you can bake her a cake, or I can even order one from the bakery if you'd like. We'll give her a nice gift. What about an add-a-pearl necklace? Why do we need such a fuss?" Frank felt his argument failing, his voice placating instead of insistent now.

June's fist tightened around a pair of Angel's anklets. "She's growing up too fast. Before we know it, she'll be in high school. I can't see what's so wrong. That is, I want to make a fuss. I want to celebrate, invite Mom and Dad."

"Your parents are here almost every Sunday. It's not like we never see them."

"That's a sarcastic thing to say." June threw the socks in the basket and yanked her blue blouse off the clothesline. "You just never want to do anything fun. Not since the war, not since...."

"What are you talking about? Didn't we go bowling last weekend? June, I just don't understand you sometimes. I try to make you happy. It just seems like no matter what I do or say, it's not enough. Listen...." Frank held out his arms to take the clothesbasket from his wife, but she glared at him and sidestepped his advance. "I'm just saying that it seems like you're going overboard here. That's all."

June did not look back as she headed to the door, the clothesbasket thrust in front of her. She held the door open with her hip to give her room for the clothesbasket, then let it slam behind her.

In the end, Frank acquiesced. Most times it was just easier to give in.

1950

June and Angel surveyed the fabrics at Marlene's Stitch 'N Sew. Angel wanted all of her new school clothes to come from the store, but June convinced her daughter that a few homemade things, a couple of skirts and a few blouses, would stretch their dollar considerably, so she would actually be able to have more clothes. June had hoped that Angel would still be able to wear most of her seventh grade things, but very little still fit. Angel had not only grown taller in the past year, but more womanly as well.

"Now Angelina, no one's going to know your clothes are homemade. I can sew as well as any New York designer."

Angel had no doubt her mother could sew a blouse or a kilt or a dirndl skirt, but even she couldn't pull off the felt poodle skirt and angora sweater Angel desperately wanted. Angel thought of Brenda, a girl in her class who had been forced to wear a crumply, hand-knit cardigan her mother had made. It was simply awful, but Angel had told her how swell it looked.

"Ooh. Look at this cute print. Aren't the tiny roses sweet? I think this would make a lovely blouse, maybe a Peter Pan collar?"

"Mom. I'm not in third grade. Jeepers."

"Well, you don't have to be mean. I just thought it was a sweet print. What do you like then?"

Angel resisted every choice, but eventually gave in and chose light pink for one blouse and plain white for another. They settled on a red-and-black tartan plaid for a kilt-style skirt.

At the cutting table, as Marlene herself unrolled the bolts and lined up the fabric along the yardstick at the edge of the table, June watching carefully to be sure she wasn't being shorted, Angel asked about shoes.

"Of course. You'll need those as well. God knows where you got those feet. And I suppose a few underthings. A couple of new bras?"

"Mom!" Angel said, embarrassed. But Marlene, who either didn't hear or didn't care, kept her eye on the fabric she now cut with sharp shears.

June smiled at her modern daughter, so concerned about what others thought of her. She supposed that was normal, though she could not remember ever being so self-conscious. Of course, when she was thirteen, she didn't have breasts. When June was thirteen, she was also lucky to have two skirts. Many of her friends wore their one skirt to school all week and to church on Sunday. It got washed on Saturday to be ready for another week. No one cared about clothes. Not at her school. No one felt inferior or superior. Times were hard. Everyone knew that.

At the shoe store, the clerk measured Angel's foot. As the girl placed her right foot on the metal measuring plate, June sat beside her, clutching her purse in her lap.

"Seven-and-a-half, just slightly under, but I'd go with an eight to give her a bit more room to grow," the thin, bespectacled clerk said.

Angel found a pair of black patent Mary Janes and held them up. At the same time, June held up the brown-and-white Buster Brown oxfords she thought would work best. Clearly the two had a different style in mind, but June did not wish to engage in a standoff with her daughter, not here in the store. Roxanne Gluck from church was with her youngest son, and June did not want to be gossiped about. June waved to the back of the store where Roxanne waited to acknowledge her. Roxanne smiled, and June sent back an expression that implied, "I know. Shopping with the kids is awful." But of course, she didn't mind shopping with Angel. Not really. Angel could be obstinate now and then, but the two normally came to agreement without too much consternation.

June tried a different approach with the shoes. "Those are stunning, Angel," June said, and Angel's faced beamed. "I supposed they're a bit fancy for school though, aren't they? You could wear those to a dance, or a wedding." June looked at the Buster Browns again, then said, "I suppose these look too childish, don't they? All right. What about something in between?"

Angel conceded. She went back to where she found the black patent Mary Janes, set them regretfully back on the display table and picked up the same style in cordovan. She liked the reddish brown much better than basic brown and held up the compromise pair for her mother's appraisal.

"Very nice. Stylish. I think they'll work well with all of your new clothes."

The clerk brought out the eight along with an eight-and-a-half. "This style is running just a bit small," he said.

Angel slipped her foot into the eight-and-a-half and the clerk fastened the gold buckle for her. "Plenty of room in the toes, but not too much," he told June. He told Angel to walk around a bit. "Make sure they feel good on your feet." He pointed out the slanted floor mirror. She saw that her ankles looked slim and the shoes did not make her feet look too big.

"I like them," Angel said.

June said she was glad.

At the cash register, the clerk suggested they might like a tin of cordovan polish, and June agreed they would, so he added it to the bill and put the polish in their bag. She thanked the clerk for all his help, studied his crooked smile and sweaty upper lip, and wondered if there was a Mrs. at home, suspecting there was not. There was no gold band on his left hand, but many men did not wear a wedding band. No, he just seemed too uncomfortable in his own skin. She imagined him going home to a one-bedroom apartment, heating up something from a can for dinner.

June had a soft spot in her heart for misfits and loners. She sometimes felt that she didn't really belong where she was, that she was playing, had been playing, all the roles of her life. Oh, she did it well. No one ever suspected that she wished almost all the time to be someone else, to be somewhere else. She was not sure what she expected life would be when she married Frank, but she thought they might travel or go to parties or meet interesting people. He'd come from the city, and he seemed so exotic when she first met him, so dark, so romantic. And he'd had big dreams—back then. And yet if she were to go back and have the chance to begin again, she knew the girl she was at nineteen lacked the imagination or knowledge of the world to choose anything different from marriage to a good man. So now, even though they were foolish, and she knew they were foolish, her daydreams of being on stage in New York or of working as a missionary in China erased, at least for a time, the ever-increasing feeling that she was not living the life she was born to live.

June took her change, tucked it into her coin purse, and sighed wistfully. At least I'm not frumpy Roxanne Gluck with three pimply-faced boys, June thought gratefully.

June and her daughter stepped out onto the sidewalk. It was a sweltering day that was in dire need of a rain shower to clear out the humidity.

"Let's head over to Jumes for a treat, Angel," June said when they had put all their packages in the car. "Maybe a root beer float? Would you like that?"

"Yeah," Angel said, feeling excited at the prospect, feeling less like thirteen and more like nine.

"You should always say 'yes,' dear, not 'yeah.' 'Yeah' sounds vulgar."

Angel twitched her mouth in an "I don't get you" expression, but did not give her mother any backtalk. Her mom could be so weird at times. Then again, like now, buying her a treat for no reason, she was pretty nice.

The sat in a booth near the window and looked out onto 8th Street. It was a busy back-to-school shopping day, and June and Angel watched mothers with two or three children in tow, arms sometimes bursting with packages.

Angel twirled her straw in the frothy brown foam, then lifted it and licked it clean. June lit a cigarette and leaned back to relax. "I think those clothes will look very smart, Angelina. You'll be the prettiest girl in school."

Angel blushed. "You have to say that. You're my mom."

June laughed. "Oh, I suppose that's right. And I suppose it is also true that if I told you that you really, truly are beautiful, you would not believe me. You're going to be a stunner, my dear. And I think I will take some of the credit in that regard."

June inhaled gently, held the smoke in a long while, then turned her head to exhale slowly. She imagined having a maid at home, scrubbing the marble floor in the front foyer while she and her daughter sipped tea and nibbled shortbread cookies. Her daughter, recently engaged to a Texas oil heir, had suggested this New York shopping spree, but not for the wedding. All that would come later. This little trip was just for the two of them.

Moments later, their teenage waitress headed to their table, her crisp uniform swooshing as she walked. "Is there anything else you want?" she asked before blowing a bubble with her gum.

Angel slurped the last drops of root beer from the tall glass and looked to her mother, who seemed not to have heard. "Mom? Did you want anything else?"

June, back now in the present, felt the weight of her disembodied thoughts.

"Mom?" Angel said again.

June smiled at the plump blonde girl. "We'll take the check, please."

Outside, June slipped her arm around Angel's waist and pulled her tight. "This was lovely. You know, we ought to do this more often. We should just tell Daddy that we're going to have Mother-Daughter days once a month, maybe even once a week. Would you like that?"

"Sure, Mom," Angel said. "That would be fun."

1977

"My mother was a beautiful woman, Sophie. I wish you could have known her. She had the prettiest blond hair, thick and wavy. As she got older, she got prettier, I always thought. Some women get thick around the waist and develop oxen-like legs and ankles, but not her. She worked as hard as anyone, but she stayed slim. Like you. You're like her that way. Not your wild dark hair though. That must come from your Papa." Closer to the truth was the possibility that Sophie had inherited all of her coloring from Ruben Miranda, but Angel did not bring that fact to light.

The nurses had been busy with a new patient, so Sophie had helped her mother to the toilet and was now settling her back in her bed. The fifteen-foot trip had been arduous. Angel was still weak, but it was either walk or use a bedpan, and Angel refused that option.

"What made you think of her just now?" Sophie said, adjusting the blankets.

"I suppose it was you taking me potty." Angel laughed. "Who would have thought I'd need help doing that again?"

"You should take a nap now, Mom. You really should rest."

"I will. I'm just—I hate to leave my memories, you know? I mean— Well, soon enough there will be no one who remembers June Schneider Catalano. I need to. I want to remember her while I can."

Sophie suppressed the pang in her chest and exhaled deliberately. She stood near the edge of the bed, held her mother's hand, and nodded. "Tell me your best memory of her," she said.

"My best memory? Well, let me think." Angel closed her eyes and raised her chin, pressing her head into the pillow. The room was dead quiet. Angel yawned. Her brain darted in and out of dark rooms, remembering strong impressions. June hovering and yelling, June grabbing her by the arm and twisting, June's face nearly touching her own, speaking low and mean. Angel closed her eyes even tighter and shook her head to erase the darkness. Christmas lights. A long green cord laid out on the living room floor. Screwing in new bulbs. Keeping the pattern: white, blue, yellow, red, green. Plugged-in bulbs glowed on the carpet. They got warm, hot. All bulbs fixed now. "Help Mommy, little Angel. Let's surprise Daddy by having the tree all pretty." The radio. Mommy singing, "O Holy Night." The drapes closed. No lights but the tree. Snuggled on the sofa. Mommy smelled like beer. Snuggle. Sing. Sleep.

Sophie brushed her hand over her mother's forehead, leaned down, and kissed her cheek. Later, she would ask her if she had thought of something, if she had remembered her favorite thing. Sophie closed the drapes to darken the room, and as there was nothing else she could do, she sat in the green chair, head back, eyes fixed on the dim ceiling, and listened to her mother breathe.

1951

"You're in a good mood," June said, kissing her husband, who had just come home from work.

"I should be. I got a raise today."

"That's wonderful, Frank. You deserve it."

Near the end of the previous summer, Frank had realized his hardware store job did not pay well enough. While he enjoyed the work and was happy helping customers, he knew he needed to find something that paid more. His pride would not let him go back to furniture, and an acquaintance from church who worked at Vollrath, a company that made stainless steel cookware, suggested he apply there. Frank liked that idea. The plant was near enough that he could walk to work. He started working there right after Labor Day, and so far things were going well. The work was clean, and his natural sense of loyalty to the company showed in the quality of his work. He missed the casual banter he had enjoyed with his regular hardware customers, but he was making more money, and now, he'd earned a raise after only a year. The change had been the right move.

"Dinner will be ready in about an hour. Meatloaf okay?" The question was a courtesy, for there was no alternative if he wanted something else, which he never did. He ate what was served to him. He was grateful to have someone cook for him, and even though he knew his way around the kitchen enough not to starve, he did not enjoy cooking.

"Where's Angelina?"

"She's at Alice White's house working on a school assignment. I expected her by now. The new *Life* magazine came today. You always enjoy looking at that. Why don't you put your feet up for a while? Can I fix you a drink?" It was common for both Frank and June to have a cocktail before dinner these days. Frank reasoned that if June drank a bit out in the open, she would not feel the need to be secretive.

"Sure, but I'll just have a beer."

Frank headed to the bathroom to wash up. "Are these new towels?" he yelled out.

"What did you say?" she shouted back from the kitchen.

He was in the living room now, in the new gold club chair, settling his feet on the matching ottoman. June handed him a bottle of Pabst. The chair was new, bought to replace an old side chair that had finally broken badly enough that even Frank could not repair it. He had chosen the chair, upholstered in patterned brocade, with the intention that it would be his chair. He knew it was a bit more extravagant than seemed sensible, but he also enjoyed its comfort every night after work, and at this time in his life, he felt he deserved it.

"I asked if those were new towels in the bathroom."

"Yes. Do you like them? I think they brighten things up."

Frank had passed caring about the towels but smiled as June chatted about the sale at Prange's. She was a good bargain hunter, he decided.

"I had lunch with Mother today," June said. "They're well."

He nodded and said, "Good."

"Well, I'll let you enjoy your beer. I'm putting a tossed salad together," she said, heading back to the kitchen. He heard her make herself a drink.

Twenty minutes later, fourteen-year-old Angelina came home. The teen was nearly 5'9" now. June was worried she would get too tall if she kept on growing. Women shouldn't be too tall, June felt. They should always be shorter than their husbands. It didn't look right otherwise. A new couple at church proved her point. He was nearly six inches shorter than his wife, and when they stood next to each other, June almost wanted to laugh, they looked so odd. It didn't help that she was also too plump. But they were nice people and June guessed that was what really mattered.

"Hi Daddy," Angel said, letting her book bag drop to the floor. She wouldn't need it anymore tonight. She went to her father and messed up his hair.

"Hi there," Frank said, pushing the black fringe off his forehead and looking up at his daughter. "What have you been up to?"

"Just practicing Spanish vocabulary at Alice's. We have a test on Friday. "Hola Padre," Angel said grinning. "¿Cómo estás?" Learning Spanish made her feel cultured, even worldly. "And Alice and I are the freshman representatives on the Homecoming committee. We're helping to decide how to decorate the gym for our dance. Isn't that a kick?"

"Oh, it's a kick all right," Frank said.

"But the best," she said, turning pirouettes, her arms out like a ballerina, "the absolute best is that I'm going to the dance with Johnny Steinmetz. He asked me in school today. Isn't that unreal?"

Frank's bemused look turned to a scowl. He set the newspaper aside and looked sternly at his daughter. "Now Angelina. I wish you had asked your mother and me about this first. You did not tell the boy yes, did you?"

"Of course, Padre. Why not?"

Frank tilted his head. Wasn't the answer obvious?

"Because you're too young to go to a dance with a boy."

Angelina stood with her arms on her hips. "No I'm not. I'm in high school now."

"That may be, but you're still too young to date. I'm afraid you'll have to tell him tomorrow that you can't go with him."

Angel's face turned dark. She couldn't believe what she had heard. "You're not serious, are you? All the girls in my class, all the pretty girls anyway, have dates for the dance. I am too old enough."

"And I say you are not." Frank's voice boomed and he pointed his finger at her, controlling the trembling anger he felt within. "You will wait until you are sixteen before you go on a date with a boy."

Hysterical, Angel ran to the kitchen to tell her mother. "Did you hear?"

"Hear what dear? I've got the radio on. Here. Let me turn it down. My goodness. What's wrong?"

Angel retold the scene, and by the end of the story Frank was standing in the kitchen.

"Frank. What's the problem? Can't she go? He seems like a nice boy."

Angel nodded and blurted out, "He's a really nice boy."

"Honestly Frank, I don't see what's the harm. It's a high school dance. They're not planning a romantic escapade. I think we can let her go."

Angel brightened. Her mother understood. Her mother would make it right.

"No," Frank said, his voice low and growling. "I am not going to be overruled on this one, June."

"I think—"

"I said, no."

June dropped her chin.

"Angelina," Frank said to his daughter, whose eyes were ringed with red, cheeks blotched pink. "Come on," he began plaintively, hoping a softer tone would calm her. "You're just too young. I know you don't think you are, but you are. I just want to protect you is all. You can go with a group of girls. I will even buy you a new dress, but you will not go with a boy, not alone with a boy. If he's there, I'm sure it won't hurt to dance with him. There will be chaperones, I assume?"

"You're being impossible, Daddy. Everyone else has a date. I'll be the only one. They'll all laugh at me."

"I don't care about everyone else. I care about you and your reputation. It's not a good idea for you to be out alone with a boy."

June tried again. "Now Frank, surely it will be all right. He can pick her up here. We can meet him properly. We'll set a curfew…."

"I said no. I give in on every other goddamn thing around here. You two get what you want all the time. But not this. You're my only daughter, and it's my job to protect you. That's final."

Angel ran to her room, crying. "You're so unfair!" She slammed her door.

Frank was about to head down the hall when June stopped him.

"Just leave her alone. Let her cry it out at least. What did you expect her to do? Of course she's upset. Do you have any idea how hurt she is?"

"Better hurt than pregnant."

"Oh my god. That's a pretty big leap. Don't you trust her?"

"I suppose I do, but I don't know him. I don't trust any teenage boy."

June sighed. Her parents had never imposed such an arbitrary rule on her, but even if they had, it would not have mattered to June, who had never been boy crazy like Angel was. June blamed TV. Girls today thought nothing of openly flirting. June turned the oven off and set the meatloaf on a wooden trivet. She would have to serve dinner soon and knew getting Angel out of her room was going to be a monumental feat. Angel would probably say she wasn't hungry, and June would completely understand.

"You're just going to make her more rebellious, you know," June said.

"Oh, June. You always know everything, don't you?"

Frank opened another Pabst.

1952

"Angelina! Hurry the hell up. We're going to be late for church again, goddamn it." He slipped his finger under his stiff white collar to loosen it.

"Frank. It's Sunday. That's no language to use on Sunday."

"Don't even start, June, don't...." His head was pounding. He had slept badly. Lately his stomach had been keeping him awake at night. "What's so hard about being on time?"

The screen door slammed behind her as Angelina ran to the car, still carrying her black patent Mary Janes, running over the pebble-littered driveway in her white anklets, the untied blue sash of her white eyelet dress a ribbon waving behind her.

"Sorry, Daddy," she bleated as she got in the back seat, sliding over the smooth leather upholstery and pulling her shoes to safety as her father slammed the door.

The engine was already running as Frank slid behind the wheel and yanked his own door closed. As he stepped on the brake and shoved the Fordomatic shift lever into reverse, he exhaled a hostile grumble. In the street, he braked hard, shifted into drive, and squealed the tires on the already-warm pavement.

"Roll down the window, Angelina," Frank barked. "If you don't, you'll melt back there."

"But Daddy...." She was worried about her hair being blown to frizz.

"Just do as your father says, Angelina." June did not feel well either. It was only the fifth day since she'd given up drinking—this time for good. The first two days had been horrendous, even worse than the other two times she had tried to quit. Getting older, it seemed, made it harder to persevere. She failed to admit that it was not age that worked against her but the sheer amount she had been drinking. Telling Angelina she had the flu, June spent the first day shivering under blankets, running now and then to the toilet to vomit, fearing at times she wouldn't make it and worrying over that humiliation. Frank had shown little patience. He had hoped, of course, that this would be the time she really succeeded, that she could find the strength to quit for good, and he had told her so, but June knew she had let him down before, so she did not blame him for his lack of faith. On Thursday night, the nightmares attacked her. Sharp-toothed gremlins the size of small dogs raced ferociously around her, twisting her, biting at her nightgown, growling in her ears, the sound choking her. She'd wake, panting, and gulp water by the handfuls from the bathroom faucet, splash her face, let it drip down the front of her gown. In the dim nightlight glow, she had glared at her reflection in the mirror, half expecting to have turned into the hag she felt like. Reluctantly in bed, she feared and longed for sleep.

So this morning, after tea and toast, June was happy to contend only with a mild headache and the slish-slosh nausea that she could control with steady breathing. It took all of her will to stay calm and not appear agitated, but she had no tolerance for Angelina's snippiness.

Angelina glared at her parents and slumped down in the back seat, her arms folded over her cramping abdomen, her head throbbing with the headache that had kept her tossing in her bed since before the sun had come up. The two or three bites of oatmeal she'd been able to gobble felt queasy on her stomach.

They went only to the Lutheran church now, which was within walking distance, but Frank insisted on driving. Saturdays in summer he washed and waxed his turquoise '51 Ford Fordor sedan until it gleamed like the day he drove it proudly off the dealer's lot almost a year ago. The car, with its showy whitewalls, represented his years of his toil and sweat. It was his American trophy, and if he were to be honest, the car was the only reason he went to church.

June still couldn't believe that her husband, the one who was usually so concerned about every cent, had splurged on a V-8 model when other, cheaper models would still have been very nice and would have served them just as well. However, she had to admit she also liked the car, and she never tired of hearing its muscular rumble. After Frank had first driven the car home, he insisted on taking June for a drive in the country. They had left Angelina home by herself, and they took the county roads west into the rolling Kettle Moraine. June did not mind at all that Frank was quiet. While he concentrated on the road, seeing what the car could do, June stared off into the countryside. At times she imagined herself behind the wheel, out alone for a drive, no particular destination in mind. When Frank turned onto County Road A and drove the winding forest roads near Greenbush, June wondered why they did not come out this way more often. Filtered sunlight flickered through the trees, flashing now and then off the gleaming surface of the hood—it was all so beautiful.

This morning's hurried drive could not have stood more sharply in contrast. Frank's horrid mood did not help, and Lord, was it hot. June loosened the front of her ivory brocade jacket, grateful for three-quarter-length sleeves, took her gloves off, and cooled herself with last Sunday's bulletin, which she found already folded into a fan in her purse. She decided she would not be drawn into whatever was bothering Frank.

"Awful hot for the beginning of May, don't you think, dear? The tulips have withered already, and I swear I could plant peas this afternoon with no worries."

June was not deterred by the fact that no one answered her. She smiled consciously. "Yes. Awful hot. Did you hear that the Schmidt's new car has air conditioning? Wouldn't that be something?"

"Humph. What for?" Frank grumbled. "Roll the windows down.

Half the time it's too damn cold by the lake anyway."

Maybe Frank sped up because he took June's remark as an indictment, or maybe he was afraid the men who leaned against their own glistening fenders in the church parking lot—enjoying their last Pall Malls before the call to worship bell summoned them—would have already ground their butts beneath their polished oxfords. He eyed the intersection ahead as a competitor, and, tossing his half-finished cigarette out the window, he put both hands on the smooth, chrome steering wheel and stomped his foot to the floor.

"Frank!" June shouted in alarm.

Angel, who had been wondering if she would have to sit next to Bad BO Arnold Wright again—the Wrights always sat in the last pew so Mrs. Wright could take their newest colicky baby into the vestibule—was startled by the lunge. Her eyes opened wide and her heart pounded. The car, as an extension of her father, growled. Angel instinctively pushed both feet flat against the back of the front seat, one behind each parent, her hands grasping the edge of the seat.

"Frank! Slow down!"

But Frank, who had won the first charge, felt empowered to test the traffic light two blocks ahead. He saw no cars in front of him or on his tail. He ground his teeth in determination, eyes straight ahead. A quick side glance mid-block revealed a red-headed kid in dirty T-shirt and baseball cap, standing as he pedaled his bike, bounding off the curb and into the street. Reflexes sharp, Frank braked and the tires squealed in warning to the kid who now pedaled furiously. The impact averted by a split second, cool pricks of nerve tingled at Frank's temples. Angel sat in mute fear, muscles tight and throat clenched.

"Good god, Frank," June gasped, her hand clenching the door handle, her knuckles white. "You nearly hit that child."

He ignored her. Nearly? He was in total control. Not even close to the kid. Adrenaline cleared his vision. The light glowed yellow like a demon in front of him. Foot pressing the pedal to the floor, he raced through the intersection. All so clear in his mind, the scene played out before it happened, and the man who beat the clock saw himself standing jovially and proudly among his admirers, who patted him on the back and pumped his hand. In the parking lot, sun glinted off the hoods of polished sedans, off the tortoise shell-rimmed spectacles of men in black suits, white shirts, and thin black ties.

The impact of a pickup truck loaded with a rusty ringer washing machine pulled Frank out of his reverie and knocked Angel to the floor, where her head hit the driver's side door. She was already unconscious when the car swung around and slammed against an oak tree, shattering the window and raining glass shards upon her. When she opened her eyes minutes later, the sunlight was clouded with dust, and her father was sobbing. "June. Junie, sweetheart, wake up." Angel dabbed at her lip with her tongue and tasted blood. Her head hurt worse than it ever had. A shadow eclipsed her curled form, and the hand of the shadow reached into the car to touch her father's shoulder.

"Sir? Hey, mister."

"Oh, Junie, Junie. What have I done?"

"Help is here now, mister."

A siren came closer and Angel's eyes closed against her will.

1952

Grandma Schneider died a week after Halloween and Angel knew that her world was infinitely smaller. It felt to Angel as if her mother had died all over again. At the burial, Angel stood between her father and her grandfather and wept endlessly. How could God give her so much pain?

The day itself mourned with its dismal sky, steel gray painted thickly in the west, thin, pathetic clouds the only brightness. On the way to the gravesite from the church, cold rain spit against the windshield. Frank drove slowly and deliberately, as he would for the rest of his life.

Angel shivered as the minister finished his prayer, the words only sounds to her ears. A squawk overhead drew her attention to where a red-tailed hawk circled. The corner of Angel's mouth lifted slightly. Grandmother loved watching hawks. One year a mating pair had built its nest on top of the old the telephone pole in the alley behind their house. "A good omen," Grandmother had said. When Angel was six, Grace had given her *Audubon's Field Guide to North American Birds* for her birthday.

Her head still with the circling hawk, Angel had almost forgotten where she was and why she was there, until she felt the warm squeeze of her grandfather's hand. "It's time," Wally whispered, his eyes glazed and red. The pallbearers, Frank among them, lowered Grace's casket into the ground. When it came time for the mourners to toss a handful of dirt into the grave, Angel stood stiffly and refused. Frank, who did not see why she must comply, nevertheless respected tradition, so he tried to force his daughter to cup a handful of earth, but Angel glared at him. Then, as if she were a child and not nearly a woman, she broke away from him and ran from the gravesite to the line of parked cars, where she sank to the ground, sobbing.

Frank looked at Wally and mouthed, "I'm sorry." But Wally did not feel there was a need to apologize. He wished he could follow the girl. Lowering his Gracie into the ground was the beginning of the end of his life, and he knew it.

Frank had not been inside the house at 6th and Lincoln in years, and being there now felt oppressive. Every photograph of June or of him with June and Angelina, every knickknack, every hint of June's childhood felt to him like a judgment. He had taken their daughter from them. Once when he married her. And then the second time.

And yet Wally, the gentle soul, saw none of that. He had never blamed Frank. He put the blame on the truck driver, who could not have been paying attention. He put the blame on chance and bad luck. But not on Frank. Wally had always felt an affinity for Frank. The two of them knew what it meant to go to war. The women had never understood that. But Wally did. And anyone could see that Frank was a good father and had been a good husband.

Angel led Grace's friend Sylvia to the mahogany buffet where the dessert service was kept. Then she helped her set the twelve gold-trimmed white china plates on the table. Angel felt her mother at her shoulder, telling her to be the lady of the house now. As a child she had always been expected to help her mother and grandmother on occasions like this one, and even though she felt numb in the process, she moved about the kitchen and dining room with ease, as if she'd been hosting funeral receptions her entire life. Angel was grateful this reception would be simple and small. Wally, who felt out of place in his own home, watched Angel glide about the room and was grateful for her presence, knowing he would fumble it all if it had been left to him.

"Hey Grandpa," Angel said now, the table all set, her work done for the moment. She was a good inch taller than her old grandpa, who stood at the living room window and stared blankly out onto the street. She put her arms around him and held him tight. He was in no hurry for her to break the embrace.

"I already miss her so much," Angel whispered in his ear. The old man's eyes filled with tears. Later, she led her grandfather to the table, and, as if he were a small child, she helped him fill a plate with a ham roll, a few of the little sweet pickles he loved, and a small corn muffin. He wasn't hungry.

"Thank you, my little Angel. I don't know what I would do without you."

Six months later, when a neighbor called to say they'd found Wally dead on his front porch, saying he must have sat down to watch the squirrels and just died, Angel knew there could be no god.

1952

Month after month, father and daughter did little but go through the motions of life. Each evening, Angel would, or Frank would, if he had to, make dinner, and father and daughter would sit across from each other at the kitchen table, eating, being civil, politely asking one another to pass the salt or the green beans. After dinner they would read, or she would do homework. He might watch TV, or the TV would be on. He might drink too much. And they would go to bed early because there was nothing else to do. And each morning, he'd awaken, would shave and dress and get himself to work, and the robotic depression would continue. And she would head to school and do her lessons because that was her job. It was expected.

Since her mother's death, Angel had tried to stop blaming her father for the accident, but she had not been able to. Angel felt if she could only say the words, could only tell him it was okay, things might get better. But, whenever she thought she might go to him and say something, she found she could not say what she did not believe.

At Christmas, Mrs. Merton brought over a fruitcake. She stood on the dark porch with the foil-wrapped loaf, and Frank flipped the switch to turn on the porch light.

"Guess the bulb's burned out," Mrs. Merton said, shivering and hoping to be invited in.

Remembering, finally, his manners, Frank stepped aside and waved her in.

"It's not much, but I do remember June always appreciated my fruitcake. Said she liked how I put in extra cinnamon." Mrs. Merton smiled, but she saw how much effort it took for Frank to return her smile, and she wished she had resisted the urge to be neighborly.

Angel, who had been in her room reading, came out when she heard Mrs. Merton speaking. Seeing her mute father facing the fruitcake, Angel took pity on their neighbor.

"Thank you so much, Mrs. Merton," Angel said as she took the loaf. "It's really nice of you. Can I get you something? I could put some coffee on."

"Oh goodness, no. But thank you. I just wanted to drop that by and wish you a Merry Christmas. Know it won't be the same and all, but we're thinking of you."

Frank thought only of the burned out porch light and was grateful Mrs. Merton made her exit only moments later. In the basement he found a 100-watt bulb, much too bright for the porch, but it would have to do for now. He'd go out and by a pack of 60-watt tomorrow. He screwed the bulb in the socket. Back inside, he flipped the switch and the light flooded the snow-covered front lawn, creeping out even into the slushy gutter.

That night as he lay in bed, Frank realized he had no idea how long that bulb had been out. Before long, if things didn't change, it would be more than a bulb. The shutters would be falling off the house and people would start to talk about the poor widower and how he'd just let himself go.

1953

Frank felt unaccountably sweaty, sitting in the school counselor's office, listening to the litany of grievances against Angelina. We understand, the young man was explaining, how difficult, mother dying. The words battered Frank's consciousness. Late to class four times. A D- in math, an F in science, and a C- in art, her favorite class. These were not his daughter's grades. This was not how she behaved.

"What...what can I do?" Frank stammered.

"Well, that's not...that is, I can't really suggest what can be done. My job is to bring you in, make you aware. We wouldn't want you to be surprised with a negative report card."

Frank scowled at the counselor, annoyed now that he had taken time off from work. He may as well have learned all this through the report card. Why on earth did he have to be there in person?

"Well, we'll see what we can do," Frank said and stood up.

The counselor seemed relieved to have the meeting come to an end as well. At the door, he said something that nagged at Frank all the way home. He'd suggested that while these grades are alarming, good grades are not as important for girls as they are for boys, and what really matters is that Angelina begins to feel better about herself.

The unavoidable scene at home did nothing but create even more distance between Frank and Angelina. All Frank had to say was that he'd been summoned to the school and Angelina felt she knew all the other words that would follow. She ranted about how meaningless school was. Why did it matter?

All of it Frank took as punishment. All of it he felt he deserved. So he let her rant and said only that he hoped that she knew that he just wanted the best for her. He had never expected straight A's. He had only wanted her to do the best she could do.

Things did not change much until Angel went back to school after the Christmas holiday and was assigned a new lab partner in chemistry class. When Mr. Johnson first paired Angel with the new boy from Chicago, she was embarrassed. She found it hard to talk to him. Her throat would tighten and her heart would pound. She'd never worked with a boy before. Well, she had been paired up in math class with Todd Miller, but that was different. Being paired with Ruben Miranda was something else entirely. He was a lean boy with glossy black hair and dark chocolate eyes. He smelled like moss and radiated heat.

From the moment he met Angelina Catalano, Ruben Miranda could think of little else, her long, cinnamon-blonde hair, sometimes tied up in a ribbon, sometimes bouncing off her shoulders, her soft chestnut brown eyes. The soft, soapy scent that hung in the air she moved through never left him, nor did the motion of her hips as she walked down the hall towards her next class, looking now and then slightly over her shoulder at him. She was not like any of the other girls he had known, girls who huddled together wherever they went, always twittering gossip. Angelina was a woman in a girl's dress. She just didn't know it yet.

"We moved here mostly for my little sister Ana," Ruben told Angel as he handed her a beaker. "She's only a little eleven-year-old punk kid, but she's already trouble." No matter what Ruben said, Angel adored listening to him. He sounded so different from Sheboygan boys. As he read their lab notes, she thought it sounded like poetry.

Technically, according to her father's ridiculous proclamation, Angel would not be old enough to date until her sixteenth birthday in a few months, but when Ruben asked her to go with him after school for a burger and a root beer, she did not think twice about her father, other than knowing she would have to invent stories about where she was and who she was with.

Her father was also not in her thoughts that night, long after she had reluctantly let go of Ruben's hand and walked the three blocks home from where he'd dropped her off. She could not get him out of her mind. In bed, she lay awake long into the night, restless and anxious. When she finally gave in to sleep, she found herself floating and naked, her limbs tangled with Ruben's, her heart pounding, her mouth dry, her eyes glassy and on fire.

At the lunch table a few weeks later, Angel was telling Alice that Ruben was hinting about going steady.

"I don't know, Angel," Alice said. "He seems like a fast boy. I don't think you should. He will probably want you to…you know."

Angel knew exactly what "you know" meant, and she had wondered many times about what "you know" would be like. With Johnny, with other boys, too, but now, with Ruben, she longed to know. It thrilled her to think of it, and it terrified her. Angel held her head high and told Alice she didn't know what she was talking about.

Alice reddened. "I'm only looking out for you," she said. "You don't want to get a reputation."

Angel shocked Alice when she fired back, "Well, maybe I do."

Alice said nothing then. She only looked across the table at her friend with a blank expression.

Angel rose with her tray, lifted her chin, and turned her back on Alice, but as she made her way to the return counter, Angel felt her knees wobble and her stomach sicken. If she had not been in school, she would have crumbled to the floor and cried.

1977

Sleet from yesterday's storm remained on the grass, but the sidewalks and streets below were wet and clear. The temperature was rising and predicted to soon be back in normal range for May. Earlier, the doctor had asked Sophie again about a nursing home for her mother, saying Angel had improved enough to move and they really could not keep her in the hospital much longer. Sophie had felt embarrassed that she had no answer. So despite her reticence, she knew today was the day to get things settled.

Sophie helped her mother back into bed after she had been up to use the toilet and wash her hands and face. "My hair's a bird's nest," Angel had said, looking at her haggard reflection in the mirror. Sophie promised she would brush it for her.

"Put that extra blanket on me, Sophie. I'm freezing."

Sophie covered Angel with not one but two blankets, then, once her mom began to feel warmer, Sophie brushed Angel's hair, making it look only slightly better. It needed a wash in the worst way.

"Listen, Mom. We have to decide about a place. The hospital needs to know."

"Ouch," Angel yelped.

"Sorry. Guess I didn't see that knot." Sophie laid the brush on the bedside table and sat on the edge of the bed. "I know this is hard," she began.

"No. You don't."

Sophie lifted her head in surprise. "What?"

"Now you listen, Sophie. You don't know. Truth is, neither do I. I have never done this before, any of it. I have never had to put an aging, or sick, relative in a nursing home. Besides, I've always thought of those places as death's waiting room. I mean, come on."

Sophie remembered the old men and women in the nursing home she had visited long ago with her Brownie troop. She could not argue with her mother's reasoning. But in this case, they had no choice.

"Yes, but...."

"No. No buts. This is my life. My death, more so, and I will not go to a nursing home."

"But the doctor."

"Sophie," Angel shouted. "You're not hearing me. I want to go home. I want to lie down in my own bed. I want to see the sun come in my own window. I want to be among my own things. I have that right, don't I? Can't I choose where I want to be when I die?"

The question, put like that, was impossible for Sophie to dismiss. So despite having no idea how she or they would manage, Sophie made arrangements with the hospital care coordinator and Dr. Winter. He would send home pills, instructions for general care, and a list of emergency numbers in case things got so bad Sophie needed help. In addition, they would arrange for a visiting nurse to stop by every few days.

Yes, of course. Angelina would go home to die.

1954

"Why do I have to go?" Angel whined, sounding more like six than sixteen. "I barely knew her."

Frank said it didn't matter. He almost said "she was your grandmother," but he knew his mother had never been a grandmother to his child. "She was my mother, and you will go with me. It will be expected." Angelina looked so much like June these days that at times it hurt him to look at her. It hurt him to be stern with her, but goddamn it, the girl was like her mother in other ways, too. She was infinitely exasperating.

It wasn't that he did not sympathize with his daughter. How many funerals could she be expected to bear? If he was truthful, Frank dreaded the prospect of this funeral every bit as much as Angelina did. Maybe more. The family and his old neighbors would expect Angelina to be reticent, but from Frank they would expect a show of grief, which he did not feel. When he was in the hospital in London and learned that his father had died, he felt grief then. But now? He felt mostly guilt, knowing that his mother's death gave him relief. He would no longer have to make the hollow call on Christmas or Easter. He could, from now on, place his mother into memory. He resolved, however, to be kind enough in that memory. He could afford to be. Memory was easy. It was the living that was hard.

The service at St. Rita's was longer than necessary. Christ, Catholic masses, Frank thought. The priest's homily described his mother in terms Frank felt more fitting for saints, though even he admitted his mother did what she could for others. After he and Robbie had left home, his mother turned her maternal needs to the church. She cooked food for funeral dinners, organized clothing drives for orphans and the poor, and once even shamed the archdiocese via a scathing letter into replacing frayed altar cloths. She was formidable. Frank would not dispute that. And those who did not know how she had shunned her daughter-in-law or how she gave up on her son—who had betrayed her by moving away—those people might think Maria Catalano *was* a saint. He guessed it would harm no one to go along with that idea now.

After leaving the church, Frank drove past the tannery. He wanted to show his daughter something of his old life. "It was an awful job, Angelina. I don't know how my dad did it for as long as he did. Talk about saints. He really was one. You know me. I don't mind hard work, but that was worse than hard. When a man can't breathe, that's not work. That's something else."

Angel heard the words slaughter, bloody hides floating, vats of stench. Her stomach turned over. She liked seeing the old neighborhoods, though, and hearing about who lived where, and about some of her father's boyhood escapades. She wished he would talk to her like this more often. As he told the story of the clubhouse he had built with his best friend Jimmy, his voice became animated, and it was fun to listen to him. Still, Angel couldn't stop thinking how odd it was to imagine her father as a boy. Especially lately. He seemed so old.

As they pulled up to the brick row house where Frank had lived his entire life before moving to Sheboygan, he felt almost as a foreigner seeing a new city for the first time. It had been so long since he'd been home. Angel, who was used to bungalows and colonials set on wider, tree-lined streets, thought her father's boyhood home looked old fashioned. The constant traffic along the street, too, so different from Sheboygan. But she could somewhat imagine, as she viewed this neighborhood and the rest of what she had seen of Milwaukee, a bit of what her father's childhood might have been like.

Inside Frank showed Angelina the second floor room where he and Robbie slept when they were boys. The room was small and narrow, but the ceilings were high. "What's upstairs?" Angel asked.

"It's a separate two-bedroom flat. My best friend Jimmy lived there. He died after the war." Frank paused now to think of Jimmy as he was, as they were, back in '35 when they'd taken off for Sheboygan. It was easier to think of Jimmy in the place where they had been boys.

"Does his family still live up there?" Angel asked.

"No. I heard they moved to Florida, and after that Mom decided not to rent the apartment out anymore. Said she just couldn't imagine having strangers living above her."

Buoyant laughter beckoned Frank and Angelina back downstairs. Robbie and Lucy had arrived with their three boys. They stood just inside the door, stomping their snowy feet on the rug in the tiny foyer. Aunt Lucy waved hello, and Angel waved shyly back. Two women from the church came in right behind, each carrying dishes of food. Angelina followed her father to the dining room. Frank noticed that all four leaves of the walnut table were in use, and it was covered in his mother's favorite white tablecloth. A huge antipasto tray from Glorioso's served as the centerpiece. Salami, prosciutto, provolone, mushrooms, pepperoncini, giant green olives glistening. It had been a long time, Frank realized, since he'd seen one of those trays, and his mouth watered. Of course, someone had prepared his mother's meatballs and sauce. Nearby was a bowl of ziti tossed in olive oil, ready to be topped. As they filled their plates, Frank helped Angelina make sense of the offerings.

The biscotti looked like toast, she said.

"It's a cookie," he told her. "You'll love it."

After moving to Sheboygan, Frank learned to eat German or standard American meat and potatoes meals. He could cook a brat like anyone, and he enjoyed brats, but he missed this. Summer sausage was not salami. It just wasn't the same.

"Did you get a cannoli?" Robbie asked. "Lucy made them," he said.

Frank's plate was already full. "Maybe later," he said.

Even the strong coffee tasted better. June, like her mother, had always made it so weak, and he had gotten used to it. But this, *this* was coffee. He promised himself he would start adding a couple more scoops to the pot. Why not? Life was short.

After the priest led the group in one last prayer, he donned his cap and coat and said goodnight. After that, others felt free to start heading home as well. With the party breaking up, Angel hoped to be in the car soon, so when her father told her he had a job to do first, she got a bit ornery.

"I don't think it will take that long, Angelina. Robbie and I just have to go up and bring down Grandpa's trunk and get it loaded into our car." It was a matter of doing it tonight or making another trip. He wanted to handle it right away. "You want another piece of cake?" Frank said, trying to sweeten the situation.

"Ugh. No. I'm stuffed." She had her eye on the sofa in the living room.

"It won't take that long. Promise." He smiled.

She sighed and shrugged her shoulders. Moments later, Angel sat on the sofa and pulled her feet up behind her. Then she realized she had her shoes on and put her feet back on the floor. She really wanted to lay her head down and close her eyes.

Frank headed over to the table where his brother was eyeing up the last cannoli on the plate. "You sure you wanna eat that? Gonna weigh you down so's you won't be any help at all." Frank found himself falling easily into his boyhood cadences.

"Guess yer right," Robbie said. He motioned to Angel on the sofa. "She gonna be okay down here alone with the natives?"

"I hope so."

In their mother's bedroom, the men felt again like boys and tiptoed across the carpet as if she were downstairs and could hear them "snooping." The old trunk sat in the alcove, where it had been put to use as a table for plants. Above the trunk, three bay windows looked out onto the dark street, one dim streetlight illuminating the sidewalk below. The snow heaped onto the curb lay in soot-covered mounds.

"I feel kinda bad about takin' the trunk, Robbie. That is, it means a lot to me that she left it to me, but don't you wanna, I don't know, roll for it or something. Make it more fair?"

"Yer the oldest, Frankie. Seems fair. It's just a beat up old trunk. Probly filled with a bunch of old junk, war medals maybe. Seems right you should take it."

"You mean you never opened it?" Frank asked.

"Jesus, no. She wouldn't let me near it, like it was radioactive or somethin'. Heck, I used to think she must have been stashing money in there or—I mean who knew with her. Anyway, guess I just gave up caring about it a long time ago."

Frank took the key and turned the lock. A whiff of mothballs filled the room. The glare of the ceiling light cast shadows into the cavernous interior. Lying on top, wrapped in tissue paper, was their parents' wedding portrait that their mother had put away many years ago.

"Jesus. Ma was thin?" Robbie said, holding up the frame for a closer look.

"Yeah, and even kinda pretty, too," Frank said, but it was his father's youthful gaze that held him. Would he marry her again? Would he do all of it again if he knew? If he knew how life would take and take, would he do it all again? When Salvatore Catalano married Maria Botano in 1910, did he look into the future with as much hope as his son Frank would twenty-six years later? And was there a moment in his father's life when he would see that hope dim, even see it die now and then?

Frank shuffled through, sifting his way to the bottom. "Sorry, Rob. Appears there's no horde of cash."

Robbie sighed. "We coulda been millionaires."

"Yeah, sure. Millionaires." Frank smiled. He knew money never really solved anyone's problems, and even if he had been wealthy, June's never-ending longing for things did her no good.

Once the trunk was secure, Frank started the engine to warm up the car before heading back in to say goodbye. Inside, Angel, Robbie, and Lucy were the only ones left. Robbie's three boys had gone home much earlier with Lucy's parents, a moment Angel was grateful for, as the boys, aged nine, twelve, and fourteen, were starting to annoy her with their barrage of manly tricks and feats, all meant to impress their pretty cousin.

Lucy helped Angel with her coat and sent her away with a couple of leftover biscotti wrapped in foil. Lucy's hug, like all the other hugs that night, had seemed to Angel to mean too much, and once released from them, Angel was not at all sure how she should respond. She simply smiled and was glad that had been enough.

Frank and Robbie clung to each other like old women, then stepped back and held each other by the forearms for a moment longer.

"You take care, Frankie. Don't wait so long to visit next time."

"Yes. That's right," Lucy said to her brother-in-law. "We love seeing you, both of you."

"I promise," Frank said.

As they drove away, Frank said, "I hope you're not disappointed that we didn't stay the night."

Angel said she didn't mind. She was glad they didn't stay. She was ready to be home in her own bed. The day had been a confused cloud of newness, city sounds and smells, the food, the garlic in everything, the people loud and demonstrative, people who said they loved her, people she had never met throwing their arms around her, hugging her to suffocation, people who were supposed to be sad who were laughing and smacking each other on the back, people like her father who didn't want to be there. She was tired. She just wanted to go home, and the trip back to Sheboygan would be long.

Frank kept the speedometer at fifty. He was babying his cargo. He hoped it would not snow before he got the car safely into the garage. He would unload it in the morning.

Had he a truck, he could have brought home tables, chairs, a sofa. Robbie and Lucy said they didn't need any of it. "Neither do I," Frank said. He had no intention of turning his house into a replica of his mother's. The brothers decided they would give it all to the church to sell or donate.

A small, round side table that Frank had made for his mother when he was in high school was the only exception. That he wanted. He was still proud of the fine work he had done. After all these years it still did not wobble one bit. The yellow pine table fit nicely in the back seat. It would be for Angelina, though he did not tell her that now. She might shrug it off, treat the gesture as unnecessary and spoil it. He would wait. Someday he would present it to her. Someday, he hoped such things would matter to her.

They were headed north on Highway 57, and just a little past Mequon, Frank looked over at Angelina, already asleep, her head resting on a folded blanket laid over the armrest of the door, her hands tucked between her drawn up knees, the soft rise and fall of her breathing. He was glad she had come with him. He was glad his aunts and uncles had met her and had seen for themselves what a beautiful girl she was.

1955

Frank had held his tongue for over a year, reminding himself every time he wanted to warn his daughter about her relationship with Ruben Miranda that such a warning could push her away. The past year and a half had been agony for him. Even mentioning other boys, nice boys, young men a father could be proud of, would send her into s a tirade and Frank would have to backstep, saying he hadn't meant anything. Did she know the boy is all? Then last Saturday, Frank had witnessed a scene that had forced his hand.

Ruben and Angel stood on the sidewalk a few houses down from Angel's house. They did not see Frank sitting in the dark on the front porch, did not see the end of his cigarette glow red now and then. But he saw them. It was typical of Ruben to park his noisy hot rot down the street, especially when it was late. That night, a full hour and a half after Angelina's supposed curfew, there they were, oblivious to the world around them. Surely others could see them. Frank fumed. No one would ever say to him, "Oh, by the way, I saw that loose girl of yours the other night with that boy." They would not say, "She should be ashamed of herself." But he would feel their words in their knowing looks. It was his own fault, Frank reasoned. I should have been doing more to teach her about these things. A mother is the one....

In the quiet summer night, Frank heard his daughter's soft giggle, then watched as Ruben's hand crumpled Angel's skirt, inch by inch, raising it enough for him to slide his hand underneath. Frank watched as her hand grabbed Ruben's, slowing the inevitable. Their faces so close the streetlight barely penetrated the gap. There he goes again, Frank witnessed. He felt he should not be seeing what he saw, but he could not unsee, and he could not move. What if she realized she needed her father, called out, slapped the boy, and ran? Then, the boy chasing, she struggling? Frank would be on that boy in seconds, pummeling him to the ground, but never once raising his voice. Almost under his breath, he would say, "If I ever see you with her again, I'll kill you." Then the boy, lifted to his feet, would wipe his face, taste blood, feel fear. He would nod assent and limp off. His daughter would be ashamed but grateful. She would always remember how close it had been, how her father had saved her from her weakness. But it didn't happen.

The next morning Angelina woke early, but she was so comfortable, so happy, that all she wanted to do was lie there and listen to the birds and chattering chipmunks. At 8:25, Frank opened her door and told her it was time to get up and that he didn't want to hear any excuses. He hoped he said it playfully enough that she would know he wasn't angry.

Today he would tell her, finally, that she was humiliating herself. He was afraid. But this was what being her father meant. It was his duty to make her see the truth.

He added two more scoops to the percolator basket and filled it with fresh water. It was rare to make a second pot of coffee, but he'd been up since 6:30, and with Angelina drinking a cup or two these days, he thought he had better make more. While she slept, Frank had made oatmeal muffins, topped with brown sugar and cinnamon the way she liked. They were cooling on the table now.

Angel plodded out to the kitchen in her robe and slippers, last night's ponytail loose and off-kilter. Frank had set aside the Sunday comics section of *The Sheboygan Press* for her.

"Coffee?" he asked.

"Sure. Yeah."

Frank hated when she, or anyone, said "sure." Worse than slang, it was no answer at all. Today he let it pass.

Frank set the cup before her, and she measured a heaping teaspoon of sugar and stirred it in.

"Muffins? What's the occasion?" Angel peeled the muffin paper and bit into one as if she hadn't eaten in days. "Good," she said, her mouth full.

Frank waited until his daughter had finished two muffins and poured herself another cup of coffee. He patiently read the sports section. That is, his eyes saw the photographs and the words in the sports section. He had no idea what was reported there, not today.

How would he begin? He imagined scolding her: You were late, almost two hours after curfew. I was worried. You were late. Does curfew mean "come in whenever you want"? Angel, I wish I hadn't seen what I saw last night, but I.... You will never see that boy again, do you hear me? I forbid it. He had played all of that and more in his head since early this morning when he'd made up his mind to confront her.

She noticed her father's unease. "What's wrong? Is something wrong?"

He took a deep breath and felt almost as he did when charging toward the enemy, knowing as he ran forward that everything he knew could come to a sudden and remarkable halt, that everything he knew about the world could end.

"You were out too late with Ruben last night."

She started to make an excuse, but he cut her off. He would not let her flank him. "I was on the stoop. I saw you."

The hair on her neck stood up. She blinked.

"If I saw you, who else saw you? It was indecent, what he did. A goodnight kiss is one thing, on the porch, under the light. People expect a little kiss. What you were doing is not something done in the open, and not by young girls, not by unmarried girls."

"Dad...." Sometimes Ruben took things too far. Her father had seen them? Her stomach lurched at the thought. Even so, it was nothing to make such a big deal about.

"I have always thought that boy was trouble. He obviously doesn't respect you or your reputation. And that car of his. Boys like that...I have known boys like that." Frank wanted to say it, to pronounce the ultimatum he had rehearsed. He wanted to point his bayonet in her face and force her to surrender.

"Now Angelina. I love you and I only want what's best for you. You wait and see. That boy's going to end up in jail. He's no good. I do not want you to go down with him. I...from now on, Angelina, I...." He couldn't do it.

Angel exploited his hesitation.

She was on her feet. Her tears were hot, boiled up from powerless anger.

Standing over him, she leaned down into his face. Her robe hung loose, and her arms thrust out at her sides. "How can you say that?" she shouted, her eyes narrowed and sharp. "You don't even know him." Her voice strengthened like a storm cloud. "You have never tried to know him. From the beginning you have judged him. You. You have no right to judge him. You're not perfect, you know. Maybe Mom would have been better off not marrying you. She would probably still be alive. You're horrible. I can't believe you. I hate you. I hate you."

Frank watched her as she ran down the hall, her robe sailing behind her, then slam her door in fortification. And now, as with so many things, he felt consumed by his impotence. It was not just that he had failed. It was not just that he had made things worse. But in the moment his daughter stood screaming over him, she had embodied her mother's worst, most unraveled moments, and in that moment Frank felt that he had never had control over anything in his entire life. As he sat with his head in his hands, he had no idea what to do next.

1955

Their plan was to head to California, find jobs, and live like Bohemians in a surfside bungalow. Ruben could cook or he could fix cars, and she could wait tables or work in a store. They didn't have much money, but they had enough, they believed. Two can live as cheaply as one. Wasn't that the saying? Until they got a place to rent, they thought they could even sleep in the car. In fact, neither one had any real idea about what it would take to live life as an adult. Of the two, Angel romanticized the experience. The trip itself would be an adventure, she thought. She imagined the Pacific breezes, the sound of waves crashing. She had never seen an ocean. Lake Michigan's broad expanse and sometimes-violent waves were all she knew. Pictures from *National Geographic* and *Life* magazine informed her imagination. She could not wait to discover what salt air actually smelled like.

They drove west on two-lane highways bordered by narrow shoulders, long white rulers down the middle of gray, sometimes reddish pavement. The Chevy seemed to enjoy the open miles, and Ruben loved the sound of his engine pushing itself to the limit.

Angel was the designated navigator. With a notebook and maps on her lap, she charted the course. Their plan was to drive straight west. Then, according to the map, Denver, Colorado was a good place to begin heading southwest. They were excited they would be driving through Utah and Arizona on their way to Los Angeles or San Diego. Angel thought it would be fun to see what Hollywood was like. Ruben agreed. They thought they might spot some movie stars. Even if that didn't happen, they knew they wanted to live near the ocean. They wouldn't be too picky otherwise.

About an hour after backing out of the Catalano driveway, they crested the hill on Highway 23 and looked down into Fond du Lac's broad valley, the southern shore of Lake Winnebago visible to the north. Even that view was a revelation to the two, who had never traveled farther west from Sheboygan than Plymouth. At that point, Angel and Ruben set their first goal to make it somewhere well into Minnesota before finding a wayside where they could pull over and sleep for a few hours. Both had agreed not to spend money on a room for the night until they absolutely needed one.

It was now late afternoon, and although they hadn't done anything but sit in a car, they were ravenous. Onalaska, Wisconsin, on the edge of the Mississippi River, looked to Angel like a good place to stop for a meal. Sitting opposite each other in the diner, waiting for their food, glasses of Coca-Cola sweating on the white Formica table, Angel and Ruben agreed they were not in any real rush, so it would be okay to pull over on both sides of the Mississippi River. It was Angel's idea. She wanted to look across at Minnesota, and then back at Wisconsin. She wanted snapshots of both shores. Ruben thought it was silly, something only a girl would want to do, but she was his girl, and he wanted her to be happy.

They stood now and looked westward from Wisconsin, where Minnesota's shore rose up in a forest before them, a mass of green obscuring the horizon beyond. French Island blocked their view of the Mississippi, with the Black River tributary only hinting at what they soon would see. Minutes later, as they drove over the bridge, the landscape opened up to sky and water, the Mississippi wide and mighty below.

But it was not until she looked eastward from the Minnesota shore that Angelina understood how definite and distinct the river stood as a demarcation between her old life and her new life. "It's so beautiful here," she said, feeling as if she were discovering something new, as if no other person had seen the expansive river before. Looking north, she saw several small fishing boats anchored in Onalaska Lake, a wide bulge in the river. A tug pushed three white barges southbound, its red and white wheelhouse glowing in the dusky light. She heard the rhythmic chug of a freight train hugging the shore as it headed north. Angelina and Ruben were not the only ones with a destination.

Angel did not want to move when Ruben said it was time to get going. Her feet were weighted to the ground. She looked down into the broad Mississippi valley, across at French Island, at the little green fingers of land stretching in the water, sparkling rivulets flowing between them.

"Yeah, I know," Ruben said, pulling her toward the parking lot. "It's nice. But we gotta go. We're gonna see lots of nice things, mountains, the ocean."

"You're right," Angel conceded as she looked one last time at the vast edge of her home state, resigned now to never see it again, or at least not for a very long time. Looking into Ruben's dark eyes, Angel had never been more certain that this future was meant to be.

About an hour later, the Chevy began to sputter steam, so they pulled over and Ruben topped off the radiator with the jug of water he had stowed in the trunk. He frowned as he stood with the hood open, peering in at the engine. "We'll let 'er cool down just a bit before we start up again."

"You bet," said Angel, who knew nothing about cars. She had full confidence in Ruben's ability to manage all of that for them. While they waited, they leaned against the trunk and stole kisses whenever there were no other cars on the horizon. Twice a car slowed and pulled over, but Ruben walked over to the driver's door to let him know they were fine.

Five miles out of Austin, Minnesota, steam hissed out of the hood again. How could it be dry already? Ruben wondered. "Shit! That's not right." He put in the rest of the water from the jug. It was not enough, but it would have to do. Then he babied the car to a service station on the edge of town.

"No mechanic on duty now," the gas station attendant said. "He'll be in tomorrow mornin'. Up the road's a motor lodge. Purty nice," he said. He took Ruben's name, scratched it on the back of an old receipt with a dull pencil that had been sharpened with a knife.

"The mechanic'll give you folks a call tomorrow at the desk there, okay?"

The news was not good. Hole in the radiator. "Not surprised you couldn't see it," the mechanic said. "She's down underneath. Probly got hit by a stone or sump'n. Anyway, pistons overheated, so...." The parts would have to be ordered. But worse, the repairs, while not as major as they might have been, would surely strip them of most of their cash. Angel joked they could rob a bank like Bonnie and Clyde, and even though Ruben laughed, he didn't think she should be kidding around at a time like this.

Later, when the car was fixed, Ruben tried negotiating with the station owner. "Couldn't you just let us take 'er and we can send you the rest of the money later?" Ruben suggested.

The stout, feedbag-stomached man smiled broadly. "Now son, I could do that, but if I did, I'd be out of business in no time."

"We're good for it," Ruben added, trying again to be convincing.

"I'm sure you are. I'm sure you are," the man said, though he knew if he handed over the keys, he wouldn't see Ruben, his pretty girlfriend, or any more money.

"Now, look, son. I am not as heartless as you think. My brother-in-law's a bigwig over to Hormel and I could call him to see if there's any work. Lots of local folks work there. You ever heard of Spam?"

Ruben said he had.

"We make it right here, in good old Austin."

Ruben did not seem impressed, but he saw that he was stuck. "Sure. You can call him for me. We're paid up at the motel for a week. Old lady who owns it felt sorry for us and gave us a discount."

"Oh you bet," the station owner said. "She'll do that. Course you can tell she's not getting ahead either. Light's been burnt out on the 'L' in her sign for nearly a year. We call her place The Pines Mote. Anyway, son, I'll give Roger a call and we'll see if we can get you some work."

Later, in the little motor lodge kitchenette, Angel spread Jif and Welch's grape jelly on white bread, then cut Ruben's sandwich in four wedges, the way her mom had always done for her when she was little. To save money, Angel made her sandwich with only one slice of bread, telling Ruben she wasn't that hungry. "It's going to work out just fine," Angel said. "I'm disappointed too, but we can work for a few months and get ahead, then take off like nothing ever happened." She already could imagine her child tottering about the house. Their house. She held in her heart all her hope for the future.

As he bit into the soft, doughy bread, Ruben thought the sandwich tasted like defeat.

1955

After Angelina told her father she was pregnant, before she and Ruben left for California, Frank had tried to convince her that she did not need Ruben. "He's no good for you, Angelina. Why do you even have to tell him about the baby?" Frank had pleaded. "You can keep on living here with me. I'll take care of you both."

But instead of seeing the offer as generous and kind, Angel resented her father's interference in her life. Finally, he had pushed too far and she had raged at him. They were in the kitchen after breakfast. She raised her tremulous fists and gritted her teeth. "This again. What is wrong with you? Can't you understand? You'll never understand."

"No, it's you who'll never understand," Frank hurled back. "Not until it's too late, not until after he hurts you. That boy is not the fatherly type, either. You mark my words."

"Were you? Were you the fatherly type?"

She could always find the words to slice into his heart. So like her mother that way. Then she told him that she and Ruben were headed to California. Going to start a great life out there.

"You can't be serious," Frank said, truly astonished.

"Why not? Just cuz I was born in Sheboygan, that doesn't mean I want to die in Sheboygan."

"Angel, come on, now. Be reasonable. I know that since your mother died, you and I have...."

"You say that like she got sick or something instead of.... I mean, Jesus, Dad." She just stared at him, then shook her head and told him it didn't matter. Her mind was made up.

Frank felt desperate. "Just stop. I mean it, Angelina. Stop all of this. You are still my daughter and I forbid you—"

At the word "forbid," Angel screamed. More than that, she wanted to break, to destroy. She threw her nearly-empty coffee cup and watched its shards bounce off the floor.

"Jesus Christ!" Frank shouted, his face red, his eyes glistening with rage. "That make you feel better?"

After she threw the saucer to the same fate, she screamed, "No!"

Frank kicked the chair and sent it on its side to the floor. "Do you think I'm just going to rush in and rescue you when he leaves you or worse?"

"I don't think anything, Dad," she said deliberately.

"Get out of here, then. I can't do this anymore. Just get out of here," Frank said, slumping in defeat to pick up the chair.

He did not help her pack, nor did he help her load her belongings into Miranda's ridiculous car a week later. But he did not stand in her way, and when she climbed into the front seat and turned back to wave goodbye, Frank raised his hand. With a smirk, Ruben Miranda closed her door and walked around the front of the car, his chest puffed out in victory. Then he got behind the wheel and drove away.

At that moment Frank Catalano felt instantly older. He consoled himself that at least they were not screaming at each other as she left. At least that was something.

Now that she was actually gone, Frank felt unhinged, and he was not quite sure how he would begin to live life alone, truly alone for the first time in his life.

That first night, he heated up a large can of pork and beans for dinner. As he ate, he laughed at himself. He saved the one small lump of fatty bacon for last. Tomorrow, he'd cook some brats on the grill, or "fry out" as Wally would say. He could make a bunch and keep the leftovers in the fridge. Looking up, he said, "Probably what I deserve, eh, Junie?"

Frank thought about his daughter every day and could not help but worry about her. When he became overly anxious, he repeated the phrase June had always said when she wanted to push worry away: "no news is good news." If his daughter had been found dead on a remote highway somewhere, he would be told. If that delinquent abandoned her at some small town diner, she'd call. If she got sick or needed money? He had to work hard to push such thoughts out of his head. Keeping busy helped.

Frank sat on the front stoop in the steel spring lawn chair he'd fixed up the weekend before. With a wire brush, he'd got most of the rust off. He chose a deep red Rust-Oleum enamel. Frank did not consider himself to be good with a paintbrush, but it had turned out well. Sitting in that chair on nice evenings became habitual. Neighbors walking their dogs would wave. Those who knew him shouted out "Hi Frank," but they respected his privacy. Close neighbors knew. A few had watched from behind their blinds as Angelina Catalano handed her suitcase to that boy, got in his car, and drove away. They knew, and they pitied him. First the wife. Now the daughter.

Frank lifted the top off another Pabst. He thought about when he was young. He remembered the row house, the years with Ma and her rules. It wasn't all bad there, at home, but there were times, he knew, when he couldn't wait to get away. Frank smiled to himself when he recalled the moment he first saw June. He stood in line to pick up his paycheck, his very first from North Shore, and there she was behind the counter, a low parapet of a railing keeping her and the stack of envelopes separate from the workers. She was the reason he had left Milwaukee. He was sure of it. Their daughter the second reason. And now, he had lost them both.

1955

On a dismal December 5, at 2:30 in the afternoon, Sophia Rose Miranda slipped from her mother as easily as a blanched tomato from its skin. There had been some pain, of course, but not what Angel had feared.

"You're a lucky one," the nurse told Angel. "Most women would kill to have it so easy. You might not gloat to your girlfriends about what a piece of cake this was," she said, chuckling. "You'll probably have a flat tummy in a month, too." The latter comment was accompanied by a bitter note.

Angel was in love. The wrinkly, dark-haired baby sucked noisily. "You're a hungry girl, aren't you?"

Ruben hadn't stuck around for feeding time, which unnerved him. Earlier, he'd come into Angel's room to try out his new role as proud father. He told Angel she looked pretty good, considering, he said, what she'd been through. Hell, what a thing, he realized. Then, to his daughter, he said, "Hey little one. I'm your daddy." He touched her tiny, wrinkled hand, marveled at her long, slender fingers.

As Ruben took up the baby, Angel coached. "Be careful. Hold your hand under her head." He cradled his daughter in his strong hands, then began to rock her, gently at first, then almost widely.

"Give her back," Angel barked. "You'll drop her."

"Take it easy. I got her. I got her. Right little one? She looks like me, I think."

"Babies look like babies."

"Well, she could do worse than take after me." To be honest with himself, Ruben had wanted a boy. But his little girl, her dark hair already wild and unruly, could not have been more beautiful.

The first weeks at home with Sophia in their half of a side-by-side duplex were more tiring that Angel could have imagined. Nursing Sophia every three hours or so took a tremendous toll on Angel's body. And she couldn't stand letting the baby cry, a strategy one of the nurses suggested. "Let her stretch those lungs," the nurse had said. But it didn't feel right. It felt like allowing her baby to be miserable on purpose. So instead, if she couldn't calm Sophia by rocking and cooing, Angel fed her. Eventually, the baby cried less and Angel's method worked out just fine.

At first their life in Austin, once the two of them realized they were stuck for a while, was just as blissful as Angel had dreamed, minus the ocean. She loved caring for her husband and keeping a neat house. They had married at the courthouse in September, before Angel began looking obviously pregnant. Two of Ruben's coworkers were witnesses, people Angel had never even met. Years later it would occur to Angel that a wedding without family was not a true wedding. At the time, she had only wanted to get it over with.

Ruben's job at Hormel paid the bills, and he said he didn't mind the work. The temporary custodial job he got after the car broke down had turned into a permanent job on the production line. He was making Spam, or at least part of it. He joked that it was his job to add the pig snouts. Dented cans or label misprints were discounted in the employee store, so the Miranda's shelves were full of Spam cans. Angel had learned to cook it in various ways. Ruben liked it sliced right out of the can, slathered with mayo on a sandwich. She liked it mixed into macaroni and cheese.

But it was not long before Ruben began feeling tied down, and he started socializing a couple of nights a week with coworkers. While Angel didn't like that he wasn't always home, she didn't want to criticize him.

He worked hard and deserved to relax. She feared she'd push him away if she complained. In November, before she had started to feel too fat to go anywhere, he took her out for dinner and gave her a pearl necklace. Of course they weren't real pearls. They didn't have the money for that, but Angel thought the gesture was awfully sweet.

Once Sophia arrived, Angel realized she missed her mother more than she had in a long time. Two days out of the hospital, Angel could not stop crying, no matter what. Ruben brought home a little pink cap and bootie set a friend's wife had crocheted and she burst into tears.

"Don't you like it?" a confused Ruben asked.

"I love it," she said, having no idea why a bootie set would make her cry. If she had been able to call home, talk with her mom, she knew that they'd laugh about it. Eventually her days of spontaneous tears ended as abruptly as they began.

At Christmas, because she felt obligated and a little guilty that she had not done it before, Angel called her father. She had let him know about Sophie with a pink-and-white birth announcement depicting a little baby girl held in a diaper that a stork carried like a hobo's bindle pack. But she had not heard her dad's voice since the day she had left. She wasn't even that angry anymore. It's just that she didn't know what she'd say. The longer she put off calling, the easier it became not to.

The phone rang ten times before Frank finally picked up.

"Hullo? Frank Catalano speaking."

At first her voice caught in her throat, but she managed to say, "Hi, Dad. It's—" she was going to say "Angel," which is what she called herself, but remembered her father preferred her full name. "It's Angelina."

There was no sound on the other end of the line but his breathing. Angel understood that silence and allowed it, accepted it. She gave him time. Then he cleared his throat. "You there?" he said.

"Yes, Dad. I'm here. How are you?"

"Okay. I'm okay, I guess. You?"

"We're…I'm fine."

"Good."

"Your granddaughter is fine." And at the thought, Angelina burst into a flood of information. "She's so pretty, Dad. She has your dark hair and eyes. Mom's nose. Or maybe it's my nose. She loves to cuddle and coo. I just can't bear to let her out of my arms, even to put her in her crib at night. She's just perfect."

Silence again.

"It's been a long time, Angelina."

"I know. Yes. It has. Are you all right? Did you have a nice Christmas?"

Frank let out a concealed laugh, more of a huff than a laugh. Christ. The girl. What kind of question was that? Robbie and Lucy and their boys had come up, brought ziti, biscotti, and a small antipasto tray. He had no wine. Only beer. But no one cared about that. "Gee, Uncle Frank, you're swell," the boys shouted when they opened their presents from him. He'd gotten each one of them a football. They were boys. Seemed like an easy enough decision.

"Yeah. Nice. You?"

"Well," Angel gushed, "I guess I got the best Christmas present ever."

Frank cleared his throat. "Hmph. I guess I better get a present in the mail for her. For Sophia," he said. He realized just then he had never spoken his granddaughter's name out loud. He had not even told Robbie and Lucy about the baby. He guessed he didn't really feel much like a grandfather.

Silence hung between them.

"Well…I…I just wanted to say hi and Merry Christmas," she said.

"Okay. Thanks."

"Dad, I…."

"Well, Angelina. I have to check on my pork chop now."

"Dad. I called to talk. All you care about is your dinner?"

Her tone. Just the same old Angelina, Frank thought. Did she forget she was the one who left him? Did she forget she was the one who had hurt him, who had turned her back? Now, he had a granddaughter. When would he ever see her? Frank sighed loudly. He wished there really was a pork chop on the stove.

"You still at the same address? The one on the birth announcement?"

"Yes, it's the same, but Dad?"

"What?"

"Well, you sound like you can't wait to get off the phone. I mean, don't you want to talk to me?"

What's there to talk about, Angelina? Frank thought. What's there to say? Leave that shit heel and move home. Bring me my granddaughter. Admit you were wrong. Is that what we should talk about?

"Sure. Yes. I do."

But she heard in his voice the words he did not say. She didn't get angry. It was Christmas. She didn't want to yell at him. Why did he have to be so stubborn? Honestly! "Well," she said. "Like I said, I just wanted to say hello and wish you a Merry Christmas."

"Okay," he said. "I can send the baby something then?"

"Sure. Yes. That would be very nice."

"Okay, then. Goodbye."

"Bye, Dad." She barely finished the syllable before the line clicked. She set the receiver on the cradle and looked at Sophie, who slept in a borrowed bassinet. "You bitter old son of a bitch," she said. In her heart, a heavy lump would not move.

The second week in February, a small box was delivered. Inside was a little yellow dress, already too small for her growing daughter. Angel would write a gracious thank you note and pack it away for her next baby.

1956

Thinking it would seem unhelpful to sit on the front stoop and watch others work, Frank stayed in the house, and watched the parade of furniture as the muscular movers guided it gently from the truck into the house next door. His new neighbors were an older couple, both white haired and thin. He imagined the woman barking out orders like a platoon leader. June would have done the same.

About a week later, Frank arrived home from work and saw the old couple on the front lawn, scrutinizing a rather scraggly shrub under their living room picture window. They heard his car and looked his way. Frank realized he would need to meet them now or seem unfairly standoffish. So after setting his lunch box on the front stoop, he walked over to them.

"Hi there. Something wrong with that bush?" Frank said to start the conversation.

"Hello. I'm Ruth Perlman, and this is my husband Josef," the woman said, extending her hand to their new neighbor. "Not so much wrong as neglected. I think Joe can prune out all that brown, and then we'll see. He's our green thumb."

"Happy to know you," Joe said, extending his hand as well.

"Frank. Frank Catalano," Frank said, not sure why he felt nervous. "So, how do you like the place?" he asked.

"We like it fine. Some things need attention. The realtor failed to point out a few obvious problems. The kitchen sink drips. I won't be able to tolerate that very long," Ruth said.

Close up now, Frank saw that Ruth Perlman was taller than her husband by about four inches. She was also the more gregarious of the two. Both were well dressed. She wore a crisp sea-green dress, belted at the waist. Josef was in wool trousers, a white short sleeved oxford shirt and tie. He was not a factory man by the look of his hands, or maybe he was retired.

"We will find a handy man, Ruth. I can ask around. Maybe Mr. Catalano knows of someone?"

The Perlmans looked at Frank expectantly.

"Well, sure." He could put them in touch with someone at Wilson Hardware. They could give the old couple a name. Or he could fix it himself. It was probably a matter of a simple washer. Joe was obviously not able to fix it if he thought to hire someone for a dripping faucet. "Or, well, why don't you let me take a look?"

"Are you handy, Mr. Catalano?" Ruth asked.

"They tell me I am. Let me get my toolbox."

As Frank headed to his garage, Ruth and Joe Perlman watched with the hopeful look of truly helpless people who continually find themselves amazed at what others are able to do. Fifteen minutes later, Frank turned the faucet on and off, testing his work. "Should be good now," he said. "Is there anything else you'd like me to look at?"

Joe's gentle laugh sounded almost child-like. "Well, Frank. That's awfully generous. Is there, Ruth? Is there anything else Frank can fix?"

Ruth hesitated only a moment. There's just this outlet here. When I plug in the vacuum, it doesn't stay in tight. Is that something you could fix?"

"I'll need to see if I have an extra receptacle, but I probably do." A half hour later, Ruth was fully satisfied with the repair, and while Frank put his tools away, she stood ready with her purse.

"What can we pay you for your trouble, Mr. Catalano?" Ruth said.

"It's Frank, please. And put your money away. I'm happy to help."

Ruth could see arguing would be fruitless. "Well then, you're staying for dinner, and I won't accept 'no' for an answer."

It would not be the last thing Frank fixed for the Perlmans, nor would it be his last meal with them. Frank discovered that he enjoyed both of the Perlmans tremendously. Just as it had pleased him to guide new kids on the line at North Shore, just as it had pleased him to fix lawn mower motors at Wilson, just as it had pleased him to pump up bike tires for neighbor kids or glue "good as new" Angelina's music box, Frank found a peaceful satisfaction in making things right for Ruth and Joe. And not since his mother had he known such a good cook as Ruth.

Frank also found in Joe a new friend, he realized one afternoon later that summer, as the two sat on the Perlman's front porch listening to Earl Gillespie on the radio, who had just announced, "The pitch to Henry Aaron. A swing and a drive back into center field!" Frank had not had an honest-to-goodness friend since Jimmy.

"Need another one, Frank?" Joe said, holding up an empty brown longneck.

"Don't need one, but I s'pose I'll take one if you're offering."

Joe hoisted himself up and headed inside for the beer. The Braves would win this game, which was good as they were neck and neck with the Dodgers in the race for the pennant. Jimmy had loved baseball, too. Jimmy, whose life had really ended in the Pacific, even though he did not die until three years later, when, unable to face another day, he hanged himself in his childhood bedroom. Frank felt his failure as a friend to be a cosmic judgment at that moment. Maybe he had a second chance to get it right with Joe. He would reach out and help the old man whenever he could.

June would have loved the Perlmans. They were generous and caring people. Ruth brought Frank extra raspberries picked from her patch. "I love them, myself, but Joe says they give him problems. She patted her stomach to indicate that nature of the problems. I can't eat them all, and it's a shame to let the birds have these," she said handing Frank a brimming pint. Eventually, Frank helped Joe till a space for a bigger garden. Joe's love of gardening reminded him of Wally Schneider. When he lived with his in-laws, Frank had cared little for the garden, for its value, or even for the fruit of their labor. But now, somehow, alongside Josef Perlman, he enjoyed even weeding. Planting meant something. Tucking the kidney-shaped bean seeds under the loam and patting the earth felt so hopeful. The entire process was an act of faith.

1958

Angel loved being a mom, but she wanted more than that. Six months earlier, she thought she was pregnant again, but it had been a false alarm. After that disappointment, her daily life, which had long been tedious and uninspiring, suddenly revealed the truth that she needed more than a two year old's company to occupy her. So Angel cooked Ruben's favorite meal and afterwards showed her husband the brochure for the two-year nursing program at Austin Area Vocational-Technical School.

Ruben was against the idea entirely. He tossed the brochure aside and argued loudly, waving his arms in the air as he spoke. "I'm the man of the house, Angelina, and I will pay the bills."

"It's not about paying bills. I want to do something, too. I have always wanted to be a nurse. Why can't I do it? I don't think it is for you to say what I can do."

That night in bed, Angel hugged the edge of the bed and cried silently. She was disappointed, but she would not give up. She cajoled, presented arguments, even used sex to persuade, and eventually she wore him down.

When classes began in September, Angel dove into the rigorous coursework full of good intentions. For most of her life, she had been a good student, and she found now that some of her old study habits returned to her easily. Harder was balancing schoolwork, childcare, and housework, not to mention keeping Ruben's sudden mercurial moods in check. Many nights after Sophie and Ruben were asleep Angel slipped out of bed and studied until one or two o'clock. When it was hard to pry her eyes open in the morning, she never complained.

Eventually Ruben made peace with the new arrangement. He tried to help out more around the house. In addition to cooking dinner several nights a week, he took on more of the childcare tasks, things he had not really been willing to do before. After picking up Sophie from the babysitter, he was in charge of giving her an early bath. One less thing for Angel to do later on. Angel told him again and again how much she appreciated all his help. He would always smile rather weakly when he replied that she was welcome.

After the first year, classes were on hiatus for the summer. Angel insisted they celebrate her achievement. "Let's get a babysitter and go out. It's been so long since we went somewhere together."

Ruben agreed. He knew a place they could get a drink and go dancing, and then later…. It had been a long time for that as well.

"Treat me to a steak dinner, first," she said playfully.

The second drink turned Angel's lips numb and made her brain fuzzy. She almost never had alcohol, and she wasn't used to it. Ruben was already on his third. "You better sit down, baby. You don't look so good."

"I think you're right," Angel said. He led her to a table and after getting her a Coke, asked if she minded if he stayed up at the bar to talk with some friends from work. She said she didn't mind, but it was a lie. They were supposed to be on a date. Still, she wasn't really feeling like great company just then, so she figured it wouldn't hurt if he spent a little time with them.

Angel drank her Coke and nibbled on pretzels. After her head felt a bit more normal, she walked without too much wobbling to the ladies room. When she emerged minutes later, she was ready to dance. Ruben was no longer sidled up to the bar. Where was he? She scanned the busy club for her husband. She spotted him, finally, on the dance floor, his arms slung over the shoulders of a petite blonde in a tight red dress, her hands working their way to places they definitely should not be going. Then Ruben slid his hands down, first tight against the blonde's waist, then smiling, unaware that his wife was watching, Ruben sank his face into the crook of the woman's neck, and as he did so, his hands slid lower, curving over the woman's butt, when he pulled her in a thrust tight against him.

Blood rushed to Angel's head and she felt she was going to be sick. The room spun and she reached her table, balancing herself on the back of the chair before sitting down. Angel dropped her head down between her knees and breathed heavily.

When the song ended, she lifted her head. She felt less dizzy now. Her stomach had settled. If she could see her blotchy face, she'd want to powder it, but at the moment she did not think about how she looked. At the moment her gaze was fixed on her husband, who sauntered jovially toward her.

"Hey baby. Feeling better?" he said.

"Not really. Can we please go home now?"

"Now? The party's just gettin' started, baby. C'mon. A couple more drinks?"

"Ruben," she said forcefully. "I want to go now." She shot him an "I mean it" look. He had seen it before.

He shrugged his shoulders. "Whatever you say."

When they got home, she went directly to the bathroom. Ruben paid the babysitter, who lived across the street. He was glad he didn't have to drive her home. He was feeling ready to get into bed with Angel and didn't like the idea of being slowed down on that road. At the fridge he popped open a beer and chugged half of it, then began humming the song he'd danced to with that sexy girl from the packing line. "Ooh, mama," he said out loud.

"Angel," he called. "Hurry up. Your old man's waiting for you." His voice sing-song-y and playful.

When she didn't answer, he went to the bathroom door and knocked gently. "Hey, honey. You okay? You been in there a long time."

She opened the door. Her face was scrubbed clean and her hair was wrapped in a towel. She glared at him and padded down the hall. Before going in her room, she peeked in on Sophia, who was soundly sleeping. Angel planted a gentle kiss on her baby's head. Now moving into her room, she bent over, took the towel from her head and rubbed her damp hair before tossing the towel on the floor. Ruben sashayed in after her, his hips swinging side to side, still dancing.

She ignored him. Angel turned down the bedspread and folded the sheet and blanket back. Then she went to the closet and pulled a blanket off the top shelf. She grabbed Ruben's pillow off the bed and shoved it and the blanket at him.

"Hey," he said, taking the hint. "What's this about?"

"You're sleeping on the couch tonight. Unless that whore you were dancing with has room in her bed for you."

He dropped the pillow and blanket on the floor and came closer to his wife. When he moved in to put his arms around her, she pushed him away. She stood with her arms crossed over her chest, her feet hip-width apart.

"Now Angel, we were just dancin'. She's a nice girl, really. I know her from work. We were just—"

"Just nothing. You can't talk your way out of this. I saw you grab her ass, you son of a bitch. That's not dancing. And you were kissing her neck. If you think that's nothing, you and I have a completely different idea of what nothing is."

"Okay, okay. I admit it. I got a little frisky with her, but I was just thinking of you, baby. About coming back home to be here with you, my Angel baby."

"Get the hell out of here, Ruben. I cannot even stand to look at you right now."

She held her hands out and pushed against his chest, she the locomotive, he the stalled train. "I mean it. If you don't get out right now,

I don't know what I'll do."

He saw it was no use arguing. He leaned down to pick up his pillow and the blanket and headed to the living room. He sat on the sofa in the dark for over an hour. In the morning, he begged her to forgive him. He promised he would never do anything like that again.

She let him back into her heart, and for awhile, he honored his promise.

1959

Frank and Joe sat at the picnic table in Frank's backyard, already on their second beer. Ruth, who was not much interested in listening to a football game, had been in the garden gathering summer squash and end-of-season pole beans. She thought it might freeze one of these nights, and she did not want to lose her hard work. She had five nice pie pumpkins that she'd let lie as long as she could.

After rinsing her hands under the outdoor faucet, she headed over to see what the men were up to. Overhead a flock of Canada geese honked and called her to attention. She looked up, watched the lead change, and wondered how the geese knew to fly in a "V" formation. How did any creature on this earth know to do what it did?

The Green Bay Packers were playing the Detroit Lions at Lambeau Field. It was a mild, overcast Sunday, and with a light sweater on, it was nice to be outside. Now and then when the sun crept out, the yellow leaves on the towering maple in the far corner of Frank's yard sent golden light down from its canopy.

"Whoo, hoo," yelled Frank. "That's the way, McIlhenny! We'll show 'em!"

"Did you hear that, Ruthie?" Joe said. "McIlhenny just scored a touchdown and Hornung kicked the extra point. We're up 14 to 0 now."

"That's nice, dear. Do you boys need anything to nosh on? Seems like you ought to have something to go with that beer."

"Pretzels sound good."

A few minutes later, Ruth returned with a bowl of pretzels and a glass of ice water for herself. She took a seat near her husband.

"Thanks, Ruth," Frank said, grabbing a handful of pretzels.

"You're very welcome."

Ruth stretched her long legs in front of her and closed her eyes. Her ears took in the sound of the radio even if her mind tuned it out.

"So the players are doing well?" Ruth asked a few minutes later.

Frank smiled. Joe shook his head. "Women just don't know how to talk about sports, do they, Frank?" Frank was not about to agree with him.

At halftime, Frank and Joe got up to stretch their legs, and Ruth asked if Frank had a moment to look at one of their shutters that had come loose.

"Yeah, sure. I can fix that for you," he said. "After the game, I'll get my tools."

"Ruthie, do we need to trim this old shrub?" asked Joe, who seemed always to be finding work for her to do.

"I'd like to tear that hideous thing right out of the ground and maybe plant a nice climbing rose. But that's not going to happen before spring."

"She's never satisfied with how things are. Always wants something else."

"Joe. Stop teasing me."

Joe slipped his hand around his wife's waist, pulled her toward him, and made smoochy sounds with his lips. That old man got fairly silly on a couple of beers, Ruth thought. She pushed him away, not wanting Frank to witness their intimacy. But he did see, and he missed, in that moment, his Junie more than he had in a long time.

"So, Ruth," Frank said, changing the tenor of the moment, "how's Lev doing?"

"Ach, that boy," Joe chimed in.

"Now, Joe. You be nice. He's doing very well. Thank you for asking, Frank. Joe and I are going to drive out to New York and visit next spring.

Aren't we, Joe? He can't come home for Hanukkah. He's so busy. He just got a new part in a play."

"He should be managing people's estates, not prancing around on a stage," Joe said.

Frank felt he ought to commiserate with his friend. "I'm frustrated with my daughter, too. She had so much going for her, but she hooked up with a guy who is not anywhere near good enough for her. What are you going to do?"

"I hear you, Frank," said Joe, who laid his hand on his friend's shoulder. I never imagined my own son would throw away his college education on the vagaries of the stage." Frank did not know what "vagaries" meant, but he decided it wasn't a good thing.

"Oh, just stop it, you two. To hear you. Are they suffering, our children? Are they sick, destitute? Didn't we sacrifice to give them a better life so they could become the people they wanted to become? It's not the duty of our children to live out our imaginations of their lives. It's the duty of parents to love their children enough to give them all the time and space they need to find their own way. I thank God they live in a world where they aren't begging for scraps of food or crawling under wire to escape persecution."

"Holy smokes, Ruth. I didn't mean anything. I was just—"

"I know, Joe. You were just. But one of these days you're going to need to accept and love your son for who he is, not for who you wish he was."

In the fourth quarter, Max McGee caught two touchdown passes from Lamar McHan, one for forty-one yards, the other for thirty-six. The final score was 28-10.

After the game, Frank fixed the shutter and helped Joe dig out the shrub and its gnarled old stump. The shutter was a promise. The shrub was penance.

1977

"Where'd that thing come from?" Angel said, barely one foot inside the front door. She pointed to the hospital bed that was situated in the living room in front of the picture window.

"The visiting nurse who will be working with us said you would be more comfortable," Sophie said. "And easier for when we have to care for you." Visions of bedpans and sponge baths and god knows what else were still unsettling to Sophie, who struggled to imagine herself as her mother's round-the-clock nurse. She changed the tone and tried to sell the positive attributes of a living room view. "We can raise and lower the bed, raise up the head end. And," Sophie continued cheerfully, "it will make it much easier for you to see outside. See? Lev even filled the bird feeder for you." Sophie smiled and thought, please Mom, please just be cooperative.

"I want my own bed," Angel said petulantly.

"But, this is for your own good."

"No buts. I'm sleeping in my own bed."

A week later, Sophie and Lev moved Angel to the living room despite her objections. Sophie had bought cheery new sheets and a bright yellow bedspread, hoping to further sweeten the prospect. The new bedding and the wide window view pleased her mother after all. Plus, Lev had argued that if Angel were to remain in her own room, Sophie would not be able to spend as much time with her as there would be too much Sophie would need to do elsewhere, but if Angel were situated in the living room, Sophie would be around all the time.

"You sound like a lawyer," Angel had said, a smirk on her face. She knew she was beaten.

Now that Angel was set up in the living room, it *was* easier to include her in everyday life. At first she was not confined to bed, though as the days passed, she spent fewer and fewer hours out of bed. In the living room Angel could watch TV whenever she wanted. Or listen to records.

One of the hardest adjustments to the new arrangement for Angel was giving up her role as the woman of the house. But she found she enjoyed watching her daughter take on that role. As Sophie prepared food, cleaned the house, or folded laundry, her mother watched with pride. Angel observed life outside their house as well. From her view, she kept a curious eye on the comings and goings of many of their neighbors. Her reports amused Sophie and Lev.

Sophie learned to manage. They all learned to manage.

Lev promised that when things got really tough, he would arrange it so he could be there when she needed him. She knew already she couldn't have managed this far without him. He had stayed home the day the bed was delivered and rearranged the furniture to make it fit. "I'm going to be here for you, Sophie, and for her," he had told her.

"I'm so grateful," she replied. "I don't think I'll ever be able to repay you."

"What? You act all of a sudden like we're ordinary neighbors. You're like my little sister, you know." He'd given her a brotherly sock in the shoulder then as if to prove the fact. She smiled. Sophie knew in her heart that she could ask anything and he would do it. He would give it. But she also felt she should not take advantage. She should not take him for granted. He wasn't really her brother.

On Saturday morning, Lev came over to visit before leaving town that afternoon. He was flying out to Los Angeles to film a scene in the new detective thriller he had been cast in. It was a small part, but his resume was building, and in LA, at least, he was sometimes recognized when he was out for dinner or a drink. Angel had a hundred questions. She wanted him to name all the people in the movie. Who did he know that was famous? What was it like? Do they really say "action" and "cut"?

"Oh, Lev. Do one of your lines for us. Please?" Angel made a pouty face and said "please" again as a helpless waif.

"Well, okay," Lev said, giving in easily. "I played this grimy outlaw once. They ended up cutting my scene, but I liked that role. I had only one line, but it was fun playing such a bad guy. I was so dirty. Oh, and you will not believe how my teeth looked. So horrible, brown and rotten. So anyway, my gang had chased down a guy, forgot why, but we had him, and as the others held him, it was my job to stare the guy down, spit in the dirt and sneer, then say, 'String 'im up, boys.' We did it in one take. I thought I did great. I don't know why they cut me."

"String him up boys," Angel repeated, then laughed. "Oh Lev, what a fun job you have. I envy you."

That evening after dinner, Angel told Sophie that she did not want Lev seeing her in "not nice" situations.

"What do you mean, 'not nice?'" Sophie asked.

"Well, you know, like if one of these days I can't get to the toilet. I would just die if he had to help with that. Promise me, Sophie."

Sophie promised. But her promise was hollow and she knew it. If there came a time when she needed to lift her mother or turn her or, God knows what else, she would need help. If the visiting nurse were available, that was one thing. If not....Well, if she needed him, she would ask for Lev's help.

"I get what you're saying, Mom. But you know, he's not going to be embarrassed. He would understand."

"What about me? What about me being embarrassed? I'm embarrassed just thinking it might happen."

Angel began to color, and she did not generally let things like this get to her. But she had read an article about a woman in just her situation, end-stage breast cancer, and god, at the end it was just horrible.

"Seriously, let's not talk about this," Sophie said. "I promise. If something not quite nice happens, I'll be able to take care of it all by myself. You hardly weigh anything anymore as it is." Sophie slipped her arms around her mother, the way the nurse had showed her, and pulled her mother's body toward her. "See. I can move you, as long as you don't fight me. When you're zonked out on your meds, you are dead weight anyway."

"Don't say dead weight, Sophie."

She'd heard it, too. The moment she said it. Not her best choice of words.

"Speaking of being zonked out, you can barely keep your eyes open. You and I both need to sleep soon. Come on, let's get you settled." Sophie removed Angel's bed jacket, laid it over the end of the bed, pulled up the extra blanket, and adjusted the head of the bed a bit lower. Angel could still see the TV, which she would watch or stare at for about ten minutes, if that long. Afterwards, Sophie would lower the bed a bit to make her mom more comfortable. If it were a good night, Angel would sleep five or six hours without needing more medication. Sophie learned to take each good night as a gift, knowing they would not last.

Sophie clicked on the TV. A repeat of *The Waltons* was on. Both she and her mother liked that show. In this one, John Boy began to write stories about life on the mountain. At the commercial, Sophie got her bed pillow and a blanket from her room. She decided she would sleep on the couch tonight. She found she slept better when she was closer to her mom. She worried less.

In the TV's flickering blue light, Sophie snuggled herself under her blanket and paid half attention to the family on the mountain who dealt with life and death and illness just like everyone else in the world. Angel was asleep now, her breathing slower, deeper. A made-for-TV movie about a teenage girl alone in a house came on next. She'd end up dead, or rescued at the last minute. Last week there was a movie about a haunted house. Angel loved scary movies, but not Sophie. She did not understand why someone would want to be afraid on purpose. It made no sense. Sophie wished she had one of those fancy controllers that would let her change channels, but she didn't. Before she turned the TV off, she clicked the dial to see what was on the other three stations. Nothing she cared about. You'd think that with four choices, one of them would have something she would like to watch.

She lay back on the couch now, covered and comfortable. Moonlight seeped into the living room from the front door sidelight and the kitchen windows. The drapes were always drawn at night so that Angel, as she put it, would not "be on display for the neighbors, lit up like the evening show." The refrigerator hummed. Outside sounds, the echoing voices of neighborhood kids calling out in the dark, found their way inside. Shouldn't they be inside on a school night? A car now and then shooshed down 13th Street.

"Not-quite-nice," Sophie said softly to herself, followed by a quiet laugh. Her mom could let the blue language rip when she was in the mood. Sophie had known the word "shit" from the time she could remember. Now all of a sudden Angel found it hard to talk about the real thing? And what about me, Sophie thought. What about how embarrassing it might be for me to clean up if you mess all over the bed? No, Sophie did not need scary movies. She did not need to invent situations that would haunt her. They would come. They would come soon enough.

Sophie flipped herself so that she faced the back of the couch, pulled her knees up, and crossed her arms about her chest. A block away, a siren wailed, headed east on North Avenue to the hospital six blocks away. Then quiet again. She closed her eyes and sighed deeply.

"Good night, John Boy. Good night, Mary Ann. Good night, Momma."

1959

Ruben Miranda veered right and took a turn on a country road. Passing woods and farm fields, he drove aimlessly down roads he had never taken before. Car windows down, it was nearly dusk on a humid August day. Crickets chirped and wires buzzed.

He had tried, hadn't he? Ruben thought, consoling his own guilty feelings. This wife and kid thing just...he really had tried. He'd even changed diapers, for Christ sake. Angel was too demanding, not the fun girl he had run away with. She wanted him home every night. She wanted him to help her cook dinner, even. Do women's work.

He was against her going to school, but she threw a tantrum over that so he gave in, which meant she had less time to take care of the house and less energy to take care of him. There were things a man needed and she couldn't understand that. He had been careful. Thought he had been careful. Shit, that woman could throw a fit. He supposed he didn't blame her. But she did not understand that a man has needs. And women didn't need it like men did. Hell, he was not the first man to get something on the side. It didn't mean anything.

He told her it didn't mean anything, but that had only made her angrier. He couldn't breathe. It was like being home again with his mother. Constant demands. Angel didn't even care about California anymore. Shit. That whole beautiful dream, gone. He was only twenty-four years old and he felt like goddamn fifty. He felt death breathing down his neck, a chill of certainty.

He pushed the gas pedal to the floor and sped ahead on the gravel road, dust a billowing cloud behind him.

1960

An Easter basket for four-year-old Sophie sat on the kitchen table.
The large basket woven of pink and white plastic was stuffed with green
cellophane Easter grass and piled high with candy. Crumpled foil wrappers
lay near the basket. Someone had already eaten two chocolate marshmallow
bunnies. And while a mound of colorful jellybeans caught Sophie's eye, she
was told she had to wait until after breakfast.

"Plus, you've got to go out and hunt for your eggs first, sweetheart,"
her mother said. Angel finished tying her straggly hair up into a ponytail,
then quickly transferred all the candy to a metal bowl. She sorted through
the jellybeans for red ones and popped a few into her mouth. "There," she
said, handing the basket to Sophie. "Now you can put all your eggs in here,
all cozy in the Easter grass."

At the front door, Angel pulled her robe around her. "The snow is
a nice surprise, sweetie, don't you think? You can pretend to make bunny
tracks."

"I don't want to go out," Sophie whined.

"Now, Sophie, Mark hid the eggs for you. He got up early. You should
be grateful." Angel put her cigarette down, skewed her mouth, and blew the
smoke off to the side. She grunted a bit as she bent to tie Sophie's black-
and-white Buster Browns, which she'd found at a rummage sale for only
two dollars. They'd needed new laces and the toes were slightly scuffed, but

otherwise they were in good shape. Angel thought briefly about putting plastic bags over the shoes to keep her daughter's feet dry, but she doubted Sophie would stay out that long. There were only a dozen eggs for her to find.

"Now come on, let's get your coat on." The sleeves of Sophie's lavender wool jacket no longer covered her wrists, but they'd gotten an extra year out of that coat. Angel pulled the hood's drawstring tight and synthetic white rabbit fur encircled Sophie's stern face in a halo. "Stop pouting, Sophie. Hunting for Easter eggs is fun."

The snow began to fall again, in puffy tufts. Angel laughed, "I guess that stupid groundhog was wrong. This is going to be a late spring." She coughed, coughed harder, took another drag on her cigarette, then remarked as she pushed her daughter out the front door, "Looks maybe like Jesus is having a pillow fight, huh, Sophie. Go on now. Have fun!"

Angel shivered and shut the door. As Sophie stood reluctantly on the front stoop, a distant memory came to her: her father's hand warming her own, bending low, peering under a rose bush, a pink and purple egg.

Sophie stood alone on the stoop, shrugged her shoulders, looked up at the falling snow, and stuck her tongue out to catch the cold flakes before setting off on the forced quest.

Inside, Mark crept up behind Angel, leaned in to kiss her neck, then pinched her rump.

"Knock it off!" Angel barked. "Go get a shower and get dressed. We're taking Sophie to church this morning."

"Again? We just went last week." He pulled Angel close. "Come on. We've got time. She won't even know. She's having fun out there. See?"

Angel watched her daughter walking alone in the yard, head down, her tiny feet making erratic prints in the snow.

He bit her earlobe. "You owe me. You know I hate church. Favor for a favor? Hmm?"

Sophie found the first egg easily. It was on the sidewalk near the stoop and looked like a bump in the snow. She picked it up and brushed off the snow. It was white. Sophie scowled. Easter eggs were supposed to be colorful. Sophie carefully put the egg in her basket, looked up at the closed front door, sighed, and started to look for other bumps.

At the end of the driveway, trash was stuffed into a banged-up green metal garbage can. Angel had missed Friday trash pick-up again, and no one had moved the can back to the garage.

"Stinky," Sophie said, pinching her nose, but glancing down, she found another snow-covered egg at the base of the garbage can. She headed back to the front of the house. Her footprints looked like a treasure map in the snow. She found two more eggs by the bushes under the front window.

Sophie snuffed up her runny nose, rubbed her hands together, and headed toward the backyard. The wiry bushes along the garage yielded two more. Sophie counted 1-2-3-4-5-6.

The snow had stopped, and the bright sun was warm. Sophie started to feel sweaty in her coat. She opened the backyard gate and kept her steps close to the edge of the fence, where scraggly grass and browned weeds from last year still clumped. There were four more eggs hidden unimaginatively along the fence. Back near the garage now, Sophie pivoted near the gate and started walking with her toes out, making little vees in the melting snow. She was ready to go in, but she knew she needed one more egg.

A squawky bird flew overhead. Sophie shielded her eyes and looked up. A smaller black bird was pestering a hawk. She felt sorry for the hawk. It was then that Sophie realized she had not searched around her swingset, so she walked in her little vees over to the swingset, where, sure enough, the last egg sat in a little puddle at the top of the shiny metal slide. She stopped climbing at the middle step. Sophie did not feel comfortable on the ladder. She reached and grabbed the egg. With the egg in one hand, she held more tightly with the other hand to the ladder, and even though she was not that far off the ground, Sophie felt unbalanced. She looked down at her feet to place them carefully, but as she set her foot on the next rung, she slipped. It happened so quickly. Sophie dropped the egg so she could grab the ladder with her other hand. Her feet on the ground now, she saw the last egg's golden glow, bright against the snow.

Angel heard the door squeak, and, tying her flimsy robe about her, she hurried to help Sophie inside.

"There you are, sweetie. Did you have fun? Did you find them all?"

"Yes, but one bwoke."

"You could have brought it in anyway. It would still be good."

"I couldn't, Mommy. It was wet and goopy."

Angel scowled, then looked in the basket. White eggs? "Mark!" she yelled. "You idiot! You hid the wrong eggs. You hid raw ones, not the ones I boiled and colored."

"How was I supposed to know?" he shouted from the bedroom.

"I wrote 'Easter Eggs' on the carton. Are you...?" Angel restrained her language in front of her daughter.

"Well, I hid the damn eggs, didn't I? What difference does it make? Scramble 'em. I'm starving."

1977

The early morning had been cloudy, but around ten o'clock, a warm west breeze blew the gloom away and the sun shone so brightly that Angel asked Sophie to close the drapes, just for a while. The bright light was giving her a headache. In the dim room, quiet except for the soft plodding of Sophie's feet as she busied herself in the kitchen, Angel was once again asleep.

While her mother slept, Sophie puttered about outside, clearing dead leaves from flower gardens. On the north side of house, the forsythia was in full bloom, yellow spurts of flowers aglow against the golden brick. Sophie found a pruning shears in the garage and snipped off several dozen sprays. Inside she arranged a vase for her mother. She hoped Angel would appreciate the flowers as well as the gesture. A second bouquet brightened the kitchen table. This one is just for me, Sophie thought, pleased with the idea. It was a bit early for lunch, but she had not eaten breakfast, so she sat at the kitchen table now and ate a ham sandwich. The florescent light above the sink hummed loudly.

After her lunch, she washed her plate and milk glass before going to check on her mother, who was beginning to wake. Sophie opened the drapes wide again. The house was too gloomy with them shut, and by now the glare of the morning sun was gone.

"You hungry?" Sophie asked after helping her mom to the toilet and back into bed.

"No, but I suppose you're going to make me eat something," Angel said.

"I suppose I am."

Resigned to the fact that she had to try to eat, Angel asked for a bowl of corn flakes with extra sugar. Sophie set the bowl on the tray table and sat on the couch while her mom lifted the spoon to her mouth. With her mouth full, a drip of milk on her chin, Angel remarked on the flowers. "I never thought about cutting forsythia, but it sure is pretty in here. Sort of makes the whole room glow yellow, doesn't it?"

Sophie agreed but took note of the fact that her mom had not thanked her for bringing her flowers.

In a bit Angel pushed the bowl to the side. When Sophie took it away, she was pleased to see her mother had eaten all of the cereal. She would remember to put more in the bowl next time, maybe fatten up the milk with heavy cream, anything to get some calories in her.

"Can you come back and sit with me?" Angel called out to Sophie, who was in the kitchen putting the cereal box away.

Sophie returned with a cookie for her mom, which she had broken into bite-sized pieces. "You can just nibble."

"You're a sly one, daughter. You'll make a good mom someday."

Sophie rolled her eyes. The very farthest thing from her mind was having kids.

"Hand me that *Family Circle* magazine, would you?"

Sophie gave the magazine to her mom. "Okay if I stretch out a bit and put my head down?" The girl did not wait for approval but situated the orange throw pillow beneath her head and lay on her side.

Angel licked her finger and turned the pages, and Sophie worked hard to keep her eyes open. Only minutes after she dozed off—or could it have been seconds?—her mother spoke, jarring her awake again. Sophie's heart pounded loudly in her ears.

"Here's a recipe for rhubarb pie, like my mother used to make, I think. I never had her recipe. She'd just tell me as she was making it, blathering out the ingredients, and of course I never thought to write any of it down. We should cut this out so you can make it sometime."

Sophie yawned and said she would do it later. She probably would not actually use the recipe as she did not care for rhubarb, but she would clip it and put it aside nevertheless. What mattered was that her mother saw her cut out the recipe.

Angel laid the magazine down and gazed out the window. If she felt up to it later, she would ask Sophie to set a chair on the front stoop. She would like to sit in the sun and feel it burn her face and hands and arms.

"I never told you much about your father, did I Sophie?"

Sophie blinked in astonishment. From rhubarb pie to her father? Sophie's throat felt dry as she spoke. "No, you never did say much of anything," she said, even though it was not in the least true. Her mother had told her quite a bit over the years. From time to time Angel would blurt out some story, sometimes in a half-conscious alcohol haze, sometimes when she needed someone to blame other than herself, sometimes, but not often, when Sophie asked. The stories changed from one time to the next, and at some point Sophie realized that her mom had not even remembered telling the previous contradictory story. Sophie had been told her dad died in a car accident. Another time, she learned he died in the Korean War. Another time Angel said he had just left them, just up and left them. The last story sounded the most real, but it also meant that her dad could still be living somewhere, and if he were still alive, why hadn't he called her or sent her birthday cards or Christmas presents? It had been so much easier when she had thought he was dead.

Sophie started to sit up.

"You don't have to get up. Let's both just lie here and talk."

Sophie stretched and pulled the afghan down to cover her legs and feet.

"You know why I made that stupid rule about you not dating until you were sixteen?"

The rule, which seemed arbitrary and straight out of another century, had not really upset Sophie, who, when she'd heard the rule for the first time, was only eleven and had felt no interest in boys whatsoever.

"Well?" Angel said.

"Well, I guess you wanted me to be safe? Not get pregnant or something?"

"Yeah, or something. It's hard to be a mom. Hard to be a dad, too, I guess." Angel glanced up at the ceiling. "You hear that old man? Yeah, I said it. I admit it. I was a horrible daughter and you tried your best."

Angel paused so long Sophie thought maybe she ought to say something when her mom spoke again.

"I mean, you get better at it, at being a parent. At least I hope you do. But you shouldn't start out too young. I had you too young. I think if you had not been born until I was twenty-five, or even older, I think I would have done a better job. And maybe I would have married someone who could support us better, so that would have helped. I think then you would have had a happier childhood."

Sophie squinted at her mom, amused by her flawed logic. Still Sophie got her overall point. "I don't think I had an unhappy childhood, Mom." Sophie was unfailingly generous on this point now.

"Well. Not unhappy," Angel said. "But it could have been better." She turned her head at the sound of a dog barking. A short, fat woman with tight, curly hair was being pulled past their house by a big German Shepherd. That dog's taking that woman for a walk, she thought. "Well, I supposed we can't go back and have a do-over, can we? I met your dad in high school." She felt a twinge in her side and grimaced. "He was a year older than me. So cute, you know?"

Sophie didn't know.

"When I look back, I can see now that I might have been, in a way, trying to hurt my dad even just by dating your father."

"What do you mean?" Sophie asked, but she knew, or at least she had seen her mom say unkind things to her grandfather, almost like her mom wanted to cause a fight.

"I suppose I hadn't really forgiven him for the accident that killed my mom. I knew Ruben was not the kind of guy most girls like me would marry." Angel laughed a regretful laugh.

"What's funny?" Sophie asked.

"Not funny. I was so damn mule-headed that I wouldn't listen to anyone, and look where it got me." There were times she wondered if her cancer was punishment for all her bad decisions.

Angel inhaled deeply, then let out a controlled moan.

Sophie rolled off the couch and now stood at her mother's side.

Angel's face clenched, and her eyes closed in a spasm. Sophie checked her watch. It wouldn't be time for morphine for another hour, but clearly her mother was hurting.

Sophie put pillows under her mom's knees the way she liked, taking some pressure off her spine.

"Better?"

"A little." With Sophie's coaching, Angel took slow deep breaths. Then, moments later, breathed a long, satisfied sigh.

Sophie stood at the side of the bed, still worried.

"You know, I was younger than you are when I left home. We were going to go to California…."

"But what about him, Mom? Did he die?"

"Where on earth did you get that idea?"

Sophie did not explain. She just shrugged her shoulders and let her mother continue her story.

"Things were great with us at first. We were excited about the future. Then, well, I suppose a leaky radiator is to blame, but then, when you came along so fast and we had bills to pay, and…. I suppose he must have felt trapped or something."

"By me?" Sophie interrupted.

"Oh, don't look like that. It wasn't your fault if that's what you think. I didn't mean it to sound that way. Your dad…he just wasn't strong."

"I don't know what to say," Sophie said. It felt good, at least, to know the truth. "But he was a good guy? You loved him?"

"Sure. I loved him. I loved him a lot. Then...."

"What?"

"Well, I'm pretty sure he was cheating on me, even before you were born."

Sophie shot a quizzical expression toward her mother.

"Yeah. Shitty, huh?"

"Yeah, shitty," Sophie agreed.

Angel smiled, then a spasm took her. She tightened her grip on Sophie's hand and cried out. Sophie leapt off the bed and in seconds unscrewed the pill bottle, dumping the capsule onto her palm. After she put the pill on Angel's tongue, Sophie helped her mother lift her chin to the water glass and sip.

"Oww," Angel cried.

"Breathe, breathe. It'll be better soon, Mom. Soon," she said, in a soothing voice. "Close your eyes now. Just rest. We'll talk later."

The next evening, Sophie gave her mother a quick sponge bath to calm her before bedtime. The warm cloth felt good against her skin. Angel moaned in deep pleasure, and Sophie was glad this was something she could do for her mom.

Out of nowhere, Angel blurted out "You think you might want to try to find him? You know, after I'm dead? Your dad, I mean."

"Jesus, Mom. I don't know," Sophie said, rinsing out the washcloth in the old enameled basin.

"I'm not saying you should or anything. But if you wanted to, someday? Well, I just want you to know that it would be fine with me."

"Yeah, okay," Sophie said, now fumbling to button her mom's pajama top.

"I feel so much better, sweetheart. Thanks for all you're doing for me."

"You're welcome," Sophie said. Sophie inhaled slowly and patted her mother's shoulder, then leaned down and kissed her on top of the head.

After Sophie dumped the basin and hung up the washcloth to dry, she fixed herself and her mother a glass of ice water, plopping a bendy straw into Angel's glass.

"Come here, sweetheart." Angel let her left hand fall limply off the edge of the bed to beckon her daughter to her side.

Sophie set the glass on Angel's bedside tray.

"Can I get you anything else right now, Mom? You should go to sleep, and I'm beat."

Sophie hoped her mother would not sense her distance, would not feel the confusion that hovered in her heart. The way her mom had spoken in such a matter-of-fact way about her dad, and to finally learn that he was a deadbeat, a loser—and then to come out with the idea that she might want to find him? It was an idea she had toyed with her whole life, but now...? What would be the point of trying to find him? It was all just too much for her. Sophie tried to compose herself. She was no longer a child wondering about a dad that may or may not have been alive, a dad she didn't know, couldn't know. She needed to get past the emptiness she had felt her whole life, never knowing why she, among all her friends, why she was the one who did not have a dad. Sophie looked over at her mother and felt the ball of emotion billowing within her about to combust.

Angel interrupted Sophie's thoughts. "I should have told you about your dad a long, long time ago," she said. "I should have, but Sophie, you have to believe me. I never wanted to hurt you. I just wanted to keep him from hurting you."

"I know," Sophie said, holding back irrational tears, holding down the flutter in her chest that would betray her. "It's okay. It's okay. Go to sleep now. It's time to rest."

Angel closed her eyes and sighed deeply. She would sleep for hours.

Sophie turned away, faced the dark hall that led to the bedrooms, and scorned the single tear that fell. Just one. She would not cry. She would not cry. The minute her head hit her pillow, Sophie buried her face in the down and sobbed.

1960

Angel would always consider it to be a failure of spirit that she moved back to Sheboygan to live with her father. On the other hand, at this point in her life, her father was really the only man she was willing to have anything to do with. Mark, Roger, and the others she had not even invited home weren't looking for a long-term commitment, and they did not want to be stepfathers. At first she kept her standards high, but as the bank account ran low, her waitress job and inconsistent tips just couldn't pay the bills anymore. Ruben had taken off with their only car, so she'd had to buy another. If she could have tracked Ruben down and got him to divorce her, she could have had child support. Calls to his father in Sheboygan got her nowhere. It seemed they were keeping her from him. What kind of lies had he told them?

Because of one thing or another, she just couldn't get ahead. She would sock away some money for tuition hoping she could take a few classes at least, but then Sophie would need to go to the doctor. A toothache sent Angel to the dentist, who told her she had four cavities. So, when she realized that she could trade her assets, so to speak, for the temporary monetary support these men gave, she felt she had to do it. The result was that she descended further and further into self-loathing, and the Easter episode was the last straw.

Angel scrambled those eggs all right, scrambled them and dished them out, hot, onto Mark's plate, slapped butter on a nearly burnt piece of toast, and stood behind him, smoking, tapping a nervous foot.

"You not hungry?" he asked.

"Nope. Not hungry." As usual, it would take him forever to pick up on her tone.

Fuming, she watched him eat. Stubbing out her cigarette in the ash tray, she next scooted Sophie out to the living room and turned on the TV, found *Rocky and Bullwinkle*, and set the volume louder than normal.

Back in the kitchen, Mark asked if there was any more toast, as if she were his personal waitress.

"Nope. All out." There was an entire loaf of bread in the fridge, but he would not know it. "Are you done, then?" she said with impatient fury.

"Sure baby," he said, still in the afterglow of their morning, a morning Angel would regret for the rest of her life.

"Then get up, get your things, and get the fuck out of my house."

"What? What's this?"

"You heard me. I'm done with lowlife losers like you."

"Now wait a minute. You've got no right to—"

"I said get the fuck out. Now."

"Watch your language, baby. The kid," he said, jerking his head toward the living room.

"Oh, now you care about her?" Angel laughed scornfully. "She's fine. She won't even remember this. She sure won't remember you. Hell, I might not remember you."

Angel had no idea what would come next, except that it was clear she could no longer manage on her own. If she moved back to Sheboygan and lived for a while with her dad, it would be easier to get ahead. She was not positive her father would accept her, but if she turned up with Sophia? Of course he would take them in. He would be a good grandpa. She would simply not have to care that her tail hung so low between her legs.

On his part, Frank would always consider his daughter's move home to be an implicit apology, and because he believed it to be so, a part of him breathed more easily. Learning to get along with his daughter again after a five-year absence was something he would need to do without dragging along their past. She was an adult now. She was a mother. They were beginning again. It was as simple as that.

Angel soon began waitressing at Alexanders restaurant. The diner served big breakfasts. Their brats and hamburgers were served on Sheboygan hard rolls, and a sign in the window boasted they had the best malts in the world. All their soups were homemade. It was not fancy, but the kitschy décor appealed to Angel. The owners were Greek. Really kind people, and if she needed to be home with a sick child, they said they understood. They hoped it would not happen too often, but they understood. And they hoped she would understand if they needed her, only now and then, of course, to work an extra shift?

Frank was still working the day shift at the Vollrath factory. Their neighbor, Mrs. Perlman, might agree to watch Sophie, he suggested. "Oh, she's nice," Frank said. "Joe, too. They moved in next door about five years ago. They're in their 70s. Dunno exact ages. I never asked. Not polite to ask a woman's age, anyway, is it?" Frank laughed. He realized that he was trying too hard, even in these simple, functional, conversations.

Ruth Perlman was enchanted with Sophie the moment she met her. "What a dark-haired beauty," said the tall, graceful woman to Angel. "You must be a proud momma. Frank, you never told us your daughter was so pretty." To Angel she said, "If we can ever get our son Lev to visit, I'll introduce you. He's about your age, well maybe a little older. I think you two would hit it off. Lev lives in New York. An actor. At least he's trying to be."

Angel's first impressions of Ruth were also positive. The woman seemed sincere and down to earth. "Josef isn't home just now. You'll meet him soon." Ruth took them into her home so Sophie could begin to feel comfortable. The house was tidy, not cluttered, furnished well with fine, old pieces. Clearly the next-door neighbors enjoyed a higher standard of living than they did. If mother were still alive, Angel thought, things in their home would be nicer, too. Her father's house, her house, seemed just as she had left it, which was exactly as it had been the day June died almost ten years ago. Angel pushed her bitterness back to its dark corner.

"Sophia," Ruth said, stooping to Sophie's level, "you can call me *Bubbe*. Would you like that?"

Sophie nodded shyly.

Ruth perceived Angel's confusion. "It means grandmother, but if you'd rather not? It's just a word, but whatever you think is…."

"No, no, it's fine," Angel said. "It sounds sweet." Were they Jewish, Angel wondered. Perlman? Hmm. Well, if so, it didn't matter. Growing up here, many of their neighbors were Jews. The synagogue was only a few blocks away. "And she's Sophie, though Sophia is fine, too. Whatever you like. My father likes formal names. He calls me Angelina, but I'm pretty used to Angel these days." She smiled at him. She had not meant to judge or suggest it was a fault, but she could see that he took it as if she had.

Arrangements were made to drop Sophie off at Ruth's each day before Angel went in at 10:30 for her lunch and dinner shift. Frank would pick her up as soon as he could after work, usually no later than five. When Sophie began kindergarten, they'd figure out a new plan. If Frank had to work later, Ruth didn't see a problem. His days of heading to the tavern were over, and since he'd become friends with Joe, he didn't do that so much now anyway. Frank accepted his new role gladly. He was excited to get to know his granddaughter. He felt younger around her. Even though she was dark-eyed and dark-haired, he thought he saw his Junie in her face, June's high prominent cheekbones and her little kitten nose.

While Angel would not say that her relationship with her father was entirely repaired, they were getting along, neither one making too many demands on the other. Neither spoke about the day Angel left, or about the accident, or about anything else from their past. They measured their comments carefully and treated each other with kindness. If it felt unnatural to either of them, they did not let on, but each one knew that if it were not for Sophia, things might not have been the same.

At first, Frank would accept no money for groceries from his daughter. The mortgage had been paid off for over two years, and Frank managed his other expenses just fine. Angel didn't even need to work if she didn't want to, Frank insisted. But *she* needed to work, she said. She wanted and needed to earn her own money. Angel eventually forced her dad to accept a contribution for expenses. Without telling his daughter, he put her money directly into the savings account he had begun for Sophie the day after he had received the birth announcement.

Angel began once again to plan for her future. She began to save money, which she hoped to put towards nursing school, something she would not be able to do if her father were not also supporting them. She was grateful. She truly was.

The first Sunday she was home, Angel roasted a chicken, made mashed potatoes and gravy, and even a lemon meringue pie, which she knew her dad was partial to. As the little family sat at the table around the feast, Frank smiled a true, honest smile. His eyes crinkled and his heart felt full.

That night, he tucked his little Sophia into her bed, and though it was nothing he did himself, he guided his granddaughter in a bedtime prayer. Children should say prayers, Frank thought.

"Do you think you might like to call your old grandpa 'Papa,' Sophia?" Frank asked hopefully. "When I was a boy, that's what I called my grandfather. Although he lived in Italy and I never got to spend much time with him. But you and me? We'll be good friends, won't we?"

Sophie liked the warmth of this man, how his body felt warm against hers. He was always picking her up and hugging her. He tousled her hair and laughed whenever she spoke. He looked at her as if she was hard to see.

"Good night, my little princess," Frank said, pulling her covers up around her neck.

"Good night." Sophie hesitated. "Papa."

As he softly closed the bedroom door, Frank had never felt happier.

1961

Dear Angelina,

Your back in Sheboygan living with your dad I hear. I'm happy about that. Sheboygan was never home for me, but I think you belong there.

I'm writing because I owe you a explanation. Or an apology. Both I guess. I can't fix what I did to you, cheating on you I mean. I wasn't cut out to be a father either I guess. Little Sophia scared me, how she was so perfect and all. I was afraid all the time I would hurt her.

Not a good reason to leave tho.

I'm out in California. I got a job on a ranch near Fremont. Being the city kid, I knew nothin about horses, but I love them and have learned to manage them pretty good. It's like I can talk to them softly and they listen. I don't get mean around horses like I can sometimes with people. If I never had to be around people again I think it would be a good life for me. I don't drink any more either.

Here is two hundred dollars. I know it ain't enough to do anything with. But maybe you can put it in the bank for the kid. It is something from her dad anyway.

I know you will have a good life, Angelina, because you were always the one who could see a bright way ahead when I never could.

I will send more money if I can, but please don't come out here.

Oh, you will smile to hear that Corrina left me. She called me a deadbeat. I guess when two women think your worthless, you probably are. The horses don't ever talk bad about me though. Ha ha.

Please kiss the kid for me. I think about her alot. I see the stars sparkling at night and think of her pretty eyes. She deserved better then me, but I did love her.

Take care of yourself, Angelina.

Ruben

After Angel read the letter, she ripped it to pieces. She put the money in her pocket. Ir would be crazy to destroy that, too, no matter how spiteful she felt.

At first she tried to forget about Ruben's letter, but instead of putting it out of mind, Angel began to obsess about the money he'd sent. Carrying out plates of meatloaf and mashed potatoes, smiling her "work smile," her head furiously wondered how on earth he could think, after all this time, that two hundred dollars was going to pay for new glasses or for braces? Then one day her absent-mindedness caused her to overpour a man's coffee. Angel stared blankly at the brown river surging towards his lap, motionless until he shouted and worked furiously to sop up the spill. He scowled at her apologies, and she didn't blame him when he called her a "nitwit."

Later she got it in her head that she could hire a private detective, but reasoned that would cost a fortune and it would be money she probably wouldn't get back even if she did find him. She had to admit, Ruben hadn't been what she would call ambitious. Of the two, she was the one who had wanted to make something of herself. He only cared to have a little money ahead, enough to pay for what they wanted or needed now.

She knew now it was time to finally confront Ruben's parents and demand to know where he was.

The following Saturday Angel drove slowly past their house on 15th Street twice before stopping. She was having second thoughts. If she had not destroyed the letter, she could have used it as evidence to pressure Ruben's mom and dad and force them to give her his exact address in Fremont. How stupid not to have seen that possibility, she thought.

Now, with Sophia in hand, Angel walked up to the front door and pushed the button. She heard the bell "ding dong" and her heart fluttered. Why the hell was she so nervous? It wasn't like she had done anything wrong.

A young woman answered the door. She wore her hair up in a French roll and her lavender pedal pushers set off her long, tan legs. She held a small, white curly dog that looked at Sophie and growled. "Hush, Bruno," the woman said.

Angel smiled. Bruno? The name seemed more fitting for a large dog, a German Shepherd or a Great Dane, not a fluffy little lap dog.

"May I help you?" the woman asked.

"Hi. I may have the wrong house. I'm looking for Mr. or Mrs. Miranda? I thought I had the address."

Bruno whined. He wanted to get down. Sophie looked up at him, wishing she could pet him.

"Oh, yeah. They used to live here. Moved about, hmm, guess it's been nine months we've been here."

Angel looked obviously disappointed.

"Sorry," the woman said. "I wish I could help you, but I didn't know them. Only their name from the neighbors. You could ask one of them? Maybe they know something."

Angel thanked the woman, who shut the door. Bruno barked fiercely from the living room window.

The neighbors didn't know. They seemed annoyed she was asking, so Angel drove home, not knowing what to do next.

"Your dad is a real bastard," Angel said to Sophie, who sat in the back seat thinking of that little dog and about how many times she had begged her mom to get her a dog. But Sophie wanted one like Lassie, with a silky coat. Her dog would be really smart and save people, too. And he could sleep with her and would be her best friend. She had asked her mom many times about her dad, too. Why didn't she have a daddy? But just like the questions about the dog, questions about her dad were largely ignored. Sophie did not know what "bastard" meant, but her mom sounded mean, so she did not think it was something good.

1977

"I'll be back in about a couple of hours, Mom," Sophie said. "Lev's going to keep an eye on you, while I'm gone. Are you sure I can't get something special for you? A sweet treat?"

"No, but you can open a window. It's really hot in here."

Sophie eyed her mother with concern. Hot? It was only 56 degrees outside. The weather, up and down, had taken another turn down. It was supposed to get abnormally hot and humid over the next few days, so Sophie didn't mind it being a little cooler, but 56 was ridiculous for June.

"I've got it," said Lev, who did not want Sophie to be late for her hair appointment. It was Lev who insisted she go, mainly to get her out of the house for just a few hours. Not that she felt she needed it, but she supposed she could have her split ends trimmed, and it would be nice to get away. Sophie's plan was to pick up a few groceries afterwards.

"You sure?" Sophie said. "I don't have to—"

"Go. Right, Angel?"

Smiling, Angel waved her daughter away. "Right. Go get yourself beautiful. I mean more beautiful."

After Sophie reluctantly closed the door, Lev opened a window. Then he got a basin of cold water and a washcloth. He wiped Angel's face, neck, arms, and hands with the cool rag. He also brushed her hair and tied it up into a knot on top her head.

"Doesn't that feel better to get your hair off your neck?"

She agreed and said she felt much better.

"You would have made a terrific nurse, Lev. Too bad men can't be nurses. Why are there rules about what people can be, anyway?"

"I'm not certain there is a rule about that."

"Well, maybe not a rule, but who ever heard of a male nurse?"

When he returned to her after dumping the water down the sink, he asked her if there was anything else she needed. He could make her something to eat, he said, reminding her that she had barely eaten anything for breakfast.

She refused food but said she needed something else. "In my closet, there's a shoebox on the floor. There are three boxes stacked on the left. Look in the one on the bottom. There's an old pair of black patent pumps in there. But also you'll find two big brown envelopes under the shoes. Bring them here, will you?"

Lev returned with the envelopes, smiling about the way they had been hidden.

Angel continued her orders. "Get me a pen. Look in the desk."

Lev handed her a pen, the third one he'd found. The first two were all dried up. Before she labeled the first envelope, Angel opened it and peeked in, verifying the contents. Then she folded the flap over and spread the wings of the brass brad. On the front, in large, nearly-perfect Palmer cursive, she wrote "for Sophie." She handed the pen and the envelope back to him.

"I need you to take this one home and keep it safely hidden. I don't think Sophie is going to be spending time at your house any time soon, but still, don't just have it out in the open. Promise me that you will not give it to her until after I'm dead."

"Promise." He smiled at her seriousness. Not that he thought the contents of the envelope were unimportant. It was just how cloak-and-dagger the whole thing felt to him, as if he was swearing to protecting government secrets.

"You swear?" she reiterated.

He held up his right hand and said, "I absolutely swear that I will keep the envelope hidden at my house and give it to Sophie when the time is right." He did not say, "when you're dead."

"Good." She told him he could put the other envelope in the top drawer of the desk, so he did that right away, and went back to her beside for further orders.

Angel looked at him as if he hadn't heard, hadn't understood what she needed him to do. "Take it home now, while she's gone. I'll be fine alone for a bit," she said.

"Oh, right this minute, you mean?" As he headed out the door with the top-secret envelope, Angel watched with a self-satisfied look on her face.

Sophie returned home almost two hours later with her long hair bobbed, somewhat like a 1920s flapper's. It was a drastic change, and Angel was not exactly pleased.

"Oh, your beautiful long hair!" The pained look on her face relayed her disappointment.

"You don't like it," Sophie said, not as a question but as a confirmation of the feeling she'd had when the shears snipped off the irrevocable first locks. And yet Sophie, so tired of tiptoeing around every second of life, afraid of displeasing her mother, had looked trustingly into the beautician's face, maybe asking for permission, and said, "I think I want this all cut off," and showed with her hands the span of eight or nine inches. How exhausting it was to be responsible for Angel's happiness.

Angel sensed she had made Sophie feel bad, so she backtracked. "Well, yes. I do like it, but it's a shock. I'm not used to it, is all. You look lovely. Of course, you looked lovely before, too."

"It's hair. It'll grow back. I thought it might be nice to have shorter hair for summer, and it'll be easier to take care of." Her new, short cut felt so free and easy on her head, so light and full of spirit, that she did not regret the impulse one bit.

Angel nodded in agreement and smiled her reconciliation. Sophie folded her rust brown cardigan and laid it on the foot end of her mother's bed. She took Angel's hand and rubbed the loose, shiny skin, then gave her a loving squeeze before letting go.

"Did you see what Lev did for me?" Angel patted the little topknot on her head.

"Smart. I should have thought of that." Sophie shot Lev a sassy look. He shrugged his shoulders and lifted his hands as if to say, "What can I say?"

"I'm sure you would have," Angel said, sensing they were back on easy terms now.

"Did you sleep at all, Mom?"

"No. I should have, but I've been watching Mrs. Merton trying to prune that snarly rosebush. She can't seem to cut anything off. It's like she thinks she's hurting it. After every teensie snip she makes, she stands back and stares for hours."

"She slept a little," Lev said.

"When? I don't remember that. I did?"

Sophie situated her mother, put her in sitting position, and slid the hospital tray table up to the bed, the usual procedure for a meal.

"What's this about, Sophie?"

"Just wait. You'll see."

"Angel, I read in the paper this morning that the ladies are playing in a golf tournament," Lev said. "Would you like to watch it? A woman named Nancy Lopez is doing well, they say."

"Oh, I don't know. I don't know much about it. I've never played golf. Is something else on? Or we could leave it off. That's fine, too."

"I'll see," Lev said, and while he fiddled with the TV, hoping he wouldn't have to adjust the aerial, Sophie brought her mother a huge, warm cinnamon roll on a Royal Doulton plate. One third of it had been sliced and cut into bite-sized bits to make it easier to eat. A glob of soft butter lay on the edge of the plate.

"I know you haven't been hungry, but when I walked past the bakery and saw the tray of these in the window, I knew I had to get you one."

Angel admitted it looked good, and once she ate a couple of bites, she felt a bit hungrier, so she ate all of what Sophie had sliced off. Before the last bite, she sighed heavily and lifted it to her mouth, but once that morsel was in her mouth she pushed the plate to the side of the tray and announced she couldn't eat anymore.

"Well, that's okay. You did great. I'll just wrap the rest up for you for tomorrow."

"Or you could have it," Angel offered.

"Do you think I didn't get one for myself and Lev? Oh, you silly mama."

Lev settled on the broadcast of golf after all. The other channels were not coming in very well. He'd have to climb up on the roof, or better yet call someone to take a look. His TV got better reception. Maybe he could bring it over for the summer. He didn't watch it much anyway.

"This is the best picture I can get right now," he said. "I know you didn't want to watch golf, but maybe you can just enjoy the scenery."

"That's fine. Sometimes it is nice to have the sound for distraction." Angel rested her head on the pillow and, listening to the golf announcer's soft commentary, she dozed off.

Sophie and Lev ate their cinnamon rolls and stared at the TV. They did not talk. Lev thought it was evidence of how much Sophie felt like family. They could just be in a room together, not needing any conversation.

About a half hour later, Angel woke and asked for another blanket. She was shivering. "It's so cold all of a sudden," she complained.

"I'll get it," Lev told Sophie, who was happy to have someone else take care of her mother, even if only for a little bit.

Lev unfolded and arranged the blanket over Angel. "Well, that should help," he said.

"Much better, so much better. Thank you, Lev."

"Listen, if you don't need me, I think I'll head home now," he said, mostly to Sophie, who nodded.

"We're fine," she said. "Thanks again for everything today."

"Angel, you be good this week. I'll be in California, so I won't be here in case you get in trouble."

"Ach. Trouble," Angel said, then shooed him away with her hand. "Have a good trip, Lev." He said he would, then closed the door behind him.

After Lev left, Angel asked Sophie to turn off the TV. "It's giving me a headache," she said.

Sophie clicked the dial. She hoped her mom would sleep most of the afternoon. She wanted to fix the hem on one of her skirts, and Sophie was hoping for a quiet hour or two. She got her wish. Not only did Sophie finish the skirt, but she also started a new novel and was well into the third chapter before Angel awoke and needed her assistance.

The next morning, Sophie did not wake until nine. She walked quietly into the living room, where her mother still slept. "Boy, she's out," Sophie thought, then headed to the kitchen to start coffee. She yawned and adjusted her glasses, which sat crooked. She would put her contacts in later.

Sun flooded through the patio door, and she slid it open to let in the morning air, already warm. Sophie was happy summer had finally arrived. She was not a winter girl. She didn't mind a little snow at Christmas, but she hated always feeling cold. And shoveling snow? Ugh. That was the worst job.

From the other room she heard, "I smell coffee."

"Be right there," Sophie called to her mother.

Angel watched TV until eleven o'clock, when she dozed off. Sophie took that opportunity to get a shower. Her new haircut was a brilliant idea. She found she could towel dry her hair, brush through the tangles, then turn her head upside down and fluff out her waves. She was happy with the way the soft curls looked when air-dried. Her hair was much bouncier now that it was shorter.

Later, as she helped her mom walk the slow walk from her bed to the bathroom, Angel told Sophie she longed for a shower.

Sympathetically, Sophie said she understood, but nevertheless, she did not think it was a good idea. "You're awfully weak. What if you fell? I'd have to call the paramedics. There's no way I could lift you out of the tub by myself. You might break a bone or something."

"I'd be very, very careful. Oh, please." Angel begged like a child in the grocery store candy aisle. Lid down, she sat on the toilet now, waiting for Sophie to get her toothbrush ready. She pleaded with her soft hazel eyes, her cheeks sunken and heartrending.

Sophie did not want to deny her mother any request, but how could she risk it? Then she remembered the shower in the hospital. Inside was a plastic seat with aluminum handles. "Okay, Mom. I've got an idea. You just sit right there. Okay?"

Angel looked up at her daughter and smiled in triumph.

Sophie returned from the garage with a plastic-webbed lawn chair, which she hoped would fit in the tub. She spread the legs and set it inside. It fit, just barely.

"You're a genius," Angel said.

"Okay, getting you in and out is still going to be tricky, but at least you won't have to stand up," Sophie said.

Angel's clothes lay on the floor in a heap, and Sophie helped her mother, naked and frail, step into the tub, then into to the yellow-and-white chair.

"Brrr. Cold," Angel said.

"Gonna get colder before warmer, I think." Sophie turned the faucet on and let the water warm before she pulled the lever to engage the shower. The first spray was icy cold and Angel's skin turned to gooseflesh. But then, then it warmed.

"Make it a little hotter, Sophie."

She complied.

"Ahh. That feels soooo good." Angel breathed deeply, the spray soaking her from head to toe. "Sooo good."

Sophie turned the faucet off, then squirted shampoo into her mother's palm. Angel rubbed the shampoo between her hands, then lifted the sudsy palms to her face. "Hmm. Smells good," she said, then she smoothed her hands over her wet head and began to scrub. "Guess my arms are too weak," Angel said. "Can you finish for me?"

Sophie set aside the washcloth she had lathered up with soap and finished scrubbing her mother's head. "You remember you used to tell me I was a soap monster when I looked like you do now?" Sophie asked.

Angel laughed. "Yeah. I did say that, didn't I. Here, hand me that washcloth and I'll try to manage my privates. Then let's get that water back on. It's getting cold in here."

The water ran in rivulets down her back, and Angel bent down now, her head between her knees, Sophie massaging the shampoo out of her hair. Angel did not want this experience to end. But it must. She was tiring, and her lower back had begun to throb.

Angel partially dried off in the tub before wrapping her arms around Sophie's neck so she could climb out onto the floor. Then Sophie wrapped a big beach towel around her mom and had her sit back down on the toilet. Once Angel was dry, Sophie helped her mother apply body lotion. They'd been lucky Angel had not developed bedsores, but her skin was dry and it sucked in the lotion quickly. A clean nightgown on, Angel brushed her teeth and stood at the mirror wondering whose face peered back at her. Her eyes were rimmed in shadow and departing into their sockets; her cheeks were hollow, lips pale.

"Come on, Mom. Time to get you back in bed. This has been quite the adventure, and I imagine you're exhausted."

Angel climbed back into bed. She wished she were in her own room, in her own bed. She wished so many things that would never come true. Such simple things she yearned for now. She was sorry she had never seen an ocean. Sorry she had never done so many things she should have done.

"Let's get you tucked in," Sophie said. "You smell good. You look much fresher, too."

Angel pulled Sophie's hand to her chest, held it between her own hands, and looked at her daughter with grateful eyes. "That may have been the best thing I have ever experienced. Thank you, Sophie. Thank you."

"My pleasure, Mom." Sophie leaned down and kissed her mom on the cheek. "You rest now. Just rest."

1961

Ruth Perlman had just finished replacing stitches on her needle after having ripped out several rows she was dissatisfied with. "One day," she told Sophie each time the girl asked to learn to knit. "One day."

Having finished writing the entire alphabet three times, the child now sprawled upon Ruth's living room floor, the floral Axminster carpet in deep red, gold, and black beneath her navy plaid skirt, a box of sixteen Crayola crayons out of the box spread before her and arranged according to color, the way she liked. Sophie was coloring the bird in its nest at the top branches of the tree she'd drawn. The finished work of art would be for her grandfather. Many times Sophie gave her pictures to Bubbe, but Papa liked the tree pictures, so she always saved those for him.

Ruth counted stitches. Sixty. Then counted again to be sure. Yes, sixty. Her brain was addled. To be more precise, she was preoccupied by Joe's erratic behavior and his increasing forgetfulness. Yesterday her husband had taken the car in for repairs, at least that's what he had set out to do. Much later that afternoon, after she'd worried and called the garage to learn he wasn't there—sorry, Mrs. Perlman, he did not come in today—Joe ambled in, a broad smile on his face, and presented her with a package of fresh whitefish from Schwartz. "Came in this morning," he beamed.

"Oh, you old man," she railed. "Whitefish! What about the car?"

"The car is just fine, Mother. Runs good."

Back now in a knit two, purl two rhythm, Ruth voiced the frustration that had tangled her head all morning, saying, "What becomes of men, then?"

"What?" asked Sophie, who looked up, puzzled, nose scrunched into her eyes.

"What's that dear?" Ruth replied.

"What did you say, Bubbe? Becomes men?"

"Goodness," Ruth laughed lightly. "I guess I let my thoughts escape. It's nothing dear. Just musing about life and its many quandaries."

"Many what?"

"Quandaries. A quandary. It's a puzzle, a question, a thing we cannot understand."

"You're funny, Bubbe," Sophie said out loud.

"Spose I am. Let me see your picture, may I?"

The child cautiously tore the page from the Big Chief Tablet, hoisted herself off the floor, and presented her art for criticism. Ruth admired Sophie's natural artistic abilities, but she also felt it was her duty to encourage the girl to try to improve. Ruth had shown her how to make tree limbs look more realistic and how to blend colors, brown and gold, for example, to add depth to the trunk. A few of Ruth's own watercolors, landscapes mostly, hung about her home, and Sophie thought Ruth was a great artist. Even the opinion of the child critic pleased her.

Ruth set her knitting aside and took up the picture. "Oh, the bird is quite nice, Sophie. I can tell it's a robin. I'm glad you used red orange for the breast instead of plain red. It looks more realistic.

Sophie accepted the praise with a smile.

Ruth stood, rubbed her left hip, and looked out the front window. It was quarter to five and she expected Joe to pull into the driveway any minute. Today she had called the garage to be sure he had arrived. He had. She hoped he would come straight home, as she had told him to. She was starting to worry. The man was nearly seventy-eight, so she supposed his forgetfulness was natural. But it was more than forgetfulness. Her Joe had once been so lighthearted. Lately he was often gloomy. If it weren't for her, Ruth was certain Joe would just as soon sit in his chair and stare at birds all day.

Well, maybe it wasn't that bad. If Frank called him over to listen to a game on the radio, he showed signs of the old Joe. Still, Joe didn't get out in the garden like he used to and Ruth had to push him out for a walk in the morning or remind him to fill the bird feeder. She even had to remind him to take care of the bristly whiskers on his face. If she complained, he would rest his hand on her face and say "Oh, Mother, you worry too much."

Honestly, there were times she felt like he were simply waiting to die. He had not tuned his violin in over five years, and when she asked him to play, he waved her off with his trembling hand and retreated back inside himself to a place she could not go, a place she did not want to go. It was hard to anticipate the next dark curtain that would fall over his eyes. She wondered now if this was just how all old men were, if sooner or later it was what they would all become.

A year and a half later, Josef Perlman would kiss his wife on the top of her head, tell her she was a good woman, and head to bed early, as he so often did. But this time, he would not wake up in the morning.

1963

Lev had moved to New York in 1950, three years after earning his BA from the University of Wisconsin-Milwaukee, an achievement he resented from the start. Accounting had been his father's idea, conceived due to Lev's excellent grades in mathematics all through grade school and high school. But Lev had also earned good grades in everything else, including English and art. What he loved best, however, was theater. Everyone who saw him as Iago agreed his was the best performance of them all. That had been his senior year in high school. So even though Lev wanted to pursue a life in the arts, he was under pressure from his parents—no, not from his parents, from his father only—to work towards a profitable career. And since Josef would only pay Lev's tuition if he earned a degree in something respectable, he was stuck. Lev graduated Magna Cum Laude and got a good job in Milwaukee.

To indulge his artistic needs, Lev had joined a small acting troupe with some players he had met at UW-M. More and more the small roles in these local plays took time away from his accounting work, and more and more he did not care. So after three years of managing people's estates and taxes, Lev resigned his accounting job. At first, he lived in a loft with friends, carefully doling out the money he had saved. A few months later, on a Friday evening after their Shabbat meal, Lev informed his parents that he and Paul, an actor friend, were moving to New York.

Josef had been furious that Lev had quit a good job to engage in a foolish whim. He berated his son for wasting his education. Ruth, sympathetic to her son, was caught in an untenable position. She hated to go against Joe, but all she could offer Lev was consolation.

Paul and Lev rented a drafty one-bedroom apartment. They worked whenever and wherever they could towards membership in the Actors' Equity Association. They worked as extras, helped build sets, did whatever they could to earn their eligibility. In those days, neither Paul nor Lev slept more than about four hours a night, but they didn't mind. They were both aching for their big break. Finally, Paul, the better singer and dancer of the two, landed a minor role in *Paint Your Wagon*. He convinced the director to hire Lev as one of the miners. They now felt they were well on their way to seeing their names on the marquee.

Lev's life in New York was not always easy, but it was finally *his* life. He and Paul found steady work one way or another. They found they were accepted as well. No one judged their theatrical flair or their love of poetry and music. The cultural melee that was New York suited them perfectly. For the first few years, Lev made it a point to head home for a week each summer, but before long, it was easier and easier to not visit.

So, even though he knew what it meant, Lev Perlman came home in the middle of August for his father's funeral. On the plane from New York, he settled into the seat, listened to the deep rumble of the propellers, and closed his eyes to ready himself for take-off, a feeling he dreaded and enjoyed at the same time. It was not for his father, he thought, looking down onto the clouds and patches of shocking blue between them, that he was headed back to Wisconsin. No, not for his father. He came for his mother and for his guilt at having been away too long.

Now at Beth El Synagogue, old men in their yarmulkes patted Lev on the shoulder, saying in one form or another, "Our condolences." What a great man, Josef Perlman was," they said. They told stories and jokes, recalled all the good times. All of these people seemed to know a man Lev did not recognize as his father.

At the gravesite, after the prayers had been said, Lev took his mother's arm and walked her back to the car. It was the way she said it that got to him. Her undemanding tone. "Do you have to go back, son? Would it be possible for you to stay?" It wasn't that Lev was unsympathetic to his mother's situation. She was a widow now. Not only that, but she had aged, more than he had expected she would. More than anything, he worried about her being alone. And as he helped her into the car, he realized that it might not be very long before she would be gone, too.

Except for theater work, there was nothing to keep him in New York. Two years earlier, Lev's relationship with Paul had cooled. Paul, whose career was now noticed by top reviewers, had begun to run with a different crowd, not just chorus actors and stagehands. At the last cocktail party he and Paul attended together, Lev watched as Paul flitted from one glamorous group to another. He was playing a role, the obsequious young man, a toy for whomever needed or wanted him, all in the service of getting where he wanted to be. A particularly ugly scene the next morning, in which Lev, dispirited and hungover, accused Paul of abandoning his principles, still haunted him.

When Paul moved out, Lev took on a new roommate, a younger man who was not interested in Lev. Lev was embarrassed he had misread the signals. So after only four months, Lev asked him to leave. From then on Lev preferred to live alone even though expenses were much harder to manage. He continued to search for roles, but he found auditions increasingly frustrating. And while he felt good about many of his prospects, jobs did not materialize, not even for Off-Broadway shows.

As he sat on the sofa with his mother, now, her thin hands folded over one another, her plaintive face pleading with him, he realized it was time. He had affairs to consider in New York. It would take him a month or so, but yes, he would move home.

After the funeral, Ruth had hired a decorator to renovate the upstairs in a modern style befitting a thirty-seven-year-old bachelor. He would have his own space and his own bathroom. Custom drapes in a blue-green geometric print were installed on the windows. The walls were painted in a light beige. She had personally chosen two paintings for his bedroom. One, his own, a sponge painting of a fish he had done in elementary school. She liked the primary blue paint on the brown butcher paper. She chose a light green mat and a walnut frame. The other was hers, one of her favorites. Lev had always liked it as well, and she thought he might enjoy her oil painting of the Onion River. Ruth had completed several paintings of the river, but she judged this one superior, the way she had been able to capture the light glinting off the rippling water.

She made up the other room, the one Josef had used as his den, as an office or lounge, a place Lev could work or read or just be alone if he chose. She knew he would need time by himself, too. Ruth cleaned out most of the personal items from her husband's desk, tossed out all the junk. She sprayed the large walnut surface with dust spray and polished it to a bright gleam. She dusted the brass lamp, wiped the green-glass shade, and pulled the chain to see if the bulb worked. Soft light spilled onto the green, leather-bound blotter. The only other thing on the desk was a framed photograph. Ruth, Josef, and Lev after his Bar Mitzvah.

On the wall Ruth hung a framed copy of a review of Lev's Off-Broadway performance as Giles Corey in *The Crucible*, the only New York play his parents ever saw him in. She had never been prouder of her son than she had been that night, seeing him bring that poor old man to life. It wasn't really Lev she was seeing on stage—it was truly Giles Corey, she told him after the show. That night, though he would never know it, his father had finally accepted that his son was born to be an actor. He has a marvelous gift, Joe had realized, seeing his son on stage.

After unpacking his things, Lev sat on the edge of his bed and wondered if he would ever look at another script. The possibility, though disheartening, was real. Perhaps he could seek out the Milwaukee troupe again. Or might

Sheboygan have a small theater group? Another possibility was that he would leave acting altogether and give up on his dreams. He conceded that the odds of that happening seemed a better bet than he wanted to admit. As Lev considered his next moves, he swore he heard a child's voice downstairs, so he headed down to investigate.

"Who's this?" Lev said, pleased to see the scene before him. Sophie, who had come as usual after school, sat at the kitchen table drinking a glass of milk. Vanilla wafers had been laid on a paper napkin.

Sophie looked curiously at the man before her.

"Sophie," Ruth said, standing behind her, resting her hands on the girl's shoulders. "This is my son, Lev. Lev, this is Sophie. She's in second grade already."

"How do you do, Sophie," Lev said, reaching out his hand. "It is very nice to meet you."

Sophie accepted his handshake, though she could not remember anyone ever shaking her hand before. She shyly said hello. She thought it odd that her Bubbe had a son who was a man. He was very tall and thin, had a long nose and thick eyebrows. His dark hair had begun to go gray, just at the temples.

Lev took in her awkward silence and remembered that he did not like meeting strangers when he was her age, so he did not feel offended.

"Well, I'm happy to know you. Maybe you can show me around the neighborhood sometime."

"Would you like that Sophie? Showing Lev around?" Ruth asked as a way of giving her consent to the idea.

Sophie looked into Ruth's eyes. Ruth smiled and nodded. Sophie looked back at Lev.

"I can show you the garden. I know all the plants," Sophie said. "Or if you wanna know where my school is, I can show you."

"That would be really nice, Sophie. Yes. I would like to see your school," Lev said. Ruth smiled proudly. She felt—although she knew she had no right to feel it, but nevertheless—she felt Lev and Sophie both were her children. "My two favorite people will be good friends. I can see it as plain as day," Ruth said.

A week later, Ruth invited the Catalanos for dinner so they could get to know Lev better. She had decided to make her mother's brisket with tzimmes, to which, in addition to carrots, onions, and prunes, she added dried apricots. While the brisket slowly simmered in its fruity-sweet stew in the cast-iron Dutch oven, Ruth had tidied the house, though it was always tidy. Later, everyone had raved about the food, and Ruth could not help but feel a little proud.

At the moment, Lev, Frank, and Sophie were in the living room. Lev had teamed up with Sophie, and they were trying to beat Frank at checkers. Angel and Ruth had just finished clearing the table and were in the kitchen.

"Why not go visit with Dad and Sophie, Ruth? I can manage the dishes," Angel said.

"I won't hear of it. You're the guest. It's you who should be out there. After all, I invited you so you could get to know Lev better. You go ahead and watch the game."

"Oh they don't want me interfering," Angel said as she set the stack of plates on the counter next to the sink. "I insist. It's the least I can do. You were so kind to have us over. How about if I wash and you dry and put away? I don't know where things go."

"Well, this is kind of you. Thanks," Ruth said. Then she smiled slyly as she tied her apron around her waist. "What do you think of my Lev, Angel? He's good-looking, isn't he? I think the little bit of gray in his hair makes him look even more handsome."

The sink filled with billowing bubbles, and Angel turned the faucet off. She looked quizzically at Ruth. She hesitated to answer, but she had to say something. "Well, sure. Of course he is." She tossed the silverware into the sink to let it soak and began washing the glasses. The second sink was filled with clear, hot water for rinsing.

"I have been thinking, Angel. I know he's older than you, a bit. You're twenty-five?"

"Twenty-six, almost twenty-seven. Now Ruth. What are you up to?" Angel swished a glass in the rinse water and set it in the drainer.

"So Lev is thirty-seven. Age is not so much a problem. Josef was seven years older than me. What's a problem is being alone. I know you have your dad and Sophie, but what about you? And Lev? I think he must be lonely, too, a bachelor all this time."

"Oh, Ruth. You're being silly."

Ruth dried another glass and set it on the counter. She looked sternly at Angel. "I don't think it's silly at all. I think you two would make a fine couple, and if you married Lev, you could give that sweet girl a father."

Ruth liked Angel well enough. No, she was not Jewish, but that would not matter to Lev. She was a good-looking woman. She was a hard worker, mostly. She could be abrasive at times, maybe even vulgar, though she had only seen such things from her kitchen window or heard them from her yard. Ruth accepted that everyone had their faults, but it was what a person was like most of the time that mattered, and most of the time Angel was kind and had a good sense of humor. She would be a good wife for her son, who sometimes seemed too quiet and withdrawn. With her final years in sight, Ruth did not want to think that Lev would live out his life an old, lonely bachelor.

"He could provide for you. You could quit work?"

Angel put the last pan in the dish drainer and let the sudsy water out of the sink. She looked at Ruth, who waited for a response, her expression quietly pleading.

Angel couldn't say exactly how she knew, but she knew that Lev would never be interested in her—not in that way—and she wanted to put this ridiculous conversation to rest.

"Now, Ruth. If Lev is interested in me, he will ask me out, and if that happens...."

Ruth gave Angel's wet hand a gentle squeeze. "You'll see. He will." She had imagined them living a happy life together. They could live in this house, or in a new house, west of town maybe, in one of the new subdivisions, or it could be anywhere, with a large green yard, gleaming white clapboards, green shutters, large, leafy trees, Lev writing a new play, Angelina pruning roses, Sophia reading or riding her bike. They would be happy.

"Come on, you old bubbe. Let's go see who's winning at checkers," Angel said, and she turned out the kitchen light behind them.

1963

One afternoon about two weeks before Thanksgiving, after Frank had gone over to get Sophie from Ruth's, he told her to head inside. He had something he needed to get from the car.

When he opened the door, Frank was holding a big box wrapped in white paper and tied with a giant pink bow.

"Well, Sophia Rosie, what could this be, hmm? Is it for Mommy? For Ruth? No, for Papa, I think. Yes, this pretty pink present is all mine."

She pretended to pout in the game they always played.

"Oh, are you sad? Well, that I won't have. All right then, it's for you."

The girl giggled and hugged him, then snatched the box away, tearing off the bow and the paper.

"Oh Papa! It's Chatty Cathy! I really, really wanted her." Sophie did not forget her manners. She laid the box to the side while she hugged her grandfather and gave him a big kiss on the cheek. "Thank you, Papa."

"All right now. You're welcome. She was in the window at Prange's and I said to myself, 'Frank, you have to buy her for Sophia.'"

Later, Angel walked in after work frazzled and limping. Her new shoes had given her a blister on her left heel. It took her less than ten seconds to notice the new doll, the very doll she had put on layaway for Sophie's birthday in three weeks.

She threw her arms in the air. "What the hell, Dad? Before her birthday? Before Christmas?"

"Now Angelina. Don't get angry. You know I can't help myself when it comes to my girls."

"Dad. We talked about this. She really doesn't need any more toys. You're just spoiling her."

"Oh, one more can't hurt, can it?"

"Christ almighty. I can't win." Angel tossed her shoes by the door and let her coat fall to the floor. In the kitchen, she got two aspirin and a Miller High Life from the fridge.

"Yes, that's right," she shouted to the other room. "I'm having a beer. It's been a shitty day and it just got worse."

Why did she have to be this way? We were having fun, Sophie and I, Frank thought. He looked sympathetically at Sophie, who hugged the doll fiercely, afraid her mother would take her present away.

Angel looked into her daughter's dark eyes, and saw the tears welling up.

"Christ, Sophie, just take the doll in your room and play."

Frank shook his head and headed for his hat and coat.

"Oh, so you're just going to leave?"

"I'm going for a brat over at Shultz's tonight. Should be leftover stew for you and Sophie," Frank said, and he walked out.

The next night, after Sophie was in bed, Angel decided to confront her father about the doll. She asked him to sit at the kitchen table with her, told him she'd like to talk. She was so commanding that he felt as if he were a child again in his mother's house, she about to scold him for something he had done, her heavy, dark frame hovering over him, her voice filling the kitchen, her hands the orchestra of her words. He should never have let his daughter rule over him in the same way.

"Dad, about the doll...."

"Why do you care so much, Angelina? I would think you would be happy that she's got nice things. I was always such a miser with you and your mom."

"That's just it. When did you become so generous with money? I never got a new bike. I had to make do with old ones you fixed up. My swing set was a rusty old hand-me-down. Sure, it may have been sturdy, but it looked old. And Mom, you always made her scrimp. Look around. The nicest furniture came from Grandma and Grandpa, like the walnut coffee table. The rest is mostly factory seconds."

At this severe misapprehension, Frank had to step in. "No. He didn't."

"He didn't what?" Angel tapped her cigarette on edge of the green glass ashtray.

"He didn't give that table to her. I made it for her. It was a birthday present. Now, Angelina…."

"Well, sorry. I guess. I just. Sorry."

Frank nodded to accept her apology. He felt hurt that Angelina thought that way about their house. He guessed it was true that he had not bought anything new in a long time, but if things weren't worn out, he saw no reason to replace them, especially just to keep up with the latest style.

"I guess I'm just angry because I had put that same doll on layaway."

"I couldn't have known that," Frank said. "I'm sorry to…."

"Anyway, Dad, the point is, we don't really have the money. That is, maybe you do, but I don't. Sure. I would like to give Sophie a lot of nice things, dolls and clothes and whatever she wants, but I don't make that much. I'm still trying to save enough to afford to go back to school. You know that."

"We're not poor, Angelina. You act as if we are. We're not rich, but we're not poor. I can cover household expenses and you can surely afford tuition on your own. I know you've been saving, so…."

"That's for Sophie," Angel said defensively. "For real college someday, maybe a good school out east, or wherever she wants to go."

"Well fine, I understand. It's just…."

"Just what?"

"Well, you keep saying you want to go back to school, and I've explained to you that I am happy to pay if you really want it, so I'm starting to think you're not really serious."

"That's not fair."

Frank saw that he was into this fight now. He had made the first stab. He would say what had been on his mind for a long time. "How is it not fair? Have you even checked into the cost of tuition? Or when classes begin? Honestly, you use going back to school as a bargaining chip, but it's wearing thin. What's the real problem?"

The specter of his mother had vanished. In her place now lay a wounded animal, quivering, ready to bite.

"That's a hateful thing to say. How do you know what I want? You stopped caring about me a long time ago. You abandoned me, and now you think you can make things right by buying my daughter toys." Angel felt her chest heave and her throat tighten and ache, but she would not cry. She was hurt and angry, and years of unsaid feelings roiled within her, but she would not cry.

"I never abandoned you. Never. If you recall, you're the one who left, or did you forget that fact?"

"I had to. I had to get away. You took my mother from me. She was the only one who really loved me."

Frank wanted to shout, "Grow up Angelina and face the facts. She was a drunk. She left you alone. She sometimes couldn't get out of bed all day. Sometimes I mended your clothes. Sometimes I packed your lunches. Me. The one who covered for her all those years. I loved her. God knows I loved her, but she was not always the best mom to you." But he couldn't. He could not destroy his wife a second time.

"I always loved you, Angelina. Always. I do now. I will try harder to do things your way."

He stood, walked behind her, laid his hand on her shoulder, then headed down the hall to his room.

And Angel, who felt the warmth of that touch deep under her skin, convulsed in sobs she had no power to control.

Since Angel had Thanksgiving Day off, she decided to smooth things over with her father by cooking dinner. She honored the Schneider family tradition of eating the big meal mid-afternoon to have plenty of room for pie later on, but it meant getting up early to cook. Angelina set her alarm for six o'clock and was soon as busy as June Cleaver. On the stove, the giblets simmered in seasoned water for broth. She washed the sixteen-pound bird, patted it dry, and set it in the shallow roasting pan. She dumped the chunks of old bread she had been drying out all week into a large bowl and added chopped onion, celery, and apple—her grandmother's secret ingredient— then salt, pepper, and rubbed sage. In a smaller bowl, she beat two eggs. When the broth cooled a bit, she would temper it into the eggs and then moisten her dressing with the liquid.

While she waited for the broth to cool, she preheated the oven and took out the ingredients for pumpkin pie. Grandmother Schneider made hers from the pumpkins Grandpa grew, but a can of Libby's would have to do for today. She could still turn out a crust, though. Her mother had taught her that. Start with lard, cut it into the flour, don't forget a pinch of salt. Then add the icy water slowly. If the dough is too wet, the crust will need more flour, and the more you work it, the tougher it will be. Angel rolled the dough, laid it in the pie plate, patted it carefully into place, cut off the excess, and fluted the edge. It was lovely, much lovelier than the pies she served at Alexanders. I should be baking their pies, she thought, then laughed at the idea. Angel was so busy that she did not notice Sophie standing behind her in her nightgown, still half asleep and rubbing her eyes.

"I smell dinner," Sophie said. Angel looked confused. Oh, the broth, she remembered.

"Well, I guess you do. It's too early to be up, honey. You should crawl back into bed."

"I can't sleep."

Angel clapped her floury hands over the sink, then wiped them on a towel. Okay, silly girl. Why don't you cuddle up on the couch then? Angel turned on the TV. Later the Macy's parade would be on, but right now it was *Davey and Goliath*. Sophie liked that one.

"Okay? All set? I have to get back in the kitchen. Papa will be up soon and you two can watch the parade together. How does that sound?"

Dinner turned out well, even better than Angel had hoped. The week before, knowing she would cook this peace offering, Angel had bought a light gold tablecloth at the Penney's pre-holiday sale. She even splurged on matching napkins. After all, Angel had Ruth Perlman to impress. Once the table was set with her mother's good china and stemmed glassware, she stepped back to admire the elegant effect. As she brought the turkey to the table and set it before her father to carve, Angel felt her mother and grandmother surging within her.

Frank was pleased as well. He admired his daughter's ability to pull this off. He had tried last year to cook, hoping to do something special for his girls, and while his turkey was good, his dressing was soggy and the pie was a genuine disaster. In contrast to earlier in the week, today Angelina's ebullient demeanor set him at ease. As it had been with her mother, when Angelina was in a good mood, when she was happy, everyone was happy. Still, Frank was grateful she had invited the neighbors for dinner. Happy-go-lucky Ruth could always be relied on to ease any tense situation. It would be good to see her happy, too. He knew she still grieved for Joe. They talked about it now and then when they met outside, puttering in the yard. But he also knew that she seemed younger than ever now that her son was home.

Frank passed the mashed potatoes to Lev, and as he handed the bowl off, he asked, "Are you settling in okay, Lev? How's the job?"

Lev took the potatoes, spooned a small portion onto his plate, made an indentation with the spoon, and passed the dish to his mother. While he waited for the gravy boat, which Sophie was struggling with, he told Frank things were going well.

Lev worked part time at Marshall's Menswear, a small shop downtown.

While Ruth insisted there was no need for Lev to work, he enjoyed the work. And he was good at it.

"Lev, tell them about the television show," Ruth said proudly.

"Oh, Mother, they don't want to hear about that."

"And why not?" Ruth set her fork down and began to fill in the details. "He's modest, but his old friend Paul, who lives in Los Angeles now, is a movie actor. Can you imagine it? We know a movie star."

"He's not really a star," Lev corrected. "He's had a few minor roles."

"Well I am impressed, let me tell you. So, Paul, he calls Lev and says to him, Lev, you need to come out here. You tell them, Lev."

Angel's face brightened at the brush with potential stardom as well. "You're going to be in movies, Lev?" she said.

"Oh no," Lev said lightly, as if the idea seemed unimaginable to him, even though when he had heard about Paul's first small movie role, he had been instantly jealous. But Paul had not forgotten him. Lev liked to think the invitation from Paul to go out to LA was an attempt to mend the fence Paul himself had finally destroyed.

"Maybe television," he continued. "I was out there last week and auditioned for a small part in *Bonanza*. I expect to hear one way or another this week." He knew it was a thin thread that he grasped, but in his daydreams, his what-if imaginings, he pulled it closer and closer. When he moved in with his mother, Lev was resigned to make the best of it in Sheboygan. But this unexpected opportunity set him upside down, and he wondered if he could live a dual life. If it came to making a choice, he knew he would not leave his mother again. Truthfully, he wasn't sure he was prepared for all the rejection that seemed inevitable in a future of acting. No one said, "You're not quite right for..." when you picked out a shirt and tie for them. The flaw might lie in the tie itself, not quite the right design, a bit too pink, but not in the salesman. Still, another part of him pulled him toward the precipice of risk. He missed it. Acting. He missed it a lot.

"That's so exciting," Angel said, and Frank agreed.

Sophie said excitedly, "You gonna be on *Bonanza?*"

"I hope so, Bubbala. Wouldn't that be fun?" It would be more than fun, Lev thought. Maybe New York was not supposed to happen. Maybe that wasn't his time. Maybe Lev needed to grow older, earn some wrinkles to give his inexperienced face gravity. He was sure the young man who first auditioned in New York would never have even been considered for a "swarthy outlaw." He almost looked the part now, without theatrical makeup or awkward prostheses. TV wasn't like the stage. The camera came in close. One needed an authentic look.

Lev stabbed at the last bit of turkey on his plate and coated it in cranberry sauce the way he liked it. In a way, Lev felt all this talk would jinx his chances. He didn't believe in sharing news until there was news to share. It had felt good to audition, but he was so rusty, he was sure his awkward reading had not hit the mark. And yet, there were high points, too. The gravelly voice he'd added as texture. That was inspired, he thought. "We'll see," he said. "Dinner is delicious, Angelina." Lev stuffed the turkey into his mouth.

"Yes, dear. It is quite good," Ruth agreed.

Frank raised his glass of wine and the others followed his lead. "To my daughter, Angelina," he said.

The gesture, so unlike her dad, pleased her nevertheless. Her humble "thank you" was so quiet she almost could not hear it herself.

1977

Angel's eyes fluttered in the light. She breathed deeply. Sweet, freshly cut grass. Breezy. Cold. Dark. She opened her eyes. She worked to set in her mind the architecture of the living room, beige drapes, off-white walls, green, gold, and brown floral sofa. Her gold club chair and ottoman, wide rolled arms—her father's chair.

She felt the room move about her, furniture lifting itself off the floor, shifting left, right, left. Dizzy. Eyes heavy. Her arms grew larger. Floated beside her. Breathing. Breathing. The kitchen door to the garage. Opened. Closed. The door grew larger and opened and closed, opened and closed. Sophie now at the sink, running water. The sound cooled her. She was thirsty. She was in the dark. She was hot. Sweating. Eyelids sweating. Heart, thump thump. In her ears. The door opening, closing.

At 7:30 a.m., Sophie heard her mother crying quietly. The sound, so helpless, brought Sophie out of a weird dream. She'd been stuck in the garage. Outside it was snowing, and swirls of snow blew in under the garage door. In her pajamas, Sophie had shivered on the dirty, grease-covered concrete floor.

Sophie stood at her mother's bedside now.

"Mom?" Sophie laid her cool hand on her mother's hot forehead, which was wet with perspiration. She pulled the blanket back. Angel's nightgown had shifted up into a tangle about her hips. The gown felt wet, too. More than sweat. Sophie would get a clean gown later.

"Mom? Can you hear me? Want to try to wake up?"

In the bathroom Sophie wet a washcloth and brought it to the living room to smooth over her mother's face and neck. She washed over her hands, too. Angel quietly moaned her pleasure.

"Mom. It's morning."

Angel blinked and took in the room with her eyes. Then closed them. This slow waking was normal now. Sophie had been under sedation when she had her wisdom teeth pulled when she was seventeen. She remembered that slow, groggy return to consciousness. It was weird, being both in and out of reality.

Angel's eyes opened fully now, but she looked terrified, her eyes darting right and left. Then, fixing on Sophie, Angel took a deep breath and looked alert at last.

"Well, there you are. Good morning. Sure wish I had it as good as you and could just sleep in whenever I wanted."

"Thirsty."

Seconds later, Sophie returned with a glass of water for her mom, a bendy straw bobbing up and down, and guided the straw to her mother's lips.

"Oh. That's so good." Angel took a deep breath and looked around her. The room already so brightly lit. "Pretty day."

"It should be a beautiful day. How about later we get you outside for a bit?"

Angel said she would like that and fought the strong urge to close her eyes. She did not succeed.

Sophie opened the lawn chairs and set them on the front stoop, which was just large enough to accommodate them. In her clean nightgown and robe, for she no longer put on regular clothes, Angel held onto Sophie's arm as she stepped outdoors. She was also grateful for the help as she lowered herself into the chair. Sophie covered her mom's lap and legs with a blanket.

Angel breathed in deeply. "It's so nice out here. Thank you for thinking of it."

"Well, we should be doing this every day, right?"

Angel smiled and said that would be nice, but lately she would often just rather stay in bed. It had only been a few weeks since she had been in the hospital, and even though she'd come home feeling pretty well, she could tell she was losing strength every day.

Sophie read *The Sheboygan Press* while Angel sat quietly and watched life on 13th Street more closely than she could through the window. In some ways, the neighborhood looked exactly the same as it had when they moved into this house. She had been only twelve years old. I thought I was all grown up then, she thought. I had no idea that I had already lived more than a quarter of my life.

Without a thread to connect to, Angel began talking, to Sophie obviously, but more as if she were talking to no one but herself.

"Lately I have been thinking how lovely it would be if there really were a place like Heaven. Wouldn't it be something to be whisked off in flowing robes to a golden paradise where you would see again all the people you've loved and have missed your whole life? It would be something to see Mother again. Father, too. Especially, him. I have a lot I need to say. And then, you would be there, too. Of course, not for a long, long time. We would all be waiting for you. Papa and me. Mostly me." Her voice softened. She stared at a hazy image of houses and trees, seeing them not as they are but as they were.

Angel continued. "Oh, it is a lovely idea. I guess I just don't think it exists, or even God. I suppose if I'm wrong about that I'm in trouble. Course, I don't believe in Hell either. When I die, I will be dust. I don't mean to be blunt, but it's the truth. And I refuse to be put in a casket underground. Cremate me."

Sophie squeezed her mother's hand. Hearing her mother talk about her own death made Sophie feel anxious. Of course she knew it could happen soon, but the last few weeks had become normalized for Sophie, and she guessed she had somehow been lulled into the idea that things could go on like this indefinitely. Sure her mom was visibly ill, but she woke each day, she was able to walk, she ate, or tried to eat. Yes, she slept most of her days. Nights could be rough. But they were managing. And one day seemed not that much different from the one before it.

In reality—and talking about cremation made it real—in reality, it could happen next week. It could happen this afternoon.

"You okay?" Angel asked.

"Yep. Fine."

"You?"

"Never better."

They looked at each other, and at the exact same moment, Sophie and Angel burst out laughing.

1964

Ruth stood in her living room, arms akimbo, surveying the chaos she'd instigated. Sophie, whom Angel had whisked over before breakfast because she forgot she had promised to cover another girl's shift, mirrored her. Several cardboard boxes with their flaps open, brown bags from the grocery store, and a wicker clothes basket served as sorting stations.

"I should have tossed out some of this a long time ago," said Ruth, who was starting to be sorry she had begun the task of cleaning out closets, drawers, and other out-of-sight-out-of-mind places. She had begun with Joe's things, feeling it was time to let go of his clothes and donate them to charity. The shirts and trousers wouldn't have fit Lev anyway, who at 6'3" had towered over his father. Before packing Joe's clothes in boxes, Ruth held them to her face. Joe still lingered in the fibers.

"What next, Bubbe?" asked Sophie.

"Let's take a look in the front closet. I know there's a coat in there from ten years ago, and I won't wear that old thing anymore."

Ruth slid the brown boiled wool coat off the hanger and saw Joe's rubber galoshes, which she directed Sophie to put in the clothes basket, as well as a pair of shoes he'd worn to cut the grass. On the shelf was a box of odds and ends, including a cheap plastic menorah. "I can't even remember where this ugly thing came from," she said. "Joe saved the oddest things. He thought such things would 'come in handy' someday." Ruth decided the entire box was full of junk, so she set it by the back door. At Sophie's suggestion that she could hold a yard sale like their other neighbors sometimes did, Ruth scoffed and said she would not have anything from her house out on display like that. It was unseemly.

Ruth climbed the stepladder to reach into the corners of the shelf and found a fold-up plastic rain bonnet, which she tucked into the pocket of her spring coat. That, she decided, just might come in handy. An old wool scarf that Joe had never liked went into a box. She then wiped down the empty shelf, embarrassed at the grime left on her rag. Now clean, it gratified her to see the empty space. She would leave it empty for now. Lev might want to store something, scarves or gloves, perhaps books. She would offer the space to him later.

Ruth saw that Sophie had climbed into the closet and had nearly disappeared into the coats. "You having fun, you silly girl?"

Sophie fingered the white wool coat with the mink collar that Ruth now wore in the winter. "I like this coat. It's pretty." She slid inside the slippery satin lining and breathed in Ruth's warm scent. Can I wear it?"

"Oy, no. Now stop futzing and come on out of there. We've got to get this all squared away before Lev gets home from work today. I'm going to ask him to pack it all up in his car."

It was nearly 1:30 when Ruth taped the last box. Everything was neatly in place by the door, ready for Lev. She wondered if he might have to make two trips to the resale shop and hoped he would not be annoyed if that were the case.

"I'm tired. What about you?"

"I'm hungry," Sophie said.

Ruth's eyes opened in alarm. She had completely forgotten about lunch. "Well, I suppose you are. What shall we make today?" Ruth opened the refrigerator and surveyed the possibilities. A pound cake covered in waxed paper tempted her, but she didn't dare feed that to the child for lunch. Leftover noodle kugel she might like, but so would Lev. She pulled out a loaf of bread and directed Sophie to get the peanut butter from the cupboard. There was just enough raspberry jam left for two sandwiches. Ruth poured Sophie a glass of milk while the girl set the plates on the table.

"So you like Bubbe's coat, do you?" Ruth said.

"You look like a rich lady when you wear it."

The comment made Ruth laugh, although she admitted it was a fine coat. Joe had not spared his pennies on it. "Well, maybe I'll leave it for you when I die."

The comment had not been intended to upset the girl, but Ruth could tell by Sophie's eyes—which suddenly reddened and glistened, her cheeks pink with emotion—that it had.

"I don't want you to die," Sophie said, working very hard not to cry.

"Oh, my sweetheart. I'm sorry. No, no. Don't you even think about it. Your bubbe's not going to die."

Ruth deftly steered Sophie's attention away from morbid thoughts. "I was thinking I might make cookies in a bit. Would you want to help? Lev likes to have something sweet before bed. I could make extra and send some home with you?"

Sophie found the recipe in Ruth's wooden box and then helped her gather the ingredients. Ruth wiped out the milk glass mixing bowl before using it to cream the butter and sugar.

Sophie would need more practice at cracking eggs. "Be sure you get all that egg shell out of the bowl," Ruth said, smiling. Ruth remembered her own mother losing patience with her. She wished her mother had known that children need time to learn.

Sophie spooned the stiff oatmeal raisin dough onto the cookie sheet. Ruth reminded her to scoop the same amount for each cookie so they would bake evenly. Good job, girl, Ruth thought proudly, and after the last batch was in the oven with the timer set, it was time to begin cleaning up. Sophie stood at the sink washing the mixing bowl and beaters, the measuring cups and spoons. Ruth rinsed and dried.

I would tell her, Ruth thought, if I had enough courage, that this is what our life is. Making cookies. Packing away the past. And no matter how much we love each other, we all die. She smoothed her warm, damp hand over Sophie's dark, shiny hair. I will die before you are a married lady. I will hate to miss seeing you walk down the aisle. I will die before your first child is born. Oh, would I love to see that, your little baby, so new and perfect. But I can't think about it. I can't think that you will have to be there when they bury me. I can't think about how sad it will make you. That is just how it is. Some of us die too young and some of us live too long. We can't choose. I'm glad we cannot choose. No one should know they are going to die. It's much better when death comes as a shock.

The kitchen timer buzzed. Ruth thrust her hand into the oven mitt, pulled the cookie sheet out, and turned the oven off. "Let's keep the oven door open just a bit to let that nice heat out into the house. She transferred the cookies to the counter, placing them onto a sheet of newspaper lined with waxed paper. Sophie was already eating her second cookie.

"Good?"

"Mmm."

"All right then, my little bubbala. I'm pooped, as Joe used to say. How about if we rest now? I'm going to lie on the sofa and you can turn on the TV if you keep it low."

Sophie helped Ruth cover up with the knitted throw. Before Sophie headed to the TV, Ruth held her small hand a moment. "I don't want you to worry about me, Sophie. I'm as healthy as can be. And I don't plan on dying any time soon. And I would be so, so sad to leave you. Okay?" She gave Sophie's hand a hard squeeze.

The girl smiled. "I love you Bubbe."

"I love you, too. Now. I'm just going to close my eyes for ten seconds."

An hour later, Angel arrived. Sophie met her at the door and held her finger to her mouth. They left Ruth snoring softly on the couch. Lev would be home any minute.

1964

Sophie had been on the couch watching Saturday morning cartoons while Frank cleaned up after breakfast. Angel had another early shift and had been out the door at 5:15 a.m. Frank eyed his granddaughter and knew she would watch TV all morning if he let her, so after wiping the table and rinsing out the dishrag, he decided to put her to work building something in his small workshop in the garage.

"Get dressed, girl. I've got a surprise for you. Put on some old play clothes."

Sophie looked up at him but didn't budge. He wiped his hands dry on the towel and folded it neatly on the towel bar. He did not like to use an authoritative approach with Sophie. He preferred to be more playful, but sometimes the child did as she wished, and if he wanted to make her mind him, he sometimes needed to be more stern than he liked to be. She stared with wide eyes as he bent down to turn the TV off.

"I wanted to watch that," she whined.

"I am sure you did," Frank said. "But you can't find out what my surprise is by staying on the couch all morning."

"What surprise?"

"Sophie. You weren't even listening to me. Now, come on. Go change into some old play clothes."

She pouted, but felt defeated with the TV off, so she slumped off to the room she shared with her mother and got dressed as she was told to do.

"What's this one?" Sophie said, picking up another tool, lifting it like a weight. "It's heavy."

"That is a pipe wrench. See the threads there, under that bead. Turn the bead. Yes, like that."

"Oh, it gets smaller."

Frank showed Sophie how to set a smaller, everyday wrench around a nut to tighten it. He introduced her to various hammers, and she decided she liked the slender tack hammer best. She was quick to learn the difference between a flat-head and a Phillips head screwdriver.

Frank's hand-built workbench was a modest two-and-a-half by five feet, but it held all the tools he needed as well as a good supply of standard hardware. His design featured six dovetailed drawers, a mounted vice at the left edge, and a hutch with narrow shelves on each side of a pegboard center where hanging tools were neatly organized. There was not a rusty tool among his practical collection. Lately he'd only come to the bench for a screwdriver or a hammer to make a repair. It had been a long while since he had been excited to build anything, but this morning some old impulse fired within him and he longed to teach Sophie at least a little bit about building something with wood. She was a naturally creative child. She liked to draw and make up stories, and all of that was fine, but he felt strongly that a person needed to build things that people could use. And learning to use and respect tools would be something she would always have a need for. Even a woman should know how to make repairs in her home.

Sophie practiced driving screws into a soft piece of pine while Frank leafed through a couple copies of *Woodworker* until he found what he thought he remembered. Simple plans for a birdhouse. *Building with your sons is fun and rewarding*, the article said. Frank smiled. How about granddaughters? Frank generally did not need plans and could design most things he wanted to cobble on his own, but he reasoned that a child just learning would benefit from the illustrated plans. As for tools, they would use the power drill with the hole saw to bore the entry hole and a 5/16" bit for the dowel that would serve as a perch, but the rest could be managed with a small hand saw and hammer and nails. And, of course, she could paint it if she liked. Any color, though they would have to go to the hardware store for a can of enamel.

"Ooh, neat," Sophie said when Frank showed her the plans. "Will birds really live in it?"

"We can hope so. Maybe after we hang it we can put out a 'for rent' sign."

"Oh, Papa. Birds can't read."

"Oh, they can't? I guess that won't work then."

"You were just kidding, right?" Sophie asked, just to be sure he didn't actually think birds could read. He just grinned.

"We have to read the plans carefully, draw out the lines, and measure twice before we cut. Do you think you want to try the saw?"

Sophie nodded enthusiastically. Frank showed her how to position the vice so she would have a good angle for cutting. She tightened the pine plank into the vice. She struggled to get the saw to work, but Frank did not take over. He kept guiding her, the way he used to teach the new workers on the line. "No one learns by watching someone else. You have to do it yourself," he told Sophie.

Her first cut wasn't perfect, but Frank assured her the birds wouldn't care. The next one would be better, and the one after that better still. Sophie progressed with confidence. When it came time to assemble the pieces, Sophie was pleased that she did not need the plans to know where each piece went.

"It's obvious where they go, isn't it, Papa?"

He said he thought it was, but maybe not everyone would agree. He said he guessed she was smart about how things worked, and she liked that idea.

"This is fun, Papa."

Frank gave Sophie a small claw hammer to use. She took it and drove some nails into her practice board. She held each nail carefully upright, gave the head a few taps to set it, and then hammered confidently as Frank had instructed. "How's it going?" he asked, even though he had been intently watching her.

"Easy," she said. "This hammer is kind of like a kid's one. It's not heavy like yours."

"It's part of a tool set I bought for your mom when she was your age, maybe even younger."

Frank judged it would be safer for him to use the power drill, but he let Sophie hold on while he made a hole in her practice board. She said it made her hands buzz.

All the pieces assembled, it was time to dab the dowel with glue and set it in place for the perch. "The glue should be in the middle drawer on the left, Sophie." She was about to open the drawer when the door to the kitchen creaked open. Her mother stood at the top of the step, her work apron over her arm. She stepped down into the garage.

"What's going on here?" she asked.

"Me and Papa are building a birdhouse. Well, mostly just me." Sophie ran to her mother and grabbed her hand and pulled her over to the bench. "Look. Isn't it nice? There's a hole for the bird to go inside, and I'm going to glue this little stick—"

"Dowel," Frank corrected.

"—dowel, into this little hole, and that's where the bird can sit if he wants to. I'm going to paint it red."

"Well, it's very nice. But Grandpa made most of it didn't he?"

"Nope. He only made the holes with the drill, but I did the sawing and the hammering."

Angel glanced up at her dad with a skeptical, even worried look.

"All her. She's a gifted woodworker already."

"Very nice, sweetheart. You did a great job. I'm going in to get a shower and try to get the smell of bacon out of my hair. After that, you can tell me more about your day.

After Sophie was sound asleep that night, Angel sat with her father at the kitchen table. He had dealt his second solitaire hand and she was polishing her nails in shimmering pink.

"Wasn't it dangerous to let her use tools?" Angel finally said what had been on her mind. "She's only eight. And hammering nails is a boy thing."

"I'm surprised you feel that way. Aren't you always saying girls can do anything boys can do?"

"Well, I don't want her getting hurt."

"You sound a lot like your mother. She was always worried about you playing too rough. Remember those Stowe boys? She did not like you playing with them at all, but I...." Frank paused when he remembered that one of those boys had drowned and how upset Angelina had been. He tried to finish the thought quickly. "I never thought playing with boys would harm you."

Angel nearly knocked the Cutex bottle over. "I haven't thought of Tommy Stowe in a long time." She tried to ignore brief flashes of that awful day. She was also thinking how ironic her father's statement was: playing with boys wouldn't harm her. It was he who wouldn't let her date until she was sixteen, though he never knew, at least she didn't think he knew, that she'd disobeyed his rule several times. She also supposed the final irony was on her, as playing with Ruben had hurt her. And Mark, and all the others. They didn't know how to play without causing harm. Boys were dangerous, just not in the way he meant—well, not in this context. And it wasn't so much that she minded Sophie hammering nails. It was kind of cute, and the birdhouse was adorable with its jagged edges and two or three bent-over nails. But why had he never taken her into the garage to build something like that. Why hadn't he wanted to teach her about tools? Her eyes burned.

"You're right to be concerned," Frank said. "But you know I was right there. I would never...."

"I know, Dad. I know. You're good to her. You're good with her." Angel did not want to sound jealous, but she could not forget the scene she walked in on, her father and her daughter, head to head. She could not remember a time when he had just wanted to be with her like that.

"That kid of yours is pretty amazing. I'm getting older and...."

"You're not old, Dad."

"Not old, but older. Old enough to know how fast kids grow up. It won't be long before she would rather be out with her friends than hanging around with her old grandpa. I guess I just want her to know me. I want to know her." Frank sensed that at some point parents and children grow out of sync with each other. For a time, their trajectories in life are parallel. They head forward along the same path, pausing at the same moments, until the time when the child's step falters on her own for the first time, when she feels the significance of that step, knowing she owns it. From that point forward the child veers by increments toward her separate path, the shadow of her parent growing dimmer with each step.

Angel shook her left hand gently and blew on the nails. Why did this bother her so much? Jesus. She was ready to burst into tears.

Frank noticed his daughter's glistening eyes. "What's wrong? What's the matter? Did something happen at work? Did I upset you by mentioning that Stowe boy?"

"No. Jesus. No." She closed the polish bottle tightly.

"What's the mat—"

"What's the matter is that you never showed me how to build a birdhouse. You never let me hammer nails. You do so much with her. It's like she's your daughter and I'm, I don't know what, but you... It would have been nice, that's all. You..."

"I tried. You didn't want to. I..."

"It's my fault? You were hardly ever home. Not the war. Well, I missed you then, too. But I don't mean that. I mean after. When you got back. You were at work or down at the VFW. Or if you were home, you were in the basement or in the garage a lot. You were just not there for me. You are for her. But you weren't for me." Angel sniffed up her tears. She would not cry. She would not.

Frank felt that Angelina was being too hard on him. He had tried to do things with her, but for whatever reason, he and his daughter did not get along, not like he and Sophie did. But there was no use arguing with her, no use reminding her of the time he wanted to teach her how to swing a bat. She tried to hit five balls. Five. But instead of trying harder, instead of keeping her eye on the ball, she threw the bat to the ground and whined. Frank absent-mindedly played a two on the ace of hearts, his head hung low, nodding. "You're right, Angelina. You're right."

How was it, she wondered, that *she* suddenly felt guilty? The man was a better dad with Sophie than he had been with her. It was a fact. Then Mom. The accident. It was as if her life had ended then, too. But Angel also knew that after the accident she had shunned her father's attempts to love her for a long time. She knew she was not blameless. Only since Sophie had she realized she no longer wanted to shut him out. And she was trying. She did try. Probably she shouldn't have said anything. Just kept it bottled up, like so many other things. But it hurt that he was so close to Sophie. It shouldn't have, but it did. Yet, look at him. Jesus. The man was so easily hurt. She didn't want to wound him. She didn't. She got up, went over to him, laced her arms around him, and laid her head on his shoulder.

"It's okay, Dad. We're...well, all that was a long time ago. I'm not mad."

He gave her arm a squeeze but did not speak.

She straightened up, then bent again to kiss the top of his head, still so full of hair. From this perspective, he looked young, except for the hunched curve of his shoulders.

"Good night, Dad. Don't stay up too late."

Angel padded softly down the hall to her room, and in the moonlight undressed and slipped into her nightgown. Sophie's one-eyed teddy bear was on the floor between their twin beds. Angel picked him up and tucked him gently under her daughter's arm. She smiled and thought how that same arm had built a birdhouse this morning. "Good night you amazing kid, you," Angel whispered, then crawled between the sheets. She lay there a long time thinking about Tommy Stowe, about his ocean-blue eyes, his white hair, even his arms, those strong, tanned arms she longed, even as a very young girl, to touch, and how he never got to grow up. "Maybe you were the lucky one, Tommy," she said quietly. "Maybe."

1977

Sophie and Lev were in the kitchen playing Gin Rummy. Angel slept on and off, murmuring a quiet word now and then. Sophie glanced at the clock on the stove and decided she would wait another half hour before waking her mom for more pain pills.

In her dream, Angel held her father's hand, and she stood with the tips of her toes on the edge of her mother's open grave. Looking down into the black and endless hole, she felt dizzy. Somewhere far, far below the earth lay her mother's casket, and inside it, her mother. Angel felt her hand slip from her father's, her arms flailing as she fell, he bending and reaching and calling, "Angelina, grab my hand, An-ge-leee-naaaa," his voice becoming an echo. She fell and fell and fell into the endless black.

Angel's eyes fluttered. A streetlight glowed in a hazy yellow circle. A sharp twinge in her chest and a quick gulp of air forced Angel awake. Her brain and tongue felt fuzzy. She surveyed her surroundings. There were times when she woke surprised to find herself in bed in the living room. She had to think hard to reposition herself in the present.

She heard Lev's deep laugh and sighed. Angel was grateful that Lev was here, helping Sophie, keeping her company. Angel enjoyed having him around, too. He was a gentle man who was doing everything he could for them. He knew how it felt, dealing with death, and he would know what to say and do to help Sophie.

"Hey there, sleepyhead," Sophie said. "Or you old slug-a-bed, as Ruth used to say."

Lev closed the drapes and turned on the living room lamps. "We're hungry for ice cream, Angel. What about you?" Lev said.

"Is there any Hershey's syrup?"

"Of course," Sophie said.

In the kitchen now, Lev scooped vanilla ice cream and drizzled the chocolate syrup.

Angel set her pills on her tongue, sipped water from the straw, and swallowed.

"Thank you, Sophie."

"Here you go, your majesty," Lev said, setting the shallow bowl and spoon on Angel's tray, moving it into position so she could manage easily.

Sophie clicked on the TV and the three of them watched *Hawaii Five-O*. Sophie noticed her mother lay her spoon down and told her to try to eat a bit more. Angel acquiesced, even though lately nothing tasted good. How awful it is when even ice cream doesn't taste good, she thought.

After the show ended, Lev said he needed to be heading home. Angel waved from her bed and Sophie shut the front door. Another detective series was on TV now, which they left on in the background while Sophie got her mother situated for the night. They were still walking to the bathroom, and Sophie hoped that would continue until the end. The idea of a bedpan intimidated her.

"Stay with me till I fall asleep," Angel said. Sophie pulled up the rocking chair and listened to her mother talk, at first with some energy, later slower, until eventually, she would lose her thoughts.

"Did you know your grandpa Catalano bought this little house after the war through the GI bill? I know you'll probably sell it, but if you do, I want you to take a lot of pictures. Take pictures of everything, so you won't forget it."

Sophie realized at that moment that she had never even thought about the house. She knew she was born in Austin, Minnesota, but she remembered nothing about their house there. This was her home. The idea of selling it, of living somewhere else came as a shock to her.

"If you move away and then visit later," Angel said, "the new people will have changed everything, just like at my Grandma and Grandpa's house. I loved that big old house, but after they died, it was just not the same. I suppose that tomorrow we should talk about the stuff of mine that I want you to keep." Angel thought just then that none of this was really hers. It had all belonged to her parents, and to her grandparents before them. She had bought very little on her own.

"Do you remember that time when we made homemade strawberry ice cream? Grandpa let you turn the crank. The sound of the churn twisting in the ice and salt...."

When Angel was finally asleep and Sophie was in her own bed, she lay awake a long time trying to remember making ice cream with her grandfather. She was sure it had never happened.

1964

Only an hour before clocking out to go home, Frank was updating the production log for his shift crew when a black shroud covered his eyes. The room spun briefly, then he fell. He was dead before he hit the concrete floor.

1964

Sophie was sprawled on the living room floor. Her mom had been home all day with a cold. Angel lay on the couch, covered in blankets. The radio was on in the kitchen and the disembodied voices created unnecessary noise.

The phone rang, but Angel did not want to get up. Seemed like every time she raised her head, it grew four sizes. "Sophie. Can you get the phone?"

Sophie let it ring one more time before Angel yelled, "Sophie. The phone."

The child picked the heavy black receiver off the hook. "Hullo?" she said.

"Hello," the man's voice said. "Is this Sophia?"

"Yes. Who's this?"

"I work with your grandpa, Sophia." The man didn't say anything for a moment. "Sweetheart, is your mom home?"

Sophie held the receiver out to her mom.

"Mom. It's for you." The radio voices buzzed in the background.

"Who is it?" Angel complained. What was it now? She'd had two calls from salesmen during the day while Sophie was in school. She just wanted to rest.

Angel plodded across the living room to the hallway table. She took the receiver from Sophie and shooed the girl away. Taking her time, thinking the caller was another solicitor, Angel finally spoke.

"Hello. What can I do for you?" she said caustically.

"Angelina?" The man cleared his throat.

Sophie, who had not been shooed away, wondered what the man was saying. She looked up into her mother's face, saw her mother's brow tighten, saw the color drain from her mother's face, saw the hand holding the receiver fall to her mother's side, saw her mother drop the phone and fall like an old rag doll to the floor.

Robbie came from Milwaukee for the funeral and served as a pallbearer as did Lev. Angel, Sophie, Ruth and Lev Perlman, Robbie, Lucy, their three sons and their wives and kids, and seven of Frank's co-workers, only one of whom Angel knew, stood at the gravesite. On the way to the cemetery, the November wind picked up and an icy rain fell. Later, the rain would turn to snow. The priest offered words of consolation and said earnestly that such a vital man should never be taken so young. He was only fifty-one. That fact made Angel realize just how young her mother had been when she was killed.

Angel buried her father next to her mother. She was grateful that her parents had purchased the double plot not long after they bought the house on 13th Street, though she was sure they felt it would be many long years before they would take up residence there. She was grateful also to Ruth, who had planned the post-burial luncheon. It was one more obligation that seemed to prolong the difficulty of the day. She did not know how she would have managed all of this on her own. As it turned out, she had very little to do beyond taking care of herself and Sophie.

Sophie stood as still as a little black statue. She's so brave, adults said of her. The truth was, she had not yet understood that all of this ceremony meant her grandfather was gone from her forever. At the church and at the gravesite, she mewed quietly, but in the backseat of Robbie's car on the way home, the certainty that she would never see him again struck her like a pinch and she cried loudly for her Papa. Angel held her daughter close, her own tears now silently falling.

Angel thought about how her complex relationship with her father had changed over time. As a young child, she adored him and he adored her. They were her two peas in a pod, Mother often said. She remembered when she was sick with scarlet fever and he pulled a chair near her bed and read from the *Blue Fairy Book*. When she had measles he was away for the war, and as she lay in bed covered in the itchy rash, she missed him horribly. She knew her mother loved her, but sometimes Mother would be distant and cold. Sometimes Mother would lie in a dark room all day with a headache. But Father had never pushed her away. Angel had felt nothing but love from her father.

But after the war it was different. When he walked into the house in his uniform, leaning on his cane, the purplish scar on his chin, she had run to him: "Daddy, Daddy! You're home." She remembered her mother having to pull her away from his side that night, telling her it was time for bed. She was afraid he would go away again. "Never again, Angelina," he had said. "Never again."

But more and more he said he needed to be alone. He found things to fix or work on, and she was in the way. So from the time she was eight or nine years old, Angel spent less and less time with her parents. Of course she was older and she did not need them to watch her each minute.

Angel looked down at her daughter, whose head lay in her lap. She stroked Sophie's dark hair, her father's hair, and realized something else had changed during the war. Something harder to define. It was the way he used to look at her, the way he looked at Sophie, she suddenly realized. Exactly like that. Maybe such a look from a parent or a grandparent for a child is reserved only for small children. Maybe Angel had simply outgrown her right to that look. She didn't know about that, but she knew that for many years she longed to be outwardly loved by both of her parents, the kind of demonstrative love she got only from her grandparents.

Then, after the accident everything changed. It was after the accident that she, yes, it was she who had done it, that she closed off her heart to him. She knew that now. Why does it take years for people to understand why they do or say the things they do? He was driving too fast and it happened. She blamed him. He must have been as devastated as I was, she thought now.

Robbie swerved slightly to avoid a pothole. Jarred momentarily from her contemplation, Angel leaned nearer to Sophie and smiled weakly. Those years after the accident were a hard, hard time. She took a deep breath trying to calm her urge to cry, squeezed her eyes tightly and leaned her head back against the seat. They had stopped for a train. The signal lights flashed and clanged.

Angel remembered that for two weeks after the accident, she refused to go home, so she stayed with her grandparents until Frank came one Saturday morning and told her flatly, "You are coming home with me now." Wally and Grace did not argue. They agreed that the girl should be with her father, though Grace especially could see it would take months for the two to learn to live alone together. While each of them grieved, it must have been hardest of all on a young girl to lose her mother.

Oh, Sophie. Papa is dead. At twenty-seven years old, Angel felt like she was fifteen all over again.

The rest of that winter and into spring, Angel left things in the house as they were, not sure what to do, but eventually she realized it was silly for her to continue to share her small childhood bedroom with Sophie. On her day off, while Sophie was at school, Angel decided finally to clear out her father's room.

She began in his closet, folding clothes and layering them in paper grocery bags to take to St. Vincent de Paul. Angel slid a blue chambray shirt off the hanger and remembered she had bought this one for him last Christmas. Tags still hung off the cuff. What else had he never worn? The blue pinstripe? That was an expensive shirt. No tags. She remembered now, she'd made a big deal about him wearing that one, so he had worn it to Josef

Perlman's funeral. She held it to her face. It smelled like him. After all this time? It was harder for her to lay that one in the bag. At her hesitation, she reasoned it would be foolish to keep it.

Onto his chest of drawers now. In a tray on the top were his Sunday cufflinks that he had not worn in years, his military dog tags, and a string of pearls that belonged to her mother. She set all of these things on the bed in her "to save" pile.

She pulled open the next drawer and found two brand new shirts that had not even been removed from their plastic wrapper. "Dad," Angel said out loud, peevishly. "Ugh. I guess I should have stopped buying you shirts." Those gifts, she acknowledged, had never been personal, only easy.

In her father's nightstand, she found two paperbacks: *For Whom The Bell Tolls* and *The Long Goodbye*. She had rarely seen him reading anything other than the newspaper or a magazine now and then, but he must have. Inside, the books were inscribed: To Frank, Love, June. Then again, maybe he saved them for the inscription only. She would save them, read them one day. Mother would like that, wouldn't she? Or Sophie, the little reader that she was, would certainly like them. Angel decided she needed to begin a "save for Sophie" pile.

She looked around the room. It had taken her 45 minutes to sort through all of her father's personal belongings, at least those he kept in his bedroom. Someday Sophie would be going through her things too, keeping some, tossing most of it out, although Sophie would be an old lady by that time.

Angel lit a cigarette and popped open a cold bottle of Schlitz. She hauled the bags out to the garage. She would take them to the thrift store on Saturday. Maybe Sophie would like to help her.

Angel decided she would reuse her father's chest of drawers. There was no money to buy new bedroom furniture anyway. She could paint it someday if she felt like freshening it up. For now, she got a dishpan of warm, sudsy water and scrubbed down the insides of each drawer. She pulled the tissue out from the bottom drawer and found something she'd not seen before. "What's this?" she said out loud. She held up a small wooden box, about the size of a pack of cigarettes. An elephant amidst palm trees was carved onto the lid, which was hinged with tiny brass hinges. She lifted the lid and smiled widely. Inside, a key, nothing more. "Oh my god," Angel said. "I can't believe it." She knew immediately what it opened. Angel held the key before her eyes. The key's open oval head was stamped, but she couldn't make out what it said. Was it in Italian? The shaft was still smooth, not pitted, as were the two flag-like teeth. She had always liked the look of old keys. They stood in her mind for far-away places.

She remembered that horrible trip to Milwaukee for Grandmother Catalano's funeral and how she shivered in the cold while her dad and Uncle Robbie struggled to hoist the steamer trunk into the car. She had not wanted to go, but her father had forced her. He had said family is still family. She did not know what that had meant.

Angel remembered what her father had told her when he'd brought the trunk into the house the next day. "It belonged to my father. He was only twenty-two years old when he packed everything he owned in this trunk and set off for America, not knowing what the future had in store. That takes courage, don't you think, Angelina?"

Angel felt nervous—anxious but excited to unlock the old, black leather-and-brass steamer trunk at the foot end of her father's bed. She never really believed he kept only old blankets in there. Why would he keep it locked if that were the case? And now she would find out.

The cigarette pinched between her lips, Angel slid the key into the lock and turned. The lock clicked easily and the latch flipped open.

1964

Angel took the mail from Sophie, thanked her, and asked, as she always did, "How was school?" And as always, Sophie replied, "Fine." Angel usually didn't press for more. If things were not going well, she would hear about it.

"How's Ruth? Anything new with her and Lev?" Angel said as she tucked an envelope with a Fremont, California postmark into the pocket of her uniform apron. She hoped Sophie hadn't noticed it. Then she sorted through the rest of the mail: utility bill, phone bill, a card from her bosses, a postcard offering 5% off new windows. In December?

Sophie answered her mother's question. "They're fine. Nothing new. Oh, well, Ruth got her hair dyed today. It was supposed to take away the gray, but it looks kinda purple-y. I told her it looked nice. She said she didn't know."

Angel smiled. Plenty of older women came into Alexanders with various tints in their hair. The blue fairies, she called one group of widows who met regularly for breakfast on Fridays. They were generous tippers and were never condescending like some old ladies could be.

"Well, it's just hair. It is probably just a rinse, not permanent, so it will wash out soon."

"Yeah. A rinse. That's what she said."

She opened the card from Alexanders. It was religious, as always, a manger scene crowned by a deep blue, star-filled sky, the Christmas star the brightest, flecked with gold glitter. Inside it read, *For unto you is born this day in the city of David a Saviour, which is Christ the Lord.* Hand written below was *A blessed Christmas to you and Sophia from your Alexanders family.* Angel set the card on top of the curio cabinet next to the secular holiday card from Ruth and Lev, which featured a lovely snow-filled landscape, fir trees adorned with colored lights, and inside a simple *Seasons Greetings* in a brush script. Angel liked that the Perlmans, who did not celebrate Christmas, always mailed them a card instead of hand delivering it, and that they always bought Angel and Sophie a small gift for the house. Maybe her favorite gift from them was the four-foot-long, red mesh stocking full of candy they gave Sophie every year, and even though Sophie was nearly too old for such a gift, the girl always reacted as if they had given her a diamond ring.

Later, Angel warmed up the rest of the casserole that Ruth had made for them yesterday. Even though Angel had insisted she didn't have to feed them, Ruth would not hear of it. She knew how hard it must be now without Frank and she wanted to do it for them. And honestly, Ruth's toss-together meals were so delicious, not to mention the fact that she didn't have to cook, that Angel accepted gratefully. She was not looking forward to the inevitable day when she would have to do it all on her own again. After being at the restaurant all day, the last thing she wanted to do was cook.

After they'd eaten and cleaned up, they watched TV, *Mr. Novak*, a show about an English teacher that for some reason Sophie liked. Well, that young actor James Franciscus was awfully good looking. Maybe that was it, though Angel did not like to think that her nine-year-old daughter was already thinking about the opposite sex. Later, after Sophie was in bed, Angel would watch *Peyton Place*, which she liked. It was far-fetched, certainly, but entertaining. And yet Angel often fell asleep during the show, so she rarely saw how things turned out. It didn't matter. The other girls at work were hooked on the show, too, so they would fill her in.

Sometimes after Sophie was in bed, Angel would treat herself to a glass of wine or a vodka and seltzer and read a magazine. Tonight it was wine. No TV. And the card. Angel slid the letter opener under the flap and zipped it across neatly. There was no return address, just the postmark, but she knew who had sent it.

The card featured a Western Santa Claus wearing a cowboy hat and sitting atop a horse. He looked like Hoss Cartwright with a white beard, and his saddlebags were bulging with toys. Angel snickered at the silly card. Guess that's California, she thought. Inside, the card read: *Be dadburned good this year guys and gals, or Santa will not ride up your trail. Merry Christmas.*

The piece of loose-leaf notebook paper was folded into fourths.

Dear Angelina,

I heard your dad passed away. I hope you believe me. I am real sorry to hear it. I know he didn't care to much for me, but I am sure it was not easy for you or the kid.

I still think of you. I hope you are doing okay. I am. I just wanted to send my condolinces. Tell Sophia hello from her old dad. I know you don't want me to, and I know I ain't got a right, but sometimes I think I would like to see her. She probly looks all grown up by now.

This $5 bill is for her if you want to buy her a present from me. Merry Christmas, Ruben

Oh why did he even have to write? Angel thought. She guessed it was nice of him to contact her about her dad. Obviously someone from here had let him know. Angel sighed, folded the letter, and tucked it back in the card, which she slid into the envelope and back into her pocket. If he really wanted to do something nice, he could divorce her and pay child support.

Five bucks? She considered her daughter asleep in her room, completely unaware that 2,000 miles away her father was thinking about her. She tucked the cash into her pocket, too. Maybe a Barbie? Or some new Barbie clothes. She might tell Sophie that Papa had bought it for her before he died? Or maybe she would just put it in her petty cash jar. Fewer problems that way. Yeah. She didn't need this hanging over her head right now. Without her dad, it was going to be a shitty enough Christmas.

1977

While Angel would generally be asleep at 2:00 in the afternoon, today she was agitated, even anxious, which had put Sophie out of sorts. Sophie had woke that morning with a stuffy nose, and now she ached all over. All she wanted was a nap.

"You should be sleeping, Mom."

"I know. I will, but first I have to talk to you about something."

"About what?" Even Sophie heard the impatient tone in her own voice.

"Well," Angel said, "if it's that much trouble...."

"Oh, come on. Don't be that way."

Angel huffed.

"I'm sorry. Okay? I'm just tired."

Angel said she understood.

As directed, Sophie opened the desk drawer and found the envelope she'd been sent to find. She knew darn well it hadn't been in the drawer last week, when she'd taken out a slip of notepaper to start a grocery list. Sophie headed back to Angel's bed and held the envelope out to her.

"No, you take it. And sit down."

Sophie did as she was told and thankfully was able to make herself comfortable on the couch.

Angel squinted and drew in a sharp breath, then exhaled slowly. She rested her hands on her abdomen, closed her eyes, and took several slow, deep breaths. Then she looked at Sophie, who was feeling self-conscious. She had a feeling what this talk was going to be about, and she'd almost rather it did not have to happen.

"Okay, so after that first fun visit to the doctor when we got the happy news, I realized I should make a will, so nearly as soon as I sent you back to school, I called the lawyer I met with after your grandpa died. So I called, but I found out he was retired. Wouldn't you know it?"

Long story short, Sophie thought to herself.

"Well, so, anyway, I got an appointment with a different lawyer. Young guy. Boy is he good looking." Angel held her chin down and looked into Sophie's eyes. "I told him about you, Sophie. But I found out he's already married."

"Mother, please," Sophie said, rolling her eyes.

"Sophie, please." Angel mimicked her daughter, then laughed. "Married or not, he was very helpful. Now, don't get too excited Sophie. You know I'm not rich. As for things, there's not much that's worth anything in this house. Oh, there is the furniture Dad made, the dishes, other keepsakes from my mother and my grandparents, mostly sentimental value I suppose. And God knows I could have been less of a penny pincher and got a few new things now and then, but that's not the point. The point is…."

Angel winced again and gasped audibly. Sophie checked her wristwatch and realized she had missed her mother's medication time by nearly an hour. No wonder she was in pain. Sophie bolted to the kitchen and fumbled in her haste with the pill bottle.

"We can do all of this another time, Mother," said Sophie, as Angel swallowed her pill. "Really. It can wait, can't it?"

"Wait for what, Sophie. If you hadn't noticed, one of us is running out of time. I just have to tell you about a few things. Then I'll rest. I promise."

Sophie nodded. "Okay, but if you get worse, we will stop."

Angel nodded, then continued her speech. "Sophie, I know you don't know this, which is why I'm telling you now. There is money in a fund for you. Your papa started it when you were born. I don't mean the money he gave you for college. This is separate. Apparently, the lawyer said, he'd been putting all the rent money I paid him over the years into the account as well. The old sneak."

Sophie worked consciously to mask her astonishment. How much money? she thought.

"So you'll have to go see them, the lawyers, about that trust fund. They also have the deed to the house and the title for the car."

"I also have a small life insurance policy. Usually a person doesn't get much benefit from those, but I guess you're the lucky winner. Point being, you won't have to worry about money. Unless you do something stupid with it, but you wouldn't."

Sophie's head was spinning. Insurance policies, funds, money. All these years they had lived so meagerly, her mother's self-denial practically a source of pride, but it made sense, sort of. Actually, it made no sense.

"His name is Arthur Haber, the lawyer. His card should be...."

Sophie slid it out from under a paper clip and held it up.

"Good. Now he's been paid for your first meeting with him, so don't let him charge you again."

Sophie smiled. Her mother had even thought of that?

"If you need help, I'm sure you can ask Lev."

"I might need to," Sophie said, knowing she was far more comfortable with words than with numbers. She could not help imagining herself in the good-looking lawyer's wood-paneled office, him sitting behind his massive mahogany desk, looking sympathetically at her—

"You listening?" Angel said.

"Yes. Of course," Sophie said quickly. "This is all just a lot to think about."

"You can say that again," Angel said.

The bright morning had started out warm and muggy, and now the outside temperature was 81 degrees. The humid air had settled into the house, making everything, even the papers Sophie held in her lap, feel wet.

The drapes began to billow. Out the window, tree tops waved wildly.

"It looks like a storm coming," Sophie said, and she got up to close the windows.

"Oh, let's leave them open a while, can't we?" Angel pleaded. "It's so stuffy."

"It might rain in," Sophie said as she turned on a lamp.

"It might, but a little rain won't hurt anything," Angel said. "And it will smell so good. I love summer rain. Did I ever tell you, Sophie? I used to be able to smell rain way before it got here. When I was little, I'd smell it and tell my mom and dad. At first they'd tell me that no one can smell rain. 'Look at the sky,' my mother said. 'It's not going to rain.' And later, when it did, then they believed me."

Just then, thunder rattled the house. Sophie stuck her head out the front door and looked off to the west. The sky was as black as night. "Mom. I think we should." Sophie thought about what she would do if the tornado siren sounded. There would be no way she'd be able to get her mom to the basement. At the very least, maybe she could try to get her into the bathroom, away from the big picture window. In that bed if the window broke....

"Mom. I think this can wait. The storm is...."

Angel responded sharply, "No. It can't wait. Sit down and let me finish. It's just a storm. I've been through worse."

Sophie felt she had been scolded. All she was trying to do was help.

"Sorry. Didn't mean to bark. At least I didn't bite," Angel joked.

Sophie sighed.

"Oh, come on honey. Don't be so sensitive."

Sophie did not appreciate the tone. She wasn't being sensitive. She was being sensible.

"Just finish then. I'm listening. What else?"

"Well, it's about my funeral. The white envelope in there."

Another tremendous burst of thunder, louder than Sophie imagined thunder could be, rumbled long and loud. The lightning strike flashed upon their faces.

"Most important," Angel continued, "it's all planned. And paid for. There's nothing you need to do except call Roland Wilson at the funeral home right away. He told me that's all you'll need to worry about. He'll take care of everything. His phone number is on the main page of those documents."

The drapes filled with air but, constrained by Angel's bed, did not fly like flags over the living room. The rain hit the roof, pounding at the shingles.

"It's raining monkeys and parrots out there," said Sophie, using Great Grandpa Schneider's silly twist on the old phrase.

"Smells wonderful, though, doesn't it?" Angel said, breathing in the sweet, clean smell she loved. Things like this she would miss. How life sometimes smelled so good. Rain. Cinnamon. Roses. Pumpkin pie in the oven. And life so beautiful to look at, too. Even this storm. She imagined it. Dark, billowing, blowing leaves and twigs all over the neighborhood. It was hard to not think of it as a kind of beauty.

"Listen, Sophie. I need you to understand all of this." She paused and looked into her daughter's face with an earnestness that Sophie could feel. Sophie's face warmed and her pulse raced.

"I was younger than you when my mother died," Angel continued. "I have never, ever, been able to forget her funeral. It was horrible. They made me look at her in the casket. And she didn't look at all like my mom. Worst of all, my father made me kiss her goodbye. I didn't want to. He told me that if I didn't kiss her goodbye, I would regret it forever, so he made me." In a moment more Angel added, "She was so cold."

Sophie did not know what to say, but she felt just then almost motherly, and instinctually, she felt the urge to hold her mother tightly in her arms. Instead, Sophie quietly said, "Oh, Mom. That's awful." She did not move an inch.

"I knew I did not want any of that for you. I know I've told you this before, but it's in writing now. No casket for me. No one, but especially not you, will be gawking at my ugly, dead face. They're going to cremate me and put my ashes in a vase. Later you can scatter me somewhere, or not. It won't matter to me."

Sophie scowled.

"What?" Angel said.

"I just don't like talking about this," Sophie said.

"Well it isn't exactly my top choice of sparkling conversation either."

"Sorry."

"Don't be. I would feel the same if I were you. I wish we didn't have to talk about it. Sorry. Anyway. I'm done. That's it. I just wanted you to know all of this now, while I still have my wits about me."

"Oh, Mom. When have you ever had your wits about you?"

"You brat!" Angel said and then laughed. "I love you."

The rain had stopped. And the drapes hung still. The sky had begun to lighten. "See? Just a little ole storm," Angel said. "Nothing to be afraid of, my little Sophie."

Sophie leaned down and kissed her mother on the forehead. Before Sophie could rise, Angel slipped her arms around her daughter and held her there, as tightly as her weak arms could manage. She whispered in Sophie's ear, "I don't want to die."

Sophie whispered back, "I know. I know."

1964

A week before Christmas, the restaurant was busier than usual. Downtown shoppers weighted down with bulging bags were stopping in the diner for coffee or a late lunch. Cindy had called in sick, again, so Angel had started work early. Practically the entire day she had run from table to table, sometimes forgetting to breathe. She glanced quickly at her watch, puffed out her breath, and told herself to hang in there. She had only an hour and a half to go.

At a corner booth designed for six, two women looked over their menus. The elder of the two, dressed in a smart blue skirt and jacket, wore a pillbox hat. The younger, a fiery redhead, was dressed more casually, almost as if she had not intended to leave the house. Angel smiled broadly as she set two glasses of water on the table. She greeted the women and recited the day's special: "an open-faced beef sandwich on toast, slathered in homemade gravy." The gravy was actually something new the boss was trying, from a can, but it said homemade on the label so….

"Is it you, Angelina?" the redhead said. "It is, isn't it?"

Angel cocked her head quizzically.

"Janet. Janet TerMat. From high school?"

Angel smiled. "Well, hi there. Of course. Sorry. I'm just—how are you?" How did Angel not recognize Janet immediately with that hair? Tamer now, in high school it moved about her head like Medusa's snakes.

"I am well, thank you. Angel, I'd like you to meet my mother, Betty. She's treating me to dessert today. Isn't that decadent?"

Angel wiped her greasy hand on the skirt of her ice-blue uniform before extending it. As for that, her appearance on the whole was less fresh than she wished it were, especially to greet a face from the past. How light and lovely Janet looked.

"How are things, Angelina?" Janet asked.

"As you can see, working mom." She laughed uneasily.

"Oh, you're a mom? How great. Boy or girl? Or maybe one of each? Where's your husband work? Do I know him?"

The questions shot out of Janet's cannon mouth and Angel felt wounded by them.

"One. Girl. She just turned nine. Her dad died in a car accident," Angel blurted out. "We were living in California at the time. After that, well, I guess I just missed home too much, and my dad, so we moved back. He. Not sure if you saw it in the paper, but he just died. My dad, I mean."

Betty squirmed. They'd come in for pie, not this woman's tragic story.

"I'm so sorry to hear that," Janet said, then hung her head slightly. When she looked up again, Angel shifted the mood for which Janet was grateful.

"Thanks. Anyway, enough about me. What are you up to?"

Janet said her husband was now a full partner in a local law firm.

"Wow. That's great. You must be proud." Angel suddenly felt stupid. "Well, so, you didn't come in here to chat all afternoon. What can I get you? Not sure what you like, but the pecan pie is scrumptious."

Janet and Betty felt they owed it to Angel somehow to accept her recommendation, so they ordered pecan pie à la mode. They left her an extravagant tip, which made Angel feel even dirtier.

At home, after she kicked off her shoes and rubbed the bunion on her right foot, Angel unscrewed the vodka bottle, not at all concerned that it was only 3:30 in the afternoon.

1964

Years later Sophie would drive the route from her house to the nursing home where her Girl Scout troop had been singing Christmas carols and discover that what she had thought was five miles was really only 15 blocks. At the time, those blocks had seemed endless.

Camille's mom had asked again as Camille climbed into the back seat of their car if she couldn't drive Sophie home, too. "No trouble, of course." Camille lived four blocks to the east of Sophie and her mom. Sophie and Camille were friends in school, too.

Sophie shook her head no. "Thanks anyway. My mom is coming, and I better wait for her."

As they drove off, Camille rolled down the window and leaned out to yell, "See you in school tomorrow, freckle face."

Sophie stood outside the glass front doors of the nursing home in the spotlight of a soft yellow overhead light. She waved back, hoping she was right, hoping her mom would be there any minute to get her. She tugged her mittens on, pulled her hood up, and began humming the tune from her favorite carol, which they had sung so well this afternoon. Then she sang quietly, "What child is this who, laid to rest, on Mary's la-ap, is sle-e-ping." Car headlights lit the black street, wet from the falling snow that melted as it hit the pavement. At five o'clock it was so dark it might as well have been midnight.

"Whom angels gre-et with anthems sweet, While sh-e-pherds watch are kee-ping?" She knew she sang well. Her music teacher had told her she had a clear, natural voice. Sophie thought back over the party as she waited there, starting to feel the cold. Besides singing carols, the girls had helped the old men and women decorate their tree. They served them cookies and punch and delivered hand-made cards. Sophie had decorated each of her cards with multicolored sequins, which she used as ornaments on her crayon trees.

Sing it two more times, Sophie told herself. Then she'll be here. But after the third time, it was clear that Mom was not just late.

Sophie began to walk. She felt sure she knew how to get home. She could see the steeple of St. Paul's. Her house was not too far from there. She looked up at the dark, hazy sky, gray clouds lit by streetlights.

This was the shortest day of the year, they'd learned in school. Ritchie had pushed Sophie out of the way so he could be the first one to trace with his finger the lines on the globe that divided the world in half. They were called hemispheres. Sophie giggled out loud remembering Ritchie's answer to Mrs. Greene's question: "Which hemisphere do we live in, boys and girls?"

Everyone laughed when he'd shouted out "The south one." Sabrina got to write "solstice" on the chalkboard, even though Sophie had wanted to do that. "Solstice" was a nice word, she thought. It was fun to say. "S-O-L-S-T-I-C-E," she spelled out loud.

Sophie watched carefully as she stood at the intersection of 8th Street and National Avenue, waiting until no cars were in sight before she crossed, still hoping the next car would be Mom's. A sudden, sharp wind blew Sophie's hood off her head, so she stopped, took her mittens off, and tied her hood strings tighter. It was getting colder. She thought maybe she could run a little and get home faster, but then she tripped on a bump in the sidewalk. She stood up, embarrassed. She felt certain the drivers in the passing cars were laughing at her. She'd torn a big hole in the left knee of her tights, and the hole's frayed, white edges colored slightly with blood.

In some parts of the world on the shortest day of the year, her teacher said, people celebrated. Sophie thought about the pictures her teacher had shown them and wondered how you could build a fire in snow. Wouldn't the fire melt the snow, and then wouldn't the water put out the fire?

Camille's house had a fireplace, but it wasn't a real one. They turned it on with a switch. Even so, the flames were warm. They got to have it on one night when she had slept over. Camille said it was just like camping. Sophie didn't know what camping felt like. Angel thought sleeping outside on the ground was a ridiculous idea. "Why on earth would we go camping?" she had said when Sophie asked her once if they could go.

Sophie began to feel like she'd been walking a long time, though she had no way of knowing how long it had been. She wished she had boots on. Her feet were cold and her toes were numb. She jumped up and down a couple of times thinking her feet would feel better, but it did not help.

Soon she began to see houses and places she knew. Sophie passed the little corner grocery where her mom sometimes bought bread and cigarettes. She wasn't far from home now. Sophie had fallen last time she had tried to run, so she did not do that again. Instead, she walked as fast as she could. The snow fell heavier now. Fluff balls like dandelion flowers fell upon her. Warm yellow lights from the houses she passed flooded out onto the lawns. Colored lights tacked to gutters or strung on trees glowed in the dark. Her mittens were soaked through now, and her fingers burned.

When Sophie reached her house, all the lights were off. Not even the porch light was on. Bubbe's house glowed like a jack o' lantern, and she would go there if her mother were not home.

Inside she stepped into the warmth of her house and took off her wet coat, mittens, and hat. She took off her shoes and her soaking wet tights. Her red hands burned hotter now. Just then she heard her mother gasp for air, as if she had stopped breathing, and Sophie realized her mom was on the couch.

Sophie tiptoed to her mother, who was still dressed in her uniform.

The ice in her empty vodka glass had not fully melted yet. Carefully, so she wouldn't wake her, Sophie covered her mother with the afghan. In the dark, Sophie made her way down the hall to her room. She turned on her bedside lamp and changed into her nightgown. She was getting warmer now. Sophie slipped her feet into her slippers and made her way to the kitchen. The glow from her bedroom gave her enough light to manage, so she decided not the turn the kitchen light on. Sophie made herself a peanut butter and jelly sandwich and poured herself some milk. There was only about half a glass of milk left. She shrugged her shoulders and was glad she wasn't that hungry. They'd had frosted Christmas cookies at the party. Sylvia's mom had made them. She had piped zigzag frosting garland on the trees and used little silver candy balls for the ornaments. When Sophie's mom frosted cookies, she just smeared it on. "They don't have to be fancy to taste good," Angel would say.

Sophie closed her bedroom door, not all the way. She left it open just enough to hear her mother's snoring, just enough to hear if she needed help, and slid under the covers. She realized it was too early to go to sleep, so she read her favorite Lois Lenski book, *Strawberry Girl*, for about an hour until her eyes got heavy. Then she put the book away and turned out the light. She tried to sleep, but she couldn't. It was still early, still before her normal bedtime. And she was angry with her mother. No one else's mom forgot their kid. Camille's mom probably had a chicken in the oven or maybe even just grilled cheese and tomato soup. Sophie had dry bread and peanut butter and hardly any milk.

Sophie lay on her side, pulled up her knees, hugged them, and sighed. She closed her eyes and decided she would imagine a different ending to the day. This was something she had begun to do lately, especially when Mom was having a bad night. She would curl up on her bed, close her eyes tightly, and pretend something else. It was like she was writing a different story for her life and she got to choose everything. She could make her mom be happy. And she could imagine a dad.

Sophie imagined that Mom had picked her up, just like she had promised, and when Sophie got home, she practiced her spelling words, getting them all right, just like she always did. Mom had a pork roast in the Dutch oven, not her favorite, but Dad loved it, especially with applesauce on the side. Sophie added that detail because Papa loved that dinner. After dinner, she and her parents would watch TV for a bit. *Bewitched* was her favorite. Aunt Clara was funny. If she were a witch, Sophie thought, she'd wriggle her nose and really, truly make her life perfect.

In this story she imagined it was bath night. Sophie took a deep breath and saw herself all alone in the bathroom, redone how she would like it, aqua seahorses on the shower curtain, a fluffy white towel to dry with, and a bubble bath, something she was rarely allowed. An overflowing capful of Mr. Bubble added to the water first, the rush of water pounding into the pink gel made mounds of glistening bubbles. Sophie lowered herself into the tub and slid down so the water and bubbles covered her shoulders, then she submerged her head, felt her hair fan out in the water. She was a mermaid, fluttering her feet, her tail, in the foam. Lathering her hair with shampoo meant the bubbles would disappear, pop, popping one at a time, retreating like a wave on a beach. So she would wait awhile before she did that and make shapes out of the bubbles. But then the water got cold, so she washed and rinsed her hair. Sadly she lifted the lever and listened to the water gurgle down the drain. She wrapped her hair in a towel, like her mother did. And by the time she was finished brushing her teeth, her hair would be at least a little bit dry.

She pictured herself wearing a brand new pink polka dot flannel nightgown with ruffled cuffs and hem. Then she got into her bed, a full-sized bed, not a twin, yes, a big bed with a canopy, a white eyelet canopy, her menagerie of stuffed animals at the foot. Sophie would snuggle under the covers and make room for Dad, who sat on the edge of her bed.

"All set there, sweetie?" he would say, or maybe he'd call her "honey," but he would use a word that was not her name. And then he would say they had time only for one story tonight as he was tired himself, but it would always turn into two stories. She pictured herself snuggling next to him, his deep voice humming inside her as he read. And she'd feel the warmth of her father's body radiating into hers. Breathe in his smell, not like her own Prell or Mr. Bubble smell. She thought he might smell like leaves.

"Sophie?" came a weak call from the living room. Sophie's skin prickled with anxiety.

"Sophie, baby…?"

Would her mother be sick, like after Papa's funeral, and tell her to quickly get the dishpan from the kitchen? Would she have to help her to the bathroom, where she would throw up again? Would she have to listen to her mother cry and say how sorry she was? Would she have to listen to things she did not understand, about how life was not fair, or worse, about how she wished she had never married Sophie's father?

"Sophie?"

The child slid from bed, a twin bed with no canopy, and with bare feet on the wood floor, she plodded out to the living room. Moonlight weakly lit the hallway, but Sophie's eyes were already adjusted to the dark. Sophie thought then about her fall. She'd not been hurt badly, but what if she had been? What if she had not been able to walk? What if she had been lying on the sidewalk all alone?

What if I had needed you, Mom? the girl asked herself. What if I had been sick?

Sophie stood near her mother now and willed herself to respond kindly. "What do you need? Are you sick?"

Angel reached out and rubbed her hands against her daughter's legs. "You've been in bed? Jammies on, right? Did you remember to brush your teeth?"

Of course she remembered. She remembered everything. The next morning her mother would not remember that she had needed her daughter's help to get into bed. She would not remember that she had forgotten to pick her up from Girl Scouts or that she had never made dinner. She would not remember any of it. In a way, Sophie preferred the forgetfulness because it meant that she did not have to listen to the apology, did not have to feel that she should say something that would make her mother feel better. It was just easier.

1965

Clouds and freezing drizzle had made themselves at home for the past week and a half, so when the sun finally broke through late in the morning on Wednesday, Angel's day off, it was as if a light had been turned on in a dark room with no time for her eyes to adjust.

It wasn't just her eyes that needed time to adjust. Angel had been, like most people after a long, dreary winter, a victim of her own sluggishness, and while the golden glow brought her a rush of happiness, she needed a bit more than a clear blue sky to get herself moving. After all, the thermometer said it was still only about 40 degrees, and snow remained hunkered down in low, shady spots. March could be a cruel month in Sheboygan. True spring would not arrive until late April, if then.

Her goal was to wash the dishes she'd let stack up in the sink, pick up the clutter, and run the vacuum. First, she opened the living room drapes as wide as they'd go, scattering dust motes into new territory. I should wash the windows, too, she thought, but she knew another year would pass before she even considered that possibility again. One thing at a time. Emerging from hibernation doesn't happen in an instant. She cranked up the radio, blasting "You've Lost That Lovin' Feelin'."

Committed to doing a thorough job, Angel tossed all the old magazines in the trash, wondering what on earth she'd saved them for. Most were old hand-me-downs from the restaurant anyway. Maybe she thought she would try out a new recipe or two. But that had not happened. She found a nearly-empty can of Pledge under the kitchen sink and used a clean dust rag to polish the end tables, taking extra care with the two valuable pieces of furniture she owned—a honey pine side table, which she kept next to her father's chair, and the black walnut coffee table. Her father had made them both, one for his mother and one for his wife. They were hers now and would be Sophie's one day.

Next, Angel ran the vacuum over the carpet. Getting her arms into the motion, back and forth, felt like dancing. The sun now poured aggressively into the small, off-white living room, and Angel was hot. She tossed her sweatshirt on the gold chair and cranked open one of three small windows under the picture window.

"Oh man, it smells so good. Spring air. Yes!" Angel shouted over the music.

She decided it would be a good idea to get under the couch, so she pushed the coffee table out of the way and pushed the sofa back so she could vacuum under it. Popcorn seeds ping-pinged as she sucked up the detritus from months of neglect. Might even have been last spring that she'd moved the couch, she thought, feeling a bit ashamed, but no one would know. She sure couldn't brag about her housekeeping skills to anyone. She put the attachment on the Hoover and lifted each of the three cushions, one at a time, finding forty cents, more old maids, and a red crayon broken in half. She ran the brush over the cushions, the arms and the back of the couch, too, all the while singing along to the radio.

"We can forget all our troubles, forget all our cares. So go downtown. Things will be great when you're downtown—"

Angel did not hear the doorbell ring, not the first time, not the third. When she eventually pivoted the vacuum, she saw Ruth Perlman standing inside her house on the rug near the front door, a worried look on her face.

Angel waved, turned off the vacuum cleaner, and then, begrudgingly, the music.

"Sorry to let myself in," Ruth said. "I rang and rang."

"Oh, no. That's fine. I guess I had it cranked up pretty loud. What can I do for you?" Angel asked, barely concealing her annoyance.

Ruth thrust a business-sized brown envelope toward her neighbor. "In my mailbox by mistake, I'm afraid. I thought it might be important."

Angel pushed the hank of bangs off her forehead as she took the envelope and quickly scanned the return address. Only paperwork from her father's lawyer. She got quarterly reports from them.

"Thanks," Angel said, quickly, wondering why Ruth looked at her so queerly. Of course. Ruth would know that Schuster, Shulman, and Haber was a law firm. What fantasy would she be cooking up in her brain right now, Angel wondered.

"Well thanks for bringing it over. Mailman must have been asleep, eh?"

"Angel," Ruth hesitated, looking around as if she agreed that the place surely did need to be cleaned. "Not bad news I hope."

Ruth looked down at her shoes, then back into her neighbor's eyes. In Ruth's experience, letters from lawyers rarely brought good news.

"Now Angel, I know I probably shouldn't say this, but if there's anything wrong and you need...if you need help?" Ruth would do anything for Sophie. She would never have offered, except she worried that whatever the problem was, the child would be affected.

"Oh, this? No," Angel laughed. "Nothing bad. My dad set up a small trust fund for Sophie and they send me reports." Why was she explaining? Her finances were none of Ruth's business.

Ruth felt embarrassed. "I...well, of course. I didn't mean to pry. I...it just seemed important is all."

"Oh, I know. I would have done the same thing," Angel said, willing Ruth to go home now.

Ruth felt awkward. She wished she had kept the envelope and let Lev deliver it when he got home on Saturday. "I see I've interrupted you. I'll just get going."

Angel thanked her again. "Yeah, I should finish cleaning. I want to get to the store before Sophie comes home from school. I'm going to make her favorite dinner tonight, and we're out of a few things."

"That's awfully nice of you," said Ruth.

Of course it's nice of me, Angel thought. I'm her mother. I do nice things. Angel did not know why she always felt defensive around Ruth. Ruth was never anything but kind to her and Sophie. But somehow Angel felt that she did not measure up in Ruth's eyes.

Angel shut the door after Ruth left and watched from the sidelight as her neighbor walked with cautious steps down the front sidewalk. Suddenly Ruth wobbled and tossed her arms in the air. Then she was on the ground, looking back at Angel, pain in her eyes.

"Oh, shit," Angel shouted. She let the envelope fall to the floor as she rushed outside to where Ruth had fallen. "Oh my god, Ruth. Are you okay? Do you hurt anywhere?"

Ruth held her ankle and cried, "Owww. Owww, it hurts. Oy, what a baby I am, but it hurts." Ruth took a deep breath, squinted, then shaded her eyes and looked up at Angel who was kneeling down beside her. "Can you? Angel. If you can just help me home?"

"Of course. Then I'll call Lev. Or I can just stay with you until he gets home?" Angel could see her plans were shot now, but there was nothing to be done about it. She was not going to leave Ruth on her own.

"Lev's out of town until Saturday," Ruth said.

"Well, then taking you home isn't going to work, is it?"

"I'll manage, Angel. If you can just...."

"Don't be ridiculous. I know you're a tough old lady, but you're not that tough. Come on. It's too cold out here." Angel helped Ruth to her feet, then put her arm around Ruth's waist. Ruth draped her arm over Angel's shoulder, leaning on her.

"Okay, easy now," Angel said, and they hobbled back up the walk to Angel's front door.

"I don't know what happened," Ruth said, breathing hard, keeping her left foot up, like a prancing horse.

"Oh, that sidewalk! It's uneven. All heaved up."

Once inside, Angel slipped off Ruth's shoes and helped her hop to the sofa. "You just sit and catch your breath." She disappeared down the hallway and returned with two bed pillows. "Okay, lie back on these. Let's get that ankle up," Angel said. She stuffed a throw pillow under the wounded ankle and removed Ruth's cotton anklet, a sock Angel felt was more befitting a child than a seventy-six-year-old woman. Angel palpated the ankle, compared the left to the right, and pronounced her diagnosis.

"It's swollen all right. Probably just a sprain. I'm going to put some ice on it, okay? If it still hurts this much later, I'll take you for an x-ray."

"Oh, I hate to be such a bother," Ruth said, reaching down to her ankle. "I'm sure you're right. Just a sprain," Ruth said. "I'll rest a bit, then I am sure I'll be able to manage on my own. I'm lucky it's my left ankle, 'cause I write with my right," she snickered. Angel smiled and patted Ruth's leg, then pulled the orange-and-white crocheted afghan off the back of the sofa, the one she'd folded so neatly an hour before, and laid it gently over her patient. Angel knew that with Lev out of town, there was not a chance she was sending the old woman home to manage on her own. It was bad enough she'd fallen in front of her house, but if she sent Ruth home and she fell, broke a hip, or worse, well…she was staying and that was that.

"You're being awfully kind, Angel. I'm lucky you were watching out for me."

"My fault really, isn't it?" Angel said from the kitchen as she cracked an ice tray into a bowl in the sink. She wrapped six or seven cubes into a clean dish towel, got a second towel for insulation, then returned to the living room and set the cold compress on Ruth's ankle.

"How is it your fault, my dear? I'm the clumsy one."

"If you hadn't had to bring the envelope over, you'd still be safe inside your house, enjoying this sunny day, right?" Angel said, adjusting the pillow under Ruth's head.

"I suppose it's the postman's fault then, wouldn't you agree?"

"I suppose it is," Angel said, and the two women laughed.

"You're a good nurse, you know. Ice feels good. How did you think to do that? I probably would have pulled out the heating pad."

"Believe it or not, I was enrolled in a nursing program for a bit. Didn't finish. I had to quit."

"Ohhh, that's too bad. Seems like nursing comes naturally to you."

Angel didn't want to talk about that regret, about how the life she hoped she'd have had turned slowly into the life she never would have dreamed of. Back in the kitchen, Angel ran the faucet to get cold water, which didn't take too long this time of year, and filled one of her mother's gold-rimmed highball glasses for her guest.

"Here are a couple of aspirin, which will help the swelling go down. You can just lay your head back. Okay? Feel comfortable? Considering?"

"I guess I will rest here a bit. Thank you for taking care of me. Go ahead and continue what you were up to. Never mind me. I'm used to cleaning noise."

"Well, I'll just finish this up and put the vacuum away. Sure you don't mind?"

Ruth waved her off. "I'm sure. I'll just close my eyes a while."

Angel quickly finished the living room carpet, steered the machine down the hallway, and parked it to use in her bedroom, which needed it. God only knew what lurked under her bed.

When Sophie came home around four o'clock, she found Ruth Perlman sleeping on the couch and her mother in the kitchen, scrubbing potatoes. Angel smiled, put her finger to her lips, and whispered, "shhhh."

On Sophie's part, the entire situation was more than unusual, and it begged a hundred questions. The first, of course, which she remembered to whisper, was "Why is Bubbe sleeping on the sofa?"

"Hello to you, too." Angel kept her voice low. She smiled, then kissed her daughter on top of her head. "She sprained her ankle out on the sidewalk, and I'm taking care of her. She came over to bring me a piece of mail that she got by mistake, and on her way home, that big bump got her.

How was school?"

"Okay. I think I got them all right on my multiplication test. It smells really good in here."

"I've been cleaning. Plus, I had the window open for a while to let in some fresh air." Angel didn't mention she had not had a cigarette all day, thinking she'd finally try to quit. Already, only hours into her decision, her nerves were regretting it. "I'm thinking of making meatloaf for dinner. I had planned on going to go to the store to get stuff for chop suey, just for you, but then…." She glanced over to the couch. "So, I'm thawing hamburger from the freezer and I've got three nice potatoes to bake, and a can of green beans. I thought we could invite Ruth for dinner. What do you think about that?"

To Sophie, having her mom make dinner, real dinner, and be in a good mood, was already perfect.

"Good idea, Mom. I can help."

Angel hugged her daughter, a bit too hard. "I'd like that, honey. For now why don't you go and change your clothes. You can wear that skirt and blouse to school one more day, can't you? Maybe you can clean up your room? I'll vacuum in there after you've picked up. We will put clean sheets on your bed for our guest, and you can sleep with me."

When Ruth woke nearly an hour later, she could not believe she'd slept so long. Her ankle, she decided, did feel better, and she was no longer worried it was broken. The drapes were closed and the living room lamps had been turned on. As Ruth glanced around her, she saw the same tidy room, everything in order. Nothing seemed to have changed since Frank's death. She took a deep, contented breath. The briefest hint of the morning's spring breeze lingered. Smells good, she conceded.

Sophie was on the floor on her stomach paging through the new Sears catalog on the lookout for summer clothes—a new swimsuit at the very least.

"There's our sleepy girl," said Angel, coming into the room, wiping her hands on a dishtowel. "How's the ankle?"

"Better, I think. My goodness, Angel, what time is it? I must have been more tired than I knew. I'm afraid I've overstayed my welcome."

Ruth grunted in an effort to sit up. "If you help me up, Angel, I'll get out of your hair." Angel helped Ruth sit up, then sat beside her.

"The house looks very nice, my dear."

"We even cleaned your room," Sophie said.

Angel answered Ruth's puzzled look. "She means her room, but for tonight, yours. We've decided you'll be our house guest, for dinner and a sleepover, and there's no sense arguing about it. I'd be too nervous about you if you were home all by yourself."

"Well, that's awfully kind, but you—"

"No arguing. You're staying. If Lev were home, it would be different. But he's not, so."

Ruth ended her resistance, laying a grateful hand on top of Angel's and thanking her.

After guiding Ruth to the bathroom, Angel helped reestablish their guest on the sofa. Angel put a new ice pack on Ruth's ankle, and Sophie fluffed and arranged the pillows and the afghan.

"My very own Florence Nightingale," Ruth said as she patted Sophie's hand. "You're taking such great care of me."

Sophie blushed and dipped her chin. Then smiling, "Would you like more water, Bubbe, or we have iced tea, or would you like…?"

"Water will do just fine, Sophie. I may have tea with dinner, which is starting to smell very good. Are you the chef?"

Sophie smiled and nodded affirmatively. "Well, I helped."

On television, Walter Cronkite was telling about Dr. Martin Luther King Jr., who had led Civil Rights activists in a march from Selma to Montgomery, Alabama.

"Those poor folks," Ruth said. "If I were younger, I just might march along with them. They've got just as much right to vote as we do."

Angel eyed Ruth with disbelief. Most old people she knew—well, some of the old men who spouted their opinions at Alexanders—said such hateful things. Negroes, though that's not the word they used, should know their place, and worse. Ruth surprised her. The news showed the marchers, women wearing lovely dresses, the men in suits and ties. They were orderly. Peaceful. They only wanted what everyone wanted. A right to decide about their own lives and what affected them.

"Beware the Ides of March," Ruth told Sophie. Bubbe was always saying confusing things like that.

"What?" Sophie said.

"Oh, just an old saying, but this March seems to be full of portent, full of something about to happen, I guess. And not a good something, it seems to me."

Angel had covered the Formica table in the kitchen with an ivory tablecloth she dug out of the linen closet. She smoothed the humps from the folds as best as she could, eyed the drop so it was even on all sides, and hid the small fraying hole mid center with a pewter candle holder and one white taper. She was in this for the full effect now—as if it were a holiday dinner—so she'd got out the step stool for the china she kept in the top cabinet.

"This is just lovely, Angel. And I'm still envious of your china. It is really striking. I am not used to such fine dining," she said, even though they both knew that was not true.

"Thank you," Angel said, feeling gracious. This dinner, just meatloaf and canned green beans, the house clean and everything in order. She should do this more, instead of heating up TV dinners or bringing home a pizza. She knew she should try harder for Sophie. But most of the time she was just too tired. More than that, there were plenty of days she just didn't care. "Thanks," she said. "I wanted it to be nice."

"And it is, isn't it Sophie? But you helped of course," Ruth winked.

After dinner, while Ruth and Sophie paged through the catalogue together, Angel went next door to get Ruth's nightie and toothbrush. At bedtime Angel turned back the pink chenille bedspread, and Ruth climbed into Sophie's bed. It was easy to see this room was as tidy as the rest of the house. A small bookcase held ten or so books, a couple of board games, a stuffed bear, an Etch a Sketch, and nothing else. On top of a lovely maple chest of drawers was a ballerina music box.

Sophie grinned broadly. "You comfy?" she asked.

"Quite 'comfy,' my dear. Yes, quite."

Angel said, "Now, Sophie, tell Mrs. Perlman goodnight and then it's time to brush your teeth and get in bed yourself. You're already up too late for a school night."

"Sleep tight, Bubbe. I'll see you in the morning." She leaned down and gave Ruth a big hug. Angel could not help but feel jealous of the obvious love between the two.

"Good night to you, too, Bubbala," Ruth said, giving Sophie one last squeeze.

Ruth's ankle still hummed a bit with pain, but she did not think it would keep her awake. She settled her white head on the pink pillowcase, and Angel, still standing over her, asked her if there was anything else she could do for her.

"No, dear. I'm fine."

"Good night, then. Just call out if you need me." Then Angel pulled the door behind her, leaving it open a few inches.

Later, in her own bed, Sophie sleeping soundly beside her, Angel remembered Grandma Schneider's house and the bedroom room where she slept. The twin beds in Sophie's room came from that bedroom. It was papered in tiny yellow roses. Gauzy Priscilla curtains criss-crossed over the windows, which were left open in summer, the sound of the lake reaching her if the night were still enough. The room smelled of furniture oil and dried rose petals. The white percale sheets were always crisp and cool and she loved to rub her bare feet against them. The pillowcases smelled like the sun.

And Grandma, never Grandpa, would put her to bed. Not her mother, either. Always Grandma. "Now Angelina," Grandma would say,

"You're going to be a good girl and sleep all night, aren't you? No bad dreams. Not in Grandma's house." And Angel would nod in agreement. Everything felt right.

In the soft scent of memory, Angel felt once again the warmth she had felt earlier in the rush of generosity that had come upon her when Ruth needed her. Today Angel had been more than a good neighbor. She had opened her heart, and it felt good.

1967

Ruth no longer had thoughts about pushing her son towards Angel. She had come to realize he would never marry. One afternoon a few months past, she'd been cajoling him as she sometimes did about meeting a nice Jewish girl and settling down when a sudden memory of her mother's brother Daniel brightened clearly in her mind. Daniel, light framed and sensitive Daniel. Suddenly it all made sense to her, though Ruth did not speak with Lev about her suspicion. She could not move into that uncomfortable sphere. But from that point on, instead of teasing him about getting married, she embraced him harder, loved him more, and appreciated more earnestly the sacrifice he had made for her.

After supper, Sophie asked to go outside to ride her bike while it was still light out. Ruth shooed her away with a swat of the dishtowel. How that girl has grown, Ruth thought. Before I know it, she's going to be a teenager. As she washed the dishes, Ruth stared out into the backyard and realized she missed watching Sophie through the kitchen window. Up until a couple of years ago, she could play for hours in the sandbox Frank and Joe had built for her when she was little, designing towns or fairy landscapes with hills and rivers, making use of twigs for bridges, small leafy branches or weeds for shrubs and trees. Ruth missed her little girl.

After hanging the dishtowel on the towel bar, Ruth looked back outside and was surprised to see Sophie lying on the grass, her ear to the ground. Still as a fallen tree she lay there, and not even the sound of the screen door clicking or Ruth's footsteps disturbed her.

Ruth bent near to Sophie and said quietly, "What are you doing? Is there something wrong?"

Sophie rolled to her back and shielded her eyes from the low, orange sun. "Nope. I was just listening. My teacher told us about the Chippewa Indians today. When they were near the shore of the river, they thought they could hear Lake Superior if they put their ear to the ground."

"Are you sure, dear? Lake Superior is awfully far away."

"Oh, yes. That's what she told us. And she said the name Sheboygan means that sound, the sound of the water underground. So I'm trying to see if I can hear it, but I can't. Maybe I'm not close enough to the river. But it's supposed to be a loud sound."

Ruth smiled. Surely Sophie got some part of the story wrong, but she loved the earnestness with which she believed the legend. "I'll admit I never wondered what Sheboygan meant. I suppose I just wasn't curious enough to find out."

"We're learning all about our county and who lived here a long time ago. Did you know that before it was a city, Sheboygan was a village? But what is a village? Does that mean it was very small?"

"Didn't you raise your hand to ask your teacher?"

Sophie shook her head. "I never raise my hand."

"You don't?" Ruth said, dismayed to think Sophie might be timid in school. "But you must, Sophie. If you want to know something, you have to ask."

Sophie, now sitting, responded with a shrug. Ruth reached for Sophie's hand and helped her to her feet. "It's cooling off a bit now, isn't it? What about a piece of lemon pie, like I promised?"

In the kitchen, Sophie laid the dessert forks on the green ivy tablecloth and poured ice water into squat glass tumblers for each of them. Ruth set the plates on the table and the ladies seated themselves.

"Now. A village, Sophie. I think a village is smaller than a town and much smaller than a city. But, now that I think about it, I have no idea what a village is in specific terms."

"That's okay. It doesn't really matter."

"You know what matters to me?"

Her mouth full of meringue, Sophie shook her head.

"It matters to me that you do well in school. I don't like to think that you don't raise your hand to ask about things you don't know. Why don't you, Sophie?"

Sophie blushed and shrugged. She didn't know what to say. She just didn't. That's all. It wasn't a big deal. "We don't…nobody does," Sophie tried to explain.

It had been a long time since Ruth's school days in Milwaukee. Perhaps she and her classmates had been no different. She couldn't remember. Were she to be in school again, Ruth knew she would be asking questions constantly. Children grew out of childhood far too soon, Ruth lamented. Lev had been such a curious boy, and then, suddenly, one day he wasn't. Even now she missed his little four-year-old "why?" questions and the joy she found in answering them. She wasn't like some parents who softened life or made up silly stork stories. She didn't force ugliness upon him, either, but when he had asked what "Nazi" meant, she told him. Later Joe had chastised her for doing so. "Children should not hear such things," he'd said. Maybe he was right. And yet Ruth believed children ought to know the truth about life. It was one thing to know where the name of one's city comes from, but who teaches children how to manage their lives? Parents who work? Who neglect? No, not neglect. Angel never meant to ignore Sophie.

"Can I have another piece of pie?" Sophie asked with a pleading look.

"I think not dear. Too much sugar will make both of us fat. And before your mother gets here, I'd like to put my feet up. How about you read a bit of Anne to me before she rings the bell. I've forgotten if Matthew brought Anne home to Marilla yet?"

"Okay," replied Sophie, a bit disappointed about the pie. She folded her linen napkin, left it on the table, and carried her plate and fork to the counter.

"I'll wash those up with the breakfast dishes. Go ahead and get our book, why don't you."

The lamp on the end table glowed yellow on the pages of *Anne of Green Gables*, which was part of a set of books that Ruth and Joe had purchased for Sophie. On the green cover, an illustration of Anne Shirley with her vibrant red hair was framed in embossed gold. Ruth drew Sophie close to her on the sofa, not just to see the pages better, but also because she coveted the warmth, the nearness, and the link to fading childhood. Beyond that, Sophie read so well, and it was a joy to listen to her. At times, Ruth thought Sophie could have been that orphaned girl—or nearly so.

Ruth expressed a deep sigh, contentment and sadness, and Sophie began reading Chapter Three: "Marilla came briskly forward as Matthew opened the door. But when her eyes fell on the odd little figure in the stiff, ugly dress, with the long braids of red hair and the eager, luminous eyes, she stopped short in amazement...."

1969

Sophie and Camille ate their lunch at the picnic table in Camille's backyard. They were still in their swimming suits, all oiled and red and sweaty. They had been lying in the sun on the garage roof. Despite Camille's mother's melodramatic warnings, the girls headed up there anyway. They had climbed a ladder and made their way out onto the gray asphalt garage roof cautiously, beach towels and a bottle of Johnson's Baby Oil in hand. While they sunned themselves, the radio on the driveway below blared Top 40 hits. An hour later, Camille's mother demanded they come down. "You'll cook like a pot roast up there," she said.

"Moms!" Camille said. "They don't have any idea what it's like to be young."

In the kitchen they gulped glasses of cold water, then made their own lunch. Camille peeled and sliced a large kohlrabi and scrounged in the fridge, where she found a bag of cheese curds. "Want any chips?" she asked Sophie, who said that sounded good. She was craving salt. "They're up there, in the cupboard to the left of the stove." Camille pointed. Into two tall green aluminum tumblers, Camille poured fresh lemonade over ice.

As they headed outside, Camille's mom reminded her daughter that she had a piano lesson at 4:30, to which the girl rolled her eyes. "And you will need a shower before we go, of course," her mother added.

"You're so lucky, Sophie," Camille said, crunching a salted piece of kohlrabi. "Your mom leaves you alone. She treats you like a grown-up. She's not always badgering you about everything."

Sophie guessed that was right. She no longer needed Ruth to watch her, but she often headed over to Ruth's just for the company. And when Angel was working, or out with friends, or on a rare—very rare—date, Sophie would be left take care of herself. She could do it. That wasn't the point. Somehow her mom was under the impression that all teenagers wanted to be as far away from their parents as possible, so she sometimes went out of her way to give Sophie "her own space." But the truth was, Sophie was often lonely. She kind of wished she and her mom would do things together, even things like baking cookies, which she used to do with Ruth.

"I sometimes can't stand my mom," Camille said, "but I miss my dad." Camille's parents had divorced three years earlier and he had moved to a suburb south of Chicago, so she didn't get to see him very much. He sent money, paid for things, and got her lavish birthday and Christmas gifts, but he didn't come to visit. He was remarried. Camille didn't like her stepmother or her stepsister, though she barely knew them. She just felt she ought not to like them.

"Do you ever think about your dad?" Camille asked.

Sophie could not remember that Camille had ever asked her about her dad before. The question surprised her.

"Not really. I never knew him." The truth was, she did wonder about her father. When she was a kid, she would sometimes fantasize about who he might be. She even wished one time that Andy Griffith was her dad, and she felt foolish thinking about it now. After all, she was nearly fourteen years old, practically an adult. She really didn't need a mother or a father.

One Saturday after school had begun, Camille and Sophie went for a walk after dinner. The air was crisp, the leaves just beginning to turn in the tops of maple trees. Camille wanted to know if Sophie had heard about Bobby Fletcher's dad killing himself. "I heard they found him in the shed behind their house, his head blown all the way off."

Sophie didn't like to talk so directly about gruesome things. "I don't think it would have been all the way off," she replied.

"Maybe you're right. But isn't it ghastly?"

"Ghastly" was one of Camille's new words, and it actually fit well in this context, unlike other times: ghastly French Fries, ghastly culottes, ghastly new girl in school. Sophie agreed it certainly was. "Poor Bobby," she said.

"Yeah, poor Bobby," Camille repeated.

They made their way down North Avenue and waved hello to a lady on her front porch who was brushing a golden retriever's silky yellow coat. "Nice evening for a walk, girls," the lady said.

Sophie replied that it sure was. Half a block later Sophie said, "Hey, let's play our game."

Their game had evolved over time, but it involved walking down streets where they knew no one. For each house, or at least the most interesting ones, they would invent a story about who lived there. They would take turns beginning the story, and went back and forth inventing details. According to their rules, they had to build off what was already said. They could not erase a detail, which meant some of their stories ended up being improbably complex and unrealistic. They didn't care. The point was not to guess correctly. The point was to use their imaginations. Sophie and Camille would choose a house, then stop in front of it, considering it carefully, taking in details of the facade, the yard, the ornaments, and from this, they would create the life within, the people, their occupations, their particular oddities, their problem children, and so on.

The stucco house near the end of the boulevard, for example, was the place where the divorcée lived, and her jerk of a husband had barely left her enough to care for it. That's why the bushes were scraggly and why the shutters were peeling. They imagined she was dating a new guy, an airline pilot who came into town only once a month or so. She would have to leave the kids with a babysitter, sometimes Sophie or Camille.

"Such nice girls," the divorcée would say about them, but she did not know that Sophie and Camille knew all about the dirty magazines in her nightstand and about the liquor cabinet and the refrigerator that never had anything good to eat. They imagined the divorcée's children were quiet and afraid. They always wanted to play dress up, but Camille and Sophie said "no." That was way too childish. The teens wanted to listen to the divorcée's records, and they wanted to dance. Those kids would think we're weird, Camille had said. Sophie agreed that they probably were right.

"We'd be horrible babysitters," laughed Camille.

Today they broke their rules, and the girls chose a modest Tudor for themselves to live in. Sophie and Camille transformed themselves into two women who had married rich men. The men had gone to war and died. They did not know that rich men did not go to war. They were young, beautiful widows whose childhood friendship sustained them in their grief. Moving into the same house seemed like a natural thing to do. They had a grand life. The widows slept late, swam in their backyard pool in summer, and went to tea and luncheon at their club. They traveled often to Europe and bought all of their clothes in New York or Paris. It was Camille who insisted that the men had to have died tragically. Sophie insisted that she and Camille would be forever young and beautiful.

Later the girls headed back home. Camille thought they could watch *Rowan and Martin's Laugh-In* on the TV in her room even if Camille's mother thought the humor was too vulgar for fourteen-year-olds.

A half block away from Camille's house, they stopped, Camille thrusting her arm out to stop Sophie in mid-stride. "Who's that?" she said. An unfamiliar car was parked in her driveway. Her mother and a tall blond man were on the porch, standing close, his hand holding hers. Their heads closed the gap.

"They're kissing. Holy shit. She's kissing him." Camille's heart pounded fiercely. Her throat tight and dry.

"Oh my god, Camille," Sophie said, unable to say anything else.

A minute later the man drove off. He passed the girls but did not notice them.

"I will not have a stepfather," Camille pronounced later, *Laugh-In* over, their bowl of pretzel sticks empty. "She will have to marry him over my dead body."

"Yeah," Sophie said, having no idea what to say. Poor Camille.

1977

After Sophie had finished folding a load of towels, she put them away in the linen closet in the hall, then tiptoed over to check on her mother. Sophie needn't have been so cautious as Angel was asleep. Or unconscious, or whatever state she was in when she was not awake. It was not easy to know what kind of sleep her mother experienced. At times Angel's eyelids would pulsate, her lashes would flutter, and the lids would glide slightly open, though not fully. Such signs were often misleading.

Sophie stretched out on the couch and closed her eyes. She was tired. "Of course you're tired," her mom had said yesterday. "You're up every four hours with me. It's like I'm a baby." Sophie did not know what that was like, but she took her mother's word for it.

A heavy thump sounded, startling Sophie awake. She recognized the noise even in her frowzy brain. Another bird had flown into the glass. When she told Lev how weird it was that all these birds were trying to get into the house, he had said his mom used to say it was a bad omen, but he never knew why. Sophie checked her watch and realized she had only been asleep for twenty minutes. "Shit," she said, annoyed that she had been disturbed. She tried to go back to sleep, but she could not settle her adrenaline-charged pulse, so she lay there trying to come up with some way to keep the birds from crashing into the front window.

A few minutes later, Angel blurted out, "Goddamn it, Dad. You should have asked me."

Okay, that's it. I'm really awake now, thought Sophie, who rolled onto her side and stared over at her mother.

"It's a side effect of the morphine," the nurse said when Sophie told her that Angel sometimes talked in her sleep. Angel did not sleep talk pleasant memories or loving thoughts, but instead expressed anger, frustration, even agony. Not only was Angel in physical pain with the cancer, but she was obviously also in emotional pain and there was nothing Sophie could do to help her with that.

There were also things that Sophie needed to make peace with. She had been thinking about her own father now that she knew he was alive. Probably, anyway. And while she took her mother's word that her dad was no saint, it had still stung a few days earlier to hear Angel curse him in her sleep. Maybe he had changed. People change. The fact that her mother had given her permission to find him had set her to thinking that she might. Sophie had even begun to think about what it would be like to walk up to him and tell him who she was. Or she might begin by writing. How would she start? "Dear Dad"? Then what? And what would his reaction be?

Other times Sophie felt it might just be better to let him alone. He left for a reason. Left not just his wife. That she could understand. It happened all the time. People realize they aren't meant to be together. But he had left her, too. What kind of person decides he no longer wants to be with his child? What good could come of seeking him out, especially if he had no interest in seeing her? Right now, she had no energy to give to anyone other than her mother.

1971

I'm not kidding. You and I are doing yard work today. Camille can get along without you," Angel said, hands on her hips, eyes narrowed.

"But I told her I would be there right after breakfast," said Sophie, who now let her Cheerios swim in the milk. She was not hungry any longer. She hoped her mother would not see her toss the half-full glass of orange juice down the drain either. Her mom had a hang-up about wasting food.

"I don't care what you told her. This yard needs help and I can't do it by myself."

"But—"

"But nothing. When I was your age, I was up by eight every Saturday, cleaning my room or doing whatever else my father dreamed up for me to do. You don't have it so bad. I hardly ever ask you to help me around here."

Sophie stood and stared blankly.

"Well?" Angel said.

"Well what?"

"Well you'd better call her and tell her she can do without you this morning."

If Angel were to be honest, she knew that when she was fifteen, she had already begun to defy her father and sneak out. Even before she had met Ruben, she'd been to parties where she had learned to enjoy beer. Sophie was a dream child next to what she had been. And it wasn't like she was that demanding. She tried hard to give Sophie her own space, but today, for some reason, she had woken up wanting to spend time with her daughter. Was it so much to ask?

After Sophie hung up the phone, she sighed and plodded to her room to get dressed, all the while thinking what she would never dream of saying to her mother's face. Sophie yanked her hair back into a ponytail and secured it with a hair band. She felt her cheeks burn. You don't have to ask me to do anything, she screamed in her head. And why not? It's because I'm already doing a lot of things without you asking, Mother. You never have to tell me to clean my room because it's always clean, or hadn't you noticed? And did you ever wonder why the laundry doesn't pile up around here? No, of course not. "Arrrgghhhh," Sophie growled loudly. She pulled her bed into shape and tossed her dirty pajamas in the hamper, which was almost empty. "Thank you," she said out loud to the mother who would not hear.

Outside now, Sophie walked unwillingly over to her mother. She had pulled on an old pair of gloves, and stood with the sun blinding her eyes.

"What do you want me to do?" she said.

"Well, you can start by losing that attitude."

Sophie rolled her eyes.

"Great start, Sophie. Great effort."

"I don't know what you want from me. I'm doing what you asked. What do you want me to do?" Sophie demanded.

Angel decided not to push things into a fight. It never ended well when she did, and after all, what would be the point? This was not at all what she wanted. She took a deep breath, smiled hoping to get one in return, and said as brightly as she could, "Well, the bed on the south side needs weeding."

Sophie nodded in compliance and trudged around the house. She was glad Ruth and Lev weren't home. They were probably at the Jewish home where Ruth volunteered to set up for Sabbath dinner. Ordinarily she didn't mind taking care of flowers. She had done so with Ruth many times, with her papa, too. She actually liked gardening, and even weeding could be satisfying, making a flower bed look neat.

Angel had already stuffed one paper grocery bag with weeds and lingering brown elm leaves that had tenaciously nested under the bushes all winter. They should have done this job weeks ago. Mother would never have let her narcissus bloom among fallen leaves, she thought as she picked off the spent paper-white blossoms. She then went over to where Sophie knelt on the ground, working. One of the little marigolds Angel had put in the week before was lying on the ground on top of a pile of oxalis and dandelions.

"Sophie! What the…? You pulled out a flower."

"Not on purpose. It came out when I dug out a dandelion. I can replant it."

"If you don't want to help, then why are you even out here?"

Good grief, thought Sophie. Are you serious? She got up off her knees, and wiped her sweaty forehead on her dirty garden glove. In the front yard, she found the basket of hand tools and retrieved the trowel. Back now where she'd cleared the space of weeds, she dug a hole. She tucked the displaced marigold back in the dirt and patted the soil around it. She placed the plant deeply, having learned from Ruth that many plants will develop stronger roots if you plant them deep.

Angel supervised Sophie as she tilted the watering can and soaked the little plant.

"There," Sophie said. "You happy?"

No, she did not feel happy. If she could start the day all over again, she would have just watched Sophie scamper away after breakfast to Camille's, as carefree as a teenager should be on a Saturday morning. I guess you can't force a kid to want to be with you, she thought. But— No. No buts. It was just a stupid idea.

Without speaking another word to her mother, Sophie finished weeding the south side bed. Then she washed up and headed over to Camille's. Later, when she came home, her mother acted as if nothing had happened, and she followed along. It was how they usually set things right.

By the end of summer, that little marigold was the healthiest flower in their yard.

1977

Dr. Winter told Sophie over the phone that it would not be long now. How many times had he said that? And yet, this time Sophie felt he was right. He ordered a morphine drip and said a nurse would be by later that day to hook up the IV. From now on, he said, her mother would rarely be conscious. It will almost be like she's in a coma. She will continue to weaken until she lets go.

Lets go? Was that the medical term? She thanked the doctor.

"Sophie?"

"Yes?"

"Call me when it happens. Or leave a message with my receptionist."

"Of course." She hadn't thought about needing to let him know. Life was not the movies. There was no break in the collective consciousness when one died. People's lives did not stop. The world did not pause and suddenly take account.

"Yes. I'll call. Thanks again."

Angel felt the cold liquid begin to seep into her veins. The interior of her consciousness sparked with glaring light, then darkened. She heard low humming sounds. She had receded entirely into herself now. The outside world disappeared.

1972

More people than Angel had expected were at Ruth's funeral service. She had no idea Ruth had meant so much to so many. Beth El Synagogue was only a few block's walk from their house, but she had never felt the least bit curious about what went on there. While some people she knew enjoyed learning about others' religions, Angel had no interest whatsoever. But now, after being inside the lovely synagogue for Ruth's service and meeting a few of its members, Angel began to understand why this congregation that Ruth served so faithfully throughout her life would be present in such large numbers.

Even though Ruth's service was not overly long, Angel was glad to be outside and headed home. She was glad as well for the relatively warm December sun. She lit a cigarette. Because she had not shoveled her own walk after the previous night's snow, Angel knew she should not criticize others for their similar neglect. "Watch your step, Sophie," Angel said after nearly turning her ankle on a slippery spot.

Sophie, who was not wearing high heels, had no trouble on the sidewalk. Instead, she adjusted her white rabbit-fur earmuffs and announced to her mother that she was going to sit shiva with Lev.

"You're going to what?"

"Sit shiva. It's a Jewish custom to mourn the dead and to reflect on the loss. I looked it up," Sophie told her mother knowingly. She had first learned about the idea six weeks earlier when Lev had dropped off a beautiful challah loaf that he had made for Ruth, hoping to cheer her. Without words, for the most recent in a series of strokes had left her unable to speak, Ruth had refused it. After that, he did not want the bread either, but could not quite see dropping it into the garbage can.

"She won't last much longer, Sophie," Lev had said, knowing Ruth's death might be more painful for Sophie than for anyone. Lev was surprised by how calmly Sophie faced the inevitable truth. He had told her then about his plans to hold a shiva. While Lev admitted he was the least observant Jew he knew, he knew he wanted to honor his mother. "I think it would please her," he had said.

Angel could not possibly guess what shiva meant. "So, is this like another…funeral? Two funerals?"

"No. It's different. People come to Lev's house and mourn with him, to show respect and to reflect. Some hold their shiva for seven days…."

"Days?" Angel's eyes widened as she slowed to a stop, then turned to face her daughter. Angel pulled her coat tighter and wished she had taken the time to button it before they left the synagogue. "Listen Sophie, we attended the funeral service, and I'll make a tuna and noodle casserole for Lev, but more than that? Why? Besides, you're just a child and you're not really family, so…."

Sophie let out a frustrated growl and started walking again. After fifty feet, she turned and yelled, "We're talking about Ruth, Mom. I loved her and I miss her." Then Sophie sped up and ran the last block home.

Inside, Angel kicked off her wet shoes, sorry she had chosen to wear heels, which were not even comfortable. Sophie had already thrown herself onto the couch, lying with her back to her mother.

Angel did not speak immediately, but instead let Sophie fume a while. She saw that Sophie had flung her coat on the back of a chair, so she hung it in the closet. She was dying for a drink, but two in the afternoon was too early in anyone's book.

Sophie could hear her mother walking about, which only annoyed her more. Why didn't she just say something? Sophie started to feel a cramp in her hip, but she dared not move. She breathed quietly, staying as still as a broken clock.

Seeing Sophie lying on the couch reminded Angel of that afternoon years ago when Ruth had sprained her ankle. She thought about how good it had felt to be kind—loving actually—to their neighbor. Ruth would have done no less, and Angel realized just then that there was no reason for her to make a big deal out of this notion of Sophie's. She sat down on the edge of the couch. There was barely enough room for her, so she wiggled her butt closer, thinking she would annoy her daughter into reacting, but still Sophie did not move, not until she felt her mother's hand on her head.

Sophie shook it off.

"Oh, come on, Sophie. Let's not fight."

Sophie remained mute.

"I...I guess no harm can come of this thing Lev's going to have. Right? I mean, there's no weird religious voodoo in this... *shaver*, is there?"

Voodoo? Shaver? Really, Mom? Sophie thought. Angel was always misspeaking. Putting s's on the ends of people's names. Mrs. Johnson was Mrs. Johnsons. Not quite getting the word or phrase right. Once, when Sophie told her mother the saying was "a tough row to hoe" not "road to hoe," Angel got angry and wondered when Sophie had become such a know-it-all.

"Aren't you even going to answer me?"

"It's shiva," Sophie said sullenly.

Angel looked up at the ceiling and searched for patience. "Sorry. Shiva." She said it again and again in her head so she would remember. "Come on. Turn around. I said you could go. I am sorry. I just...." Angel placed her hand back on Sophie's head, where it was allowed this time to rest. "It's just that things like this are hard for me."

Sophie turned and faced her mom. Her eyes and nose pink. After a few quiet moments, Sophie said calmly, "You could come, too. She was more than just our neighbor."

"I know that," Angel said. You don't have to tell me." She was instantly sorry for the tone. Softer now, she said, "I know. She was much more."

Sophie felt her eyes prickle again as they welled and glistened.

"Okay," Angel said, patting Sophie's hand. "I am going to make coffee. Want some milk? A cookie?" Angel offered.

"I'd like coffee, too."

"Really?" Angel said. "You like coffee now?"

"Can't I try it?" Sophie said, hoisting herself up, wiping her eyes.

Angel smiled. Maybe her daughter wasn't a child. Maybe somehow she had become something else. But when? How? How had she not noticed?

Angel placed two cups and saucers on the kitchen table. "Cream? Sugar?"

"A little of both?" Sophie said.

"You can put some cookies on a plate and get napkins. Then, let's sit and talk about this...."

"Shiva."

"Shiva," Angel repeated, but she had remembered, and if Sophie had given her time, she would have seen that.

Just before dusk, Sophie and Angel walked their still unshoveled sidewalk to their neighbor's house. The street was filled with cars, Lev's driveway also full. The sidelight window to the right of Lev's front door glowed with a single flame. Inside the Perlman house, a man in a yarmulke greeted them and took their coats. Sophie noticed a pitcher of water and a bowl on a small table near the entryway. Paper napkins were stacked beside them. Because she knew what to do, Sophie poured water over her hands, then dried them. Angel followed her daughter's lead.

Lev, who was in the living room talking quietly with the rabbi, wore a dark gray suit, a torn black ribbon pinned to his lapel. Somehow he seemed older than he had just a few hours earlier. After the rabbi moved to speak to others, Angel and Sophie went to Lev.

"Thank you for coming," he said, his hand extended to Angel, then to Sophie. Mother would be so pleased you are here," Lev said, his demeanor overly formal.

"I see you're all set up," said Angel, feeling more awkward than necessary.

"Yes. It's all worked out well."

The living room sofa and side chairs had been moved out. The dining room chairs and others brought by members of the congregation were arranged in a semi-circle, backs to the front window, drapes drawn. Many of the chairs were already filled with mourners, but Angel noticed two that were empty in the back row. She had also seen that the mirror at the bottom of the stairs had been covered, just like Sophie had said it would be. She was proud, suddenly, of her smart daughter who knew things about life and the world that she did not know, probably would never know.

About twenty minutes after Angel and Sophie had settled into their chairs, the rabbi took his place in the center of the half circle and asked them to follow in their prayer books. Moments later he began the Kaddish, the prayer for the dead. The rabbi's voice was rich and warm as he spoke, almost singing, "Yit'gadal v'yit'kadash sh'mei raba." In response, Lev and others replied "Amen." Angel shifted in her folding chair and it squeaked. She was sure the sound drew attention to her, but no one turned her way.

"B'al'ma di v'ra khir'utei," the rabbi continued.

Angel stared ahead now, almost afraid to breathe, and listened to the foreign sounds, her heartbeat sounding in her ears.

To Sophie the rabbi's voice was soothing, even magical. She did not understand the words, but she felt the reverence they conveyed and she was comforted. Sophie missed Ruth, but at this moment, she also felt serenely close to Ruth, as if she were not only there but somehow also there with her arms around her "bubbula Sophie."

After the Kaddish prayer, a few women got up and headed to the dining room. It would have been rude to turn around to see what they were doing, but Sophie could hear the sounds of dishes and silverware. The blended smell of food and coffee intensified. They did their work without speaking.

In ones and twos, others began to stand up and move about. These mourners started speaking now as well. Their quiet conversations mingled with tinkling cups and the sound of spoons stirring.

Angel was ready to get up, but she waited for Sophie to make a move. Sophie waited for Lev. A few minutes later, Lev was up to thank the rabbi. When he turned back, he saw his neighbors still seated. Lev held his hand out to Angel to help her to her feet. "Stiff chairs, aren't they? Keeps us awake and focused on our memories, I suspect," Lev said.

Angel nodded. Her first impulse was to make a smart comment, but she kept that impulse in check. Instead she said how nice the prayer was. Lev said he agreed.

"Let's join the others," Lev said.

They filled small plates with a bit of everything. It all looked so good. Angel worried her tuna casserole in its plain Pyrex dish, which she planned to bring over tomorrow, would seem so ordinary by comparison.

Sophie flitted like a hummingbird in a honeysuckle bush, introducing herself to small groups of men and women who were delighted to meet her. Some of them had heard stories of her from the time she was a little girl.

"And who are you," a plump, white-haired woman, who had just licked her fingers, asked Sophie.

Even her own name caught in her throat as she responded.

"Oy," the woman said as she reached out and touched Sophie on the shoulder. "Ruthie loved you so much."

The woman's words pricked Sophie's eyes. Later, in bed, Sophie would hear those words again and would let her tears fall freely.

The next day, Sophie watched the Perlman house through her mother's bedroom window. The rabbi arrived around noon, but he did not stay long. By late afternoon, after visitors had dwindled to only a few, Sophie chose to return. She carried her mother's casserole dish.

Inside, she kicked off her loafers and slid them near the other boots and shoes. Lev came to greet her. She held out the Pyrex dish. "From Mom," Sophie said. "She wanted you to know she's sorry she can't be here today." Sophie did not think her mother's lie would hurt anyone, and to be honest, she was glad to be there on her own.

Sophie sat for awhile in the same chair she had chosen yesterday, and once she had settled, she allowed herself to wander back in time and think about her bubbe. She closed her eyes and saw herself at six, lying on her stomach reading picture books, Ruth knitting, the radio playing symphonic music. Again and again Sophie considered the fact that Ruth had never treated her as if she were inferior or somehow not a complete person, just because she was a child. Unlike her mother, who often just assumed Sophie would not know something or could not do something, Ruth seemed always surprised when she found it necessary to teach Sophie.

Lev shifted in his seat and felt a shiver. Without last night's crowd, today his house—for it was his house now—felt cooler. He wondered if he should adjust the thermostat, but decided it could wait.

With a sideways glance, Lev observed Sophie, who seemed to be honoring the shiva with her whole soul. He wondered then, as he often had, what blessing of fate had brought this girl into their lives. From the first, Sophie had brought them—his mother especially—so much joy and love. She was more than the little girl next door. Her presence had blessed their lives. He would tell her so, later, when the shiva had ended, or another time soon. He would tell her that his mother had loved her more than she would ever know.

He loved her, too, as his little sister. He remembered when he had first met her that she had called him "Rev." He had never met a child who communicated with adults so confidently, without the least hint of the self-consciousness he had been plagued with as a boy. Was still afflicted with at times. Even when she was little, Sophie was a person with whom he felt completely comfortable. With her, it was easy to just be himself. There were not many people he could say that about.

At home, Angel sat in the gold chair, her feet up on the ottoman, and smoked a cigarette. She was glad Sophie did not push her to go along today. So much focus on death was not good for you, but she guessed Sophie felt differently. As she drew smoke deep into her lungs, Angel considered, as she often did, that life had been unfair to her. Already she had been asked to grieve too much. Christ, she was only thirty-five and all of her grandparents and both of her parents were dead. How could that be even close to fair?

Angel stretched her neck, felt it crack, and blew smoke into the dimly-lit room. It would be dark soon. Sure, she thought, she was not as close to Ruth as Sophie was, but that didn't mean she wasn't sad. Of course she was. Though with Ruth, well, she was old. Old people die. But her mom? Her mom had not been old. Only one year older than she was right now. And her dad? Fifty-one? At least he got to know Sophie, but shit. How is it right for one family to be put through so much?

Lighting another cigarette, she shook off her morbid thoughts and instead imagined herself as a grandmother, Sophie's little tykes climbing all over her as if she were a playhouse and she giggling, tickling them. Angel smiled. She was glad she was healthy. She would live to be a hundred, she thought. Exhaling, smoke swirling about her head, Angel determined to be done with death for a long, long time.

Stiffer than a man his age ought to be, Lev wondered how anyone ever sat shiva for seven days. He had a feeling that his mother would tell him "enough of that, now. I appreciate it. You're a good son, but enough." But of course, it wasn't up to Ruth. It was up to Lev, for whom this shiva served two purposes, only one of which was selfless. He knew he had not always been a good son. He had neglected his mother, had stayed away from home for far too long, and while the years since his father's death had helped him to atone for his failures, he felt those years, his help to her, his love finally given freely, had not been enough.

Lev stood up, stretched, then stepped down the row to Sophie. He held out his hand to help her to her feet.

"Let's get something to eat. You hungry?"

Honestly, she was. Doing nothing made one hungrier than she supposed it could. The table was laid out like a buffet for forty people. Ruth's best dessert service, the silver freshly polished and gleaming. A Sterno can glowed under the chafing dish. Lev handed Sophie a plate.

"Before you go," Lev said, "you could put a plate together for your mom."

She nodded. "That's nice of you."

"Oh, that's me, Mr. Nice Guy."

"What? Why do you say it like that? You are nice."

Lev stuck his tongue out at her. She mimicked the gesture.

"You should try some of Mrs. Merton's kuchen. Pretty good. Not Mom's, but I like the almond flavor." Lev trimmed off a modest slice and laid it expertly on a dessert plate. He handed it to Sophie with a flourish. "M'lady," he said, bowing slightly.

She giggled. It felt wrong to laugh. But it was Lev's fault, so she didn't feel too bad.

Around seven, everyone else had left. With her earmuffs and coat on, Sophie held the wax paper-covered plate of food for her mom in her hands and faced Lev at his front door.

"You don't have to come tomorrow," Lev said.

"I can. I want to be here." If it had not been Christmas break, she would have been in school all week.

"No. I think I'll sit alone tomorrow, just for a while, and then I think I'm done. I can't pretend I'm a religious person. I just wanted to show my mother the respect she deserves."

Sophie said she understood, but it hurt a little that he did not want her to come. She stepped out onto the front stoop. The night air felt mild, but she could smell the snow on its way.

"Watch your step," Lev called when she was halfway to her house. With one hand, she waved without turning back to look.

Lev closed the door, and this time, he locked it. He turned off the porch light. Then he cleared the table, put leftovers into covered dishes, and set them in the refrigerator. He set the dirty dishes in the sink for the morning and returned to the living room. This time he chose the chair Sophie had been sitting in. From where she had sat, she had been able to see the watercolor Ruth had painted. A sunrise over Lake Michigan. She had captured the colors in the rosy sky perfectly. It was his mother who had given him his artistic sensibilities, not his father, Lev thought.

And yet, that was not entirely true. Josef Perlman played the violin expertly. He worked as a jeweler to "make a living." But wasn't it art to set a stone in gold? And Joe had been a good husband. He was never unkind to Ruth. Never. It was time, Lev realized, to start being fair to his father. How easily Lev had blamed his father for holding him back in those early years, but if he were to be honest, really honest, he himself had been too afraid he would fail. It was his own fear, nothing else, that kept him in that accountant's office longer than he should have been.

"I don't think you can hear me old man, but if you can, I hope you are well. Give Mother a big hug from me. I'm sure you are overjoyed to see her," he said.

In bed now, Lev stretched out fully and laughed as he always did when his feet hung over the edge of the mattress. Beds were not designed for people taller than 5"5". He continued to picture his parents, reunited now—embracing, kissing, weeping. In the dark, he saw them in light— warm, golden light. Sometimes, he thought, the improbable paradise that Christians taught their children was comforting to imagine. From that day on, Lev would think of his parents no other way.

1973

Sophia Rose Miranda was nearly late for her own high school graduation. Angel had forgotten to press Sophie's graduation gown as she had promised she would, and with her hair still in curlers, Angel now worked the iron over the creases. Flicking off the iron, Angel told Sophie to just put the gown on now to save time.

"Why are we always late? Can't we ever be on time for anything?" Sophie yelled.

"We can stay home. Is that what you want? They'll still give you your diploma, you know. So just keep it up if that's what you want."

Sophie fumed and stepped into the gown. Standing in front of the full-length mirror on the back of the coat closet door, she pinned the cap to her head, her long, thick braid reaching to her shoulder blades. She was ready to get this ordeal over with.

Ten minutes later, they were in the car headed to Vollrath Park. Of course there would be nowhere to park. They ended up walking nearly five blocks. Angel told Sophie to run on ahead and get to where she was supposed to be.

The outdoor ceremony, because it was for both Sheboygan high schools, was tediously long, but graduations, like weddings and funerals, had to be endured. They were simply part of life's obligations.

As she climbed the platform and waited her turn to accept her diploma, all Sophie could think about was not tripping and falling. She had been excited to wear her new platform sandals, but wondered now if it had been a wise choice. Falling would be so humiliating. There were hundreds of people in attendance. But Ruth was not there. Her grandfather was not there. Sophie wished Lev could have been there, but he'd gotten another small part in movie. Her mom was there, somewhere. Or not. Sophie shook the principal's hand. "Congratulations," he said, his voice deep and serious. And as he said to everyone, she was sure, he told her how proud they all were of her accomplishments.

In the post-ceremony melee, Angel elbowed her way through the crowd to where she found Sophie talking to a boy she did not recognize. Angel said hello as she slipped her arm around Sophie's waist, claiming her offspring like a lioness.

Taking Angel's arrival as his cue, the boy told Sophie he would see her later. Angel was glad she wouldn't have to make small talk with him.

"I'm so proud of you sweetheart," Angel said. "I am just so proud."

"Thanks, Mom," Sophie said, managing a brief smile. "Where were you sitting?" She felt bad now that she had thought the worst of her mom.

"Can you believe it?" Angel said proudly, "Right near the front. Fourth row, but on the end. I just sort of plopped myself down near a big family on a blanket and they didn't say a word."

Sounds about right, Sophie thought. "So you could see me?"

"You bet I could. You are definitely the prettiest girl in your class," Angel said.

Sophie lifted her eyes to the sky and hoped no one nearby heard her mom being such a mom. "Let's go home now, okay?" Sophie said. There were too many happy gatherings, classmates surrounded by family, flashcubes popping, people saying "cheese."

"No way. We're going for ice cream now. Or do you want to get dinner instead?"

"Whatever you want, Mom."

Angel sensed her daughter's sullen mood. She has a right, Angel thought. It's my fault we were late. Even so, Angel was not going to give in to the feeling, and she continued to remain cheerful despite her daughter's false smiles.

Sophie was grateful no one she knew was at Dairy Queen. As they ate their sundaes, Angel slid an envelope across the table. "Open it," she said.

The card featured colorful fireworks and the word *Congratulations* spelled out in gold glitter across them. Inside it said, *You deserve all the best. Love, Mom* was written hastily below. Five twenty-dollar bills had fallen to the sticky table.

"Thanks, Mom. That's really nice." Sophie did not bring up the fact that the card was not even a real graduation card but a generic card that fit all "great job" situations.

"Well, I didn't know what to get you. Money is always the right gift, though, isn't it?"

Sophie couldn't really blame her mother for not making a big deal of her graduation. She herself had been minimizing its importance all year, since Camille moved away. At the end of their junior year, Camille's mother got remarried, and they moved to a Chicago suburb. The only reason Camille was happy about the move was that she would be closer to her dad. But the fact that Camille would be almost four hours away devastated both girls, who had begged Camille's mom to let her live with Sophie for their last year of high school. Surprisingly, Angel had agreed to the arrangement. Camille's mother wouldn't budge. So Sophie's best friend, the only person who could make her laugh with just a goofy look, the only person she could really confide in, had gone away. It had been a horrible summer, and the entire year felt wrong. There were other girls Sophie ate lunch with and occasionally went to a movie with, but no other Camilles.

1973

Angel stood on the sidewalk outside the high rise dormitory in Madison where Sophie would make her home for the next eight months. Earlier she and Sophie had lugged five big boxes up to the fifth floor. And though Sophie told her she didn't have to, Angel insisted on making up Sophie's bed and putting away some of her clothes in the chest of drawers.

"Small, isn't it?" Angel commented as she looked over the dorm room. Concrete block walls would soon be covered in posters, but at the moment, the cream-colored walls looked cold and unwelcoming.

"I guess so," Sophie said. Sure, her dorm room wasn't fancy, but the vast view of the sparkling lake made up for it. And it was hers, at least half of it was. She was excited to be on her own, really on her own. Sophie would learn later that The University of Wisconsin was situated on the isthmus between Lake Mendota and Lake Monona. In many ways, Sophie felt she was situated on her own isthmus, with the direction to her future entirely up to her.

Now it was time to say goodbye. Mother and daughter stood outside the dormitory. The early afternoon sun shone bright and hot. Angel had no idea this moment would be so hard. Sophie could see that her mother was about to cry.

"It's okay, Mom. I'm not leaving forever."

Angel nodded and smiled.

"I'm going to try to find a ride home in October," Sophie said. "I noticed a sign on the ride-share board about going to Sheboygan for North's Homecoming. I don't care about that, but I could come home that weekend."

"Or just call me and I'll come get you. Any time. I can ask off if I know in advance." Angel paused and took a deep breath. She needed a cigarette, desperately. "You sure you got everything?"

"Yeah, Mom. I'm sure."

Angel put her arms around her daughter and pulled her close. Then she stood back and worked to keep her chin from quivering.

"Okay. Get going. I expect straight A's."

Sophie rolled her eyes then smiled. "I'll try."

"You better. Now go. I can't stand here all day, can I?" She hugged her daughter one more time.

"Bye, Mom," Sophie said, then she turned and headed toward the double doors, where she looked back and waved before going inside.

Angel barely made it back to her car before breaking into a full wail, so loud and profound that she almost could not stop. When her sobs subsided, she searched her purse for tissues. Not finding a single one, she checked the glove box and found a couple of extra McDonald's napkins.

What kind of idiot doesn't pack tissues for a college send-off? she thought. Did I think I could just say good-bye to my only child and drive away as if I had dropped off a bag of old clothes at Goodwill? She blew her nose, then fumbled for a cigarette and lit it before starting the car.

When she got home around four, Angel walked into Sophie's room and sat on her daughter's bed. How on earth had the past eighteen years sped by so, so quickly? She laid back on the bed and let the tears slide down her temples until a few minutes later she decided she was being ridiculous. After all, it was a good thing. Sophie being in college.

For her dinner, Angel heated up a can of chicken noodle soup. While she ate, she paged through the paper, considering the employment ads. In the back of her mind, there was always a better job waiting for her. She just hadn't found it yet.

Moments later she heard a cracking thump. A bird had hit the living room window so hard it left a dusty wing print on the glass. Angel walked to the window and looked out. A blackbird lay on the ground at the edge of the scraggly yew, its blue-black feathers motionless.

"Come on. Get up. You're only stunned. I would be too. Jesus. Come on," she said out loud.

But the bird remained still. If it was there in the morning, she would bury it in the backyard.

Angel tried hard to watch TV, but even with the laugh track filling the room, she didn't think anything was funny. Or she was just tired. Driving always tired her. Not to mention the fact that she'd just dropped off her daughter to live for eight months with complete strangers. Okay, okay. Don't get so dramatic, Angel told herself. Minutes later, despite her efforts to stay awake, she fell asleep with the TV blaring.

The crash was sudden. She felt the jolt that jerked her from her seat and shoved her to the floor. Glass shattered and rained down on her. She did not know whose scream she heard, but it echoed in her ears even after she opened her eyes and realized she had been dreaming.

She got up, her heart still pounding, and turned off the TV. In the kitchen, she filled a glass with water and drank it quickly.

Angel had two recurring dreams. In the first, she was locked in the basement of an old house. It was dark and damp and the musty air made her cough. She always screamed but no one ever heard her. In the second, the more frequent of the two, she relived the car crash that killed her mother. Even days after she dreamed this dream, tonight's dream, she would try hard to remember her mother's face without looking at a photograph. She could almost never do it.

She thought then about her father, falling dead at work, just like that. One minute alive, finishing up at work, getting ready to come home, then, without warning, dead. Everyone she had ever loved was dead. Except for Sophie. Not Sophie. And while Angel knew her daughter was safe, dread came upon her nevertheless, for the house was now engulfed in darkness and silence had crept upon her. The silence hovered over her, and she felt it press upon her.

1974

Yawning and dying for a cup of coffee, Sophie came into the living room, where her mother stood by the desk with a confused look on her face. Sophie took a second look and saw that her purse was unzipped and wide open on the desk where she had left it yesterday.

Angel held up a pink plastic pill container. "Care to explain what you're doing with these?" Angel said, her voice more judgmental than she had wanted it to be. When she was younger, she'd kept a nearly identical container in the drawer of her nightstand. When Angel had found the birth control pills moments earlier, her first impulse had been to slip them back into Sophie's purse and not say a word about what she'd found, but then Sophie had come into the room and had caught her red-handed.

"What were you snooping in my purse for anyway?" Sophie asked. She was more than annoyed and also a little embarrassed. She did not want to have this conversation with her mom. There were just some things you didn't want your mom to know about.

Angel glared at her daughter. She did not appreciate being interrogated. Who did Sophie think she was talking to anyway?

"I asked you what you were doing snooping. I respect your privacy. You keep all your secrets in your old trunk don't you? Have I ever broken in to your secret life?"

"I wasn't snooping. I was just looking to see if you had a couple of singles. I need to go to the store for pack of cigarettes and I'm out of cash. I haven't cashed my last paycheck yet."

"Jesus, Mom."

"Don't swear."

"Oh, that's right, because you never do."

"I just mean…it's not nice. Well, what I mean is… We're not talking about me. We're talking about you. I really didn't mean to start a whole big thing this morning, but now that we're into this, I'm just curious. Why on earth do you have birth control pills?"

"Why do you think? I don't want to get pregnant by mistake and end up wishing the kid had never been born."

"Oh, come on Sophie. That isn't fair. You were never a mistake. I loved you from the moment I saw you."

"That doesn't mean you wanted me, at least not when you found out you were pregnant. And you don't need to get all bent out of shape over it. I don't even have a boyfriend."

That comment made Angel wonder what Sophie's "social" life was like. My goodness. If the girl didn't have a boyfriend, then why…?

"So you're just sleeping around, with anybody?"

Sophie yanked the plastic pill dispenser out of her mother's hand, grabbed her purse, and stormed into her room, slamming the door behind her.

"We're not finished yet," Angel yelled. "Get out here."

Sophie did not comply.

Angel felt her irrational ire rise up out of control, and instead of taking a breath, instead of using a cool head, she screamed, "I said get out here. I'm still the mother in this house and you will do what I say." She stood rigid, her feet hip-width apart, her arms closed tightly over her chest. More than anything, at that moment she wished she could turn the clock back and start the morning all over.

When she was calmer, Angel padded down hallway to Sophie's bedroom door. "Sophie?" Angel spoke gently, her tone meant to convey her apology. Sophie did not respond, so Angel knocked softly, and said again, "Sophie?"

Sophie, who had dressed and made her bed, opened the door and faced her mother, her hands on her hips, her eyes fixed in a defiant stare.

"Sophie," Angel said. "I'm sorry. I should not have been looking in your purse. I wasn't snooping. Really. And I'm not mad. I'm just…I'm sorry I got upset. I am just surprised. Shocked actually. I guess I didn't think you'd…. Well, it's hard for me to think of you as woman, you know, in that way."

Sophie crossed her arms over her chest and huffed. "Things are just simpler if you're on the pill, Mom. If something happens, you meet someone, you know. You should actually be glad that I'm being responsible. Plus, I am over eighteen. I can make these choices for myself. It's my body."

Angel dropped her shoulders, took a deep breath, and stepped back from the doorframe. "I'm sorry, honey. I can't help worrying about you. You're all I've got and I just want you to have everything. I want you to have a life that gives you everything you deserve."

Sophie relaxed her stance as well. "You don't have to worry about me, Mom. I'm not going to ruin my future. I have absolutely no desire to get married or have kids."

"Well, someday," Angel said. Of course Sophie would have children, and Angel would be a grandmother. She would be a terrific grandmother.

"Maybe not even someday."

"Oh, Sophie. Don't say that. It's just that life is not a movie. I know young girls. When I was young and infatuated with your father, I sort of pictured our life turning out like a fairy tale. Of course, I never listened to my dad either, but I realized later that he was only trying to protect me."

"I listen to you, Mom. I know you only want the best for me." Sophie said the tired phrase in a tired voice.

Angel moved toward Sophie, her arms reached out in reconciliation, and Sophie accepted them.

"Come on," Angel said. "Let's have coffee, and maybe I'll even scramble some eggs. You can tell me all about the guy who's not your boyfriend."

1976

Sophie opened the door, ushered Lev inside, and took his armful of presents so he could take off his coat and hang it in the closet.

"Just so damp out there," Lev said. "Goes right to the bones."

The past week had been foggy, and instead of fluffy snow, icy pellets clicked against the windows from time to time.

"Well, if it isn't Santa Claus," Angel said, greeting her neighbor. Since Ruth's death, Angel and Lev thought it was important for Sophie's sake not to lose their close family bond. So for the past four years, they had celebrated the winter holidays together. Angel and Sophie would usually have dinner at Lev's house on the last day of Hanukkah, but this year the eighth day of Hanukkah fell on Christmas Eve, so they were making tonight one big party.

The first year they said no gifts, but Lev had broken that rule right away. The second year, Angel and Sophie gave Lev eight silly little gifts, one for each night of Hanukkah, from a kitty key chain to a pair of peacock sunglasses. After that, Lev bought or made Hanukkah presents for Angel and Sophie, too. Christmas presents became tradition as well. Their religious and cultural lines blurred with secular traditions, and in time the Perlman-Miranda holidays took on their own flavor.

"The house smells great, girls," Lev said.

"We've got smothered chicken in the oven," Sophie said. She had found the recipe in a magazine and decided to give the mushroom soup-covered chicken a try. They would serve it with baked potatoes and sugared carrots.

A red velvet runner covered the walnut coffee table, where plates of cookies and nuts lay in abundance. Lev had brought a plate of smoked fish and crackers as well as a tin of homemade fudge. Sophie had cleared the desk to serve as the bar. She had covered it in the white runner her great-grandmother had embroidered with red poinsettias. The menorah Ruth had given her when she was younger sat behind the punch bowl, and the flames flickered in the facets of the cut glass. For Sophie, lighting the menorah was one way of remembering Ruth. Tonight she and Lev would light the last candle together. Later that night, as she set the menorah in the kitchen sink for safety, Sophie would whisper softly, "Good night, Bubbe."

In the punch bowl, a frozen ice ring floated in pink rum punch that was a bit too light on the rum in Angel's opinion. One of Angel's favorite Andy Williams Christmas albums played on the stereo. Stacked on the floor ready to replace Andy were six or seven other albums, including Sophie's favorite: Eugene Ormandy's *The Glorious Sound of Christmas*. No singing, just music. When her mom wasn't home, Sophie played the record so loud the windows rattled, and when she had settled in her papa's chair, her eyes closed, she could imagine the entire orchestra in a concert hall.

The tree stood in front of the picture window. Lev stood by it now, and he noticed the pink light it cast into the fog. The large, colored bulbs glowed bright and warm. In fact, when he later put his packages under the tree, he could feel their radiant heat.

Punch glasses filled, the three stood in the living room and gently clinked their cups together. "Merry Christmas," they said in turn. "L'chaim."

"You both look beautiful tonight," Lev said. Lev was dressed in off-white trousers and a matching vest, the long, pointed collar of his paisley-print shirt open wide. A gold chain hung around his neck. Sophie was not sure she liked his mustache, but it seemed like every man had one now. Angel wore a pink and orange Qiana tunic over straight-leg jeans, and

Sophie, looking "very California" according to Lev, her long hair parted down the middle and released from its usual braid, wore wide-legged jeans and a gauzy light green tunic.

They worked together to clean up after dinner, then claimed their spots in the living room. More relaxed now, they turned the music down low, ate cookies, and sipped punch. As she had as a child, Sophie sat cross-legged on the floor in front of the tree. She loved Christmas. No matter how tense her family life could be, or had been in the past, Christmas was a time of kindness and forgiveness. It was the time of year when her mom and grandfather seemed truly to love each other.

Sophie, because she insisted, played Santa Claus and doled out the gifts one by one, except for her gift to her mother and her mother's gift to her. Those would be opened in the morning.

Angel gave Lev a leather wallet, which he said he needed and thanked her.

Lev gave Angel a Murano glass paperweight. She said it was one of the loveliest things she had ever seen. "It's called millefiore, or multicolored glass," he said.

"Your turn again, Lev," Sophie said. She handed him her gift, a black-and-tan plaid cashmere scarf. "I heard it might be a very cold winter," she said.

"Well, it's perfect. Thank you," he said and wrapped it around his neck.

She knew her gift from Lev was a record album. He had not tried to disguise it by putting it in a box or through some other trick. She ripped the paper off quickly. "Oh Lev, thank you. My roommate has it and we listen to it all the time, but now I have my own. Thank you, thank you." He had given her *Hotel California* by The Eagles.

When Lev left for home at quarter to eleven, Angel and Sophie turned out all the lights but those on the Christmas tree. The moon illuminated the fog and created a bright white canvas behind the tree. Angel thought quietly about the first years in this house with Mother and Dad, and she worked hard to get their faces in mind. Sophie thought of her grandfather. Snuggled in his chair, she hoped that wherever he was, he could feel her thinking of him.

"Well, you're all grown up, daughter," Angel said, breaking the silence a while later. "You're twenty-one now. Can you even believe it? Where did all of our time go?"

Even Sophie had a hard time contemplating the fact that she was so old. "I still feel like a kid, though," she said.

"Oh, yeah, I know. I sometimes do, too. There are some days that I feel ancient, don't get me wrong, but some days, on the inside, I don't feel a whole lot different than I did when I was your age."

Sophie had a hard time imagining her mother being any age other than the one she was right now.

"You know what's the best thing about having a grown-up daughter?" Angel said.

"No. What?"

"I don't worry as much. I used to worry I would screw you up, but I don't anymore. You turned out pretty good, don't you think?"

"Oh, Mom."

"I know you're going to have a great life, Sophie. You're going to have all the things I—. All the things you deserve."

The record ended and the tone arm lifted, moved across the turntable, and set itself in place with a click. Mother and daughter sat quietly now. Sophie's tired eyes filled with water, magnifying the tree lights before her.

1977

Six days after Angelina Grace Catalano Miranda had been put on a morphine drip, she was dead. During the night Angel awoke in a burst of clarity and felt for the first time in many weeks fully herself, fully aware of herself in the moment. She could see by the moonlight her daughter asleep on the sofa, covered in her grandmother's quilt. Angel listened intently to Sophie's soft breathing.

In her last moments, Angel lay in her bed almost not feeling the weight of her own body, as if she had already lifted from it. And yet, she knew she had not. Her fingers on the smooth sheets anchored her to life. The weight of pain had been lifted. She breathed deeply, her lungs remembering the crisp air of a sun-warmed winter morning. Within her head swirled purple memory and the distant aroma of cinnamon and sugar. At once she was warm, her body in perfect harmony with everything that surrounded it. She moved to her side, drew her knees up tightly, crossed her arms in a self-embrace, and closed her eyes, conscious, at last, of every atom.

When she awoke, Sophie knew. She knew before she saw the stillness. She knew before she felt the cold, unnatural touch. The room felt hollow.

She called Lev. "She's gone," was all she said. Minutes later, he stood by her side. They felt not disbelief, as they had expected of this moment, but resignation. They faced Angel's quiet body.

"I'm so, so sorry, Sophie," Lev said, then he kissed her lightly on top of her head.

Sophie nodded and wondered where her power to move forward would come from.

As her mother had instructed, Sophie called Roland Wilson immediately. She also called the doctor's office. An hour and a half later Wilson came in person with the hearse. The funeral director sat with her in the kitchen and explained the details kindly, though Sophie did not feel the need to be protected. She wasn't a child. She knew what cremation meant. The memorial service could take place on Saturday at the funeral home, if Sophie approved, which she did. Only the urn would be displayed. Angel had insisted on this, Wilson said. Her mother had explained all this to her before, but having these arrangements confirmed consoled her.

Would anyone attend the memorial, she wondered, besides herself? Lev surely, but anyone else? A few neighbors? Wilson, as if he could read her mind, allayed even that worry. Angelina had given him a list of names of those she wished to be informed, her bosses at Alexanders, a few co-workers, and people she had known in the past. Flowers would be ordered. Her mother had chosen white roses.

It all happened so swiftly, from the moment Wilson arrived to the moment he and his assistant drove away with her mother's body. She had been given a few minutes alone to say goodbye, but it felt odd to her to speak to the dead, to touch the skin that was no longer warm, to touch her own warm lips to her mother's forehead. What they say about the dead looking peaceful is oddly true, thought Sophie.

Later, Lev insisted on taking Sophie out for a burger. He thought it was important for Sophie to leave the house for a while. They drove fifteen miles west to Plymouth to the A&W. The day had been bright and sunny and now, near dusk, the air was still summer-y warm, so they drove the whole way with the windows down. Sophie enjoyed the noisy ride. The drive-in was full of cars when they arrived, and the two out-of-towners felt lucky to have found the last open spot.

"Popular place," Sophie said.

The neon bug lights, which illuminated menus posted under the canopy, cast a glow on the windshield. Sophie and Lev squinted at the small print and read their options.

"Order whatever you like," Lev said as if they were at an expensive restaurant. "It's on me."

Sophie laughed and Lev took it as a victory. "Hmm. What looks good? I suppose a cheeseburger and fries. Root beer, of course."

When the carhop arrived, she placed a greeting card-sized piece of cardboard under the windshield wiper. They were number 8.

"Good evening, folks. What can I get you?"

They placed their order and she was off, walking swiftly to the small orange-and-brown building that was set nearly on the street. It would be dark soon.

In the car next to them, a large man bellowed his order. The carhop had turned to go, but he stopped her. "I did say large root beer, didn't I?"

Lev and Sophie snickered quietly. A couple of teenage boys in black letter jackets with big orange P's on the back were sidled up to a car across from them, peering in the window, laughing now and then. It was hard to see with the setting sun in their eyes, but they both thought the driver was a girl with long blonde hair. Sophie had never come here with her friends. She didn't know anyone at her school who had.

"Well, we're both orphans now, aren't we?" Lev said on the road home.

Sophie smiled weakly. She said she guessed so. The thought made her sad. She knew he meant to make her feel better, meant her to know that she was not alone, that they shared a bond. Lev parked his car on the street in front of their houses and walked her up to her door. A bright full moon climbed in the deep purple sky.

"Will you be okay tonight? Alone? I can stay with you, if you need me."

"No. It's okay. I'll be fine."

He peered into her face, not quite believing her.

"Really. You go home. I'll see you tomorrow?"

"Yes. I'll be over. I have a couple of calls I need to make. California. Earliest I should call there would be eleven-ish. They get downright cranky if I call too early. I'll be over after that? You'll probably sleep late anyway."

Sophie nodded. "Yes. That sounds good. See you tomorrow. And thanks for dinner. That was fun."

Lev walked back to his car, started it up, then drove the thirty feet to his driveway. When he was out of view, Sophie went inside and locked the door.

She had never felt more tired in her life. She should have slept well. She should have fallen asleep the moment she laid her head on her pillow. But the silence and emptiness were too loud. It was well into the night before she fell asleep, and far too early when she woke the next morning.

The part of life where the living keep on living is a hard time, a numb time. Everything that Sophie did from the moment her mother died felt new, but in a way that felt wrong at the same time. It felt odd to wake up alone in the house, her grandfather's house, her mother's house—now, she realized, her house. Would it ever seem normal? And walking past her mother's room, it felt worse than empty, even though Angel had not slept in that room since early summer.

Sophie would have that damn hospital bed moved out today. It would be her first task, even before she ate breakfast. After she had phoned Roenitz about picking up the bed, she started the coffee, making the usual amount, more than she'd be able to drink, but it felt silly to plug in the pot for just a cup or two. Coffee was cheap and it filled the house with the morning aroma she had become accustomed to long ago.

Sophie was grateful the Roenitz truck came so promptly. One of the drivers had been in her class in high school. He bowed his head, knowing full well why the bed was being removed, but it was too awkward for him to speak, even to express sympathy, so he remained silent. The other driver was the one who asked Sophie to sign the pick-up form.

She sat on the sofa and for a time stared at the divots left in the carpet. She wondered, glancing sideways at them, if they'd ever come out or if she would need to have the carpet replaced. It wouldn't hurt to replace it. So dingy in spots and worn in front of the sofa.

Even before Lev came over, the doorbell rang. Sophie had just finished drying her hair after her shower. She expected Lev, but he'd gotten into the habit of just walking in. They had all agreed it seemed ridiculous for him to ring the bell, but maybe he'd decided that since Sophie was home alone now that it would be best to resume a more formal arrangement. Then she remembered she had locked the door. When she opened it, she found one of their other neighbors instead. Mrs. Merton, of course, ready with food, plump in her pink pedal pushers and sleeveless white eyelet blouse. She stood on the stoop with a casserole in her hands, the first float in the inevitable parade of food.

"Oh, my dear. I saw the hearse yesterday. I'd have come right away, but I just wanted to give you some time. You poor dear. How are you holding up, sweetheart?"

Sophie asked Mrs. Merton to step in and accepted the dish gratefully. "I'm okay. She'd been really bad lately. I—we knew it was coming."

"Even so, it's always hard. When my Ronnie died—he had the prostate cancer, you know—when he died, it was expected, but I always thought there would be one more day. One more goodnight kiss."

Sophie hoped Lev would pop up to rescue her. "Yes. That's true," Sophie said, not really thinking at all about how true it was or not. "Thanks for the food. It's really kind of you."

"It's the least. I haven't baked it yet. You could even freeze it now if you wanted to save it for another time. When you're ready to eat it, just pop it in the oven at 350 for an hour. If you forget, you can call me."

She stared at Sophie as if there was something she just couldn't say but wanted to. "Oh, you. Can I give you a hug? Well, I'm going to anyway." Mrs. Merton stretched out her pale, saggy arms and wrapped them around Sophie. She smelled of sweet perfume, the kind that seems nice at first but then after awhile makes you sick to your stomach. When she let go, Mrs. Merton set her shoulders back and gave Sophie a broad smile.

"Now, I know everyone always says this, but really, if you need anything, you let me know. I can come clean for you or help you with your laundry. Whatever you need."

"Thanks again for the casserole. I'm sure it will be delicious. I'll get your dish back to you soon."

"No rush, no rush," she said, then put her fisted hand up to her heart and pouted her lips. "All right. I'd better go. I have sewing circle at church in a bit. Don't want to be late."

She peeked in the Pyrex dish. Something with potatoes and green beans. Ham, maybe? It was covered in cheese. It would probably be very good, and at some point she would be grateful to have it, but for now she took Mrs. Merton's suggestion and put it in the freezer.

Later that afternoon, Lev and Sophie decided they would sit shiva for Angel, though not a true shiva, of course. It would take place right away that night. They decided that the two of them would be the only mourners at their non-traditional shiva. In preparation, Lev went to the deli and bought a meat and cheese platter, two boxes of crackers, and a plump bunch of green grapes. Then, because he thought it would make Sophie happy, he splurged on a small, heart-healing chocolate cake. It was his belief that chocolate was soul medicine. While Lev was out, Sophie ran the vacuum, trying to work out the depressions in the carpet. She covered the kitchen table with the cloth her mom used on holidays. She set out two plates, two glasses, two forks, two spoons, and two napkins for the tiniest buffet service ever.

When he returned, Lev draped the hallway mirror with the same cloth he had used for his mother's shiva. They pulled the four kitchen chairs and the desk chair into the living room and set them in a semi circle. The extra chairs were for Joe, Ruth, and Frank. Sophie secured a yellowed white taper she had found in the junk drawer in a tarnished brass candleholder, trimmed the curled wick, and set it on a table she had slid near the sidelight of the front door. At dusk they were ready to begin. In honor of Angel Miranda, Lev said the Kaddish.

Later they nibbled on summer sausage and cheese. They ate cake. And they remembered.

"She loved you so much," Lev said.

"She did," Sophie agreed. "We didn't always get along, but she did love me and she did her best to give me a good life. She was a good mom."

"She loved to sing, didn't she?" Lev remembered.

"And dance. When she was little, she was in a show in school and she played a ballerina. She told me she always wished her parents would have let her have ballet lessons, but Papa thought it was a waste of money."

Lev lowered his glance and thought of his own father, who was the same way. Too pragmatic for his own good. The old man. So much could have been…. Yet, what did it matter? Whether or not Joe was tough on Lev, demanding at times more than Lev could give. What did it matter? In the end, a person does the best he can.

Angel had done her best, too. And whether due to Ruth's nurturing or Frank's loving attention or Angel's intermittent maternal influences, Sophie had grown up to be a fine young woman. Lev was astonished at her strength. She had never once faltered. Not once all summer. He was sure there were not many her age who could have done what Sophie had done.

At 8:15 Sophie yawned and they both agreed it was time to say good night. At the door, Sophie thanked Lev.

"This was nice," she said.

Lev agreed. "If she's up there somewhere watching, I'll bet she thought it was a bit ridiculous."

"Yeah," Sophie said. "I'm sure you're right. But deep down I'll bet she loved it."

Before he left, Lev handed Sophie an envelope. "It's from your mom. She made me promise not to give it to you until...."

Sophie looked in his eyes for more, but there was nothing else.

Sophie sat alone at the kitchen table, the overhead light glaring brightly. She picked up the envelope and realized by its weight that there was something other than paper within. Why she paused she didn't know, but it felt as if she should. Sophie slid her thumb under the edge of the flap, then tore across, leaving jagged fringe. She withdrew two things, a letter and a tiny paper package, taped shut.

"She didn't want this opened fast," said Sophie, struggling with the tape. Finally, a small, old-fashioned key plunked on the table. Sophie let the key lie there while she opened the letter, but she knew full well where the key fit, and her heart pounded in excitement as if she had been given a treasure. Then she unfolded the letter.

Dear Sophia,

I never called you the name your father gave you, but I should now. Your name means "wise one." Did I ever tell you that? I don't know if we knew by looking at you the day you were born that you would be a wise young woman, but that is exactly who you have turned out to be. You're so wise. Wiser than I could ever have been even if I had lived to be 100. You just know things, about life and people. You're so smart. I want you to know that I could not be prouder of you.

I'm sure you realize the key opens your grandfather's trunk. I couldn't bear to give it to you before. That old trunk will tell you stories. I wish my father had told his stories to me. He should have. He should have told them to you. I guess he was a man who kept his secrets close.

As I write this, there is so much I want to say to you and I hope I live long enough to say it all. I have kept secrets, too.

Finally, I want to say I am sorry that I wasn't a better mom. I tried. I really did. Don't think I don't know that some days you were the one who kept the house in order and kept me going.
Think of me, Sophie. Think of me.
Love, Mom

Later, she set the letter and the key on her nightstand. She would not turn the key tonight, probably not even tomorrow. She wanted to get through the memorial service first. She wanted to have things in their place and let the future unfold bit by bit. There was a story waiting for her and she would not rush it.

That night she slept soundly. She finally slept as if she had nothing to be afraid of.

1977

The summer homework for Sophie's upcoming "Introduction to Fiction" class lay before her on the picnic table. She wrote in a dove-gray Moleskine journal, which she'd purchased as instructed at the university bookstore, and as her professor didn't allow students to write in pencil, she had also chosen a black-and-gold fountain pen and sharp, black ink. The assignment was to "write every day. Something. Anything. About your fluffy pancakes or your dog's muddy feet. Write about things you notice. About things that make you feel good or bad. But please, no private confessions." Who in the world would do that, she wondered? Sophie folded the piece of paper with her professor's expectations and tucked it into the notebook's pocket. She uncapped the pen and stared at the faint lines on the creamy page, then wrote.

I'm Kerouac, I'm Steinbeck, I'm Momaday. I'm on the road and I'm all alone. I'm 21 years old, and everyone I have ever loved in my life, except one, is dead. Okay, so my road is metaphorical, but I'm on a journey all the same. I have no idea what I will write about on this journey, but I might as well write my own story because that's about all I know. I can't imagine what I'd say about pancakes, and I don't have a dog.

Already she was dissatisfied with what she had written, but the instructor's notes warned students not to be too harsh or to mull over what they had written for too long. They were to write and turn the page and keep on writing. She capped the pen and closed the notebook. Later she would try again.

Lev's part in the television show turned out to be bigger than he expected. The director wanted his character—a sort of low-life police informant—to be developed into someone more complex that they could use as a recurring character. "I guess he liked something he saw in me," Lev had told Sophie. "I feel bad about leaving you, and I've no idea how long I'll be gone."

Before he left, Lev brought over his house keys and a list of phone numbers, people Sophie should call in case of emergency. Another yellow-brown envelope. Like her mother setting things right before she died, this felt too permanent. A half dozen eggs, a loaf of bread, a nearly-full jar of Ruth's deep claret raspberry jam, the last things of value in the Perlman's refrigerator, were now in Sophie's kitchen.

Lev and Sophie stood outside now. It was just before eight, the morning already heavy and humid. The hazy sky at least kept the sun from intensifying the heat. Lev threw his last bag into the car, and he and Sophie stood together at the edge of his driveway and stalled their parting. This was not sweet sorrow. This felt like emptiness. Lev visually rechecked his written list, and once satisfied, he folded the piece of steno paper and slid it into his pants pocket.

He did not reveal the truth to Sophie, but he knew as surely as a person can know anything that the next time he set foot in his parents' house it would be to clear it out, except for the few items he wanted to keep for himself. The cream-colored stone house was a lovely house, but as much as his mother worked to make him feel at home there, it had never been his house. He had never found it a place his truest self could breathe.

Now that Sophie was an adult, he felt sure she would be fine without him. He had really only stayed in the house for her sake. Then, to help her through the summer. He had needed to do that. But the back and forth to Los Angeles, or wherever the film crew needed him, was starting to become more and more of a nuisance. So, the plans were in the works to sell the old place and find a permanent home in LA. He would tell her later. This, he felt was not the right time.

"Call me when you get there?" Sophie said, handing him a bag of sugar cookies she had baked for him the day before.

"Yes, Mom," Lev said and smiled. She would worry. He would worry. When two people have shared life and death, returning to the unconsciousness of the ordinary has a way of magnifying moments, making them pound louder than is reasonable in their hearts. Neither one wanted to make the move.

It was hard to watch Lev drive off. When he turned onto North Avenue and she lost sight of him, Sophie headed indoors. It was supposed to be in the high 80s, and Sophie wanted to get out of the sun so she would not end up like those "prune-faced Florida women" Ruth warned her about.

Inside, Sophie dug the box of Lipton tea bags out of the cupboard and put the kettle on to boil. On her shopping list, she wrote "lemons." Today she would have to drink her iced tea without. She nibbled one of the cookies and said "good" out loud.

In the past few days, she had caught herself speaking out loud more and more. There was too much silence otherwise. If she were working on the laundry, dusting, or doing other household chores, she employed her mother's habit of turning on the radio or the TV, not to listen or watch, but just as company. Keeping loneliness at bay.

When her tea was ready, Sophie plopped herself in the big gold chair, put her feet up on the ottoman and listened to the silence. The longer she listened, the louder it got. Eventually she turned on the TV and watched it until she could no longer keep her eyes open.

That night, she went to bed early, knowing not at all what else to do.

1977

Sophie,

    New friend Mark and I took in sunset at Venice Beach last night. Picture on this postcard doesn't do it justice. Oh, I even thought I <u>saw</u> you. But she was a he. Long dark wavy hair, looked just like you from the back. You <u>will</u> come visit over Christmas? Palm trees and sunshine instead of snow and slush. Promise? You can fly. I'll pay.
Love, Lev

1977

Since Angel's death, time had passed more quickly than Sophie had thought possible. Ruth used to say, "the days are flying by, Sophie. You have to do something important every day." Sophie had gotten into the habit of staying up late, watching TV, Johnny Carson, or a late movie, or listening to records, or reading. If she got a good book from the library, she could read it nearly nonstop, sometimes until two or three in the morning. Late nights meant late mornings, too. There was no one to get up early for, so even if the sun woke her, she might stay in bed until ten.

She looked forward to the immediate plunge into a social life that would happen when she moved back to Madison for her last year of college. August had been a lonely month. By now Sophie had reconciled herself to the fact that Lev would no longer be steps away whenever she needed him, but the truth was that over the past five years, after Ruth died and Lev quit his job at Marshall's to put his heart and soul into acting full time, he was gone a lot, sometimes for weeks at a time. She was sad but not surprised when he called her to tell her he'd decided to sell the house. And she looked forward to her visits in California. The two had made a pact that they would continue to spend Christmas and Hanukkah together, and Lev had made an excellent case for a Southern California Christmas, at least for the first year.

Sophie realized after that phone call that she was free to sell her house, too, and move anywhere, live anywhere. But somehow, the old place tugged at her, and she was in no hurry to go anywhere, not just yet.

After lunch, Sophie drove out to Prange Way and stocked up on a few back-to-school essentials. She got five folders with pockets, all different colors, and five college-ruled spiral notebooks to match the folders. She tossed into her cart a pack of fine point Bic pens, black ink, and a set of four yellow highlighters. The biggest cost would be books, which she knew would be expensive. She also picked up a few things for the house, toilet paper on sale and six boxes of tissues. In allergy season, she'd need them.

At the checkout, she tossed a Hershey bar on the conveyor belt. When the clerk announced the total, Sophie made out a check for $17.42. A few weeks earlier, she had ordered simple checks, even though styles with nature scenes or animals, cute kittens or puppies, were available. She wanted her checks to reflect seriousness. She recorded the debit amount in the register and would balance the record when she got home.

After her initial meeting with the lawyer, Arthur Haber, Sophie took in earnest his advice to pay meticulous attention to her finances. He knew young people who were accustomed to "being taken care of" by their parents were sometimes so casual about things like checkbooks and bills that they found themselves suddenly overdrawn. So that day she had come home and began by cleaning out her mother's desk, tossing out all the incomprehensible junk, clippings, expired coupons, old birthday cards, a couple of keys that opened nothing, a yellow plastic whistle. She wiped the drawers clean and moved the desk from where it sat on the backside of the kitchen wall, jutting awkwardly into the living room, to her bedroom, pushing it across the carpeting little by little. The trick was getting it through the door, but she knew she would succeed if she just kept at it. She briefly considered turning her mother's bedroom into an office, but decided the desk fit well enough and looked nice in her room. People didn't put offices in their homes anyway.

Sophie began to keep a simple ledger, which Arthur had suggested. As a model, she found a thin leather-bound ledger in the bottom left drawer of the desk, with entries dated in the 1930's. Surely her mother had kept it as a keepsake. Printed in all capital letters inside the front cover was *FRANK & JUNE CATALANO*. Sophie loved the feeling of history the ampersand conjured in her mind, an elegant typographical relic. The credits and debits made in watery blue ink were surely her grandmother's work. She knew her grandfather's beautiful hand, and this was not it. It was funny to think that a woman's handwriting would look less fluid, less artful that a man's, but in her grandparents' case, it was true.

That afternoon, she headed outside with a tall blue glass of lemonade and sat at the picnic table. Shadows shifted with intermittent flickers of sunlight. The breeze carried the sweet scent of phlox from across the street where the tall pink blossoms seemed to light up the corner of old Mrs. Merton's backyard. Sophie shooed a wasp from her glass. She opened her journal and stared at a blank page. The fountain pen, uncapped, drew itself to the page and Sophie found herself inking an interlocking border of diamonds and scrolls. From high school on she had been a doodler. Would she ever get this assignment finished? She shook off her mental lethargy and began putting words on the faintly ruled lines.

> *Squirrel chattering. Chasing another up the trunk of the maple. Can hear the scratch of their "claws?" on the bark. Breeze feels great. Gotta get those marigolds deadheaded. This is not a to-do list. Describe. Notice. Picnic table needs paint.*

With her left hand, she scratched at a chip in the paint and popped off a bubble, shearing it at an angle that revealed history. She saw that the current color, a light moss green was only the newest of many layers. In the slope like a chipped surface of a stone, she saw each layer distinctly. Forest green, mint green, then underneath, brown, reddish, then rich chocolate. How many times had this table been painted? It was old. Her grandfather had replaced the plank seat she now sat on the summer she built the birdhouse. She had held the wrench with two hands, gripping it as tightly as she could, while he tightened one of the big bolts. The table had sat here in the northeast corner of the backyard, ten feet from the edge of their lot under the maple's canopy, for as long as she could remember. Grass no longer grew under it, or if it grew, if it stubbornly worked itself up through hard-packed soil, the attempt was sparse and pitiful. The ground, worn smooth by shoes and her own bare feet, was cool in summer.

Sophie ran her hand across the table's surface. Smooth in spots. Bumpy in others. "Papa," Sophie said softly. "I think I miss you most of all."

Sophie closed the journal with a slap and capped the pen. She tugged at the key that she'd begun wearing on a leather string around her neck. What did she think she would find in the trunk? Horror stories? No. Not that. But what? What was so secretive that her mother had refused to ever let her see what was inside? And why had she herself put off opening the trunk? She could have looked inside the night Lev gave her the envelope with the key. But she hadn't. She had told herself again and again that she would, tomorrow. Every day there was a tomorrow when she imagined she would sit on the floor in front of the trunk, perhaps early in the morning, with coffee, still in her white terry robe, and sift through the Catalano past.

But here it was almost September and she still had not turned the key. What was she afraid of? Surely the trunk would be filled with photographs, old cards, letters, too? All her life, she had harbored the idea that the trunk held the one secret she longed to know, the one secret her mother kept almost to her death—the truth that her father had not died in war or an accident, had not died at all, but was probably still alive somewhere. She knew that now. Yet even knowing, she had never seen his face, and maybe the final part of that mystery, a photograph of Ruben Miranda, was tucked inside that old trunk. It might be. It might be. And yet, at this moment, it was not Ruben Miranda's face she needed to see, but the face of her grandfather. At this moment, she needed something more than the picnic table and her ever-weakening memories to reconnect her with her papa.

Sophie slipped the key from her neck, pushed it into the lock, and turned. So easy. She imagined a cloud of glittering pink-and-white Disney dust to billow out as she lifted the lid. Once open, the past would rise up to meet her like a genie in a bottle, and it would take her hand and lead her into gas-lit alleys and warmly appointed sitting rooms with Victrolas and walnut cabinet radios. It would smell like candles burning and chickens roasting, bread baking and apple pies. It would smell like Ruth Perlman, sweet and powdery. It would feel like Ruth's warm hugs, too. She had nothing to fear in this past from which she was born.

When she finally opened the trunk, what met her senses was not magic, but a whiff of mothballs, and instead of glittering light, the glare from the two sixty-watt bulbs in the ceiling fixture lit the contents. What she noticed first was an envelope with her name on it. Sophie chuckled. "Oh, Mom. You and your notes." Inside was one sheet of letter paper, ruled in blue lines, and on it was written:

> *Dear Sophie,*
>   *Welcome to your Grandfather's trunk. I know you won't find everything you need here, but I hope that what you do find will please you as it did me. Enjoy the journey.*
> *Love, Mom*

She folded the note and put it back in the envelope. Next, she untied the red ribbon that secured a packet of photographs. She looked long and deeply at the faces of her mother, her grandparents, her great-grandparents. She had seen pictures of them all before, but not these particular photographs. There were even a few pictures of herself that she did not remember ever seeing.

Another packet, another red ribbon, was made up of greeting cards, a few quite old, one to her papa from her grandmother on their anniversary. Underneath *Love, June* her mother had printed her name in capital letters: *ANGELINA*, written surely when she had first learned to print. Sophie found it odd to think of her mother as a child.

A shirt box was crammed full of Sophie's artwork from grade school. She remembered making some of those things. Others not at all.

Wrapped in tissue was an old—it looked very old—lace tablecloth. Tucked inside was another note: *Made by hand in Ireland by your great, great grandmother.*

Sophie opened the box that held Frank's Purple Heart. She knew her grandfather had been hurt in the war. There were scars on his forearm and the one on his chin. When she had asked, he said only that it all happened a long time ago.

A small gray jeweler's box held a thin gold ring, set with a small, simple diamond. Inside was a tiny folded note: *Sophie, I did not have very much luck with this. Maybe you will. Love, Mom.* Sophie slipped it on her finger and it fit. She decided she would wear it on her right hand to remind her of her mother.

A few of the items did not make a lot of sense. One of these was a jar with a piece of dried grass inside. The pint jar was old with a heavy zinc lid. They didn't make Mason jar lids like that anymore.

There was a small green-and-gold cookie tin, too. The note said, *Belonged to June Schneider when she was a child.* Inside were a few small shells, a plastic whistle, and an Indian Head penny. Children collect odd things, she thought, and remembered that she herself had begun a collection of dead insects and butterflies that she kept in an old cigar box until her mother found it, had a fit, and threw her treasures all away.

Then Sophie picked up what looked to be a tubular shell on a string, but after examining it more carefully, she realized what she thought was a shell was actually a piece of bone. The nearly-white color had deceived her. The crimped, once-knotted ends of the string had been untied, so Sophie slipped the bone off the twine and held it up to the light. She saw that the bone was hollow like a straw. Without thinking, she pulled it to her lips and blew, and the bone emitted a soft, high sound.

At the sound, the skin on her chest colored in prickly awareness, and a long-ago fragment of memory came into focus. She sat in the tub with toys floating about her, listening to her mother, who, humming a familiar tune, sat naked in the steamy bathroom on a towel-covered toilet, her long, slender fingers grasping the bone that lay against her chest.

Sophie slipped the bone back onto the string and retied the ends. With an odd sense that it was something she must do, Sophie slipped the necklace over her head. The bone felt cool against her chest, and she held her hand over it, still hearing her mother's tune in her ear.

She continued looking through the trunk. There were a few books—a couple of paperbacks that didn't look that old, except that the pages were turning dark. A larger hardcover book looked very old. Sophie held it in her hands. *Around the World in 80 Days*.

When Sophie opened an old shoebox, she sensed at once that she had found the real treasure. Within was a collection of notebooks, not that different from the Moleskine journal she had purchased for her writing class. She counted nine in all. The one on top was the oldest.

Its sable-brown suede cover looked bitten off in the lower right corner, but it was as smooth as a bird feather. On the first page was written: *Frankie P. Catalano, 1923*. And below that, *The sea is everything. It covers seven tenths of the terrestrial globe. Its breath is pure and healthy. It is an immense desert, where man is never lonely, for he feels life stirring on all sides. ~Jules Verne*

Inside, the browning pages were filled with drawings of birds, tall buildings with slender smokestacks, and ships at sea. There were diagrams and designs for things to build or make. Now and then a list: *1) Find copper wire 2) See if there is a book at the library on wireless receivers 3) Ask Ma if I can have the old pony blanket for our hangout*.

Each successive notebook was dated.

"Oh my god," Sophie said out loud as she read the date on the last notebook and the inscription inside the cover: *Frank P. Catalano, June 1, 1961, Angelina and Sophia*. She turned the pages. This was a true diary, with two to four entries per page. Now and then an illustration, but mostly this was a record of their lives, of his life with them. Here he wrote about how proud he was of her mom working so hard. *I wish she would learn to forgive herself. I have. Or maybe it's that she cannot yet forgive me. The girl is such a joy. Such a little dark-haired beauty. I do not know how I stand being at work each day without her.*

Dated November 12, 1963: *Who would have thought a goddamn doll would have caused so much trouble. I cannot figure her out. So like her mother at times I just don't know what to do. I only wanted to make the child happy.*

Sophie had never forgotten that day. She had not understood her mother's reaction. It made her even sadder now to remember that after her grandfather died, that doll was one of the things they had donated to charity. Well, maybe somewhere, some little girl had enjoyed playing with her.

Sophie clasped the notebook to her chest. This was better than a hundred photographs. This was better than cuff links or a Purple Heart. This was better than anything. In these notebooks, her papa had given himself to her forever.

Throughout her life, Sophie would read and re-read the notebooks and study the drawings. She would research the references to events and places he wrote about. She learned as much from what he said as from what he didn't say, and at times, what she read broke her heart.

Within the trunk lived her history, and years later, after her children had married, and while her husband tinkered in his wood shop, Sophie would find herself drawn again to the world within the trunk and the rich stories she longed to put into her own words.

1978

Sophie's first few months of teaching English at North High School, the school she had attended, were going well, even better than she had hoped. As a student teacher in a high school south of Madison, Sophie had been subjected to multiple horror stories involving first year teachers from veteran teachers who were probably just trying to be funny. During lunch in the teachers' lounge, those veteran teachers, mostly white-haired men but also a few wizened women, smoked and laughed. Sophie had learned to smile politely, nod her understanding now and then—even at the more salacious stories that turned her cheeks red—and eat her lunch while they joked that she was far too pretty to waste her life trying to teach teenagers to write.

But so far nothing catastrophic had happened, and her looks, pretty or not, had been as irrelevant as she had hoped. The staff at North High was younger and more supportive than at her previous school, and she was grateful. Some of the teachers she'd had as a student were still teaching, but quite a few had retired in recent years. In fact, it was her favorite English teacher that Sophie had been hired to replace.

Two days before her students arrived, the principal had led Sophie up the familiar old stairs to the second floor classroom where she had first learned how to diagram sentences. It was there that she had first read *Romeo and Juliet* and poems by Robert Frost and had been told she had a "way with words" and where, one bright January day, looking out at the blue sky instead of at the conjunctions on the board, she had first realized she needed and wanted to be a teacher.

Despite the ominous warnings she had been inundated with as a student teacher, not once had Sophie come home in tears, desperate to quit. She had come home those first two weeks desperate to lie down for a quick nap before setting herself to planning lessons and grading assignments, but there had not been one moment when she thought she had made a mistake. Bubbe would say of her fortuitous job opportunity that it was meant to be, getting a job so close to home. Her mother would say it was simply stupid luck. Either way, she did feel lucky. And happy.

As one of her first writing assignments, she had asked her sophomores to draw out a map of their neighborhood as they remembered it from when they were younger, anywhere between six and ten years old. She smiled to hear a few of them complain, "that was a long time ago. I can't remember back that far." Sophie told them their maps should include their own house, of course, as well as the houses of their friends and neighbors and any other important buildings, like synagogues or churches or schools. They were to draw landscape elements and label them. Trees, tree houses, hedges, gardens. They were even to add things they thought were insignificant, like doghouses, potholes in alleys, flags painted on mailboxes, empty bird feeders. As an example, she showed them the map she had drawn and pointed out her own house, Ruth's house, Joe's garden, her sand box. She drew and labeled the picnic table in her backyard, Ruth's raspberry patch. She pointed out that it wasn't important to be a great artist. "See?" she said. "Mine is fairly rough." While they drew, she walked around the classroom and observed their maps. "Be detailed. Put it all in. Don't forget. Label everything. Remember? My map said 'Ruth's raspberries: eat them right off the bushes.'"

The visual map, she had learned, was the key to unlocking memories. Step two, she told them the next day, was to find a story buried in the map. On a separate sheet of paper, students listed their ideas, or if a strong story presented itself, they were to just begin writing. At the table in the front of the room, Sophie sat with her map, her paper, and her pen. As her students worked, she worked, too. They knew she would never ask them to do something she was not also interested in doing, and seeing her write alongside them gave her students encouragement to do their best. They would have more class time to compose, but she urged everyone to add at least one more page to their stories by Monday.

Sophie walked home from school now, glad it was Friday. The days were growing shorter, so each moment of warm autumn sun was a blessing she did not take lightly. She'd be shoveling snow before she was ready for it.

On the porch, she lifted the stiff lid of the mailbox and removed three envelopes. Two were bills. She would pay them first thing tomorrow. Sophie had become an obsessively conscientious homeowner. The other was a letter from Lev. She smiled.

The new next door neighbors were very nice, a young couple with a two-year-old boy and a baby on the way. But they were not family. She missed Lev more than she thought she would. They wrote to each other often, and he would call now and then. He still felt the need to check up on her, to make sure she was doing well. He worried about her living alone. And yet he had to admit that solitude seemed to suit Sophie. He, more than anyone else in her life, understood that about her.

Inside her house, little was changed. She had repainted all the rooms and had finally torn out the worn living room carpet. Underneath she discovered a golden oak floor that she could not bear to cover again, so she hired a man to refinish it. It gleamed now in the afternoon light. Other than the floor and the paint, the house was as it had been when her mother had come home to die.

Wriggling out of her blouse and skirt, Sophie threw on a pair of beat-up Levi's and one of her grandfather's old flannel shirts. She tied her hair up in a ponytail, grabbed a tall glass of ice water, and headed out back to enjoy the dwindling afternoon. The wires hummed and crickets chirped, and Sophie let out a long, satisfied sigh.

After she had read Lev's letter, Sophie thought about the story she had begun to write. She was six, in Ruth's house, not her own. Why was it that when she looked back to happy memories, she nearly always ended up in Ruth's house? She remembered putting on Ruth's coat, the one with the soft fur collar. Ruth had laughed because the coat dragged behind her like a queen's train. The satiny white lining felt cool and smooth. In the story, Sophie played up the fact that she had been pretending to be a queen. Truthfully, about all she really remembered was the touch of the lining, the collar, and the smell. It was Ruth, and she missed her desperately. She had always been able to tell Ruth whatever was on her mind, and Ruth had never belittled her or made her feel foolish. Ruth, even more than Papa, and so much more than her mother, had loved her just as she was.

On Monday morning she would tear it up, every bit of it, and consult her map for a less sentimental story, one that would not come across as silly as this one surely would.

1978

Sophie rose early on Sunday, and after her coffee, she was glad to see the clouds begin to lift. The forecast had promised mostly sunny skies. She dressed as if she were going to church, wearing a navy A-line skirt and a pale pink rayon blouse. She pulled the long collar ties into a low, loose bow. The pantyhose she'd washed out on Friday were still on the towel bar in the bathroom. She glided them over her legs now. She slipped two bangle bracelets onto her left wrist, spritzed a bit of cologne behind her ears, and glanced one more time in the mirror.

The square cardboard box she had found in the basement yesterday sat on the kitchen table. She cautiously set her mother's urn inside the box, then padded it with kitchen towels so it wouldn't wobble. She set the box on the passenger seat and drove to Kiwanis Park. She drove cautiously because of the urn, but she was anxious to get there. She had thought about this morning for many, many Sundays.

There were not many people in the park at 9 o'clock, just a father and son playing catch and a few small groups of people setting up for picnics. She was happy for the solitude. Sophie took only the urn from the car and carried it in her arms like a baby. The grass in shady areas was still wet from the morning's heavy dew. She set her sights on a spot about thirty yards south of where she'd parked the car, to where an open view of the river looked promising. The act would need to be inconspicuous.

Sophie had decided weeks ago that she did not wish to recreate one of those overly dramatic movie scenes that often took place at the apex of a bridge or on the edge of a cliff so the ashes could burst forth in a showy cloud. That was not what she wanted.

Instead, she sat along the cool river bank and worked the lid off the urn, twisting and pulling gently till it was free. Inside, her mother was dust, but Sophie would not send her back to dust. She would send her back to water. Sophie lowered the mouth of the brass urn so it was near the surface of the river and moved it slowly back and forth so that the ash and grit that had been her mother fell gradually. The ash lay for a second upon the water's surface before saturating and sinking. Except for the lightest particles. Those almost-golden specks lingered longer on the water and swirled downstream atop sparkling ripples until they were out of view.

Sophie dunked the urn in the river three times. After, she sat in stillness for a while, hugging her knees, listening to a cardinal's song. The urn lay on its side in the mossy grass, water droplets clinging to the brass. A yellow maple leaf dropped onto the water as lightly as if it were made of air itself. Behind her, more and more families came into the park, claiming cooking grates and picnic tables. A whiff of burning lighter fluid assailed her nose. She should leave before someone approached. This spot would be a good one for fishing.

But she could not move. Not yet. Sophie stretched out on the ground. She lay on her side and pressed her left ear to the earth, covering her right ear with her hand. Sophie had heard that robins find worms by listening for their vibrations. She listened now with the heart of a child who believes that a human ear can hear things, the vibrations of earthworms, the sound of water in far off lakes, and voices. Then, as if respecting Sophie's purpose, everything around her turned silent, and in that moment, she listened as hard as she could for the whispers of those she would never forget.

Acknowledgments

I would like to thank Signe Jorgenson of Signe Jorgenson Editorial Services and Co-Editor in Chief of *Stoneboat Literary Journal* for her careful and thoughtful feedback. When I got stuck early on, Signe helped me push through.

Thank you to my friend Peggy Weiner Smith, a former English teacher and voracious reader, for her feedback and for helping me with a variety of cultural references. Thank you as well to my friends Lee, Sue, and Eric, who were my earliest readers, for sharing their knowledge of Sheboygan with me. To Marilyn, Georgia, Sylvia, Maryann, and Nancy—my poetry "posse," who listened to early chapters and told me to keep going—thank you for all of your honest feedback and encouragement.

I would be remiss if I did not acknowledge my teachers' impact on my development as a writer. From high school to college, they nudged me toward the road they saw I had no choice but to take.

A Hollow Bone is about family, and I want to thank mine. To Kris and Jennifer, thanks for liking Angelina and Sophie and for getting caught up in their story. My parents, both good storytellers, maybe even writers in another life not thwarted by time and circumstance, provided helpful feedback, and I thank them for their insight. I also want to thank Michael for his love and support and for understanding that writing is a solitary endeavor. Kevin and Laura, Shana and Lucas, Olivia, Ella, Shelby, Mya, and Ian, if I had no other words, if I had no other stories, I would still have your love.

Lastly, thank you to my little Mika, who brings me so much joy.

About the author

Dawn Hogue is a Wisconsin writer who lives in a 19th century house near the rolling Kettle Moraine, not far from Lake Michigan. She taught high school English for 25 years. In addition to writing, she enjoys reading, knitting, quilting, and gardening. *A Hollow Bone* is her first novel. Learn more about her at www.dawnhogue.com

Water's Edge Press

Book Club Discussion Questions

1. Should Grace Schneider have been less severe with June in the opening scene? What could she have done instead of scold her child about the clam?

2. What is your idea of a romantic marriage proposal? Was Frank on the right track?

3. Was Frank right or wrong to enlist in the Army without first discussing his plan with June?

4. When Frank returns home from war, he is unwilling to visit his old friend Jimmy, who desperately wants to see him. "Frank knew it was wrong, but he could not help thinking it was nevertheless true that very often human beings were repulsed by each other's misery." What do you make of Frank's assessment?

5. What are things parents can and should do to help a child in the event that one of the child's friends dies?

6. If June had not lost her twin boys in the miscarriage, what course might her life have taken?

7. Angelina's mother gives her the bone necklace as a talisman for strength. Why do you think Angel chooses not to pass the gift on to her own daughter?

8. What effect was created by juxtaposing scenes between Sophie and her mom with the family's historical chronology?

9. Discuss the Perlman family's role in the novel. Who was more vital to Sophie's well being: Ruth or Lev?

10. Discuss the role of mental illness in the novel.

11. Should Sophie have insisted her mother move to a nursing home where professionals could care for her? Why or why not?

12. Discuss the role of water in the novel. Why are lakes and rivers important? What other natural elements in the novel struck you as symbolic or crucial to understanding the book's themes?

13. Discuss the female characters' childhood experiences and the impact their experiences had on them as adults.

14. In what ways did Angel's choices enrich or diminish her life?

15. Discuss the value of Frank's trunk for both Angel and Sophie. What value do you think the trunk held for Frank?

16. Which character do you most empathize with and why?

17. What questions do you have about Sophie or Lev's lives after the last pages of the novel? What do you think happens to them?

18. Which scene in the novel stuck with you the most and why?

19. How important was the setting to the plot and characters? In other words, what was the value of "place" in the overall novel?

20. In what ways is *A Hollow Bone* a novel about ordinary life and the search for the American Dream?

Made in the USA
Lexington, KY
03 August 2017